THE CALAMITY OF A CHOICE

DIMITRI ROGERS

The characters and events portrayed in this book are fictitious. Any similarities to real persons, living or dead, are coincidental and not intended by the authors.

ISBN-13: 979-8-88993-013-6

TABLE OF CONTENTS

CHAPTER 1

A dependable person.

Yeah, that's what I used to say whenever someone asked me the painful question of what my goal was in life. To be a dependable person. The kind of person that can be depended on. A beacon of light and hope. But, of course, you can't just go out and say something like that, can you? I mean, you could, but then you'd get weird looks and people would start to think you're crazy or just plain stupid. Though it wasn't an incorrect answer, it's obviously not the answer that people looked for when they asked you that question—even I knew that. It didn't take long for me to find out that giving that answer had the exact opposite effect I wanted. Giving an answer like that often causes people to think you're undependable.

So, I shut up.

I kept that desire to myself and spared everyone the trouble of hearing about it.

I started to give the basic answers people expected: a doctor, a lawyer, and an astronaut. I even said I wanted to be the president, if I was feeling adventurous.

Now, I don't want you to think that I was ashamed about my goal or dream or whatever you call it. Truth was, I didn't really care what I was, as long as I was dependable. That's all I wanted.

Because that's how she was.

She was the one that saved me, and as a result, that's the way that I had always envisioned her; an unwavering paragon of reliability and trustworthiness.

It didn't matter that I never honestly believed I could be that way. You can say you want something all you want, but that doesn't have any bearing on whether or not you'll actually get it. Take my word on it. I'm speaking from experience. Some people just aren't meant to be that way. For there to be dependable people, others had to need someone to depend on, and I was part of the latter.

Nevertheless, that wouldn't stop me from trying.

I didn't ever expect that I was going to get what I wanted, but that didn't mean I was planning on giving up again either—especially when she never did.

However, I know this is all starting to sound an awful lot like lip service and grandstanding, so I wanted to come out and say, before you get the wrong idea about me, that I had no idea how I was going to do it. I really didn't. I was clueless. Didn't know the first step. And that's exactly how I felt when I happened to encounter the first of my trials. That girl sitting alone at a bar on a Sunday night. A girl who looked like she had a host of problems of her own she needed to work out, and me who unceremoniously fell right into them. But I soon realized she was merely the starting point of a long and arduous journey.

Sounds basic, right?

Well, that couldn't be farther from the truth.

The dominoes were about to fall.

CHAPTER 2

"So? What's the deal, Chris? Are you going to do this thing or not?"

Before I even had the chance to answer Brad's series of questions, his massive hand hit me right between the shoulder blades. The tremendous force of his blow nearly caused me to spill my drink all over my favorite pair of jeans.

"I don't know," I choked out painfully. "And can you not do that? It hurts."

"What are you talking about? What hurts?"

"My back."

"Well, it's not going to hurt as much as missing such a fine *opportunity* over there. So, suck it up and get your game face on! We've got a babe hunt to conduct and you're getting laid tonight!"

"Don't drag me into this."

The man who towered over me and who seemed to take pleasure in my agony was Brad Cutter, my college roommate. But I guess it wouldn't be too accurate to use the term "towered," as if he was physically some giant, hulking figure. No, in reality, he was roughly my height, and on some days when I decided to stand up straight, he was actually an inch or so shorter than me.

However, Brad's immense size didn't come from anything physical. It was his charisma and presence that defined him and made him feel like a person bigger than he was. I couldn't quite put my finger on why, but I eventually settled on the idea that he was just fundamentally built differently than I was. While I was born with an overdeveloped sense of neuroticism, cynicism, and pessimism, and a bunch of other -isms, he seemed to lack any of those faculties. It made for an interesting dynamic between us, and one that I wasn't wholly opposed to.

The main difference between the two of us was that he was extroverted. What I mean by that was that Brad was *actually* extroverted. If I didn't know any better, I would have believed that he may have been the very origin of the word itself. The concept behind the word's creation. He might have been extroversion embodied and personified in human form. He lived and fed off the energy of those around him like a leech. I had no doubt that if we hadn't been assigned to the same dorm room our freshman year, we'd have still crossed paths somewhere along the way.

I can still remember that day, too.

It was move-in week before our first year started three years ago, and it was a wet one. Rain had been pelting against the window ever since I'd arrived at our room. I had gotten there first, so I picked the side of the room that I wanted and unloaded all my stuff, just the way that I liked it. After I finished, I thought I might as well take a quick nap before I decided what I wanted to do with the rest of my day.

That's when it happened.

Brad burst into the room. His black hair was shiny underneath the light of a single uncovered bulb from the ceiling, and his clothes were drenched in water, mud, and some other mystery substances that I really didn't care to ask about.

At that point, I was already tucked into my covers, too stunned to move. All I could do was caution a peek at the door over the top of my blanket and meet the eyes of my would-be assailant.

"Yo! You must be Chris! I'm your roommate, Brad. Nice to meet you! Now give me a hug!"

And before I could protest, Brad had peeled off his wet clothes until he was standing in front of me in his white briefs. Immediately, he slipped into the covers beside me—as if to live and feed off my energy as extroverts are known to do.

He said he enjoyed being the big spoon, and we'd been close friends ever since.

You really do meet a lot of interesting characters in college.

I wouldn't describe myself as a big decision maker, so most of the time I found myself carried around in other people's current.

And Brad was the reason I found myself at this bar on a Sunday night.

The place was a prominent hangout for our college town. Well, that was an assumption I was making based on what Brad told me and what I heard. This wasn't my scene. It was my third year enrolled at Oceanside, and I hadn't been here once.

Located a block from the campus' main entryway, students and faculty would congregate here after classes to cut loose, drink, socialize, and generally act unsightly and rowdy. Plasma TVs lined the walls displaying a host of different sports that I didn't care about and the pool tables at the end of the room were occupied by loudmouths that yelled and screamed every time they pocketed a ball.

With sensation having finally returned to my upper vertebrae, I stood up from my seat and quickly glanced across the room. I wanted to see if I'd made a fool of myself in front of the girl I had been eyeing most of the night, and through the crowd of young and old faces, I was just able to make out the brunette hair of the woman sitting at the far end of the bar. She was still engrossed in her glass—as if the answers of the universe were hidden away at the bottom.

Luckily for me, depending on how you looked at it, she hadn't noticed a thing at all.

She probably hadn't noticed me at all either, for that matter.

I guess you could look at it as one of those glass half full/half empty situations, something that was very common to me.

Based on my completely unbiased and manly intuition and the top-secret data I'd been trying to gather throughout the night, I could tell that the woman was beautiful. Even from this distance across the bar. Noticing a woman's beauty was something that happened naturally. It's a feeling. It's a scary thought if you think about it. Being able to tell the physical attractiveness of a person from across the room, not even having to look at their face. It's as if to say your silhouette or very presence can be found to be appealing, so you always had to be on your guard. Every time the thought crossed my mind, I couldn't help but straighten my back and flatten out my wrinkled shirt.

That's not to say that I hadn't seen her up close yet. I had. A couple times. On a few back-to-back trips to the restroom that lay in the hall behind her. I'm sure she didn't notice. I was being sneaky and inconspicuous. These trips did have a functional purpose besides emptying my bladder. I was trying to build up my courage, bit by bit. Asking a woman out is probably one of the most fear-inducing things that a man could do next to breaking up with one. Whenever I've gone in unprepared, I've always managed to get my foot stuck in my mouth. You had to ease into this sort of thing.

The first trip was to get myself used to walking in her direction.

The second was to plan out my route, i.e., where I would stand and sit when I went up to talk to her.

And on the third and most recent trip, I took things a step further. While I was behind her, I bent down to tie my shoe. Actually, untie it first, then re-tie it. I even managed to force out a cough too.

All that effort was for the purpose of getting used to being in her presence and proving to myself that I could in fact muster a sound while I was around her.

"See. There you go ogling again," Brad said before taking a sip from the amber liquid in his glass. "If you want to meet people, you have to actually go and meet them, you know. You do that by talking, not staring. Nothing gets done if you sit on your ass acting like a total creep."

This guy was too damn perceptive, but he was right.

I held my gaze on the woman for an extra second before turning back to my roommate. He was frowning and the crease on his forehead was two shades darker than it usually was.

"I was planning on it," I said. "Just give me a second, will you? We haven't even been here that long. Just let me finish my drink and then I'll go. It'll give me the last bit of courage I need."

I lifted the plastic cup and swirled the clear liquid, rattling the two remaining ice cubes.

"That's just water."

See! Way too perceptive.

"Yeah, so what? I'm thirsty. And I love water."

"This is a *bar*. You buy alcohol here. Only a weirdo goes to a bar and just sits around staring at people and drinking water. People may start getting the wrong ideas."

"Who are you calling a weirdo?"

"You," Brad said. "I'm trying to make sure we have a good time and you're being a total dick-in-the-mud."

"What did you just say? I think I misheard you."

"You're being a total dick-in-the-mud," Brad repeated, emphasizing the word dick by pointing directly at me.

"Who's being the dick?! Plus, you're saying it wrong. It's supposed to be 'stick.' A stick in the mud. And even if you were doing it on purpose, how does drinking water make anyone a dick?"

Brad shrugged. "I'm just saying, bro. You need to loosen up a little. I think a long, hard, stiff one could do you some good."

"Okay, you're definitely doing it on purpose."

"I'm talking about a drink."

"No, you weren't," I said. "And this water is more than enough. I'm good."

"Come on! That's what I'm talking about. Why are you so against it? It's just one drink. It won't kill you to have one drink. You've been holed up in the apartment for three months lying around in bed doing nothing, but you're finally doing stuff again! This is when we should be celebrating, bro. This is like your coming-out party."

"You know I'm straight."

"Your coming-*outside* party then. Just drink with me."

"This feels a lot like peer pressure," I retorted.

"I see it more as an intervention."

Oh.

That was good. I'd have to give him points on that one. But I still wasn't going to let up.

"Haven't I told you why I don't like drinking? We've known each other for like three years. I'm almost certain it's come up at least once."

"No, you haven't."

"Are you just dumb? Yes, I have!"

"Well, I forgot so explain it to me again."

"And you don't have to be such a stick about it either," he added.

Great.

He wasn't just going to let this one slide. Brad would pester me all night until he got his answer.

It's not like I was opposed to alcohol. I've tried some on separate occasions. A sip here and a sip there. It tasted okay. Obviously, it was an acquired taste that I hadn't built up yet. If that was all it was, then I could see myself becoming an avid drinker, not an alcoholic, but someone who wouldn't have been opposed to throwing a few back at a barbeque once in a while. Of course, there was more to it, though. Things could never be explained as simply as just that.

What I was opposed to was the way people started acting once they'd started drinking. They were too wild. They made idiots of themselves. They acted like buffoons. And it always ended up like that. I should know. This was a common sight on our campus, especially prevalent on game days. Football was big at Oceanside, not that I cared. I only cared because I knew that on those days, I wouldn't go outside unless it was completely necessary. Seeing people act irresponsibly—I didn't like it.

Besides, she never drank either.

"I don't like anything inhibiting my thought process," I told him after a second. "It's as simple as that."

"That's it? One drink won't even do that. In fact, it'll lower your inhibitions. Sounds like a win to me. Live a little, why don't you? Take a chance. Go out and kiss a girl! Jeez, bro."

"I'm good. I don't want to risk it."

Brad sighed and threw his hands up in defeat. "Okay, fine. Do whatever you want. Just know you're lame."

I smiled and graciously accepted the victory. "Better safe than sorry."

"This wouldn't by chance be because of Zoey's influence, would it?"

My grin dropped immediately.

He'd actually said it. The name of the girl in question. The forbidden name that we swore to cross out from either of our vocabularies. People had been killed for doing less, but Brad had gone and said it so nonchalantly. Why was I so surprised? This was exactly the sort of thing that he'd do. He always had to have the last word.

In all his perceptiveness, Brad must have noticed the color leaving my face as he simply shrugged his shoulders.

"Oh, did I say something I shouldn't have?"

"You... promised."

"My bad." Brad paused to give me a once-over. "So it is still bothering you. I thought as much, but I wasn't sure."

I nodded.

A situation like that one. The one I had with Zoey. I couldn't just let it go, no matter how many times I sang that song. It just wasn't that easy.

I wondered if she was doing okay.

"Didn't *you* break up with *her*?" he asked.

I nodded at the half-melted ice cubes in my cup.

"Bro. I love you and all, but I hope you know I'm never going to let you live that down. Never in a million years. I'll be laying on my deathbed and still be bringing that up. I didn't even think it was possible for such a perfect person to exist. Zoey was pretty, attractive, hot, beautiful, sexy, cute, handsome, gorgeous, a knockout, a stunner, nice-looking and... did I mention pretty?"

Geez, Brad. I could see what you prioritize in a woman.

"I guess she was also smart, caring, and had a pleasant personality," he said. "I know you like that sort of thing too."

"Yeah, I know. I dated her."

"Way more than just that."

"What do you mean?"

"Dated? That's an understatement if I ever heard one, especially with how long you two knew each other. Same hometown. Childhood friends. High school sweethearts. Decided to attend the same college together. It was like you were always together. You two were practically married."

"Don't go that far."

"You guys were practically conjoined twins."

"That's even further!"

Brad's eyes softened, and he leaned forward onto the counter, propping his head up with his hand. The band around the arm hole of his sleeve hugged around his tanned bicep tightly. If I didn't know any better, I'd say he was flexing at this very moment. Those swim practices had been paying off for him.

"So, why'd you do it exactly? You never actually told me," Brad threw out cautiously.

"Do what?" I feigned ignorance, my most commonly used tactic. It almost never worked.

"You know. Break up with her."

"I don't know."

"I don't mean to press you, but come on, bro. You're always so quick to run away from the conversation whenever we bring it up. Just give me something. Then I'll shut up. Scouts honor." Brad raised a hand with three fingers and put on his failed interpretation of a serious face. He looked like he was suffering from a brain freeze.

I sighed and massaged the bridge of my nose.

Here this grown man was, sitting in front of me with his hand raised like a middle-schooler, thinking that his little gesture would give him any more credibility. The whole thing made *him* look like the weirdo. If anything, this would have made me more inclined to think that he was lying. Especially since he had just broken our promise to never utter that forbidden name.

Yet, whether I was a masochist, or I just had nothing to lose, I gave him what he wanted—parts of it anyway.

"I wasn't good enough. I couldn't become the person I thought she deserved, so I didn't want to give her any more trouble." I stopped and took another sip of my water. That was all I was willing to give at this point. Any more and my mind would end up swirling down to that dark place in the back of my heart. It probably wasn't enough to satisfy Brad though, so I was mentally bracing myself for the barrage of questions that were inevitably about to come my way regarding my cryptic wording. He wasn't the best at reading between the lines. He enjoyed taking most things in life at face value.

But as the seconds of silence ticked on, the questions never came.

Instead, Brad stood up and stretched his arms as if he had just woken up from a long nap before thrusting his fist out. "Say no more. Say no more. That'll conclude the depressing talk for today. I'm just happy that you agreed to come out with me tonight. I was getting a tiny bit worried about you... I wasn't sure if I should even bother asking you to tag along with me on our little babe hunt."

My fist connected with his.

"No. You made the right choice. Thanks for inviting me out. I appreciate it. I really do."

"No problem, buddy."

It was moments like this, fleeting and few, that I felt an actual shift in our mental acuity. Whereas I usually felt more attuned emotionally to things, when Brad was able to show this level of emotional intelligence, I realized that the scale was tipped just a bit more towards the neutral position than I thought. That being said, it still favored me and nothing he said or did would ultimately change that. I just didn't outclass him in this aspect as much as I thought.

But despite all that, there were still things I wasn't willing to tell him yet regarding that topic. I only told him what he needed to know. Situations were never as simple as they appeared.

At this point, Brad flashed me a devious grin. "And you know what they say, Chris."

"What?"

"The ass is always greener on the other side."

"Nobody says that but you! That doesn't even make sense."

"Don't overthink it. That's a bad habit you have. You're being a sour pussy."

Eh. I couldn't even be that mad.

With all these idioms he was butchering, I was beginning to think this was a systematic problem rather than an issue with Brad himself. Somewhere along the way our education system had failed him.

But with all that out of the way, we had better get back on topic.

From across the bar, the woman had remained seated for the duration of our conversation, intermittently taking sips from her drink and tapping away at her cellphone. Even those simple gestures she made so elegantly. I'm sure she would have even looked good clipping her toenails. The way she grabbed her glass and brought it to her lips—it was all just so gentle and delicate. An angel wouldn't have been able to do it any better. She was clearly someone that existed on a separate plane of existence compared to us lowly commoners.

That's partially why I was so nervous.

I mean, could you blame me?

I'd be the first to admit that I'm not exactly the most handsome guy in the room, not by a long shot. I'm lanky and tend to walk around with my head down, and shoulders hunched forward. I tell people it's because I have to carry around the weight of all my thoughts, but in reality, it's those long nights leaning over my desk doing homework with terrible posture, among other things.

However, putting all physical characteristics aside, there was something else that drew me to that woman.

The first thing I noticed about her—that woman who I knew nothing about—was how sad she looked.

The woman didn't glance around, and she didn't try to converse with anyone. She might not have even been fully aware of her surroundings at all, her silence standing out against the backdrop of loud rock music and laughing faces. If her melancholic expression wasn't enough to put up those walls around her, then the way she just kept her attention focused on her glass and phone did just that. It seemed to me that she was cut off from the rest of the world.

I was able to recognize that because I felt the same way—even now.

It takes one to know one, as they say.

What could have caused her to make a face like that?

I wanted to ask her.

That's what Zoey would have done.

But I'm nothing like her, am I? So there wasn't any point in trying.

"I don't know anymore," I finally said. "I think I'm just going to pass this time around. I'm just not feeling it."

"Wow, just shut up. You're doing this whether you want to or not," Brad said, bouncing up and down as if he was warming up before a race. "You're getting me all worked up now. Just go. She isn't busy."

"What if she doesn't like me, or I say something stupid?"

Brad pulled his ankle up to his thigh, stretching his leg. "You're the smartest guy I know. You couldn't possibly say something stupid."

Thanks for the vote of confidence, buddy. I appreciate it, but that faith is completely misplaced. Do you even know who I am?

I sighed. "No, I think I'll pass this time."

"Okay, fine."

"What?"

"If you won't, then I will. I'll bring her over here to talk to you. Just sit back and relax. I'm the ultimate wingman." Brad gave me a thumbs up and started making a beeline through the crowd.

"No!" I grabbed both of his arms in an attempt to hold him back.

"Don't do that!"

Brad stopped and turned around. "Either you go, or I go. It's your choice. I'm trying to help you. This might be the only way for you to get over your ex. To be frank, that's actually the real reason why I brought you here today."

I took a deep breath.

And another.

And another.

Ugh.

Why was this so hard?

"Brad, I don't think I can do this."

"Bro, what do you want me to do? Hold your hand?"

"No, but..."

That would have helped. It would have at least moved me in the right direction.

"What if she's waiting for her boyfriend to show up? And he's huge. What do you expect me to do if he picks a fight with me? I'd get squashed." I threw out this feeble excuse hoping that it would deter him from advancing.

"If that happens just run. Though, if he was here, we would have seen him by now. Just go before she leaves. Now's your chance!"

Wasn't he supposed to be helping me?! He was enjoying this way too much!

Slowly, I pulled my plastic cup up to my chest. The ice cubes had melted and drops of perspiration were trailing down the sides. I couldn't tell if the water was shaking because of my trembling hands or the beating of my heart. I knew I had to make a move soon, but I needed a second to try and compose myself.

Come on, Chris. You can do this. You can do this.

And with one more breath, I took my first step towards the lion's den.

Yeah, I *can* do this. I got this. What could go wrong?

And that was my first mistake.

Saying those famous last words.

"You got this buddy! Go get her!"

Before I could turn around, a hand slapped me between the shoulders in the same tender spot that I was previously subjected to. The transference of all that force into my lanky, frail, poor, hunched over frame was almost too much for my body to handle. I found myself stumbling forward, frantically waving my arms to counteract the inertia before I made a complete ass of myself. And, luckily, I succeeded.

To a degree, at least.

Depending on how you looked at it.

Another one of those glass half full/half empty situations that I told you that I find myself in way too often.

I succeeded in stopping myself from landing face first on the hardwood surface. That was a win. It was just at the cost of spilling my drink all over my pants, leaving a dark blue wet patch conveniently where my crotch was. Way too convenient. Just like a scene from a Hollywood movie. You couldn't say that the situation was any more perfect unless I looked up—straight into the brown eyes of that sad, brunette who was suddenly paying a great deal of attention to me.

I was in the lion's den now... I just never knew that lions had such beautiful eyes.

CHAPTER 3

"Ah."

The word sprang from my mouth without my consent. It wasn't at all what I wanted to say, obviously. If I had a choice, I would have preferred something like "Hey," or "Nice weather we've been having lately, right?" Both options would have been more friendly and easier to transfer into a conversation.

Maybe next time.

Both of us remained suspended in that moment, clearly unable to decide on what to do. She was staring down at me from her stool at the bar, while I looked back up at her. My body was already shaking.

Now, I couldn't tell for certain, maybe it was just my perception or my embarrassment, but it seemed like she was staring at my crotch for an exorbitant amount of time. An awkward amount of time. And to make things worse, the ray of light reflecting off the bottles of fancy liquor adorning the shelf cast a multicolored spotlight on that very spot. My groin was now front and center—the star of the show. It wouldn't be until she spoke a few seconds later that the magic of the moment was broken.

"I'm sorry."

Her first words were as soft and gentle as her delicate movements. Just the right amount of tone and pitch that prevented them from falling into the monotone category, but somehow, they still held with them a caring quality.

But why was she the one apologizing?

Did she not just notice me almost crash into her?

I honestly didn't know how to even respond. It really was just a bizarre thing to say.

"For... what?"

She pointed at my crotch.

"That."

"My groin?!"

Her brown eyes flicked back up to mine and she raised an eyebrow, as if she didn't expect such an answer, even though she was the one still pointing directly at it.

"You spilled your drink on your pants."

"Uh, yeah. But that wasn't your fault. You don't have to apologize. I should be the one apologizing to you. It was my bad."

Standing up to my full height, I took the next moment to get a good look at the girl in front of me.

She was dressed simply. By that I mean there was nothing extravagant about what she wore. There wasn't any semblance of style either. No accessories and no color. She wore a long-sleeved black shirt that had faded slightly to give it a grayish hue, a dark pair of jeans, and her hair fell past her shoulders in a way that resembled a black veil. Everything about her seemed to tell me that she wasn't trying to draw any attention to herself.

Still, despite her plain appearance, none of that detracted from that pleasant and kind face or her large, brown eyes—eyes that were still fixated on the wet spot below my belt.

"Hey, it's rude to stare," I said.

"Oh, sorry," she apologized again, looking flustered. "But do you want me to help you with that? Somehow, I still feel it's my fault."

She grabbed a small stack of napkins from a dispenser off the table and reached her hand out until it was mere inches away from my junk. I almost let her do it too, but then reason returned to me at the most opportune—or maybe inopportune—moment.

"Whoa, hey, what do you think you're doing?!"

"Drying that wet spot," she said innocently. Her eyes were wide now, as if she was confused. As if this was a completely rational and normal thing to offer. As if I was the one being the weirdo.

What was up with this girl?

"No, I'm good. You don't have to do that. I can do it myself." I grabbed the napkins from her hand and started dabbing the area myself. The moisture had long since soaked in, so the endeavor seemed ultimately pointless, but I continued anyway because I didn't want her to get any more funny ideas.

"I'm sorry if I offended you," she said. "I wasn't thinking."

"It's okay. It was an honest mistake. Happens all the time." I stuck out my unoccupied hand. "My name's Chris, by the way."

She took my hand.

"My name is Bernadette."

"It's, uh, nice to meet you, Bernadette."

"Likewise."

I released her hand just a moment before it would have been considered too long, and let my arm drop to my side.

Silence.

Now what was I supposed to say?

The commotion from the happenings around the bar only seemed to amplify the stillness between us. Unable to maintain eye contact any longer, my attention fell back down to my crotch. The wet spot still looked just as dark, possibly even darker than it did a few moments earlier.

Making conversation with a stranger. You don't really remember how hard it is until you're put in a situation where you're forced to do it. Didn't help that I was out of practice too. Over the last couple months, I had mostly only talked to Brad, Mom, and my academic advisor. I had forgotten that I was never a good conversationalist to begin with.

Through the locks of my own black hair, I glanced up to see how Bernadette was faring in this awkward situation I'd put us both into. Seeing her squirm would have calmed me down and built up a sense of rapport between the two of us who were going through this ordeal together. She was probably just as socially awkward as I was.

Or so I hoped.

But you don't always get what you hoped for. You probably don't even get it half of the time.

To my left, Bernadette had turned back towards the bar and her eyes were now fixated on her cup. There was not a trace of nervousness about her. No wasted movements. No fidgeting. No nervous tick of any kind. Her body looked frighteningly still as if it were cut from marble. Pale skin peaked out and contrasted with her dark clothing and hair. It seemed as if she had drifted back into her own world, making no sign, from what I could tell, that she was even still aware of my existence.

"So, uh…" I threw out the words like a piece of bait, praying that she'd at least nibble it, if not give it a little tug. My main goal was to try and transition the conversation into a more conducive direction about our interests or why we were at the bar on this night. Normal small talk topics, but she didn't respond. It left me utterly dejected and embarrassed. Was this one of those hints that guys never seemed to pick up on?

I was on the verge of cutting my losses and retreating to Brad when she raised the cup, threw back her head and downed the remaining liquid in one fell swoop.

The simple gesture made something that should have been so obvious click in the back of my mind. Maybe this was her way of throwing me some bait of her own.

So, I decided to bite.

As a fish would.

Already raising my hand to signal to the bartender, I said. "Hey, looks like you're finished. Let me buy you another drink."

She waved my request off with a hand of her own.

"Oh, no, you don't have to," she said. "It's just water."

Water!

The word hit me with enough force to rival one of Brad's slaps, and suddenly I was able to understand what he meant about weirdos who sat around drinking water at a bar alone, one's who didn't interact with their surroundings in any meaningful way. If we used Bernadette here as an example, he had a point.

She must have noticed my shocked face because she added, "Sorry, is that weird?"

"No, not at all. That's perfectly normal," I lied.

Even if I believed that she was weird, that didn't mean I was going to say it to her face. That's just plain rude. And to admit it would be to put me in the same boat as her.

"What a relief." Bernadette sighed. "I was actually disappointed that they didn't have the drink I wanted, so I chose this instead. It was the next best thing."

"Oh, what's your drink of choice?"

"Tea. A cup of jasmine tea."

"Okay, that's weird."

Did they even serve hot tea at bars? Especially at a sports bar down the street from a college? I wouldn't know. But at least in my opinion, it was weird in the sense that it was incredibly uncommon to hear someone request that. Weirdness can be interpreted as merely going against the norm of what people believe to be natural, after all.

"Is that so?" Bernadette said. She sounded disappointed this time.

"Yeah, but if that's what you like then go ahead and drink tea. I'm not trying to stop you."

"Okay."

"Are you not much of a drinker?"

"I drink things all the time."

"Uh, like alcohol and stuff." Her answer threw me off for a second. I couldn't tell if she was joking.

"Ah, I don't drink any alcohol."

"Thank you! Me neither."

Finally, it seemed like our conversation may have been going somewhere, and I was getting excited, but my hopes were killed when she didn't follow up at all. Once again silence had fallen over us. Unlike last time though, things had somehow become more awkward than before, but I wasn't going to give up yet. A force inside of me was telling me to try and press forward and see where I can lead things.

Bernadette was staring off blankly into space. She looked deep in thought. Seeing that expression reminded me of what I'd found mesmerizing about her in the first place. All of her features were slightly turned downwards. The corners of her lips. Her eyebrows. Her eyes.

Even her shoulders. It might have been personal business, but I felt the urge to ask her about it anyway. Maybe she needed someone to talk to. I'd felt the same way not too long ago, so I could sympathize with her on an emotional level. But on the other hand, maybe it was nothing at all? I didn't know her.

"Hey, Bernadette."

She didn't respond, so I tried again.

"Bernadette?"

"Oh, yes?"

"Penny for your thoughts?"

"Sorry, I don't need the money. Maybe a while ago I could have used it, but I have no use for them anymore. There's not much a single penny can do in the grand scheme of things anyway. Did you know that it costs more to make a penny than they're worth?"

"Are we talking about economics now?! I meant that judging by your expression, it looked like you had a lot on your plate."

"You must be mistaken. I'm not very hungry right now."

"I wasn't asking you about what you wanted to eat either!"

There was no question about it, this girl was weird. I was willing to give her the benefit of the doubt before, but this sealed the deal. She must be making fun of me. Was this some overly convoluted way to reject someone? Had I been away from the outside world for too long? What year was this?

On the other side of the counter, the bartender who must have heard my outburst looked between the two of us, then glared at me.

"I'm sorry, if I upset you," Bernadette said. "I tend to do that sometimes... I-I'm bad at reading situations. I've always been like this."

"I'm not upset. Just surprised."

"Because of what I said?"

"Uh, yeah?"

"So... it's still a problem?"

Still a problem?

I didn't know about all that.

But maybe I was the one that was really at fault for all of this? This whole situation could have been chalked up to my own social incompetence as much as hers. It would make just as much sense if I was the one to apologize to her for my outburst.

"Hey, Bernadette look—"

I stopped mid-sentence.

No, I was interrupted before I could finish.

Something threw me off my train of thought.

It was a sight that I really didn't want to see.

In front of me, tears were welling up in Bernadette's eyes. Big wet ones. They threatened to spill forth at any second.

Where did those come from?!

That couldn't possibly have been me!

I grabbed a fresh wad of napkins from the dispenser and pressed them in her direction. "Here! Don't cry! Please don't—"

It was too late.

Bernadette started sobbing. Two streams of tears were riding down the slopes of her face until they merged at the point of her chin. From here they dripped down into her lap, soaking into her cwn jeans.

"Please stop crying! What's wrong?!" I pleaded, but my words didn't seem to reach her. She continued to cry, her shoulders bouncing to the rhythm of her sobs. Bernadette wasn't being loud or anything, but my commotion was attracting a lot of unwanted attention and lingering eyes from those around us. In particular, the bartender who was staring angrily at me now.

It's not my fault, man! This girl started crying on her own—I promise!

"Bernadette, it's okay. Don't cry. People are staring at us!"

At that, her head snapped up. She glanced around at all the different faces looking at her—at us. The whole scene must have looked terrible for my image. Any way I sliced it, I came out looking like the bad guy. They must have thought I was an abusive boyfriend berating his tender and loving girlfriend until she started crying in public. With this narrative already forming in their minds, I didn't see any way that I'd be able to make them think otherwise.

Luckily, I didn't have to.

"I'm sorry. I'm sorry. I'm sorry," Bernadette repeated over and over. With each new apology, she faced a different group of people who were just as confused as I was. "I'm sorry for bothering you and ruining your night!"

The display from the tearful girl seemed to have its intended effect as the onlookers started turning away from her awkwardly, and before I knew it, everything had returned to normal, to the point right before she started crying. It was like it never happened at all.

What a chain of events.

After another minute, Bernadette had dried her face with the napkins and was now sitting with her hands folded neatly in her lap.

"Thank you, Chris. I appreciate it."

"For what?"

"For the insightful conversation."

"Insightful? In what way? This whole conversation has been completely incoherent. I'm so confused."

"Anyway."

"Are you ignoring me now?!"

Bernadette smiled gently.

"I've just been thinking about a lot of different things lately..." she said, moving the conversation along, definitely ignoring my question.

"No kidding."

"Yes, I'm serious. It's been...hard for me." She fiddled with her empty glass, taking her time to find the words she was looking for. I'd decided against pressing her and instead waited for her to speak again.

"Do you ever get that feeling where it seems like everything in your life is a complete mess? That's what I'm dealing with currently. There's just so much going on that I can't focus. I don't know how I'm supposed to clean it up."

More so than I'd like to admit, honestly. In my case, it was the rough last year I had. Breaking up with Zoey had messed me up, and I only just now felt like I was recovering from it. For the better part of three months, I'd virtually never left the apartment I shared with Brad. All I did was lay in bed and stare at the ceiling. I didn't want to move. I couldn't move.

But here I was now attempting to be social at least. "Attempting" being the key word.

Even then, things didn't feel completely normal for me yet. And I didn't know if they'd ever will.

"If you don't mind me asking. What kind of problems are they? The ones you can't focus on," I asked.

Bernadette thought for a moment. "Family."

"Okay, that sounds normal. I actually had family issues when I was—"

"And boyfriend."

"Ah..."

My heart sank.

Well, I guess it made sense. I knew that there was a possibility going in that Bernadette was taken. However, I still couldn't help but feel a tad bit disappointed by this revelation. Despite all the mental turmoil I was just subjected too, I was still hoping to get her number at the end of all this.

"Yeah, I'm just having a hard time deciding how I feel about him. I like him, and I see his many good qualities, but I think... I think I'm going to end up breaking up with him."

My ears perked up.

Did I have a chance?

"What makes you want to do that?" I asked.

"Father and mother don't approve. I've always tried to make them happy."

For better or worse.

"I see."

"There's more to it, though. I don't want any conflict or trouble. I don't want to hurt him or disappoint my parents. I just want everyone to be happy, but I already know that isn't possible. Last time I tried to do that, I hurt someone very dear to me. So, I know at the end of this, someone is going to be let down."

"Uh huh."

"Yeah, that's basically what I've been contemplating for the past week." Bernadette's finger traced the swirling designs on the countertop round and round. "What do you think? Any thoughts? I'd like to hear what you have to say."

"Me?"

"Mm-hmm. After all, you're insightful. We've only been talking for a few minutes, and you've already pinpointed one of my biggest flaws. That means you must be smart. A social genius even."

You're giving me too much credit, lady. Anyone would have been able to notice that.

But—

She wanted my thoughts on the matter? Huh... That's a difficult one.

Would she have still asked if she knew anything else about me and my shoddy choices? Not likely. Asking any stranger for advice in this situation seemed like a farfetched idea to be honest. A stranger wouldn't know the whole context of the relationship and all the minute nuances. It's things like that that make asking a stranger for advice a bad idea. They may have lived through similar situations, but they couldn't possibly understand.

"You want my advice?"

She nodded. There was a hopeful look in her eyes as she leaned forward on her stool.

"I don't know."

"Huh?"

Bernadette's mouth fell open. Such a blunt answer was not something she anticipated at all.

"I can't help you. It's better if you figure out how to solve your own problems. And, also, you wouldn't want my advice anyway. It'd probably screw things up even more than they already are. That's *my* biggest flaw."

"That's—"

"Like I said, I don't think I can help you in any way, shape, or form."

"..."

I'm sorry, Bernadette. It's for your own good. Though it's not wrong to ask for help, you have to make sure you ask the right person. A dependable person. I don't see myself that way yet, so that shouldn't be me. After all, if you're drowning, what good would it do you to ask another drowning person for help?

Bernadette stayed silent.

Maybe she was thinking about what I just told her, or maybe she was offended. I couldn't tell. Her expression had returned to that sad quality from earlier.

I turned away and tried to pinpoint Brad's location in the crowd. I thought now would be a good time as ever to gently excuse myself, but I couldn't seem to find him. Knowing Brad, some other girl may have caught his attention, so he was distracted.

"It's just... confusing."

Bernadette's soft voice caused me to turn around.

Her hands were folded in her lap again. Hunched forward on her stool, she resembled a child who'd just been scolded. My natural reaction to seeing this was to look into her eyes. It might make me sound like an asshole, but I didn't want her to start crying and cause a scene again. However, her eyes were dry. She was just staring down at the counter.

Something about that sight caused me to recall an event from my past, and it was that recollection that made me reconsider my response.

I sighed and looked up at the ceiling, as if the answer I was looking for was hidden somewhere among the water stains.

"Yeah, I feel that," I answered.

Bernadette immediately perked up.

"You do?"

"I think everyone does at some point. It's a common thing."

"It is?"

"Uh, of course. That's just life. But people have been overcoming those kinds of feelings and situations for thousands of years."

"They have?"

"Yup, and I'm sure you will too, only if you keep at it. Don't give up."

"I will?"

"Sure. In one way or another, I hope everyone can."

"We can?"

"Yeah, that's what I believe."

Ultimately, I didn't expect her understanding of what I was trying to say to match her ability to use pronouns, but I hoped it came close. I wanted her to grasp the essence of it at least. I didn't actually know if she'd be okay, but I gave her the answer I thought she needed at the moment. Despite their overall naivety, they were affirming words and that's all some people needed to pick themselves up. To hear that things weren't entirely hopeless. In fact, Zoey had told me similar things on numerous occasions whenever I'd let my thoughts get the best for me. I don't think I'll ever be able to shake the strong impression those words always had on me, or her either for that matter.

She was the one that saved me, and as a result, that's the way that I'd always envision her. The paragon of unwavering dependability. A responsible and respectable person in every regard. The light at the end of the tunnel. She'd much rather let herself down than the ones who put their faith in her.

I'd broken up with her, but even now, I still wanted to emulate her example.

"That was profound. Did you think of that yourself?" Bernadette asked.

"No, I was told the same thing before."

"Did it help you?"

"Yeah, and it still does."

Bernadette smiled. It had a hopeful quality to it. "Well, thank you, Chris. Your words put me at ease. They really did. I think I know what I need to do. Thank you so much." She stood up abruptly and started to straighten herself out, grabbing her purse. "I'm glad we had the chance to meet like this. I'm going to call my parents right now and try to talk things over with them and explain."

"No problem, it was nice to meet you too, Bernadette."

"Call me, Adi. It's easier to say in conversation."

"Sure thing, Adi."

That was a cute nickname. It fit her well.

She smiled again and spun around as elegantly as a ballroom dancer, and slowly began to walk away. From behind, her black hair bounced with each of her steps. I didn't know why, but I felt like I was forgetting to do something. Something important. What could it have been...? Oh, yeah, that's right!

"Wait!"

Adi, who'd already taken about five paces towards the exit, turned back around to face me.

"Yes?"

"This may be a bit forward," I said, scratching the back of my head. "But... but, uh, I was wondering if I could get your number."

"My number?"

"Yeah, your cellphone number."

Adi gave me a curious look. She seemed to be considering my request.

"No."

Ack.

Her answer was merciless and abrupt. There wasn't even the slightest attempt to put me down nicely.

"Didn't I say I had a boyfriend?"

"Yeah, I guess, you did."

What was I even thinking? Of course, she wouldn't have given me her number. That was so stupid.

Adi watched me silently, her head tilted slightly to the right. A moment later, she was back at the bar. She whipped out a pen from her purse and scribbled something down on one of the napkins on the countertop. When she was finished, she brandished the napkin in front of me with a graceful flourish.

"This is my twin sister's number. Her name is Yasmin. I think she'd be interested in meeting someone like you. She's not seeing anyone. At least, I don't think she is."

I slowly took the napkin from her, a beautifully written number adorning its surface in black ink. There was no question as to what each number represented. Her handwriting was clear as could be.

"Ah. Thanks."

Adi nodded before turning back around. This time she made it to the exit without any other distractions, but I didn't know that for sure. I wasn't watching her that closely anymore. My eyes were glued to the napkin that I now held delicately in my hand as if it was some sacred cloth I needed to protect.

The thin paper felt damp between my fingertips.

I wasn't going to take any chances, none whatsoever. Knowing my amazing luck, I'd end up losing it. I needed to save this number now.

Pulling my phone from my pocket, my thumbs flew across the screen, pattering the sequence of numbers I was given. It was baffling how fast my fingers were moving.

Contact saved.

I smiled and stared at the screen for a few seconds.

Hm.

You know what? Maybe I'd just send her a text right now? I was feeling pretty good about myself. I didn't remember the last time I felt this confident.

I opened my contacts and used my thumb to scroll all the way to the bottom of the list. That may have sounded like it would take a while, but it didn't. I only had a few other numbers saved on my phone. I wasn't a popular person like Brad. I hardly received any text messages anymore.

After less than half a second of scrolling, I was already at the bottom of the list where Yasmin's recently created contact was waiting for me, but it wasn't the only one that I saw. I just couldn't help but notice another name sitting right under it.

Zoey.

The letters of that familiar name glared back at me. If you saw my face, I must have looked like a deer caught in cellphone lights.

I hadn't deleted her number yet. I was too scared to do so. To relinquish that last connection would have meant things between the two of us were over for good. That wasn't something I was ready to do. And it was that thought I was having, which made me think that maybe I wasn't ready to start talking to anyone else either.

CHAPTER 4

The sky had darkened considerably by the time I'd left the bar. The occasional breeze that blew through the shopping district of Oceanside exacerbated the frigid night air, causing the hairs on my arms to flutter in the wind. I guess the upside was that it helped me stop thinking about Adi.

I had been abandoned.

The phrase could have many different interpretations. Sometimes good—most of the time, bad.

I guess the obvious question would be how being abandoned could ever be a good thing. By its very definition, the word elicits negative feelings, even more so than other similar words. For instance, to say that you were abandoned sounds much worse than saying that you were sad. Abandoned is more of an umbrella term that encompasses a range of different emotions, including sadness.

Being abandoned could only be a good thing in very specific scenarios. And most of the time, it was only after the fact that you realize that the abandonment was a blessing in disguise. Sometimes it would be years down the line, but in some very special cases, it was sooner than expected.

My father abandoned my mother and me when I was younger.

He just walked out the door one day. The really messed up thing about it was he told me he'd be right back. That he had a surprise waiting for me.

Naturally, a small part of me, a part that gets smaller with each passing day, is still waiting for him to return. I wasn't waiting in the sense that I still expected him to walk through the door with that surprise in hand, but it was more of a longing—a lingering feeling down in the deepest recesses of my heart.

Or maybe his leaving was the surprise he was talking about?

I didn't know, and I'd probably never find out. It was a question that frequently crept into my mind.

Well, that's okay.

It might not be obvious from that little anecdote, but I'd already found the silver lining in that situation with my father. Uncovered that it was a blessing in disguise, you might say. And as fate would have it, it was later that week, so I wasn't that sad for very long.

But anyway, yeah, I'd been abandoned.

However, this time I'm not referencing my father. I'm talking about Brad.

He'd abandoned me to brave the freezing night air accompanied only by the fading stain on my crotch and my own thoughts.

I don't blame him, though. I couldn't blame him.

Another gust of wind hit me, and I hunched over a few inches to compensate. The pain in my lower back was entirely worth the added few degrees of warmth.

I should have grabbed my jacket before heading out. I'd forgotten just how cold it could get around here during wintertime. We don't get snow, but the temperature could still sneak up on you if you weren't careful, as was the current case. Now, I had to pay physically for my carelessness.

I could have called a rideshare service, but I decided against it. That's because I wanted to walk. Along with some light jogging on occasion, walking was one of my main sources of physical activity. If anything, it might have been one of my only hobbies as well. Of course, that was if you could consider walking a sort of hobby. For reasons previously stated, I hadn't been getting out much lately. It was too painful to leave my room, so my body had deteriorated until I was no more than a crooked scarecrow—sticks and bones. This meant that, despite the bitter cold, it felt nice being outside again. I used to go on walks because it helped me think, and this happened to be one of those times when I had a lot to think about.

After Adi left the bar, leaving me to stare at the two names on my contact list, Brad came out of nowhere and slapped me on the back for the third time that night. My phone flew into the air, and I just barely caught it in the tips of my fingers.

He'd been watching me and Adi from a spot across the bar and wanted to know how things played out. He was especially interested in what was written on the napkin she gave me. So, I gave him the general rundown. I told him how smooth I'd been. How everything had gone flawlessly. How she'd hung on every word I said. And that the only reason that I didn't get her number was because she already had a boyfriend. I ended my mostly true story by waving the little napkin adorned with Adi's handwriting and her sister Yasmin's phone number.

Brad cheered. He gave me a double thumbs up and offered to buy me a drink, which I declined.

The praise was more than enough.

It felt good.

I needed it.

"So, what's next, buddy?" Brad had asked.

"I don't know."

He rolled his eyes and groaned.

"Damn, I shouldn't even have to ask this question. But you're going to text her, right? Yasmin?"

"I'm not sure yet."

"You'd better text her," Brad said. "Only you'd have a perfectly good shot lined up in front of you and debate whether to just take it. Just do it. You're probably going to love her."

"What makes you think that?"

"Come on. You know."

"Know what?"

Brad grinned.

"Who wouldn't love, Y-ASS-min? She's going to have a big one, I promise."

"Shut the hell up."

I knew it was a terrible idea to tell him my physical preferences. You reap what you sow.

Either way, for me, taking the shot wasn't that simple. It couldn't be that simple. Acting required much more effort than simply talking about it. This was especially that case when someone else's life was involved.

"In any event." Brad pulled out his own phone and scrolled through his messages. "I'm going to head out. Crystal texted me while you were pulling your moves and asked if I could come over."

"Oh, and what are you two going to do? Study?"

Brad gave me a look and I knew exactly what it meant.

"Hey, now," I said. "Weren't you telling me about the whole thing involving your academic probation? They aren't going to let you swim anymore if you don't bring up your grades."

"Yeah, I think I might've mentioned something like that."

Something as serious as that, you'd damn well better be sure of.

"What?" Brad said. "What's with that scary look?"

"Don't you have like... two midterms Monday morning? As in tomorrow?"

"Yeah, I think I might've mentioned something like that. Anyway, don't wait up for me."

Don't wait up for him...

I didn't bother to press him any further. I already knew exactly what those words meant. It was one of many code phrases that we'd been developing since we met. Each one correlated to a different meaning or significance. The point was to allow us to say inconspicuous things in public that would otherwise turn heads or, in the worst case, get the cops called on us. Some of the others include but are not limited to: "The monkey is climbing the bars", "I've spilled the milk", and my personal favorite, "Nothing is lonelier than a coffin." Don't ask what they mean. You don't want to know. The only thing that you should know is that where we live, there are no monkey bars, we don't drink milk, and we don't own any coffins.

But, in all honesty, even though we both came up with the code phrases, Brad would be the one making the most use out of them, especially on his nightly playdates. Usually, they were no more than a warning to let me know that he'd need to borrow our apartment for an hour or two. Not that it was necessary because I always let him. During those times, I'd end up just going to the library or spending the night at Zoey's. However, in the past few months, he'd been considerate enough not to bring anyone over or kick me out.

Saying that Brad had a girlfriend wouldn't be entirely correct.

The guy had *girlfriends*.

Did the girls know that? I had no idea.

Some guys just had it much easier than the rest of us—both in terms of physical qualities and the mental ones. I didn't think I'd have the mental capacity to juggle interactions and relationships with so many people. Social situations weren't my strongest suit.

And that's why—

That's why I hesitated about texting either Yasmin or Zoey.

In my naïvety, I didn't think it would be honest for me to text them both. Not until I knew that I would be doing it for the right reasons.

I was now passing the entrance to the college campus. It was a sprawling gateway to the joys and wonders of higher education—Oceanside University. The arch, which stood above a small bridge, had taken on a green hue akin to that of the oxidized Statue of Liberty herself.

It was the sight of that arch that let me know that in just two more blocks I'd arrive at the off-campus apartment that Brad and I rented.

The night was still young, and people were wandering about enjoying the chilly, Sunday night air. Lucky for them, they all had jackets on, lined with faux fur, sherpa, cotton, and any other material made for the express purpose of keeping your body warm. And here I was, walking in my oversized short-sleeved T-shirt, each breeze constantly reminding me that there was still a wet spot on my crotch.

As I walked, I couldn't help but notice that there were a lot of couples among the people that I passed by. All of them were engaged in PDAs that spanned the entire spectrum.

On one end, some couples were simply holding hands. Nothing lewd or unsightly about that. I'd even say it was cute to see, like a pure, innocent grade school love. However, on the opposite end, things were different. I won't get into the gory details, but I encountered more than a few that were a couple bases past full-blown making out. These couples had the common decency to take it into the dark alleyways, out of view of street traffic, but after that, they didn't do much else to hide themselves. They were putting on a free private show, which some stopped to watch.

I didn't believe it at first, but it was true what people said about starting to see more couples walking around when you're single or lonely. It's as if the world was trying to torture you more than it already was, like a sick inside joke. Sure, it's not like I didn't see any couples at all when Zoey and I were going out, but in my months away from the outside world, it looked like that number had multiplied exponentially.

Or had the world always been like this, and I was just only noticing it now?

That said, I wasn't ready to jump willy-nilly into the first relationship that came my way, even if it was something I knew I needed to do. After being in something long-term, it didn't feel right. To do that seemed to lessen my previous experience. Cheapen it.

And it's not like I broke up with her because I wanted to.

It's a cliché, and I know it doesn't make it sound any better to admit that, but it was a classic, "It's me, not you" moment. I was aware of my shortcomings, and I subconsciously knew that I couldn't live up to the expectations she had for me. Not yet at least.

To some degree, I figured she must have been harboring those expectations of me ever since we'd met, which was coincidentally the week after my father had left too. Zoey was the silver lining in that situation. That blessing in disguise I was talking about. The one who saved me, and the one that I continued to hold in such a high regard.

The event in question happened so long ago it might as well have been a million years in the past. We were eight back then, which would have made Zoey eight years old as well (she was still a couple of months older than me, though, something she made sure to bring up whenever she could).

Back in our hometown, there was this small park across the street, one that they tore down a while back. It wasn't like one of those big city parks that had multiple baseball or soccer fields, the ones that always get filled up on the weekends from various sports leagues. This one was just a humble community park used by the homes in the area where mothers would congregate for playdates. The ground was covered in wood chips, and the place had a jungle gym, sandbox, swing set, and slide—nothing fancy at all, just the bare necessities.

I was alone there that day. Well, it wasn't day. It was night, and I'd snuck out of the house while my mom was in her room. In retrospect, I can see that's not what an eight-year-old kid should be doing, unless they were trying to get kidnapped, but I had to get out of the house. I couldn't stand to be inside, and any other place seemed like a better choice.

Once there, I'd climbed to the top of the jungle gym and planted my butt at the summit. The place was illuminated by a single lamp that cast a golden glow over the entire park. The warm, yellow light contrasted with how I felt at that moment.

I was there for a while. I don't remember how long, but when I finally decided to stand up and leave, I put too much weight on my leg, one that had fallen asleep. As a result, I slipped and stumbled off the dome structure. Those play structures really were metal deathtraps if you think about it, and it made complete sense that the park was eventually torn down. But, anyway, my foot ended up trapped between the bars, leaving me dangling for my life over a pit of razor-sharp bark. I was so shocked that I didn't even scream. With all that blood flowing into my head, my thought process must have been compromised because I had the bright idea to try and dislodge my foot instead of trying to pull myself up like any normal person would have. It worked.

Needless to say, I fell.

But I never hit the ground.

I landed in the arms of that girl.

She'd caught me.

That small girl had caught me.

And her first words after my feet were firmly planted on solid ground again?

"Kids aren't allowed to be here at night. It's dangerous."

"You're a kid too!" I retorted.

"Yeah, but I saw you from my window, and I came to tell you."

It was a novel first interaction and one that would forever shape my perception of her.

After that, we sat side-by-side on the swing set and talked. The first thing she asked about was why I was there. I remember debating back then if I wanted to tell her or not. I wasn't supposed to talk to strangers, but she did save me, and it was the least I could do. So, I sat there motionless on my swing seat and told her what I knew, all while she swung back and forth getting higher and higher.

Dad hadn't come home in a week. I think that affected Mom more than it did me. At that point, I still had faith that he'd be "right back," but Mom must have known the truth. Looking back on it now with a fresh perspective, she must have known the moment I told her. The following nights, after she'd tucked me in and kissed me goodnight, I'd hear sounds coming from her room down the hall. Initially, I ignored them. Maybe I was scared, or I just didn't want to get up, but I ignored them. It wasn't until the fifth night that I finally got out of bed to investigate and find out what those noises were.

Standing outside her room, I heard her crying. Through that door, Mom was crying. It was a terrifying thing for me, hearing that. That's not something that a kid might think was possible for adults to do. Adults were always the people to tell children, including myself, not to cry, after all. That things weren't worth crying over.

Eventually, after listening on the opposite side of her door, trying to make sense of it all, I concluded that this was completely my fault because of what I told her about Dad. As far as I could tell, her crying started after that. So, that meant I was the one who caused this to happen somehow and there was nothing that I could do to fix it, either. I was powerless. Reveling in those thoughts, I stood there listening for a while before walking back to my own room. I slipped into my now cold bed and pulled the covers over my ears.

It was while I was lying there in bed that I decided that the next day, I'd sneak out, so that I wouldn't have to hear her crying anymore. Instead of going to her, I'd run away.

After I finished my story, I went silent. I wanted to hear the girl's response, not that I expected it to make me feel better. She'd probably tell me that I was a wimp. A loser. A scaredy-cat. But—I was wrong. She didn't say anything. She was still just swinging beside me, not a care in the world. At first, I thought she hadn't been listening at all, and I was going to tell her off, but before I could open my mouth, at the very apex of her forward arc, she slipped off the swing and launched into the air.

She flew.

Way over anything else.

The spectacle of it caused me to momentarily forget my own problems. I watched in awe as she went higher and higher until, finally, she floated back to Earth a considerable distance away. Her blonde hair settled half a second after her.

I couldn't help but think that—

It was cool.

So unbelievably cool.

"It's okay," she said, her back still facing me. "It's okay. You don't have to worry about anything."

"What?"

She looked over her shoulder at me, just enough for me to see her smile. "I'll never abandon you."

"You'll never... abandon me?" I repeated.

With a single firm nod, she declared, "I'll always be by your side—no matter what."

She told me her name was Zoey.

And after that, we were inseparable. She led me by the hand everywhere we went.

Whenever I found myself in a bind, she was the one that pulled me out of it.

She never let me down.

Finally arriving at the door to my apartment complex, I buzzed myself in and headed straight up the stairs to the fifth floor. The elevator was usually broken, so I didn't see any point in trying to use it.

It was a cheap place that Brad and I had rented out together after our first year in the dorms. Our initial logic behind the decision was that we wouldn't be back here that much to begin with on account of all the "partying" we were going to be doing. The place would be strictly for sleeping and showering, nothing more. While he was still living up to that expectation, I was doing a lot more than just sleeping and showering here. The apartment was small. As small as physically possible, and jam-packed with only the essentials. Two beds. Two desks. Two cabinets. Basically, a twin pair of everything, except for the shared window centered in the far wall, providing the stunning view of the dead-end alley behind our apartment complex. There wasn't much light in that alley, so you really couldn't see all that well into it.

I didn't know if it was because I had just been caught up in my feelings a few moments before, but there was something lonely about being stuck in a room meant for two people. The pairs of everything just highlighted your solitude. That something was missing. The walls that I was so excited to come back to, to hide away behind, only seemed to lock in that isolated feeling, kind of like a jail cell, or more accurately—

A coffin.

Nothing is lonelier than a coffin.

It was a phrase that perfectly encapsulated my mood.

There was nothing joyous or welcoming about this place. No one was waiting for me. No one wanted to see me or cared about me. It was just cold and empty. Though I had used this place as a sanctuary; it just emphasized everything that was *wrong* with me.

I was useless without someone guiding me along.

I felt incomplete without someone beside me.

I had depended on Zoey for my whole life. Relied on her to the point that no one could rely on me, and that I couldn't even rely on myself.

That's why I felt lost.

That's also why I wasn't worthy of her and her love.

We weren't equal. From the day we met, I'd put my complete and utter faith in her, while I did nothing. And it was that mindset that led me to my lowest point.

I wanted to be like her, but I was nothing like her.

But there was another problem. One that wasn't apparent to me until recently. I didn't want to be alone—couldn't be alone—but I also didn't want to feel useless. It was the same feeling I'd experienced when I heard my mother crying. I couldn't do anything.

The only way that would change, and for me to become worthy, was if I could embody Zoey's attitude into my own actions. To become dependable. Be someone that others could look up to as well. To never let anyone down again. The old me would have been able to do that, but things were different now. She wasn't around anymore.

Yeah...

If I didn't want to be alone, I had to put myself out there.

But, most importantly, this time around, I had to make sure that I wasn't a burden. I had to take the initiative. Be a leader. Let them lean on me.

That way, I wouldn't feel inadequate. As I always had in the past.

And when would be a better time to start than right now? I'd promised myself that I would change in the months after we broke up, but I'd never found the chance until tonight.

Any small step toward that goal would result in me improving myself.

It's never too late to teach an old dog new tricks, as they say.

And maybe when I'm ready... I'll be able to face Zoey again, but this time as equals.

I emptied the contents of my pocket out onto my desk and retrieved my cell phone. Pulling up Yasmin's contact information, I immediately started typing a short text message. It was nothing extravagant or wordy, just something quick before my brain tried to stop me. When I was finished, I read the message over to make sure it was clear before hitting send.

Hey, my name is Chris.
This is a little weird, but your sister,
Bernadette, gave me your contact information
She said you might be interested in meeting
someone like me, haha.

I felt relieved, as if I'd just completed a monumental task. Like I had accomplished something.

My first step.

However, I didn't have much time to celebrate because not five seconds after hitting send—my phone buzzed to notify me that I'd just received a message.

Yasmin had already replied.

CHAPTER 5

Delete my fucking number.

Well.

I didn't expect to see that. I don't think anyone would have. I mean—where did the animosity even come from? Any way I looked at it, it was just way too aggressive and direct. I mean, she didn't even say please. What was her problem?

In a surprising turn of events, all the resolve that I'd just built up had instantly evaporated into thin air. Not a single trace of it was left. It was completely and utterly eviscerated. After such a clear and forward message—one that left zero to the imagination—I knew that there was only one thing I could do, and that was exactly the thing she told me to do. I was going to delete her number. Once I did, I'd pretend like none of this ever happened.

Without a moment's hesitation, I went through the necessary steps and highlighted Yasmin's contact in my phone, but before I could hit delete, a new series of messages came in rapid-fire, one after the other. They were all from her.

Hey

Hello?

Are you still there?

Why aren't you responding?

I'm talking to you.

Answer me

And they didn't stop there.

Her messages continued to roll in. It was an endless stream of texts, and my phone wouldn't stop vibrating from all the notifications. Yasmin wasn't giving me a chance to respond at all either—not that there was any point. Anything I tried to say would have most likely been lost in the ever-growing sea of her responses. She wouldn't have had any time to read it with how fast the screen was scrolling.

Helloooo

Hurry up

What are you doing

Im waiting

Talkkkk

Respond to me now

Heyyyyy answerrr

Give me a second, will ya?!

Now, I wouldn't describe myself as an avid texter. I wouldn't even describe myself as an occasional or sporadic one either. This was largely because I wasn't exactly the most popular guy around, not like Brad at least, which meant even if I wanted to, I didn't have many people to text in the first place. So, I should be the last person to ask about social conventions regarding texting.

That being said, this manner of texting couldn't be normal, right? It had already gone way beyond double or triple texting. She'd sent me almost fifty at this point. That was easily more messages than I'd received in the last six months combined.

Yasmin's barrage went on for another half a minute before I was able to find an opening to get in a word edgewise, as they say. I didn't know when I'd get another chance, so I decided that it would be a good idea to address my biggest concern right off the bat.

You told me to delete your number.

She was literally sending me mixed signals.

Telling someone to delete your number was basically a conversation killer. It wasn't something that a person on the receiving end could come back from at all. Yet here she was, wondering why I hadn't replied. Excluding the fact that she kept messaging me, if she wanted me to delete her number, didn't that imply that she didn't want me to talk to her? Her actions didn't make sense. Luckily, I didn't need to wait long for her next message to come in.

Uh, no, I didn't.

You clearly did!
Scroll up those 100 pages and look!

I didn't.

You did. Did you even check?
Why would I even say that if you didn't?
That makes no sense

If I didn't before, I was beginning to think Yasmin had issues just like her sister. Either that or she had a below average grasp of the English language. But it was probably a mixture of both.

Yeah, you aren't making any sense.
I didn't. You calling me a liar?

Then what did you say?

I clearly told you to
"Delete my fucking number"

You left out the "fucking."
That was important.

How was that important? The message was still the same.

Okay.
Fair enough. But I'm so confused.
If you don't want me to respond,
then why are you still talking to me?

Sheesh. Are you dumb? I was bored.
That's why. You don't have to sound
so upset. If you don't want to delete it,
you don't have to

Alright

At least she was being honest. It was all just a joke. A messed up one at my expense, but a joke, nonetheless. I could take it. I never liked people who let a simple joke get to them. But, with all that said and done, we could—

Lose it.

What?

You should lose my fucking number instead.

That'd be better. If you just deleted it,
then nothing would stop you from just

resaving it. This way it's more permanent.

How about I just block you, huh?!
This is bullying and harassment!

And I had all the evidence I needed to prove it. Pages and pages of it. She was just egging me on at this point. If she didn't want to talk, she could have just ignored me.

I'm not bullying you, you stupid moron.
Now give me your lunch money before
I give you a wedgie.

That's the definition of bullying right there!

No

What do you mean no?

Yes

That wasn't a yes-or-no question.

Maybe

It wasn't.

Fine. Fine. You're no fun. You're boring.

And you're abusive.

I don't think I'd even be this rude to my worst enemy, let alone a stranger.

By all accounts and purposes, our exchange did qualify as a "conversation." At least loosely speaking. It was an exchange of dialogue between two or more individuals, but I couldn't shake the feeling that it really wasn't going anywhere.

Much like my conversation with her sister, talking to Yasmin was a hassle, but in a completely different way. It was like I was running on a treadmill, but every few seconds it was getting faster. The catch was I could only use one leg or, rather, one foot. The wrong one. That was to say that I was seemingly always on my back foot with her, if that made sense. Eventually, I'd pass out from exhaustion, if I wasn't outright killed. My twenty-one years of life hadn't prepared me for this at all.

I took a seat on my bed and stared down at my phone. Surprisingly enough, Yasmin hadn't followed up with anything yet. She must have been waiting for me to respond, holding off until that moment to verbally assault me again, all for her amusement. To alleviate her boredom. But I wasn't going to play that game with her anymore. The only way I could win was if I didn't play. It was my only surefire path to victory.

I started getting myself ready for bed. Since Brad wasn't going to be back today, I had the whole room to myself, which was a good thing, besides the loneliness, of course. Recently, I've been a little uncomfortable changing with him around. I had plenty of experience changing in gym class in high school, but this was different. After the descent into Hell that I was subjected to a few months ago, I was more self-conscious around him now. There were things that needed to be hidden. I didn't want him to see my body, so most of the time I'd have to go down the hall to the shared floor bathroom and use one of the stalls if I wanted to change. Brad means well, but he was a nosy guy. I didn't want his prying eyes on me.

It was nearing midnight, so I was tired and wanted to go to bed. I had a meeting in the afternoon with my college advisor, Mia, and I couldn't afford to be late or look sleep-deprived. I could already imagine the look on her face if I came into her office disheveled with dark bags under my eyes. She would have been so disappointed. My ultimate goal for tomorrow was to show her that I was all better now. That I was emotionally and physically capable of being on campus. In order to do that, I needed to be in peak condition.

Having pulled a pair of sweats from out of my drawer, I quickly changed and made my way down the hall to brush my teeth. I took my sweet time, all the while eyeing my phone for any sign of activity. It was quiet though. You could have said that it was lifeless—dead even.

Once I was back in my room, I turned out the lights and slipped underneath the covers. It was warm and cozy. I sank further into the mattress with every second. In no time, I'd be drifting off to Lala land. Peeking through one eye, I glanced at my phone one last time. Should I check it again? I grabbed it.

Still nothing.

Ah...

She hadn't responded to me.

So it really was over, right?

I sighed.

I guess it was for the best. With how rocky things had started, things were never going to go the way I expected anyway. Yasmin hadn't sounded interested at all. That thought made me wonder what Adi could have meant by giving her number to me. She'd seemed sincere about it, and going off my limited knowledge of her, Adi didn't come across as the kind of person who'd knowingly throw me to the dogs. She was genuinely thankful for the vague and cliché advice that I'd given her.

Oh, well. No reason to lose any sleep over it now. In a few days' time, I wouldn't remember any of this anyway. It was all just going to end up being a blip on my radar. Nothing more than a passing thought—

Bzzt.

My phone vibrated.

Moving faster than I thought possible, I sprang up and grabbed it. My eyes took a second to adjust to the sudden influx of light from the screen, but there it was—Yasmin's message—in all its glory.

Hey

That was all she sent this time around. Just that one simple three-lettered message.

There was a lot to unpack here.

On one hand, I could just leave it be. It was obvious bait and if I took it then I'd be falling for her plan hook-line-and-sinker. On the other hand, she may actually have something important to say to me this time.

Hm.

It was a conundrum.

But I knew what I had to do.

Living your entire life questioning the motives of strangers wasn't any way to live, after all. And if I wanted to be like Zoey, then I had to be able to take the high road. Always.

What's up?

Her reply wasn't instant. The icon with the three dots popped up two or three times, showing that she was typing her message, but when they disappeared, no message came through.

What could she be trying to say?

Bzzt.

My phone vibrated again.

I told you to fucking lose my number,
but you're still talking to me.

Okay, I was done.

There was no high ground to be taken here. And if there was, it would have only led to my demise. I tried. I really did.

My mistake.
You won't be hearing from me again.
It was a pleasure getting to know you.
Take it easy out there. Bye

Wait

Wait

Don't go

Don't leave

Why?

I was just having some fun.
You shouldn't be that sensitive. It's boring.

I think only one person is having fun here.

You?

You!

Lol. Well, if it makes you feel better.
I do this to all the guys that bitch sends my way.

You aren't special.

Wow. I didn't know whether to feel relieved or hurt by that.

But, "that bitch"? Was she talking about her sister? That couldn't be, right? Adi was probably one of the least bitchy girls I'd ever met. Of course, I didn't have a large sample size to draw from in that regard, but still.

Are you talking about Adi?

Yeah

She was nice

You know nothing about her.
That air-headed bitch has issues.
It pisses me off

My interest was piqued.

Obviously, something was going on between these two sisters. The resentment was palpable through my phone. However, even though I was curious, I wasn't sure if it was appropriate to pry any further. Family matters weren't something to stumble into willy-nilly in casual conversation. Plus, it wasn't my place to intervene. I'd already done my good deed for the day in helping her sister. I didn't want to push my luck.

As I was thinking of something to say to transition out of the topic, Yasmin beat me to it.

Anyway

Anyway?

I'm just surprised

About what?

That you're still talking

We're back on this again? I could leave

Nah

I meant that most of the other guys
I've spoken to gave up by this point

Or they take forever to respond.

I'm impressed

Uh, thanks?

Let me finish

I was impressed by how stupid and
desperate you are.

Are you sitting up waiting for
me to respond?

Does getting abused turn you on
or something?

Gross

Nasty

Disgusting

Sicko

Creep

Stay away from me

How did that make you feel? Tell me

It made me feel like ending this
conversation and going to sleep.
I'm tired.

Wait

Wait

What now?

I have another question for you.

Well, hurry. I wanna sleep

Okay... why are you actually still here?

Her question caused me to stop and think.

Why was I?

I wasn't exactly sure anymore.

At least initially, I was excited about the prospect of getting to meet someone new, with the slim, non-zero chance that it could develop into something more, something romantic. Of course, that small hope had all but vanished now.

Yet, I persisted.

Like I was simply happy to have someone to talk to. Since I had no one else to talk to.

I guess it's just cause I'm so stupid and desperate.

Yasmin had conditioned me to expect an almost instantaneous reply, so I was once again surprised when her responses didn't come through immediately. As I lay back in bed, holding my phone above my face, I waited until my arm got tired. I then lowered my phone onto my chest and stared up at the ceiling.

Outside, the hum of cars on the street acted as a sort of lullaby to me. It was a relaxing sound—nothing more than white noise—but I liked it because it canceled out the oppressive silence that encapsulated my room. Ironically, without the occasional street sounds, I didn't know if I'd be able to sleep. Many times, I felt like I was waiting for it, like waiting for thunder after seeing a bolt of lightning.

I was so focused on listening to the cars that my phone's sudden vibration startled me.

Hey.

You've been a good boy.

That behavior deserves to be rewarded.

Was she treating me like a dog now?

Okay?

Do you want a belly rub or a treat?

Neither! I'm not your pet!

Lol

Well.

How about I allow you to take me on a date then?

How's that sound?

That's what you really wanted, right?

After reading her message, I jolted up out of bed. I was clutching my phone tightly in both hands.

Setting aside the pretentious way that Yasmin had put it—was she being serious? Did she actually want to go on a date with me? She even used the word "date." Not "hang-out," "get together," or "shindig." If it happened, this thing would be official.

In any case, even if I wanted to, I still wanted to approach the proposition with caution. It seemed like a trap. Something that was way too good to be true.

What's the catch?

Wow.

So distrusting

No catch

I'm just bored

So might as well

Well, what do you say?

Are you really going to turn down
a date with a fine piece of meat like myself?
I'm a real catch.

I blinked a couple of times.

Did she just refer to herself as a piece of meat? I think I heard womankind collectively groaning at such a regressive remark.

But, she had a point.

Adi said the two of them were twins, which meant that there was a high likelihood that Yasmin was bound to be a real looker too. I'd be a huge idiot to miss out on such an obvious opportunity.

Okay, sure.

Cool

We'll do tomorrow afternoon around 3. I don't have anything going on. That work for you?

Yeah, that works.

It was perfect actually. I was meeting with Mia in the afternoon, so I'd be able to head over straight after.

Great.

I'll meet you in front of the school archway.

The one over the bridge leading on to campus.

I sent her the thumbs up emoji.

You better not keep me waiting tomorrow or else.

And thus concluded the first text conversation between Yasmin and me. Maybe it was the start of a budding romance too, but I wasn't going to think that far ahead. There was already so much for me to digest.

I had a date.

CHAPTER 6

Despite it being a short walk, I was still a little tired by the time I was standing outside Mia's office—ten minutes before our scheduled appointment at one.

If you couldn't tell from my labored breathing, it would have been obvious from the amount I was sweating.

It wasn't even a hot day—if anything, I think most people would have described it as relatively cool. Clouds filled the sky, completely blotting out the sun and tucking all the blue away under a blanket of white and gray. I had checked the weather before leaving, so I knew that it wasn't supposed to rain, but I still prepared myself by throwing on an old, black bomber jacket over a white shirt and a pair of denim jeans. I wasn't going to make the same mistake I made yesterday and be caught outside if the temperature dropped all of a sudden.

But I was still sweating, nonetheless.

Partially because I had walked here, and partially because I was anxious. This anxiety had also caused me to stay up an extra two hours after my conversation with Yasmin had ended.

That's kind of why I was thankful that I got to Mia's office a couple minutes early, so that I could dry myself off and compose myself before I walked in. The last thing I wanted her to think was that I was still emotionally distraught and stressing out about things.

I was better now.

At least—I felt better. Much better.

Now, I just needed to demonstrate that to her.

But.

Taking that extra time to check myself wasn't the only reason why I didn't immediately walk inside of her office.

The other, more obvious reason was on account of the loud voices and quaking furniture coming from the other side of the door. I recognized the calmer of the two voices as belonging to Mia. She had a subtle accent—Korean, if we were being specific—but it wasn't thick enough that you had trouble understanding her. However, in this case, her usual serene voice had taken on a surprisingly more aggressive tone—one that was only directed at me on rare occasions. She must be really mad.

I couldn't hear the other voice all that well.

No, that wasn't right. I could hear it. I could definitely hear it from where I stood behind the door, and I'm pretty sure I would have heard it from down the hall, maybe even from outside the building too.

It'd be more correct to say that I had no idea *what* the voice was saying. It sounded like a jumbled string of profanities, many of which I'd never heard before.

I didn't want to eavesdrop, but I couldn't help but be interested in what was going on behind closed doors. Unfortunately, I never got that chance because the moment I was about to press my ear against the frosted glass window, I heard a resounding clatter. The kind of noise that held with it the weight of finality, signifying that the conversation was over, even if a resolution might not have been drawn.

The next moment, the door swung open and out rushed the owner of that second voice. It was a woman, or rather... a young girl? I couldn't tell on account of how short she was. She wouldn't have even reached the center of my chest if I stood up straight.

The girl had shoulder-length, jet-black hair that seemed to swallow up everything around it. Hair that fell straight until, in an utter act of defiance, the tips curled upwards ever so slightly.

I couldn't quite put my finger on it, but she did look a little familiar.

Did I have a class with her?

While I would have liked to give the question a bit more thought, that was all I had time for before she, not bothering to swerve to the side, bulldozed right through me as if I, too, was a swinging door—something less than human. I was surprised at just how strong she was considering her stature.

The punchline of the whole interaction was that, whereas any normal person would have apologized, I was left with this sweet gem as she stormed out:

"Get out of my way, you fucking moron!"

So, yeah.

She definitely wasn't normal.

You really do run into a lot of interesting characters in college.

At that point, I figured it was close enough to my appointment time, so I slipped into the office before the door closed. Sitting there at her desk, face buried in her hands, was my dear advisor.

"Mia!" I shouted, waving enthusiastically at her. That was my feeble attempt at lightening up the mood.

"Christian, how many times have I told you?" Mia must have recognized my voice because she spoke with her face still hidden in the bowl of her hands. "Please refer to me as Mrs. Lee. Addressing me by my first name is vastly inappropriate."

"No problem, Mia." I moved to the center of the room. "Anyway, what was that all about? The yelling and stuff. I almost called the cops."

"Oh, that? I think you'll be happy to learn that you're not the only person on this campus who's been having severe academic troubles."

"That's a relief. I was starting to feel a bit left out."

Mia finally took her face out of her hands.

Tracking her gaze, it was obvious that she first took note of my state of dress before looking up at my face.

"Ooh, you look snazzier than usual. I was growing fond of your disheveled look. You know how I love baggy, unwashed sweats. Did you doll up just for me?"

"Yeah, of course. I wanted to make sure I impressed my favorite advisor. And, also, uh, I kind of have a date after this too."

There was a second of delay before Mrs. Lee's face lit up and she started clapping her hands excitedly.

"That's superb! Absolutely sublime! What a lucky girl to have the chance to go on a date with such a strapping gentleman as yourself!"

Dang, she was really hyping me up. It wasn't that big of a deal.

Her praise made me feel warm and jittery, though in an embarrassing way. I got the feeling that if I was standing any closer, she would have reached out and gave my cheek a firm squeeze.

Mia Lee.

My academic advisor.

In many ways, she was like a mother away from home for me. My "school mom" if I were to put it differently. Of course, I never openly admitted that to her. I'm not really sure how she'd take it. Despite viewing her as a kind of motherly figure in my life, especially in the past few months, Mia was only a few years older than me. She was one of the people I'd leaned on to get me through that rough patch in my life. It wouldn't be an exaggeration to say that without her help, I wouldn't still be attending Oceanside University.

Mia was a tall and slender woman. She wore glasses a couple sizes too big for her face and her hair was pulled up in a tight bun. If there was anything peculiar about her appearance, it would be the long, white lab coat that she always had on that made her look more like a scientist than an advisor. She always kept it in pristine condition. Never a spot on it, which I found remarkable because a mug of black coffee was always within arm's reach.

Mia kept her office just as clean. The walls were lined with fancy-sounding degrees from recognizable schools and the books adorning her shelves were all organized alphabetically.

I guess there was one other weird thing about Mia that I should probably mention. It was how she talked. I personally wasn't bothered by it, but if you were to meet her for the first time, it might throw you off. As I mentioned before, she had an accent. English wasn't her first language. But the accent wasn't what was strange about her speech. It had more to do with her choice of words.

"Well, Christian. I'm glad we could meet under these heavenly circumstances. I could tell from the moment you walked through that door just how much more chipper you were. I know how dreadful things have been for you."

See what I mean?

She had a certain way with words.

When I made a comment about it during a previous conversation, she told me—while covering her red face in embarrassment—that before she immigrated to the States, she wanted to learn English. Unfortunately, she was on the poorer side growing up, so schooling was out of the question. The only way she was able to teach herself was from a stack of old English novels and taped recordings of TV shows from the 50s–70s. She'd been trying to transition out of that manner of speech, but it still slipped out now and then.

It was really amazing what the human brain could do. Made you think anything was possible if you put your mind to it.

"I know," I said. "That's why I wanted to check in with you. Things have been much better."

"Yes, clearly. Your grades are more than satisfactory now. I really am quite proud of you."

"Thanks. I couldn't have done it without you, though."

"Now now, stop that! Don't be so modest. You're the one who did all the work. I merely pushed you down the right path—that's all."

She was the modest one. It was her direct appeal with the dean regarding my circumstances that ultimately gave me the time I needed to bring up my grades.

"Well, let's just hope I *stay* on the right path this time."

"I'm sure you will. You're a smart young man. You shouldn't be too hard on yourself."

"Just a force of habit, I guess. Something of a character flaw."

"It's only a flaw if you see it that way. Personally, I think self-reflection is a splendid trait to have. It shows that you're willing to improve, and I know that it'll help you in the future when you decide on your plans for after you graduate... Speaking of which—have you given it any thought since our last meeting?"

"Hah, about that."

Now, it's not that I *hadn't* put any thought into it. I have. It's just that there are so many options. I was still an undeclared major in my third year. What made her think I knew what I wanted to do after I graduated?

"Is it fair to presume that I should take that as a no?" she asked.

"It's more of a 'kinda, not really.'"

"Hmm, is that so? Maybe you're not as smart of a young man as I thought."

Harsh.

"And maybe you actually should be hard on yourself. Much harder in fact."

Harsh!

"In fact, this is looking more and more like a character flaw."

"Alright, I get it! I should be thinking more about my future! I'll put it on my to-do list, right next to not having another existential crisis, something I'm very close to having right now!"

I shook my head to stave off any more negative thoughts.

Mia sighed. "Okay, I'm going to ask you a simple question. Is that alright with you?"

"Depends on if it's going to make me question my self-worth as a human being."

"Yes, that's a possibility."

"Then be gentle."

She stifled a small chuckle but maintained her stern face.

"Yes, I can tell," she said. "You are much better now. Your inappropriate timing for humor has returned. But we need to be serious. This is my question for you. It's a common one I ask all the students who walk through that door, and I'm sure it's probably one that you've heard before. In fact, this question was the one that set the missy off before you walked in."

The missy?

Mia must have been referring to the girl from before.

The one that had referred to me as a "fucking moron."

Mia paused to let the words sink in and to build suspense, probably trying to mirror all the dramas and shows she'd watched in her past.

And it was working.

If advising didn't pan out for her, then she should consider a career in Hollywood.

"Where do you see yourself in five years?"

Ah, that one.

She was right. It was a question I'd heard before. Not one I'd ever given any serious thought though. To me, five years had always seemed like such a long time. So far off. A span of time I was never able to accurately grasp.

It didn't help that whenever this question was asked, the question itself never changed either. It was always five years. No matter how long since the last time I heard it. If the years had progressively counted down from five to four to three, etc. then I believe I would have been more attuned to the answer or at least the pressure to answer it. For this reason, the question seemed like it referred to some distant future. One that might not ever come. One that I didn't need to bother worrying about now. The kind of issue you can procrastinate and put off until the last possible minute. And there were plenty of minutes in a five-year period.

But five years must have passed since the first time I heard that question. And the kicker was that I was still virtually in the same spot as I was before. Nothing had changed.

Except for one major thing.

I wasn't with Zoey anymore.

The only reason I'd even applied to Oceanside University was because of her. She told me to, and I blindly followed without considering whether or not it was the best choice for me. I guess I figured everything would just turn out alright as long as we stayed together.

"Christian? Are you okay?"

Mia's words pulled me from my thoughts.

"Yeah, I think I'll live."

"Was the question really that bad?"

"No, no. Not at all. I think my entire life might've flashed before my eyes, but I'm good. I'm good. I just had the opportunity to relive a lot of great memories."

A lot of bad ones too.

"Well, that's good," she said, eyeing me suspiciously. "It wasn't my intention to overwhelm you. I just wanted to make sure you're putting your future in perspective. To see the big picture."

"Don't worry. I see it now. It's crystal clear, in fact. I just don't know if I can figure it all out myself. Is there any way you can help me? Give me some ideas, or better yet, tell me what I should do? I'm clueless here."

Mia sighed again. At this point, I wouldn't be surprised if someday in the future I found out that she developed high blood pressure because of me.

She reached under her desk and pulled out a pile of brochures, pamphlets, and leaflets. The stack resembled a large tome.

"Here. We'll start with this. Take these and look through them. I nabbed them from the career office." She pressed the stack towards me, the top of the tower threatening to fall at any second. "It may seem daunting, but you should at least have a firm understanding of the options and resources that are available to you. You don't need to give me an answer now. But, please, spend some time thinking about it. Do you understand, young man?"

How very motherly of her.

"Yes, I will thank you."

I reached out and grabbed the first pamphlet off the top of the stack and flipped through it. On the cover, underneath the bold print title that read, "Career Opportunities," was a group of students—some looking even younger than me—smiling and laughing. Not a care in the world. It was like they knew exactly what they wanted.

After flipping through it, I tossed the pamphlet back on top of the pile and slumped down into my seat.

"I apologize if I put a damper on your mood," Mia said. "You were in such high spirits when you walked in here, but now not so much."

"Nah, it's okay. As long as it's over now, I'll recover."

"It isn't."

"It isn't? It isn't what? There's more?"

"Yes, there's one more thing that I wish to speak to you about."

I stayed silent in order to let her finish.

"Christian, dear, I'm sorry, but I do have to ask," Mia started. "You have a lot on your plate right now. Are you sure... are you sure you're *ready* to start dating again? You don't think that it might be too soon for you to put yourself back out there? What happened with Zoey really took its toll on you. Mentally and *physically*. Whenever I think about it, I still worry. You know about my reservations regarding the whole thing."

I thought about her question for a moment.

It was a reasonable one and considering that, besides me, she was the only other person that knew the full story, I couldn't fault her for asking or being concerned for my safety.

That being said—that didn't mean I had an answer for her either.

I forced a smile and nervously scratched the back of my head.

"Uh, I don't know. I really don't know. I just can't stand being alone any longer."

CHAPTER 7

I still had half an hour until I was supposed to meet with Yasmin, so it gave me the opportunity to walk back to the apartment and dump the stack of brochures on my desk. I had every intention of looking through them. Just not today. Probably not tomorrow either. I'd get to it eventually. I owed Mia that much. She was trying to help me, after all.

The meeting hadn't gone terribly. In fact, it went better than I expected, but not as well as I hoped it would. In the end, I was left with a bitter aftertaste in my mouth, similar to the imported black coffee Mia usually had brewing in the corner of her office.

Mia had the habit of asking the perfect questions at the perfect moment. To any normal person, they might have seemed like basic probing questions, the types any reasonable model adult figure might ask, but hers never failed to pierce all the way through my bullshit and hit me right where it hurt—the very source of the issue. I figured those huge glasses she wore were probably miniature X-ray monitors or something. That would be the only thing that made sense.

All in all, it made me wonder what it was she saw when she looked at me.

However, that wasn't something I should be worrying about right now. I had more important things to be thinking about.

On the way back to campus, I made sure to take as much time as I needed. The main reason was I didn't want to get sweaty all over again before I arrived. I was even more anxious than I was when I headed to Mia's office, so in order to compensate for that, I applied an extra coating of deodorant under each of my pits before I left the apartment as well as a couple spurts of cologne. It made me smell like pine trees and wood. A very manly and outdoorsy scent. Brad was the one who recommended it to me—for what it's worth. He knew more about such things than I did, so I took his recommendation seriously. Of course, this was the first time I was getting a chance to use it.

I took my thirtieth deep breath and exhaled slowly.

Stay calm, Chris.

This was nothing to be nervous or afraid about.

Having finally arrived under the arch of the gateway, I pulled out my phone right as the digital clock transitioned to three. I shot Yasmin a text to let her know I was here.

Bzzt.

Took you long enough

I told you not to keep me waiting

Loser

I'm already here

So hurry up

Huh?

She was already here?

I looked around, scanning the area. No one I saw resembled Adi. Being that it was the afternoon, there were plenty of people around, many of them on their phones. Most were walking to and from class looking like they had things to do and places to go.

Where are you?

I'm leaning against the wall

Where are you?????

I glanced up from my phone and looked around again. I didn't see anyone that was—

Wait.

There was one person.

I was barely able to catch a glimpse of her through the crowd—leaning on the stone railing on the opposite side of the walkway.

She was scanning the area, phone in hand, the same as me—the only difference being the irritated scowl on her face.

My initial reaction to seeing her was wondering how I could have missed her in the first place, but it became clear to me after a few seconds. It was obvious why.

I'd been automatically filtering out the options that didn't resemble Adi, and as a result had completely passed over her. I hadn't even considered that the person who was now impatiently tapping her foot with her arms crossed could be the person I was here to meet.

She was too short to be Adi's twin sister. Way too short.

From this distance, she resembled a young girl rather than a woman. She looked... exactly like the girl who'd rudely bumped into me outside of Mia's office, except her hair was now pulled into a ponytail, held captive by a red scrunchie.

The realization of who I was meeting caused me to involuntarily take two steps back.

Her?

That was Adi's sister?

In retrospect, considering how she was texting me, it added up perfectly, even if I didn't want to believe that it was possible.

What was I supposed to do now?

If I was going to be completely honest, I felt my desire to go through with the date slowly dissipating. I was tempted to just calmly slip my phone back inside my pocket and fade into the crowd. Once I was back home, I'd block her number and pretend that none of this ever happened.

The plan was a simple one and would probably spare me some major headaches in the future. Scratch that. It *would*.

But it was too late.

Yasmin turned her head and we made eye contact. A flash of recognition flickered in her eyes. It was like locking eyes with another trainer in a Pokémon game. A battle was imminent.

There was no way I could play this one off even if I tried.

Besides her, I was the only other person who was just standing around the gate, waiting for something, or someone. And now that she had her sights set on me, she didn't waste another moment as she plunged into the crowd with the same level of bravado she had shown when she burst out of Mia's office. In other words, she didn't make any effort whatsoever to move out of the way or be courteous to the other individuals that intersected her path. If you were unfortunate enough to find yourself in her way, you'd have been run over.

Her ponytail bounced with each step as she strutted over. A couple strands of hair hung down to frame her face on either side. Her white halter top accentuated a pair of toned and tanned arms—arms that were a few shades darker than Adi's. The pair of jean shorts she wore held true to the name, failing to pass the midpoint of her thigh by at least a few inches.

She stopped in front of me and didn't try to hide the fact that she was already judging my whole existence. And if the frown and raised eyebrow were anything to go off, she wasn't impressed.

"So, this is it? You're the guy?"

Her questions were direct and forceful. Too direct in fact. The kind of questions that people would think but not verbalize. And she'd gone and said them with no hesitation whatsoever.

What a terrifying girl.

"Uh, I'm *a* guy."

"Barely," she said. "What I meant was—are you Chris?"

"Yeah, and you must be Yasmin."

"Who else would I be?"

Yeesh.

She was a prickly one too.

A part of me wished I'd given out a fake name. I might have been able to get out of this situation if I had.

For the next few moments, we stood there in silence as people flowed around us. All the rehearsing I'd done last night was completely useless. No amount of preparation could have enabled me to deal with this monster.

No plan survives first contact with the enemy, as they say.

Yasmin crossed her arms. "So, what are we going to do?"

"Uh, yeah, right. So, I kind of planned for us to do a few things actually. I thought maybe we could start off and get some lunch or something. You know, so we could talk and get to know each other for a bit. Then we'll catch a movie. They have some chick-flicks out right now if you're into that sort of thing. Afterwards, we'd walk around and get some ice cream."

If you haven't picked up on it yet, setting up dates wasn't my specialty. You'd think I'd have a lot more experience with it, being in a long-term relationship and all, but that wasn't the case. I'd always let Zoey decide on what we should do, what we should eat, and when we would meet. That's just how it had been between us, and I had grown comfortable with that dynamic. Too comfortable.

I knew that a guy was supposed to take some initiative, so I wanted to put in effort this time around. That's why I chose some of the things Zoey enjoyed doing. You know—to use as a sort of springboard to jump off. A pair of training wheels that I could lean on. Women couldn't be that different, right? It was a well-balanced date if I did say so myself. The kind of cutesy things couples do. I knew this tried-and-true routine probably wouldn't let me down today either.

"How boring."

And just like that, my plan crumbled before me.

"Okay, what's wrong with it?" I asked.

"It just sounds boring."

"I mean, it's just a basic date."

"Exactly, it's just so mind-numbingly basic that the mere thought of it is already putting me to sleep."

To accentuate her point, she brought her hands up to her eyes and yawned. It was a genuine yawn too; she wasn't acting.

"All right. Did you have anything else you wanted to do? I'm down for whatever."

"No, you're supposed to choose."

There was no compromise with this girl, and here I was trying to be reasonable.

"Then I'm choosing what I already planned to do."

"That's boring. I want to do something else. Besides, I've already seen all the movies they're showing. They weren't any good. Let's do something spontaneous and fun."

"I don't have any other ideas."

"Yeah, I can tell."

"What's that supposed to mean?"

She rolled her eyes. "Just look at you."

I looked down at myself. Nothing seemed out of the ordinary. I honestly thought I looked pretty good all things considered.

"And what am I supposed to be looking at?" I asked, lifting both of my arms to see if I had missed something.

"Just everything about you screams boring. From your idea of a date, to the way you were texting me, to what you're wearing. All of it's so boring. Even your name, Chris, is boring. I should have known my sister was trying to screw with me. That bitch."

"..."

Okay.

I'd describe myself as a patient and kind person. I tried to see the best in people and give them the benefit of the doubt. My mother had raised me to be a gentleman, after all. But this girl. This monster. She was trying every fiber of my patience. At this rate, I think I only had a few straws left.

The only reason that I was still here was because I didn't want to give up so easily. To do that would validate Yasmin's opinion of me, no matter how small it already was. If I wanted to grow and be dependable, I had to weather this much at the least.

My next choice would be entirely reliant on if she said one more thing to piss me off. I was this close to—

"Is there anything even remotely interesting about you?"

—snapping. "I can see why you're still single."

I probably shouldn't have said that.

Yasmin's jaw fell open, and for a split second, the literal blink of an eye, she didn't look annoyed anymore. Her expression morphed into one of shock and disbelief, but only for that singular moment before it reverted to its natural state like memory foam.

"You don't even know me," she growled.

"And you don't know me either," I retorted, standing my ground.

We glared into each other's eyes.

It was a standoff.

A battle of wills.

Her eyes pierced me with a fiery intensity that contrasted with her sister's cool softness.

Were Adi and Yasmin really related? They seemed nothing alike.

As our war of attrition continued, eventually I heard a small voice in the back of my mind. It was telling me that I should probably apologize to her. Just because she was rude didn't mean I had to stoop to her level, which was almost a full foot shorter than me. She barely reached the center of my chest.

I mean, what would people think when they saw me arguing with this child?

Ugh.

I guess I should be the bigger person in this situation—

"So, are you going to apologize for what you said or what?" she asked.

No! Forget that!

Whenever I found myself about to be respectful, Yasmin found a way to tick me off even more, causing me to abandon any of my previous noble notions.

"I meant what I said," I declared. "I'm not taking anything back. I call it as I see it." I added an emphatic nod just to drive the point home.

"Same!" she snapped back. "I meant what I said too. If you weren't so boring, I wouldn't have said it either!"

"Stop saying I'm boring! Is that like your catchphrase or something? I'll have you know that I'm actually really cool and interesting. Some people even describe me as the 'Second Most Interesting Man in the World!"

"Is your mom one of them?"

"As a matter of a fact she is!"

"Well, she was lying to you!"

Seriously? A "mom joke" in this day and age? Mankind's progress must have stalled indefinitely.

"Alright, how about I make you eat those words?" I said, not entirely sure what I was thinking. "I bet I can make this the most fun date you've ever had."

"Oh, yeah? Only an idiot wouldn't take this bet. It's practically a free win! You're 'The Most Boring Man in the World!'"

What a smartass.

"Okay, so we're doing this then?"

"Damn straight we are," she said, smugly. "Now I just want to know what I get when I win."

"What you get?"

"Yeah, what're you staking on this bet of yours? I want to know what my prize is going to be. The rules should be clearly stated at the start of the arrangement. I don't want you to skimp out on me later."

"Like hell I would! I keep my word."

I paused for a minute to think up some rules and conditions. My blood was boiling and deep in my gut, a wildfire of passion threatened to consume everything else inside of me, leaving only one thing to rise above the ashes—my desire to win. To prove this girl wrong. To wipe that smug grin off her face. This was a matter of a man's pride now.

"Okay, how about this. We'll keep it super simple. If by the end of the date, let's say midnight, you don't declare the words, 'This was the most funnest, most spontaneousiest, most interestingiest and the least boringiest date I've ever been on in my entire life!' then you'll win. But if you do end up saying them, then I win. That sound good?"

"Do I really have to say that long, obnoxious, cringey, childish, pointless, nauseating, and overly redundant statement?"

"It sounds like you have no problem saying something like that! And, yeah, if I win, you'll have to."

"Okay, I guess it won't matter because you won't win anyway. Now what's the prize?"

"Well," I pondered for a second, the tip of my index fingering tapping my chin. "The winner gets one request if they win. Basically, a wish or a favor."

Once again, for a moment, Yasmin's expression changed. The hard line of her lips softened, and her eyes lit up.

"How... boring."

"Do you want something else?"

She shook her head. "No, no. That'll be fine. What are we allowed to ask for?"

"Whatever you want. But preferably something legal."

"It wouldn't be whatever I wanted if it had to be something legal. That's a cop out."

"Exactly what are you planning on making me do?!"

She grinned.

I didn't like the looks of that.

"Okay, whatever. I'm in." She pumped her fist. "You better be prepared. Once I get my wish, you're never going to want to show your face around here ever again."

She was a confident one, but not all that bright. With how interested she was now, I'd practically already won.

"We'll see about that." I stuck out my hand, but since I'm so much taller than her, I had to angle it down. "So, deal?"

Yasmin looked at the palm of my hand with revulsion. It was the kind of face you made after you stepped in something squishy and investigated the bottom of your shoe to find it smeared with dog crap. Hot, steamy dog crap.

But—she grabbed it, anyway.

I should have figured from her size, but her hand was small, barely able to wrap around my own. It was an uncanny trait that matched her immaturity.

As if reading my mind or feeling my reaction through the subtle movements of my fingertips, Yasmin gave my hand a firm squeeze. Tighter than what a normal person would consider necessary or socially acceptable.

"Deal," she said. "Now, let's get the hell out of here. It smells like someone shit their pants in the woods or something."

And so, our little game began.

CHAPTER 8

"You know," Yasmin said, "I can think of a million other things I'd rather be doing right now."

"No, I didn't know that."

"Well, you should have."

"How?"

"It should be obvious from looking at me," Yasmin replied. "You should feel lucky I'm even gracing someone like you with my presence. This is a priceless experience."

"I'm honored."

Our conversation continued like that as we walked through campus—most of it consisted of Yasmin incessantly trying to convince me that she was someone who should be praised and marveled.

I assure you that on any other day I would have enjoyed the experience of walking and letting my thoughts linger on nothing, but with Yasmin's added noise—it was turning into something else entirely. It hadn't even been that long since we met, and this already didn't feel much like a date anymore. All my previous anxiety had disappeared. At this point, I was more like a chaperone leading her around.

But that was okay.

In order to make the bet a little fairer for me, Yasmin wasn't allowed to refuse any of my date activities. She had to whole-heartedly participate with an honest effort, no matter how "boring" they were or seemed. Only at the end of the date would she tally up her experiences and give her final verdict. However, this didn't stop her from vocalizing her hatred in the only way that she seemed to know how.

"This is bullshit. Where are you taking me? All we've been doing is walking for the past ten minutes. I hate wasting time. If this was your idea of fun, then you might as well forfeit because this sucks."

"We're not walking just to walk. We're headed towards a destination. It's at the opposite end of campus."

"You're not trying to force me to some secluded area where we'll be alone and you'll have your way with me, are you?"

"I'm not forcing you at all. You can leave whenever you want. Plus, we're in broad daylight. I'd have to be a really dumb criminal to pull something like that surrounded by crowds of witnesses."

"That's the exact reasoning someone would use to get a woman to drop her guard," Yasmin retorted. "I'm starting to regret leaving my mace back at home."

"You won't need to pepper spray me. I'm harmless."

"Pepper spray? I was referring to a medieval bludgeon."

"If someone saw you carrying that they'd think I was the one in trouble!"

"I was lying," she assured me. "I don't own a mace, but I have been taking kickboxing for the past three years—so don't try anything funny."

"Strangely, that doesn't make me feel any more relieved."

I couldn't blame her for her overall cautious attitude; she was meeting a man for the first time, after all. But I still felt a little hurt by her wariness. She was the one that practically asked me out. Luckily, I'd taken all of that into account. I was taking her somewhere with lots of people, so she wouldn't have to worry about a thing.

After another five minutes of walking, and Yasmin's complaining, we finally arrived at our destination. A large green field sprinkled with tents, booths, food carts, and a multitude of other activities. The atmosphere was all tied together by the faint drone of chattering and laughter from faculty and students alike.

"What's going on here?" Yasmin asked, her eyes darting around the scenery.

"You don't know? It's the winter carnival. They have one every year," I answered. I was acting like I knew what was going on, but I really didn't. I wouldn't have known about it either unless I saw the flier for it posted outside of Mia's office.

As far as school events went, I wasn't very spirited. I was probably the least spirited person on campus. I never went to any games or rallies unless I was invited by Zoey or Brad. I wasn't opposed to them or anything like that, I just didn't care for such things.

"Oh, I've heard about this. I've just never had an opportunity to go," Yasmin said.

"What? Was it the million better things you had to do?"

"Shut up," she replied. "But this is more like it. Still painfully basic and boring, but better."

"Just say it looks fun."

"No, I'll never say it."

"Hah, we'll see."

The carnival was a standard college event. There was a wide assortment of run-of-the-mill games, the exact names of which I don't remember to be honest. There was one where you had to throw a ball to knock down some weighted milk bottles. One where you attempted to toss rings around the necks of other bottles. Another game that looked like the point was to see how long you lasted hanging from a pull-up bar. Simple stuff.

But I knew none of these would cut it. We needed to do something else. And if there was somewhere with 'something else', it was here.

Probably located in front of that densely populated crowd.

Printed on a large, white banner that stretched across a roped-off expanse of grass in bold red letters were the words: Couples Tournament.

It was such a perfect coincidence that I couldn't help but wonder if God himself had intervened in my favor.

"How about we do that?" I pointed to the sign.

"Are you dumb? It says it's for couples. We aren't a couple!"

An astute observation.

"That doesn't matter. We're a *couple* of people. You can even say we're partners if you want. No one will care. Now, come on, it's going to start soon."

"I refuse! I wouldn't want to team up with someone like you anyways."

"Trust me. The feeling is mutual. But that wasn't a request. Don't you remember the rules we agreed to?"

Yasmin went silent. Her eyes cycled from the banner to me at least five different times before settling on her white sneakers.

"Fine," she mumbled. "And just for the record, I didn't want to do this."

"Yeah, yeah. I don't care. Let's go!"

Yasmin didn't move from her spot. She still seemed reluctant.

In this situation, there was only one thing I could do. The surefire way to get someone to act.

Not bothering to wait for a response, I grabbed Yasmin's hand and yanked her into the crowd. The action seemed to surprise her as much as it surprised me.

"Let's win this thing!"

* * *

So, uh… yeah.

What happened over the course of the next couple hours could only be described as unbelievable.

The tournament consisted of three events, and the couple with the highest score across the board would be the winners and get the prize of "Best Couple" along with a gift certificate to a fancy restaurant. I didn't care about the prize; I was in it solely for the pride of winning. It was times like these when my mind would become hyper-focused on a singular task, causing all my other worries to melt away. And with such incredible focus, I couldn't help but get into it. Who wouldn't? Everyone wants to win at something.

However, by the end of the first event, I realized just how far-fetched of a dream that was.

The first challenge was a water-balloon toss with the most common rules. Each team was handed only one water balloon to use. It was a do-or-die, sudden death kind of event. I had planned to strategize with Yasmin before we started, to ensure we were on the same page in terms of strategy, but she brushed me off with a wave of her hand, a gesture that I had begun to associate with her just as much as her catchphrase.

"We don't need any special plan," she said, stretching her shoulder. "I'm a pro at dodgeball."

At that point, I should have realized just how little she grasped the rules of the game we were about to play, but before I could even question whether she was joking, it was too late.

The water balloon pelted me square in the face.

It was only the first round.

We weren't even standing a full two feet away from one another.

The same thing happened in the next game too. Not the getting pelt in the face part, but our catastrophic and shameful defeat.

The second event was a game of charades. The pairs were given a set of cards to act out and the team that got through the most during the time limit would win the game. One member from each time would act out the clue while the other tried to guess.

The obvious problem with this game was that I wasn't sure which role to trust Yasmin with. After a moment's thought, I realized I could trust my acting over hers any day. At the very least, if I acted it out well enough, there wouldn't be any way that she wouldn't get it.

Or so I thought.

We got stumped on the first card, and due to a mixture of stubbornness and pride, I resisted the option to pass on that card and attempt the next.

The word at first glance seemed surprisingly easy.

Tree.

I had more than a few ideas to start out, all of them, at least in my mind, were pretty good representations of a tree. When the game started, I immediately moved into position.

Feet together—like a tree trunk.

Arms spread out to my sides—like two long, skinny branches, even putting in the extra effort by stretching out my fingers to give the impression of leaves.

And I kept my head and spine straight and motionless to represent that picturesque and stationary aspect that you'd usually describe a tree to have.

There was probably no better portrayal of a tree out there. It was virtually a one-for-one imitation. If they put me in a play, it would have been me that stole the show and won over the hearts of the crowd.

Now it was just up to Yasmin to state the obvious.

"A scarecrow."

Okay, to be honest, that was a fair guess. I couldn't complain about that one. I merely shook my head to let her know to try again. I assumed she'd be able to get it in the next couple of attempts, but to my complete and utter surprise, her answers became more and more bizarre.

"Jesus?"

I mean, I guess?

I shook my head.

"The uppercase letter 'T'?"

What? No.

"The lowercase letter 't'?"

No!

Frustrated, I decided to change it up and pull my arms over my head in a circular fashion to simulate a large cluster of leaves, like what you'd see in a child's drawings.

"Broccoli? Cauliflower? Mushroom? Light Bulb? Hot-air balloon?"

My assessment of this girl was completely wrong. She wasn't a monster. She was a complete idiot.

"Oh, I'm a complete idiot," she said, and for a moment I wondered if I'd spoken that last part aloud.

I hadn't. It was actually her being self-aware.

She snapped her fingers like something had just clicked in her mind. "I got it now."

Hope at last?

"A ballerina."

At that point a bell rang, signaling the end of the second event, but I couldn't really hear it over the sound of my own yelling as I threw my body at her in anger.

With only one event left, it was our final chance to get at least one point, to have the right to say that we went down with a fight.

To go down swinging, as they say.

The last event was a three-legged race.

I was desperate to win and when they strapped our legs together using a piece of rope, I knew exactly what I had to do in order to achieve that victory.

Since there was such a large height difference between us. I'd be limited entirely by her short legs. Unless—

The pistol went off.

Suddenly, I lurched forward catching Yasmin by surprise and causing her to lose balance. Teetering backwards, she latched onto the only thing that was within her reach in order to maintain her stability—my waist. I waited for the exact moment that her arms wrapped around me like a belt before booking it down the strip of grass.

Now, I wouldn't say that I was dragging her along—she wasn't touching the ground at all—but it did look like she was riding my leg as I ran in a sort of straight legged galloping motion. Luckily for me, she was light as a feather, so she didn't stop my forward momentum by that much.

Ignoring everything—the cheers from the crowd, my labored breathing, and Yasmin's squeals—I raced harder than I'd ever raced before in my life. Harder than I ever thought was possible for me to do, and before I realized it, I'd passed the finish line with my little hitchhiker still intact.

Even after I untied the rope, Yasmin still clung to me with her eyes shut; the only thing holding her in place were her two slender arms, which now had to overcompensate without the aid of our binding. Basically, she was squeezing the life out of me. I was having trouble breathing.

I pried Yasmin off and she fell onto the grass with a thud, causing her to open her eyes and look around in a daze. At this point, the other couples had all begun to stagger past the finish line after us.

By all accounts and purposes, we had crossed the finish line first, so we should have won, and when I saw an official-looking man in a vest and holding a clipboard walking in our direction, I expected him to congratulate the two of us for our hard fought and well-earned victory. Instead, we were slapped with a big, fat, sloppy disqualification.

Apparently, carrying your partner wasn't allowed.

I still wouldn't admit that it was my fault. Yasmin had grabbed on to me! What was I supposed to do? Yeah, it was a three-legged race, but what was wrong with only using two of those legs?

All of these were rational questions, but unfortunately the officials didn't see it that way, and Yasmin's vehement arguing didn't really help all that much in convincing the officials either.

Slinging my two arms underneath her armpits, in a kind of full nelson position, I held her back as she cursed at the poor man and swung her feet dangerously close to the area between his legs.

It wouldn't be until I saw the two big, burly security guards making a beeline through the crowd towards us that I decided now would be a perfect opportunity for us to leave. This time I *did* drag Yasmin away, and in spectacular fashion, she redirected the rest of her frustrations onto me. I should have expected that much.

But, despite how things appeared, everything seemed to turn out for the better.

After her fit of rage, Yasmin scurried off ahead of me before I could stop her. She didn't have much trouble maneuvering through the crowd due to her small size and before long, I'd lost sight of her.

I must have looked like a parent who'd just lost their child.

It wasn't until after a couple minutes of searching that I caught a glimpse of her. Yasmin was standing in the center of a clearing with her back towards me. I could see that her head was down, and the slopes of her shoulders were bobbing up-and-down to the sound of faint sobs.

Crying? I know we didn't win, but it wasn't anything to cry about.

I reached out a timid hand to pat her on her head. Girls liked that sort of thing, right?

My hand traveled through the air so slowly it was almost as if I wasn't moving at all. In my mind I was searching for some elusive better option to comfort her, but I was drawing blanks. Oh well, I guess. Here goes nothing.

But in the next second, she threw her head back and burst out laughing, her sobs having morphed into an unreserved torrent of snickers and howls.

Now, from what I could see, if she ever had to play charades again, which I hoped she wouldn't, and she ended up drawing a card that said "laughter," she would have had that one on lock. She was pulling out every action in the book. Her arms were clutched over her stomach as if she was attempting to keep her guts from spilling out. She slapped her knee five different times. I could even see a stream of tears pouring from the corners of each of her eyes.

Hah.

Seeing her laugh like that, I couldn't help but join her.

Laughter was contagious, as they say.

After that moment, I think it was safe to assume that I had a general feeling of what Yasmin was like. Of course, after only a few hours I couldn't see all the nuances, but I had a good bead on her now.

As if unbound by some chain or leash, she let herself go and pinballed around the park with reckless abandon. I almost couldn't keep up with all that energy. No food truck was left unsampled and no game was left unplayed. She didn't even have the patience to finish most of the games I had so kindly bought tickets for before zooming off to the next shiny thing that caught her eye.

I couldn't tell if she had an unbelievable amount of self-control to have held herself back for this long or no self-control at all.

She was like a kid in a toy store.

There were some things she even asked if I wanted to do with her, including some dangerous looking rides, you know the kinds that look like they're violating at least ten different safety protocols.

I refused.

It's not that I was afraid of heights, but they just really weren't my thing anymore.

Despite my reasoning to her, Yasmin still managed to spit out that I was "boring," take my money, and stand in line anyway.

I did notice something interesting though.

At one point she did end up lingering behind the back of some caricature artist. All her energy cut off for the minute or two she studied the man's brush strokes as he expertly exaggerated the artificial smiles of the people who sat in front of him.

There was a look of tranquility on Yasmin's face which contrasted with the intense focus in her brown eyes. I noticed that her own fingers were twitching at her side to match the artist's own movements.

Her hypnotic state evaporated when I asked her if she wanted a picture of her own, which she declined before running to something off in the distance.

I didn't mind though.

It was all up to her what she wanted to do and judging by that ear-to-ear smile she had since our three-legged race—she was having a great time.

CHAPTER 9

And so, we found ourselves at the last spot I had planned for our date. The grand finale in a lot of ways. The cherry on top. Of course, I didn't really *plan* for us to end up here. The whole point of this competition was for me to show Yasmin that someone like me was capable of being spontaneous and fun. If I had everything planned out, then that would have defeated the whole purpose, wouldn't it?

But regardless of whether I planned it or not, here we were. At the beach.

It was around ten and the taxi driver had dropped us off at what he told us was a 'secret and secluded' spot. For a second, I was worried about the location, but Yasmin didn't seem opposed to the idea this time around. Originally, I'd wanted to go closer to the pier, where most people go, but the guy insisted. He said he always took "beautiful couples" such as us to the beach at night. That's what he called us the entire time. A beautiful couple.

I didn't bother to correct him. Didn't really have a chance to on account of all the talking he was doing anyway. The guy, Joe, said that he knew the perfect place to take us. He assured us he didn't just tell anyone about it, but he'd make an exception for us on account of how "beautiful" we looked together. Couples were always looking for places to get a little privacy, after all.

Gee thanks, Joe.

I was sitting in the back with Yasmin, and I could tell she was getting creeped out by the guy. Occasionally, Joe would do this thing where he'd wrap his arm around the passenger seat and look back at us before he spoke—completely taking his eyes off the road. Correction. His *eye*.

Singular. Joe only had one eye and he covered the missing one with an eyepatch. Apparently, an old flame of his gouged his eye out with a pair of scissors for cheating one night.

That's why he enjoyed taking beautiful couples to the beach, he claimed. It was his atonement in a way for "royally screwing up his chances in life." Looking back, he gave me a wink, which kind of looked like he was just blinking, and told me not to make the same mistake.

A little late for that one. I wasn't a cheater, but I'd screwed up my relationship with Zoey all the same. I breathed a sigh of relief when we finally got out of the car.

"Now that was an interesting guy," I said as Yasmin and I walked down to the edge of the water. No one was around besides us. The water had taken on a sort of murky, black hue that gave the impression of some endless dark void. Despite the eeriness of it all, the atmosphere did feel peaceful—romantic even. I couldn't help but wonder what unspeakable actions had been performed on these very grains of sand that I was currently squishing between my toes.

"He gave me weird vibes," Yasmin said.

"Oh, yeah? And what vibes do I give you?"

It was dark, but I was still able to see her roll her eyes at me.

"Boring ones."

"Still?! Looked like you were having a whole lot of fun back at the park."

"Well, you should probably get your eyes checked."

"Come on. You know this bet is as good as over."

"Yeah, for you. I'm not saying your stupid line no matter what."

Hey, it wasn't that stupid. I thought it was funny.

From the direction of the water, unobstructed by any of the buildings of the city, a constant sea breeze carried the smell of salt and wet sand. I shivered and looked around. If she wasn't going to budge, then I'd have to do something crazy enough that her only option would be to admit defeat. It would be within reason, though. I wasn't a wild animal that would vandalize property or do something illegal to win a simple bet.

I walked in front of Yasmin, stood there with my back facing the water, and smiled.

"Let's go in," I said, pointing behind me with my thumb.

"What?! You're crazy! It's freezing out here."

That was exactly what I was trying to go for.

What was more spontaneous than going to the beach—at night—when it was freezing outside and going into the water?

Not much, I can tell you that.

This was the grand finale after all. The Hail Mary. The finishing touch to my masterful date.

If she didn't completely cave in after this, then there really wasn't anything else I could do, and I'd gladly accept defeat.

"Come on, Yasmin."

"No."

"Come oooonn."

"No."

"Come on!"

"I said no."

"Come on?"

"No."

"Vamanos?"

"No! And saying it in different ways isn't going to change my mind either!"

I figured tossing in some Spanish had been worth a shot.

In any case, I wasn't going to give up just like that, but I did need to change up my tactics. You see, if there was anything I learned today, it was that, at least on the surface, my vertically challenged friend over here was pretty simple. She had been so eager to see and try everything at the carnival that she had practically been bouncing up and down in excitement, like a kid, and everyone knows that there were a few things that a kid couldn't resist. Shiny things and an insult that would attack their fragile egos. Being in possession of such valuable information, I knew manipulating her would be child's play.

"Yasmin."

"What now?" she shot back, folding her arms across her chest.

"You're being really boring right now. A total party pooper."

One of her dark eyebrows twitched.

"What did you just say to me?"

And she'd chomped down right on my hook.

"And you called me boring. Jeez, how the tables have turned."

"Shut it," she said. "I'm warning you."

"Sure, you are."

"You better stop that."

"Or else what?" I took a few steps back into the black void and immediately my feet were swallowed up. "You're not going to do anything."

"Alright. That's it. I'll show you. Let's do this thing."

"Great."

"But—" she lifted her arms and looked down at her clothes, "—I don't have a swimsuit."

That was a problem. However, it had a simple solution.

"Well, you can either go in with your clothes, or—"

I walked back onto the dry sand and slowly took off my jacket. I plopped it down beside me, and I was going to continue, but as I fingered the hem of my shirt, I hesitated for a second.

Yasmin was watching me intently from a short distance away—a little too intently if I was being honest. It was as if the weight of her eyes on my body made it impossible for me to lift my arms.

I was embarrassed, but I knew that after talking big I couldn't back down. She'd easily rip me a new one as they say.

So, I peeled off my shirt.

And then my pants.

All I had on now was the striped boxers I'd picked out in the morning.

This may seem like a strange thing to do, but I was desperate to win our bet, and it wasn't like this was my first time going to the beach at night. I had some experience. Zoey had dragged me along many times before. This was another thing she loved to do.

As I turned around to walk back to the water, I heard a small gasp behind me. When I looked back, Yasmin had her hand over her mouth.

"What's wrong?" I asked. "Are you okay?"

"No... No, I'm fine. It's nothing."

"All right. I'm getting in then. The water doesn't look too bad at all."

I said all that, but the second my toe touched the water again, I regretted everything. The water was so cold. From head-to-toe goosebumps dotted my skin in a desperate attempt to keep me somewhat warm.

Yasmin had remained in her spot the entire time, her mouth still hanging slightly open. She must not have thought I'd have the guts to actually do it.

Girl, I'm full of surprises.

To snap her out of her daze, I tried to splash her by kicking up a wave of water, but my droplets came up hopelessly short. Luckily, despite my poor display of athleticism, the gesture still had its intended effect.

Yasmin took a deep breath, and her hands went to the button of her shorts which she unfastened deftly. She didn't reach to pull them off though, instead grabbing the bottom of her shirt first and pulling upwards.

I thought I had been blinded by a flash of light, like I had witnessed something truly magnificent.

Blue. Mmm more of a baby blue. Teal or better yet cerulean.

I was kind of surprised. I just assumed because of her stature that she'd have more of an... immature... bra design, but this one looked fancy. Very lacey too.

Okay, as you know, I'm a guy. I'm no stranger to the intricacies of female anatomy. Hours of research on the internet has taught me all I needed to know, so it wasn't like I hadn't seen anything like this. But still, watching it unfold in person? It was like a mythological experience. It was like watching some forbidden act, and at any moment something was going to smite me for my insolence.

Yasmin seemed to share that same sentiment.

"Can you stop staring at me, you pervert!"

I dodged a seashell that was aimed for my head.

"Why not? They say staring is a compliment."

"As if I'd ever want to receive a compliment from someone like you!"

Geez. That was harsh. This was supposed to be a date, after all. A statement like that didn't bode well for the longevity of our budding relationship.

Weren't we supposed to be a beautiful couple?

"Then at least let me say this," I said, backing up deeper into the frigid cold, trying to put a few extra steps between us. "You really have nothing to be embarrassed about. Really. Your boobs are much bigger than I thought they'd be."

"Shut up!" Yasmin growled, lunging forward into the water, forgetting or not bothering to take off her shorts.

What happened over the course of the next ten minutes was nothing short of a fight for survival. At first, I thought she was kidding as she charged at me, practically running on top of the water, but her angry face and ferocious roar quickly dispelled that notion—as well as the jumping kick aimed for my throat. She was going for the kill. My life was literally in danger.

The worst or most difficult part about it was that my mother raised me to be a gentleman. With such a responsibility came a set of rules, codes for conduct, when interacting with members of the fairer sex. You've probably heard a few of them. "Never hit a woman," and "Open doors for them," and "Don't ask them about their weight or age,"—stuff like that. I think you'd be proud to learn that, for the most part, I followed these adages to a tee. I didn't want my mother to be disappointed with me. To think she raised some kind of brute.

However, the thing was—my mom wasn't here right now.

And there's another adage I'd been hearing going around lately.

Chivalry is dead, as they say.

Reading Yasmin's clearly telegraphed kick, I caught her leg while she was in mid-air and unable to change her course. In that single moment before I flung her head first five feet away into the water, her mouth had formed that perfect "O" shape complete with raised eyebrows and wide eyes. A look of surprise and a splash of regret. But, of course, that wasn't the only thing that splashed.

The battle wasn't as one-sided as I've been making it out to be. She ended up changing her strategy and by the end of it all, I had some bruises and scratches myself to take home as souvenirs.

It would only be after we signed our peace treaty that both of us finally retreated out of the water, exhausted, battered, and only slightly warmer than when we entered.

"That was fun." I plopped down on a rock, still only wearing my boxers that now clung to my body like a second skin. Mere inches away, Yasmin did the same.

"Yeah," she said.

"Wait? So, you admit defeat then?!"

"No! I told you I'd never admit defeat. *Never.* I was just saying that getting in the water was interesting... wait, on second thought—never mind, no it wasn't."

This girl was really something else.

"Then what does that mean?" I asked.

"It means that I win."

"No way. You're going to tell me straight to my face that you thought this date was boring, and that you hated every second of it, and that you'd have rather stayed at home and watched paint dry?"

"No, it wasn't that bad. But I would rather have watched grass grow."

"That's worse!"

Yasmin chuckled.

Sitting where we were, our shoulders were practically touching. Well, as close as they could possibly be before it could technically be called touching. If I didn't know any better, I could have sworn that in that moment I felt the tickling of one of her arm hairs brushing against my bare skin. She was that close to me.

"I will admit it did have its moments," she said.

"Thanks, that sounded like the world's most pathetic consolation."

I sunk my head in defeat.

The whole game must have been rigged from the start, but I didn't feel like there was any point trying to dispute that anymore. She sounded like she'd made up her mind.

But that was alright. I think I put up a pretty good performance myself. If it didn't sound even more pathetic than the obligatory consolation, I might have even said that I was proud of myself too.

Ah, what the hell.

I'm proud of myself.

I took in a large breath and turned to look at Yasmin.

Now it was time to do something I wouldn't be proud about.

"I'm sorry that this was the least funnest, least spontaneousest, least interestingest, and the most boringest date you've ever been on in your entire life! There I said it!"

For a second, silence hung in the air and mingled with the awkwardness brought about by the utterance of such an embarrassing statement. Yasmin just stared at me as if she couldn't even comprehend what I'd just said, and I couldn't blame her. By any standards, it would barely qualify as passable English.

"That was cringey," she said.

"Please don't pour salt on my wound. One of us had to say it, either you or me. I knew that from the beginning."

"Oh, what a gentleman."

"Yeah, my mother raised me on the foundations of chivalry. I'm basically a Knight of the Round Table. Now, have you decided what you want? What favor or order? I figure you must have been thinking about it the whole time, since you were so sure you were going to win."

"Not yet. I think I'm going to need a minute to think. I want to make sure it's good after all the pain you inflicted on me today."

"What pain was that?! You said it had its moments."

"Yeah, yeah," Yasmin asked, brushing me off. "What were the rules again? About what I can ask for. You said it could be *anything*?"

"Anything *legal*. But let's draw the line at anything sexual either. You're not allowed to have me wait on you hand and foot in the nude wearing only a bowtie while I call you master or anything like that. That's not really appropriate."

"Shut up! That was way too specific! As if I'd ask for anything like that," Yasmin said, her face flushed. "Also, you don't have much credibility saying that while you sit there in only your underwear!"

Being made aware of my near nakedness reminded me just how cold I was.

"You're right. It's getting late, so let's get dressed and head back."

With no towels in sight, we both decided to just put on our dry clothes over our wet clothes. Personally, I was thankful for that. With the effects of the cold on my male body, I wasn't feeling particularly confident enough in myself to strip off my boxers, even if we'd be facing away from one another

Once we were clothed again, I ordered another ride for us, and we headed back up to the street. The wind had just started to pick up too, as if to challenge our feeble attempts to keep ourselves warm.

"Okay, so even though you really wanted it and were practically begging, we agreed no orders of a sexual nature," I stated. "Maybe we should make sure that we're on the same page about orders involving intense public humiliation, bodily-harm, and/or death."

"First off, shut up! You know that I didn't want anything to do with that sexual stuff. And secondly, the only page there is on that kind of subject matter is that we shouldn't do any of that! What kind of person do you think I am?"

"An impulsive one. The kind of person that would proudly say what they want or present their heart's desires no matter how heinous without a second thought." I nodded my head. "Ah, but that's a shame, I was open to it."

"What? Really?"

"No."

"Fuck you."

Another gust of wind hit us, nearly knocking Yasmin and I off our feet this time. In her halter top, her arms and navel were completely exposed to the elements, as were her slender legs. She made a motion to wrap a blanket tightly around her body and rub her shoulders, except she didn't have a blanket.

"Well, is there anything you particularly want or want to do that I could help with?" I asked, continuing our previous conversation.

"Yeah, loads of stuff. I have a bucket list that's miles long. There are lots of things I want to do."

"Like what?"

"Well, there are some simple things like climbing Mt. Everest, taking a trip to Mars, and locating the Lost City of Atlantis."

"There's nothing simple about any of those!"

"Oh. What I meant was that those three are some of the simplest on my list."

"Two of them are literally impossible!"

"I'm sure I'd be able to climb Mt. Everest. People have done it before, so it can't be that hard. Don't underestimate me."

"You know that wasn't the one I was talking about!"

Either way, I couldn't help her with any of it. She was on her own. I'd expected something a bit more reasonable, like buying her lunch sometime or hopping around on only one foot for a day.

"Well, there are two things I actually want," Yasmin whispered, almost as if she didn't want me to hear it. "But those things won't ever happen."

"What are they?" I asked. "Maybe I can help."

Yasmin shook her head.

Given the tone she used, I got the feeling that she was done talking about it, so I didn't press her. Asking for details would only open myself up to the same probing questions, and I didn't want that.

We walked the rest of the way without talking, the thrum of the ocean waves playing in the background. Whether it was because the night was so quiet or because I was attuned to these sorts of things, I could hear Yasmin's teeth chattering. I looked over and saw her jaw moving subtly, confirming that I wasn't hearing things.

Hm.

The kind of person that would proudly say what they wanted, huh? It was a wrong read on my part. She couldn't even ask me for something as simple as this.

I took off my jacket and placed it over her shoulders.

Immediately, Yasmin turned to face me, but I couldn't quite interpret her expression, and she didn't elaborate.

It wouldn't be until we were finally back at the parking lot that she broke her silence.

"Okay, I got it," she said.

"Got what?"

"My order for you."

"Alright, that was quick. What's it going to be?"

Yasmin sighed.

"My order... is that you must give me an order."

"What?"

"Ugh, are you really that much of an idiot? Going to make me spell it out for you? You can tell me what you want me to do. That's your order."

With the realization of what she just said dawning on me, I smiled.

"Does that mean I win?"

"No! I'm going to make this clear enough so that even you can understand it. You didn't win anything. I won, okay? I just feel like I owe you one because you took me out and everything. And also, because—"

"Is this your twisted way of thanking me?"

Yasmin frowned.

"Take it or leave it."

"I'll take it."

Off in the distance, a single pair of headlights traveled across the winding street towards us. No one else was driving around at this time, so it made sense to assume that that was the ride I ordered. Would it be more courteous to just give her this one and get myself another one? I didn't know how this was supposed to work, especially if we lived in different parts of the city.

Fortunately, she answered my thoughts.

"Did you think of an order yet?"

"Geez, no I haven't. It's only been like twenty seconds, and I have a hard enough time deciding what I want to eat in the morning."

"Then… want to come over to my place and think about it?"

What?

Did I hear that correctly?

A girl was inviting me back to her place. At night. Didn't this kind of scenario have certain *preconceived notions*?

I mean, of course I wanted to. What guy wouldn't? But I also wanted to play it cool to not seem too eager about it either.

"Yeah, sure. What are we going to do? Play Twister or something?"

"Shut up! Also, you're still wet and if you get a cold or something because of me, after loaning me your jacket, I'd get really pissed off."

Pissed off at me? Or herself? She didn't clarify that point.

But that's what it was, huh? It made sense. I must have been jumping the gun on any other indecent ulterior motive. Not that I'd be opposed.

I am a guy after all.

"Of course. That'd be great. Thanks."

With a slight screech, Joe's car pulled up beside us and I could see his one-eyed smile through the windshield. It was like his expression was asking, "Did the beautiful couple have fun tonight?"

Yeah, it was fun. Just not in the way you were probably thinking of Joe.

Yasmin opened the door before turning back to me and pausing as if she'd forgotten something.

"Oh, and by the way, I was trying to say this earlier, but… this was fun, Chris," she said. "I've never been on an actual date before."

CHAPTER 10

I really don't know how I should interpret my current situation. There are quite a few different ways to look at it. As to whether any given interpretation is correct or not, your guess is as good as mine.

The only thing that could be said with absolute certainty was this: I was sitting on a couch in the middle of a woman's living room. Yasmin's to be exact.

And, oh yeah, did I mention that all I had on was a towel?

It wasn't even a large one either. It felt more like a washcloth and when I wrapped it around my waist, the rectangular piece of cotton resembled a miniskirt on my skinny frame.

Apparently, Yasmin needed to do laundry.

How convenient.

When we arrived at her place, the first thing she did was rush me into her bathroom to take a shower. She reiterated that she didn't want me to catch a cold and offered to take my clothes, the only set that I had brought with me, and put them in the dryer with the rest of her stuff. This towel—this miniscule towel—was all I had left to cover my nakedness now. I even had to use it to dry myself.

Now, you may be wondering if Yasmin had any spare clothes that I could have asked to borrow.

Yeah, she did, but after a few seconds of thought you'd probably realize why that was such a dumb question.

With our size difference, what could I have possibly worn of hers?

But I asked anyway.

Because I was desperate.

Yasmin offered to lend me a pair of her panties to wear as she walked into the bathroom to take a shower herself. I couldn't tell if she was joking, not that it mattered all that much. For obvious reasons.

So, here I was now, sitting on a couch in the middle of a woman's living room, in only a microscopic towel, while she was showering just a few measly feet away from me.

I shook the thoughts out of my head.

If I dwelled too much on them, I'd end up in an embarrassing situation—one where I had something to hide and nowhere to hide it. In order to combat the normal physiological reaction, I had to distract myself, so I did what any other normal person would do in a situation like this and let my eyes wander around the room of my gracious hostess.

Women really were different.

That observation seemed like a simple one, but I needed to make a certain distinction. They weren't just different when compared to men, but even among themselves.

Of course, the only frame of reference I had to compare Yasmin's living situation to was my ex, but still, women really were different.

I mean, I didn't even know women were capable of being this messy.

Scattered about was the largest assortment of random junk I'd ever seen.

Junk probably wasn't the best word to use. But it encompassed a wide range of objects and also described how those objects were treated. Your average person wouldn't call an object they treasured a piece of junk, right? Nor would they treat it in such a way.

It didn't look as if Yasmin had that kind of distinction.

One person's trash is another person's treasure, as they say.

And her apartment was a hell of a place to hold all this trash—or treasure.

Yasmin's apartment was in a fancy highrise located in the more affluent part of our town. I realized that the moment Joe's car had pulled up outside her building. A few years ago, during my initial apartment search with Brad, I'd looked at some of the listings for this place and scoffed at the prices. I thought those two extra zeros were a mistake. It was the laughter of the receptionist over the phone that made me realize they were correct. Needless to say, neither Brad nor I could afford that price range.

The apartment itself had a spacious living room overlooking the ocean, complete with a connecting kitchen, two bedrooms, and a spare room. Yasmin had explained the layout as if it were no big deal. As if this was as common as the sky being blue.

And if the apartment didn't make it obvious how wealthy she was, the junk did the trick.

Littering the floor, and any empty space for that matter, was just about anything you could imagine. Shoes, including heels, sneakers, sandals, flip-flops; expensive-looking cameras; various woodwind, brass, percussion, and string instruments; the latest gaming consoles and technology that I had only just recently seen in online ads; designer clothing laid out on chairs (were those the panties she mentioned?); athletic equipment, like dumbbells, yoga mats, and a punching bag (that would explain the strength of her kicks); cooking books, textbooks, and other instructional aids; unfinished jigsaw puzzles; Lego sets; records, cassettes, CDs; posters of random boy bands, rock bands, and even classical composers; partially eaten snack items like chips and cookies with names I've never heard of; bottles of energy drinks; and, probably the most surprising, balls of yarn with crochet and knitting needles sticking out of them.

It reminded me of a page in one of those iSpy books I used to borrow from the library all the time. The ones where you had to find certain objects. This wasn't all of it though. There were more things, but this was all I could glean with a cursory glance of my surroundings.

Hm.

I'd been sitting here for a while now, and I was starting to wonder if my clothes were done drying yet. I'd been showering when Yasmin popped them in the dryer, which meant I had no idea where the laundry room was. I didn't think she'd mind if I tracked them down; they weren't that wet, and I would be a lot more comfortable if I at least had my pants on.

Before traversing the room, I carefully charted my path. The ground was like a minefield as I stepped around objects in search of safe areas to plant my feet. It wouldn't have been an exaggeration to say that most of the ground real estate was occupied.

I made my way to the glass sliding door leading to the balcony that overlooked the city with the ocean further in the background. The twinkling city lights looked more like stars than the actual ones in the sky. It beat the dead-end view of the alley that my room had, that was for sure.

Off to the right was the closed door of the extra room she mentioned. Considering how much of a mess it was out here, I wondered if it was just as bad there. Maybe if I opened it, a mountain of stuff would collapse on top of me. Or maybe I would find the laundry appliances.

When I opened the door, the room was nothing like I expected.

Unlike the living room, this one was clean, mostly at least. By that, I mean random objects weren't lying around. I half expected it to be a guest bedroom, but there was no bed in sight. The wood paneled floor was covered with a tarp and facing the walls there were canvases lined up in a row. At the center of the room was what looked to be an easel. The white cloth that hung over it outlined a hidden canvas of its own.

Was Yasmin an artist too?

Looked that way—but something felt different about this room. Compared to the other things strewn about in plain sight for all to see, it was as if the art supplies had been separated from everything else. As if they had been locked away to keep them private.

Or maybe I was just overthinking—

"Damn, you're really nosy."

Yasmin's irritated voice from the doorway caused me to turn.

"You did tell me to make myself at home," I replied automatically before noticing the obvious. "... and where are your clothes?"

A couple feet away from me, Yasmin was standing looking less than amused, a towel wrapped tightly around her body.

And, how come her towel was much larger than mine?

"I'm still drying off," she said, "and I wanted to make sure you weren't snooping around or stealing any of my silverware. Seems I made the right choice. Now, get out of there."

I closed the door and tiptoed my way back to my spot on the couch, pushing away some of the objects that had refilled the vacancy when I had stood up.

Yasmin must have noticed how awkward I seemed because she muttered, "Sorry about the mess. Uh, I've been meaning to clean the place up for the past couple months."

"Months?!"

She shrugged before pushing aside her own pile of objects and sitting beside me.

Now, this was a strange situation.

Two adults, sitting side-by-side, in nothing but towels. Their bodies cleansed of both sand and sweat.

Two adults who were supposed to be on a date.

Was I supposed to be doing something right now?

I had no idea. None. All I knew was that my body was already beginning to react to her proximity. If Brad was in my shoes, he'd probably say this situation was leading to a perfect "Slam Dunk!" or something like that. But I wasn't him.

This may sound like a surprise, but I didn't have much experience in this regard. Not as much as someone might think.

Zoey and I never—got that far.

We dated for over ten years, and the most we ever did was kiss. And even that was few and far between. I know that may sound strange, but that was what our relationship was like. I'm not complaining, that's just how it always was between us.

So, understandably, I was at a complete loss at what to do.

"Are you thinking of something perverted?" Yasmin asked out of the blue.

"Uh, I don't know. I was... just admiring the place you have here. It's... cozy. Do you live here alone or with your sister?"

"With *her?* No. I live alone."

"Ah, I see."

It was a big place to be living alone. Did she ever get lonely? Even I felt that way whenever I'd found myself alone in the one-room apartment Brad and I shared. Despite our circumstances being different, the way she described her sister hinted that something was amiss between the two of them.

"That reminds me. You said something strange about your sister when we texted earlier. That she had *issues.* What was that all about?" I asked.

"Oh, that? It was nothing, really. Just forget I said that."

"It's kind of hard to forget. From what I've seen, you two are complete opposites. In fact, I'm surprised you're twins. Did you grow up in the same household?"

If their living situation was the same, and if both were treated equally, there shouldn't have been any reason for this kind of resentment.

Yasmin sighed. "You really are nosy, you know that? If you must know it's because I can't stand the way that she chooses to live her life. It bothers the hell out of me. Quite frankly, it's boring."

"In what way?"

She repositioned her body and brushed the streaks of damp, black hair away from her face. From this angle, I could better see the similarities in their facial structures. Their nose, eyes, and their lips. It might not have been an appropriate time to think this, but she was pretty, especially her bare legs.

Something in my lower body twitched and I cupped my hands in my lap.

"She's the perfect one. The one who always tries to stay on the family's good side. Brown-nosing and sucking up to them, you know. Been like that for years. Ever since we were little. Because of that, she was the one that got first choice on everything. Hobbies. Games. What to eat. Everything. She never shared either. I was only given the things she never wanted, which wasn't much." Her voice lowered to a mutter as she said, "Even the boys liked her better."

"You should try being nicer. That might help."

Without a moment's hesitation, she slapped me across the face.

Ouch. That one might have left a mark.

But, it made sense.

This was only Yasmin's side of the story, but I could sympathize with her.

I'd heard stories about favoritism in households before. One child getting all the praise and attention, while the other had to survive on the scraps. Naturally, you'd feel some sort of resentment toward that other sibling, and your parents too.

"Which is why I feel like I need to make up for lost time," Yasmin said, continuing as if she hadn't just slapped me. "I want to experience the fun stuff that I missed out on. Be spontaneous. See what else is out there. I've been bored my entire life. Stuck at home finding things to keep myself entertained while she did all the fun stuff. I won't be able to settle on something until I know my options. Until I've tried everything. Only then will I be able to know if anything is truly worth it."

To make up for lost time.

To experience the fun stuff.

To try everything.

How long must she have been living like this?

Looking back at the day's events with this new information, I had to interpret her actions in a different light.

What would happen if someone who was restricted by their circumstances suddenly had the freedom to live by themselves and do whatever they wanted? The perfect setting for college? Yasmin had done the only logical thing that anyone in that situation could do. To try and live her life the way she wanted.

Where my problem was that I couldn't make my mind up on what I wanted to do. Nor did I want to: Yasmin attacked everything ruthlessly, without a second thought.

Hah.

What a funny pair we made.

"And how's that working out for you?" I said, looking around at the cluttered state of her living room.

"Good, I'd say. I've had a real blast getting to try out all these different hobbies. The thing is, there's just so much to do, you know? I know I can't possibly get to it all. I just wish I hadn't lost all that time. And that's not the only problem I have. I just get bored quickly, especially if things don't go the way that I want or they're not the way I imagine they should be. And when I've lost my interest, I kind of just drop whatever it is I'm doing and just pick something else."

"I see."

She had no problem dropping things. Moving onto the next thing without looking back. Though it sounded like she had spent years competing with her sister, never having the chance to do the things she wanted, she'd also spent years idealizing and romanticizing those very same things. It would be hard not to when your sibling gets all the cool shiny stuff, and you don't. It made sense that, when she finally got her chance, they probably weren't as fun as she thought they'd be.

"That's what my meeting with Mrs. Lee was about," Yasmin said. "I should've had only one year left, but I've probably changed my major four or five times already. And don't get me started on how many classes I've added and dropped. She was telling me that if I ever hoped to graduate, I'd eventually need to buckle down and choose something. Can you believe that?"

"Well, she's not wrong. Eventually you'll have to choose something..."

Same as me.

"That's boring. I can't handle being bored."

"I had a feeling you were going to say that. Is there anything that you think isn't boring?"

Yasmin's head turned to the door at the far side of the room.

"There is one thing."

"You like doing art?"

She nodded.

I'd be lying if I didn't say I was shocked at that confession.

Didn't really seem like her thing at all. Yasmin wanted to be spontaneous and interesting. To do crazy things. Art seemed tame in comparison.

"Art's pretty cool, I guess. I love drawing stick figures."

She smacked the bare skin of my shoulder. "Shut up! I'm being serious here. I haven't told anyone that. And the only reason I'm telling a moron like you is because you already barged in there and invaded my privacy."

"It's hard to imagine us having any kind of serious conversation about privacy when both of us are sitting here in nothing but towels. Mine's barely covering anything."

"Stop it. It's not like you have much to cover anyway."

How dare she! Doesn't she know that's one of the biggest insults a woman can give to a guy?

"What?! You want to see?" I stood up and reached for the knot holding my towel together.

"Please, no. I'd rather not permanently lose my eyesight. I'll need it if I want to become... a painter..."

"Oh, so you want to be a painter."

"Yeah." She nodded. "It's one of the few occupations I think I wouldn't absolutely loathe. Art's something that's always been there for me. When nothing or no one else was. Even before I came here to Oceanside. Back then, all I had to keep myself entertained was paper, pencils, and a box of crayons. Drawing pictures and imagining happier times was all that I could think to do. Even now I still make time for it."

"Ah."

I sat back down beside her, and our shoulders touched, but neither of us moved.

Yasmin made it clear that she lost interest in things quickly, that she dropped anything that got her bored.

Things that didn't interest her, no matter how valuable, were nothing more than junk to her, casually discarded wherever she could find space in order to make room for the next thing. But her enjoyment of art was the only thing that had held her interest, and ironically, it was also her first.

So that meant the extra room, a barren space save for her easel and canvases, wasn't meant to lock in and abandon her passion, but to keep outside influences away. To keep the "boring" things from seeping in and corrupting the only thing she thought was fun.

The room was like a locked chest, and art was her treasure.

It was an overly complicated way of looking at it, and the reasoning didn't make much sense.

But that was exactly the kind of thing that a childish, headstrong person would attempt to do.

Like carefully separating your veggies from your meat—the food you like from the food you didn't—so that they wouldn't touch because the simplest touch may contaminate and ruin the whole thing.

That's the way a child may interpret the situation, or someone who was so afraid to lose that particular flavor they enjoyed so much.

"What's holding you back then?"

"I—I don't know if it'll be worth it." Yasmin looked at all the objects strewn about before staring down at her hands. "If I gave it my all and failed… I don't even want to think of that outcome. Plus, I still don't know what else is out there. What if I just haven't found something I like more? What if I start getting bored of it?"

For such a simple answer, it held a great deal of weight. It was something I could relate to.

However… this situation wasn't about me.

This was about Yasmin and what she wanted to do in her life.

Was it a good idea for me to help her make a choice that could affect her life positively?

I didn't know.

There was no way I could possibly know.

Stepping away didn't feel like the correct choice, though.

Zoey never ran away when she saw someone who needed help. She was dependable. A beacon of light and hope. A hand to guide you when you're lost.

And now, this was an opportunity for me to be just like that and offer Yasmin a hand.

People had been there for me before; it was about time I started to pay that good will back.

So many thoughts swirled through my mind that I was getting dizzy. There was also a burning sensation climbing up from my lower back, thanks in no small part to the incident from some months ago.

"You worry too much," I said coolly. "You like painting. So do it."

Yasmin scoffed at my answer.

"Hah, you make it sound so easy. You think I haven't thought about 'just doing it?' That I haven't tried? Chris, I'm telling you it's not that simple for me."

"You don't understand. I'm not asking you to do it."

Yasmin's irritation melted away into a look of confusion. "What the hell are you talking about?"

I smiled.

She still didn't seem to get it.

"That was an order."

CHAPTER 11

"So? You're really going to make me ask, bro? I was hoping you'd just come out and say it, but I can't wait any longer! How'd your date go?"

"I don't know."

"Ugh, don't give me that 'I don't know' crap. You have to give me something." Brad scooted over from his desk to mine looking very neglected. "How am I supposed to focus on all this studying for math I have to do when the only thing I have on my mind is you? I can only think about your gentle caresses and the whispering of your sweet nothings."

Okay, first of all, Brad, ever hear of situational awareness? What would happen if someone walked by and heard your dumb ass through the door? The last thing I needed to deal with right now was rumors.

"I don't know," I said.

"You spent the night, right?"

"Yeah."

"Well, did you... you know?"

"Did I what?"

Brad looked from side-to-side to check if the coast was clear. We were in our small, dingy apartment room—just the two of us.

"Get a 'slam dunk?'"

"No!"

"Sorry, sorry. I was just curious, Chris." He laughed his hearty laugh, the kind of laugh that told you that he wasn't sorry at all. "Did anything happen?"

I set my pencil down and looked up for a second, last night's events playing through my mind like an old TV show rerun. "Yeah, you could say that."

"Yooo!"

Brad jumped up, knocking over his seat in the process along with an assortment of notes, scrap paper, and old assignments. Not a second later, Brad had an arm wrapped securely around my neck and proceeded to choke the life out of me with his bicep. He topped it off with a noogie, grinding the knuckles of his free hand over the top of my head. It felt like I was being grated like a piece of cheese.

"That's my boy! I knew you had it in you! You were sitting on the bench for a while there, but now you're back in the game!"

Brad was much stronger than me, so there was absolutely no way for me to break free. This was it. This was how I was going to die. My windpipe crushed and my nostrils clogged with his body odor. Great.

However, moments before my vision went dark and I drifted off into the afterlife, Brad released me. I fell to my knees gasping for breath.

Brad didn't seem to care that he'd nearly sent me to my grave. He slipped back into his seat.

"I feel like a proud parent now," Brad said, wiping away a single fake tear that rolled down his cheek. "Would it be better to say, 'You've finally left the nest,' or 'They grow up so fast?'"

"None of those fit! You're not my dad! I'm not a baby! And I'm the more mature one out of us two anyway."

"Mhm, of course."

My words didn't seem to reach him. He picked up his fallen papers and went back to his work, still wearing that smile of his. It was like he had just achieved nirvana or enlightenment or fulfilled his lifelong purpose.

I couldn't blame him for being happy, though.

And despite what I said, one of those phrases did fit better than the others.

You've finally left the nest.

Usually such a phrase would describe someone or something leaving their home for the first time, but it held a different meaning for me.

For the span of about three excruciating months, I almost never left our apartment. I just laid in bed, partially unable to move, but also *unwilling* to move. All due to a series of bad choices on my part.

Back then, it hurt to do or think about anything. Honestly, it hurt to just sit there too, especially while Brad worried about me, but I couldn't just *will* myself out of my mental slump.

I had to venture out to speak to Mia about my precarious situation, so it's not like I was holed up in here completely. She's the only person I told the nitty-gritty details to. She picked my brain. Not even Brad and my mother know. Ironically, those two were too close to me, so I didn't want to explain everything. Having them worry wasn't going to do me any favors. I didn't even want to talk to Mia at first either, but I had no choice.

What do I mean by that?

Well, there's more to the story than those three agonizing months. They were more or less the resolution. The consequence. There's still the rising action and climax that led up to that point—things that I still don't fully understand. Simply put, I dumped Zoey. I didn't want to. Who would? She was perfect and caring in a lot of ways. You might even say I loved her, which seems a little immature if you think about it. Zoey was a first for me in a lot of ways. More ways than I'd like to mention or that I'd be willing to tell. It was to the point that, when we were dating, I couldn't even think about doing these things, even the simple things, like spending a night lying in bed, or just relaxing and watching TV, with anyone else. So, this is all just a roundabout way of saying that, ultimately, I regretted breaking up with her. It wouldn't be an exaggeration to say that I regretted it more than anything I've ever done. Even more than when I told my mother that I saw my father with another woman, which was the start of the spiral that resulted in my father ultimately leaving.

Yet, both Zoey and my mother made the same face when I told each of them what I had to say; Zoey—that I wanted to break up with her—and my mom—that I saw father with another woman.

Two different scenarios that led to the same exact expression.

And the moment I saw that look on Zoey's face, the strings of my life, mind, and body began to unravel.

That's why you might think it would be strange that I'm interested in "dating" or being "social" again, when I still wasn't completely over it all—whatever those two words mean nowadays.

Over the course of three grueling months, with nothing else to do but stare at the ceiling, I tended to think a lot. Think about the things that led me to this situation, and what I needed to do to change.

However, people aren't generally inclined to change. People like things to stay the same. You do that by going through the motions. Following habits. Not making any choice that would disrupt that balance. Usually, change requires a great deal of willpower to force yourself through that resistance. And if you didn't have that—

Chris, I'm telling you, it's not that simple for me.

Yasmin's words echoed through my mind.

Ah.

Brad was proud of me, so I was going to let him have that bit of happiness, even though the "thing that happened" probably wasn't even in the same ballpark as his line of thought.

I had just given her that order.

Not to worry about the pointless stuff. If she liked creating art, then she should just do it.

Both Nike and Shia LeBeouf have already said it best.

I thought back to last night, to the moment after I said the words.

"What?" Yasmin had said, reeling back.

"You know... the order? The culmination of the whole date. The power that you bestowed on me when we left the beach."

"What about it?"

Was she seriously this dense? Or was she just playing stupid? I couldn't rule out any of those possibilities.

"Okay, let me put it simply. I, Chris Christianson, order you, Yasmin, to not worry about the stupid miscellaneous details, and just pursue art because it's the thing you enjoy doing. Is that clear enough?"

Yasmin rose from the couch. The one arm she used to hold the knot of her towel up looked as if it might have been covering her heart. She had a whimsical expression on her face, as if her gut reaction to say one thing was having an arm-wrestling match with her rational mind. I couldn't tell which side was winning or which side was fighting for what, but the way her eyebrows crumbled together told me that the battle must have been a fierce one.

"I... you... uh," she mumbled before taking a deep breath. "Sorry. I just had a terrible series of thoughts just now."

"About what?"

"It was like an internal debate. One voice in my head was telling me that I should kill you outright for making such a stupid suggestion."

"Eh? You definitely shouldn't do that! And what was the other voice saying?"

"It was saying I should torture you for as long as possible first."

"That's terrible."

It wouldn't be a stretch to say that there might have been torturing tools somewhere underneath all this stuff. That made her threat all the more frightening.

"I mean what did you expect? This isn't a game. We're talking about my life here."

So that was the problem. She thought I was treating her life like a joke. As if all her problems could be solved easily. That after a single heart-to-heart, she'd be able to live the rest of her life in happiness and bliss. Thinking about it that way really did make me sound like an idiot—like some character from a terrible rom-com. Life wasn't that simple. She must have been wrestling with these feelings for years. As if they'd all disappear so easily...

"Look," I said, hands up in surrender. "Yasmin, I'm sorry if I made it sound that way. I was just joking around. I apologize. I am taking this seriously. We can think of a better solution."

"I wasn't finished yet."

"Huh?"

"There was a third voice," she said, staring dead into my eyes. "It was telling me that there was no way I could refuse a challenge like this. Especially, with so much at stake."

Ah.

Ignoring the fact that this girl just admitted to having three voices in her head, maybe this was the right choice after all.

"Okay," I said, "then what do you want to do then? I personally hope we follow the third voice, but that's just me."

"I'm still not sure yet. Usually if I want something all I have to do is be loud and make a big deal out of everything. That's the only way I was ever able to get anyone to listen to me at home anyway, but that won't work for this."

Like a child crying for attention.

The only thing that she could do in order to get anyone to notice her.

"You're probably just being modest. I'm sure your paintings are amazing. Can you show me?"

"Okay... But on the condition that you promise you won't laugh—even if it's terrible. I haven't shown anyone before."

"I promise."

"Pinky promise."

"Okay, I pinky promise." We locked pinky fingers.

"Cross your heart and hope to die."

"Uh, is that necessary?"

"Just do it."

"Okay, I cross my heart and hope to die," I said as I crossed my chest.

"Now, swear on your mother's life."

"Let's leave her out of this!"

"Swear on your unborn children's lives then."

"Leave them out of this too!"

I prayed that her paintings were good. A lot was riding on it!

As we navigated through her living room floor, Yasmin apologized once again for the mess.

If you hadn't noticed before, it was quite obvious that her family was loaded.

However, according to her, it wasn't always that way.

"We used to be poor. Between the four of us—my dad, mom, sister, and I—we had to share basically everything." Her voice was nearly a whisper as she added, "But I didn't mind."

Ironically, the sparse living situation allowed them to bond closer as a family and all the sharing made for some funny situations between them all. Yasmin started drawing during that time, as a cheap form of entertainment, on bits of napkins and junk mail.

She was the only one that seemed to enjoy that time though. Her family didn't go a single day without complaining about some financial issue. In the morning, at dinner, before bed, the issue of money was the most prevalent topic in her household.

And, one day, as luck would have it, their complaints were finally answered.

A winning lottery ticket.

They hit the jackpot.

A one in a three hundred million chance.

Just about any other situation was more likely to happen.

But they still won.

"The amount of money we won wasn't as large a number as you're probably thinking," she explained. "But it was close enough that we didn't need to worry about any financial issues anymore. My entire family was so happy. Even I was happy—at first."

Despite the good fortune, it wouldn't be long before the family dynamic started to change.

Money tends to change people as they say, or at the very least, reveal their true colors.

They started spending money on random things that they said they needed, wanted, and couldn't live without, but how much of that was true?

Naturally, for a family that didn't have much of anything, now that they did, they wanted to experience the fruits of life that they missed out on—very similar to Yasmin's current situation. But she hadn't seen the problem with their former life, so she rejected the drastic changes.

"And they resented me for it," she said, the darkness from her studio room casting a shadow over her eyes. "My own family criticized my behavior."

They said she wasn't being grateful.

They said she wasn't being realistic.

They said she needed to experience what else life had to offer.

Besides her, they all rejected the notion of returning to the way they once lived.

"But if you want that life, so be it," her father had said.

At that point, Yasmin was left to her own devices—only given the bare minimum as her family members flaunted all their new, expensive possessions in front of her.

All these things were so cool, they had said.

So useful.

So fun.

Only then did Yasmin start thinking that maybe this new life was better. That happiness was derived from what you owned and that shiny, expensive things were fun.

She wanted things of her own now.

However, they still ignored her—and that's when her resentment began. Offering to change for them, she thought they would welcome her into their newfound fortune with open arms.

"They gave me more, but they still rejected me," she said. "It wasn't until I came to Oceanside that I had more freedom to get whatever I wanted. I just chalked it up to my living expenses, and they didn't ask any questions."

And that has led us to this point.

Finally, she could have and do anything she wanted. She still felt like it didn't mean much. That it was boring. That it never lived up to the images that she herself had built up in her mind.

Our date had reignited some of the feelings she had experienced when she was young, when her family was still scrounging to get by. Our bickering during the couples tournament was just like the funny arguments she had with her family.

They'd shared everything.

When I put my jacket around her shoulder, it reminded her of that.

In her studio, Yasmin hesitated before pulling the cloth from over the canvas.

I didn't know what to expect, but I just hoped that whatever was there was good.

And it was.

It was a beautifully painted cityscape of Oceanside. Using the view from her window, she had painstakingly captured the essence of the nighttime version of our city. The glow from the windows of the monolithic buildings sparkled like stars. In the background, the dark blue ocean carried the reflection of the night sky.

"Well? What do you think?"

"This is way better than my stick figures."

Yasmin glared at me, obviously not amused.

"It's beautiful. Really," I recanted.

She turned back to her painting and frowned.

"Thanks."

As if motivated by my comment, she proceeded to reveal the other paintings she had facing the wall.

All of them masterfully depicted different scenery ranging from our school to the very studio we stood in right now.

Seeing the studio captured on that two-dimensional surface reminded me of how plain and sparse this room was, especially compared to the living room.

As if it might have represented a time when Yasmin didn't have anything.

"I don't see the problem. You're good. Why not just stick with this and do it?"

"I don't know. I'm not ready to commit yet. Or good enough. I feel like something is missing, but I don't know what yet."

Now that she mentioned it, the paintings, all different landscapes, did share that one commonality. Even though they looked complete, it seemed like each was missing an unknown element. I couldn't quite place my finger on it, however. I had originally just thought it was my uncultured palette not being able to fully appreciate each of the paintings' majesty.

"You can tell too, right?" she asked.

Now that was a loaded question.

"I mean... I guess?"

"I knew it."

Despite only having the light from the moon showing through the window, I saw Yasmin's expression change.

She shook her head before throwing the cloth back over the easel and returning the other canvases to their previous positions facing the wall.

"Hey, what's the matter? They're great! Don't cover them up."

"No, it's fine. Don't worry about it. I'll just find something else."

She made a movement to walk away, and I could tell that she was troubled by our conversation. It might not have been entirely my doing, but I had somehow upset her and brought her insecurities into the light.

At that moment, Zoey's image flashed into my mind.

She'd know the right words to say. The words that people needed to hear. Even if they sounded like lip service. Affirming words would be able to uplift anyone.

"Wait, don't go," I said. "Yasmin, come on. Talk to me here. Your paintings are amazing. They really are. They're some of the best I've ever seen. I'm sure you'll succeed if you stick with it. You can definitely make a living off of this."

"How could you be sure of anything?!" she shot back.

My reply died in my throat.

She sounded angry and frustrated on the surface, but I knew there was more going on. I only just met her, but even now I could tell there was a deeper meaning to her words. She wasn't the kind of person that you could judge at face value. Yasmin was softer than her hard exterior might have suggested. It was just that the hard exterior benefited her more and allowed her to get more of the things she wanted.

Despite knowing all that, at that moment, I still couldn't formulate the proper words to console her because she was right.

I *wasn't* sure.

I knew nothing about the art world or what it would take to succeed.

There was no weight behind my words. They were nothing more than false platitudes that I believed would de-escalate the situation.

"Well, idiot? Are you stupid? Say something! How can you be sure?"

"I'm... I'm not," I started, flustered by her barrage. In the heat of the moment, my mind had gone blank. "I just said it because I thought it was what you needed to hear."

"Well, you're a moron."

Yasmin pushed me aside and exited the room. I heard her footsteps trail off down the hallway before concluding with the sound of a door slamming.

Maybe this was all just another reminder for me not to get involved. Apparently, I hadn't learned my lesson.

She was someone I'd only just met. Did any of this matter?

I wasn't in the position to be helping anyone.

I needed people to help me.

I left the art room and closed the door behind me gently. Down the hall, the door to Yasmin's bedroom was closed and probably locked too, so I decided to leave her be. The slamming of her door felt like an exclamation point ending everything. However, that didn't mean I wasn't uneasy.

Clearing some space on the couch, I lay down and shut my eyes.

What did it all mean?

She said she'd just find something else.

Like what? And how long would it take to do that?

It was obvious that Yasmin was holding onto the idea that she might encounter something she loved more than painting. But that was no way to live. It was holding her back from something truly wonderful. I believed that much.

That was the thought that plagued me until I fell asleep. During that time, Yasmin's door didn't open again.

Even when I was awoken by the rays of the sun shining on my face.

Even when I tried to stretch away that uncomfortable pain in my back from sleeping on the couch.

Even when I grabbed my now-wrinkled clothes from the dryer.

But it didn't feel right to just leave, so I made my way to her door and stood there silently. My hand hovered in the air inches away in preparation to knock.

I wanted to apologize and see if she was okay, but as my hand moved forward, I heard something behind the door that stopped me. It very well might have just been my imagination, but I could have sworn that I heard something.

Sniffling.

Behind the door, I heard sniffling.

I remained still for the next few seconds, holding my breath to see if I could catch that sound again, but it never came.

Not that it mattered at that point, though.

I let my hand drop to my side and made my way to the front door.

Needless to say, I wasn't able to focus on any of my classes that morning. Couldn't focus on much of anything, really. Before I knew it, three hours had passed, and I was back in my room sitting at my desk and staring at nothing when Brad strolled in looking like he'd just received some terrible news—which he had. He'd failed his math midterm the day before. The reason why it was graded so quickly was because he'd left most of it blank.

Absent-mindedly, I told him that I'd help him study for a make-up test.

And here we were.

To be honest, I wasn't much help to Brad—I just couldn't stop thinking about Yasmin—but he'd been having a blast talking, joking, and laughing to himself.

"So, when are you going to see her again?" Brad asked.

"I don't know."

"Alright, I should have expected that one, but then how about this: do you *want* to see her again?"

"..."

Did I want to see her again? That was a more complicated question than it ought to have been. I did enjoy her company. And I did have fun. That means my answer was—

"Yeah."

"That's good. Very good, bro." Brad nodded. "Okay, next question. When's the wedding?"

"Shut up!"

"I'm going to be your best man, right? I'll throw you a badass bachelor party. Strippers and everything."

I reached out to grab something to throw, but all that I had within reach were the stack of job pamphlets I'd left on my desk. If I balled them up, they'd fly pretty good.

Taking the first one off the stack, I was about to crumple it when, suddenly, I remembered something that I saw back in Mrs. Lee's office. It took me a few seconds of hurriedly flipping through the pages before I was able to find what I was looking for.

This information would have been a lot more useful yesterday.

"Chris, I'm happy for you, but there's one thing I wanted to say."

Brad's serious tone caused me to look at him over the top of the pamphlet.

"Now that you're dating and being social again. I want to make sure to help you out this time around. I don't want another repeat of the whole Zoey fiasco. I don't want you to screw yourself over again. If you need advice, I'm here." He flashed me a bright, white smile. "I can even set you up with some other girls if you want, especially the ones on the swim team. They're hot."

Excluding that last bit, it was another one of those moments, rare and far apart, in which Brad surprised me. It sounded messed up to say, but it was a moment when his level of emotional intelligence exceeded any previous metric that I had assigned to him. Where he broke the mold that I'd placed him in. He offered to help me. And in doing so, he hoped to prevent me from falling into the same problem.

And all I needed to do was just take his hand.

Ultimately, the work would need to be done by me, but he was there to lean on.

Hm.

"I can't believe I'm saying this, but you're right," I said. "Of course, I'll take you up on that offer."

"Great! Which part? The help or the girls?"

I laughed.

"Both, I guess, because I know you won't shut up about it otherwise."

People aren't generally inclined to change. People like things to stay the same. You do that by going through the motions. Following habits. Not making any choice that would disrupt that balance. Usually, change requires a great deal of willpower to force yourself through that resistance. And if you didn't have that—

Chris, I'm telling you it's not that simple for me.

—an external force could help. Someone pushing you along and giving you that extra bit of strength. Sometimes words weren't enough.

Two heads were better than one as they say.

"Speaking of which," I continued. "I actually may need some help right now."

"Whoa, that was quick. What's up?"

I grinned.

"I was wondering if I could borrow a couple of things."

CHAPTER 12

"These are giving me a massive wedgie."

I dug my finger through the cotton of my bathrobe in a desperate attempt to rearrange what I was hiding underneath—Yasmin's surprise.

They were almost unbearably tight. Obscenely tight. The fact that I was even able to move around at all might have been considered the "Eighth Wonder of the World."

However, I knew that I had to push through this much at the very least.

How could I call myself a man if I didn't?

A little physical discomfort wasn't going to stop me. After all, I'd recently dealt with much worse. This was nothing in comparison. A passing nuisance at least. A minor inconvenience at most. These were the words I kept chanting in my mind like a mantra.

And, also, didn't they say that mental pain was much worse than physical pain?

I mean they were both similar in a lot of ways. Usually, the pain on both sides continued until the underlying issue was resolved. However, one had a slight nuance. A physical pain could be identified. Since something was *physically* wrong, there had to be a piece of equipment that could locate its source, allowing for some sort of medication or treatment to be prescribed. For mental wounds, it was different.

Compared to a broken bone, they weren't as easily diagnosed.

Therefore, they weren't as easy to treat.

A broken bone could heal in a few months, whereas a mental wound could last indefinitely.

Yasmin's ten years of bliss had ended abruptly because of a winning lottery ticket. To most, this would have been a miracle, but for her, it was a one-way trip into her own personal Hell. One she had been trapped in for the last ten years.

She was still hurting.

Nothing had healed.

It was still an open wound.

Right now, I was heading towards her apartment on the opposite side of town—the more affluent part—but it wouldn't take long to get there. It was just that the strange looks I was getting while walking down the street in a bathrobe were making me feel a bit self-conscious.

Did I really look like some kind of deviant?

From the way mothers were shielding their children as I walked by, apparently I did.

I was outside her building. Looking at the exterior didn't do it justice. If I were to describe how it looked in one word, I'd say "new." It sparkled with that modern "just off the shelf" look and the building was so tall that I had to strain my neck to look back at it, and even then, I couldn't quite spy the top. Her room was on the twentieth floor.

As I took my next step, Yasmin's voice rang in my head.

You're a moron.

Those were the last words she'd said to me before shutting herself in her room. It'd been three days since then.

Of course, I tried to call her and stuff. Texted her too. She just didn't reply. If she had, then this situation would have been handled a day ago as well. Turns out that things always had to be done in the most difficult way possible.

That's why I found myself here, unannounced. Actually. Was it unannounced when I texted her multiple times that I would be coming?

I didn't know and thinking about it wasn't going to change the situation.

The more important and painfully obvious question that you might be asking is why do it?

Why go so far for someone I just met?

If we hadn't met a couple days ago, none of this would be happening at all. Our two universes wouldn't have intersected, and life would have carried on.

So then why?

It's a difficult question. One I didn't know the exact answer too, but—

People had done the same for me.

People helped me when I needed it.

Was it out of line for me to say that I wanted to do the same?

You're a moron.

She called me that and as far as descriptions went, it was accurate. It described me to a tee. I was a moron, but that didn't mean that I was wrong.

The words I had thrown out to console her. That wasn't the wrong thing to do.

I was a moron for some other reason.

After slipping into her building as a group of people were leaving, I made my way up to her room. Outside her door, I pressed the button for the bell and then held my breath to see if I could hear any movement on the other side. It was dead silent. I couldn't hear a thing. Either she wasn't home, or she was ignoring me.

Hm.

Leaving now after all the effort I put in was out of the question, so I rang the doorbell again.

And again.

And again.

And again.

Over and over.

Rapidly, as fast as I could, my finger poked and prodded the circular button to the right of her door. I was pressing it so fast that the ringing tone on the other side melded into one long, annoying, chime.

Next, with my free hand, I pounded on the door.

"Pizza delivery!"

Knowing her fiery attitude, if she was inside, there was no way that she'd be able to tolerate this harassment for very long.

And as luck would have it, I couldn't have been more on the money than that.

"Will you please shut the hell up! I didn't order any damn pizza!"

Mid-knock, my hand still suspended in air, the door swung open abruptly to reveal Yasmin. Despite it being two in the afternoon, she was still wearing pajamas—a cute bunny onesie, complete with two long ears that protruded from the hood.

"Surprise!" I said jovially.

Yasmin's eyes opened to the size of saucers when she realized she'd been duped, and she pulled off her hood. Due to her size, she couldn't reach the eyehole to see who it was.

She turned her face away quickly. "What are you even doing here? I thought you'd get the hint when I didn't return any of your texts or calls. But I guess I overestimated your intelligence. You really are a—"

"Moron," I finished her sentence. "I know. I'm a big moron. You're right. I was honestly just thinking about it a few seconds ago, actually. Yes, I'm a moron. The biggest moron. I should have been given the title of 'The Biggest Moron in the World.' But that's exactly why I'm here right now. To apologize—dressed like *this*."

I spread my arms apart and did a twirl to show myself off to her.

I was wearing a black bathrobe. Brad had let me borrow one. He used them to keep warm and dry himself off after getting out of the pool at one of his swim practices or meets. The cotton reeked of chlorine, but it was fuzzy and soft, and it kept my body warm, especially since I was practically naked underneath.

"I wanted to make it up to you, Yasmin. I know how you're feeling. I know how much you care about your art. Your paintings. I do think they're amazing, even if something may be missing. You can succeed. I was a moron for not using my conviction to make you believe those words. I made a mistake by just saying what I thought you needed to hear. I know that isn't enough to convince anyone. And if you still have any doubts about that—"

My hands slowly creeped down to the loose knot that held my robe closed. I tugged the cotton free, and the bindings started to come apart.

Lurching back in surprise, Yasmin waved her hands in front of her.

"What the hell are you doing?! Okay, okay, I get it! You don't have to show me! Stop undressing!"

The robe fell apart and a cool, breeze traveled down my body, flowing along *all* its contours. I'm sure if you looked closely enough that the goosebumps on my legs would have been at full attention.

"See, Yasmin? What do you think?"

Both of her hands were covering her face, but I was still able to see her brown eyes through the cracks in her fingers. They weren't looking at my face or chest. Instead, they were aimed much lower.

I wondered if she understood yet.

After a second, she sighed in relief and her hands dropped to her sides.

"You had me there for a second. Where'd you even get that?"

Yasmin pointed a finger at my nether regions—at the speedo that conformed tightly to my body. The fabric stretched around all the obvious bits of the male anatomy. To the untrained eye, it may have looked like a thong. But it wasn't. This thing was built for performance.

Hence, why it was so tight.

Unbearably tight. Obscenely tight.

Brad had said the tighter the better. You didn't want to have any drag when you were in a race.

But this wasn't a race, Brad! Was it too much to ask for something a bit more comfortable?

"What do you mean? I have a million of these. I love speedos. The way they hug my body feels like a kiss from the gods," I said. To highlight my point, I kissed the tips of my fingers like a chef. "I can see why you women like these kinds of things."

"Pssh, yeah right. They look a bit tight on you. Are you sure you're okay?"

"No, I'm good. They're actually a little too big. I might have to size down. Anyway, my fashion choices aren't important. What's important is why I'm here."

To this, Yasmin folded her arms across her chest and cocked her hips as if to tell me to continue and I did.

"It's fine if you're not confident in your mad skills just yet. It's hard to be confident when you care about something as much as you do. That's why I'm offering to help you. Let this moron help you. Sometimes a little extra help is all you need to make a big change. Maybe what you're missing in your art is that spontaneous feeling you're always raving about. A different subject or perspective to capture. That's where I come in."

I struck a few different poses that I saw in Mia's pamphlet. It was a pamphlet showcasing different careers. The pictures of art models immediately caught my eye.

After coming up with my plan, I'd spent the rest of yesterday practicing in front of the mirror, trying to capture their essence and even attempting to stay in position for as long as I could. I was still working on that last bit, but even this should have counted for something.

"So? What do you think? How about we do this together?"

"Well." She paused, her eyes scanning my body. "First off, I was originally going to say that you really are an *idiot*, not a moron."

"Hah. Is that so? You should have just stopped me. My whole little speech kind of hinged on that."

"Why would I stop you? Of course I was going to let you finish. I didn't want to be rude."

Geez. Now, of all times, you didn't want to be rude? I feel so thankful that she let me make a fool of myself for the past two minutes.

"But it was... sweet," she added.

"Sweet enough for you to take me up on that offer?"

Yasmin laughed and I smiled.

It was nice to hear it again. A small part of me honestly believed that I might not ever get another chance. I'm glad that wasn't the case.

"Was it an offer? Sounded more like an order to me," she said slyly, uncrossing her arms and stepping to the side to let me in. "But, sure, why not? It sounds fun."

CHAPTER 13

"So, Christian," Mia said. "Have you done what I requested of you?"

I stood in front of her desk with my arms at my sides. Her office looked the same as always, with the fancy diplomas in a perfectly straight line, and the bookcases filled with an assortment of different texts. They weren't just for show either. The covers were well-worn, with the creases that traveled vertically down their spines like wrinkles. She'd wanted to be a writer before she became an advisor, so it made perfect sense that she was an avid reader as well.

"Well, about that," I said.

It'd been a few weeks since I last found myself here. Come to think of it, it was the same day as my first date with Yasmin. Of course, I hadn't forgotten the little homework assignment she'd given me. Remember? She told me that next time I came back that I should have at least a few job ideas that I was willing to consider. A tall order for someone like me.

"Oh dear, that doesn't sound good."

Ouch.

You're supposed to have some faith in me, Mia. Don't give up before I've even finished talking.

She was well within her rights to worry and sound disappointed.

After all, I didn't do what she asked.

I'd been busy.

"No, I haven't, but I've got a good explanation."

Mia shook her head. "I do hope so."

"Hear me out. You see, things are different now. Last time I was here, the problem was that I was having trouble making a decision. So I didn't. Does that make sense? Now, however, due to all the time I've spent reflecting and thinking about my future, all because of your terrific guidance by the way, I've decided that it'll be a good idea to keep an open mind and just try different things. It's still too early to box myself in on a choice or two, so instead, now I'm willing to test the waters. I won't just sit around and think about it all day."

Mia folded her arms and raised her right eyebrow behind the lenses of her large glasses. Her expression seemed to say that she wasn't buying the crap I was peddling.

"Very well. It seems like you've at least put a modicum of thought into it, so I won't pester you. And quarreling would only serve to bring down my mood, and I've been feeling ecstatic for the past couple days."

"Oh? Why's that? Did Mr. Lee do something romantic?

"Heaven's no. He's a stoic man who doesn't fall to the mere whims of romanticism, but that's what I just adore about him," Mia fawned like a recently wedded woman. "But, no, my elation has to do with a different problem student like yourself. Previously, I had gotten onto the wrong foot with her, and I'd felt awfully terrible about it ever since. I invited her back hoping to apologize, but much to my surprise, mind you, before I could even open my mouth, she apologized first! It warmed my heart, and we had a heart-to-heart discussion. She said she settled on a path she wanted to follow. An artist! A creative venture is a difficult journey I know, but well worth the struggle. I'm still thinking about it."

Thinking about what? Her conversation or the path of an artist? The distinction wasn't clear.

Mia nodded while tilting her head at me. "Now, if only you'd turn over a new leaf as well."

"Yeah, if only."

"Ah, speaking of which," she said, snapping her fingers. "I remember you mentioning something about a date before. How'd that go? Tell me all the details!"

"Hah, that?" I laughed. "Now that's an interesting story."

CHAPTER 14

"Be honest. Did she really say that?!" Yasmin exclaimed.

"Yeah, she totally adores you now. Sounded like you were her favorite person. She also said something about hoping to see some of the work you've done."

Yasmin laughed as she threw her arms up in victory and reclined back onto the couch. She was wearing a black tank top and gray sweatpants, her hair pulled back into a ponytail—casual as ever.

After holding a thirty-minute pose, my back was starting to kill me, so I suggested we take a break. I'd been coming over to see her about two times a week. Our dates (if you can call them that) mostly consisted of me modeling for an hour or so, after which we would get food and just talk for a while. Not that I'm complaining or anything. I think it's better this way. Building up that foundation of friendship first before taking things any further. There was still a lot I wanted to learn about her, but I was trying to do it without getting emotionally invested too quickly.

Still.

I wasn't sure what she thought about the thing we had going on either. She hadn't said a word to indicate how she felt. Which was a surprise, given that she usually said what was on her mind.

"By the way," Yasmin said, taking a sip of her sports drink, "you've been looking a little shaky up there lately. Can you hold still next time? It would be a shame if anything were to happen to you up there."

Her comment sounded way more threatening than concerned.

"Maybe it'll be better if you just take a picture. They say those last longer."

"Why would I want to do that? I'd rather feast on you with my own eyes." She smirked, using her elbow to nudge me in the ribs.

"Excuse me, ma'am," I said back. "Don't objectify me. I have feelings."

"Come on, I bet you like the attention."

Hm. She wasn't wrong about that.

I'd forgotten what it had felt like. It'd been a while.

"I don't know. Maybe," I said.

"Ahhh, see? You do like it."

"Yeah, I do. I like that I can help you and that it looks like you're enjoying it."

Caught off guard by my remark, Yasmin's eyes softened.

"And thank you for that. I appreciate it," she said.

"No problem."

Silence.

Speaking of situations, I had noticed that these awkward silences had been springing up between us a lot more often. Early on it was like we could banter indefinitely, using each of our comments to bounce off in a kind of verbal trampoline, but lately it was like she seemed to concede much more easily. I couldn't really describe it. There were also times when I was turned away and she thought that I couldn't see her. I'd catch her staring—as if she wanted to say something.

What could it have been?

Not wanting to suffocate under the weight of my thoughts and the silence any longer, I brought up a random observation. I never really liked idle chit chat that didn't amount to anything, but, at this point, even that was better than nothing.

"This place is looking a whole lot better now," I said, scanning the apartment. "I was starting to think that you were a hoarder. You know, one of those people that holds on to all their trash and things like that. I was about to throw you an intervention."

"Shut up! I told you I'd been meaning to clean up for a while. I finally found a bit more time."

"A while? Years. You told me it had been years. Sounds like a hoarder to me."

"Is your memory going out now? I told you *months.* Not years."

"Yeah, yeah. Same thing."

Yasmin seemed as if she wanted to continue the conversation, but I turned away.

Her place was not as cluttered now. No one would have been able to deny that. However, you'd have to have seen how the apartment previously looked in order to make that distinction. Sure, it was tidier, but that didn't mean it was *tidy.* Random things were still lying around. I saw a new pogo stick in the corner of the room and a unicycle in her closet that wasn't there the last time I stopped by. The thing now was the place wasn't as cluttered. You could walk through her apartment without worrying about where to take your next step.

This was all a good start.

But what was the next step?

Yasmin still had her spontaneity, thrill-seeking nature, and fiery disposition, but that was never really the problem. I'd say those were good traits to have—it was just that when they held her back that things got muddled.

And the root cause hadn't been completely resolved yet.

Her family.

She'd come to terms with them, but she had yet to address any of the fundamental issues.

We'd get to it eventually, though. These things couldn't be rushed. One step at a time.

"Chris?"

Yasmin's voice took on a lighter tone, lacking its usual aggressiveness.

"That's my name, don't wear it out."

"Shut up!" And just like that, she reverted back. "Listen, let's be serious for a minute, alright?"

"Okay, what's on your mind?"

She looked at me, narrowing her eyes into slits.

"It's just that—there are some things I've been meaning to talk to you about for a while now. I don't want you to feel like you have to answer though. I'm just... curious."

Wow. How conscientious of her.

"Are you breaking up with me?" I threw out that outlandish remark with a smile on my face. I wondered how flustered she'd get from that one.

But Yasmin didn't give the reaction I was hoping for. She didn't react much at all; instead she just frowned and massaged the bridge of her nose.

"How boring. I saw that one coming from a mile away, so I guess we'd better address that first. Chris, you've helped me with a lot of things in the past few weeks, and like I said, I'm grateful. I've told you things I haven't told anyone, and it's crazy because we've basically just met. I guess I trust you. However, I do have my pride to think about. I can't just be the damsel in distress the whole time. I want to help you too. It's only fair."

She stopped to look at me, probably to make sure I was paying attention to what she was saying before continuing. "Look. Maybe I'm doing something wrong. I don't have much experience in this kind of stuff, but I've noticed that whenever I try to bring up your life, or something in your past, you cast it off with a joke and quickly change the subject. At first, I thought it was funny and interesting. Don't go and get cocky when I say it's one of the things I liked about you when we first met. That's true. However, it's just frustrating now. I'm trying to get to know you and you seem to be treating it as a joke. It makes me not even want to bother asking anymore."

So, this was what was on her mind. I never would have guessed that.

I took a moment to think, throwing out the first five responses that popped into my head. She obviously wanted a serious answer, so I had to consciously make sure that it wasn't the least bit funny, but even then, I still had to stifle the laugh that was threatening to burst from my mouth. Why was it so much harder to hold in a laugh at times like these?

"I'm—I'm sorry," I said. "Joking around just makes things... easier. Funnier too."

At least I thought so.

Ironically, my propensity to be sarcastic, make jokes, and throw out quips wasn't something I'd spent much time thinking about. In fact, the words sort of just came out without me having to do much thinking at all. It really was just easier.

"Easier? In what way? What do you mean?"

"If I crack a joke, if I make light of the moment, the conversation becomes less serious. It makes things easier for me to talk about. Like... it's not a big deal, I guess?"

"But you're not talking about the situation, you're talking *around* it. I feel like I know your personality, but I don't know much of anything else."

"Again, I'm sorry. I'll do better in the future," I said quickly. "Anyway, I've rested long enough, so let's get back to work."

I stood up and walked to the door of her studio. I wished with everything in my being that the conversation was over. I would have walked out if I didn't think it would have left a bad impression. I still wanted to be here with her, but the pressure was building. We were getting too close to sensitive topics that I wasn't ready to talk about.

"Not 'in the future,'" she said. "Now. I didn't get to ask my real question yet."

I looked back over my shoulder at her. She was still sitting on her black couch, leaning forward, her elbows on her knees.

"Sure, ask away. I'm an open book."

Yasmin sighed, brushing a few loose strands of hair behind her ear.

"Obviously, I've seen it. No matter how hard you tried to hide it. The first time was at the beach. The thing was, I just haven't been able to get a good look at it until recently. I thought it was nothing. Maybe a birthmark," she said softly. "But I am curious about it. It looks serious."

"Curious about what exactly?" I feigned ignorance, hoping it'd work this time.

"I told you not to play dumb."

Ah, damn. I knew this was going to be a problem. I'd come up with some easy-to-believe explanations beforehand as a kind of contingency just in case anyone asked any questions, but considering our conversation, it seemed like Yasmin was on high alert. Her bullshit meter was turned up to max and pointed directly at me. There was no other way out of this. I knew I was going to have to tell her at one point, but this all felt too soon.

Yasmin slowly pointed to a spot on my lower back.

"That scar. Where'd you get it?"

CHAPTER 15

Well, I guess now would be a good time to explain a bit more about my past. Of course, if I had a choice, I wouldn't, but I don't, so I will. It was going to come out at one point, anyway, so might as well just get it out of the way.

Ugh.

It's just... I really don't want to.

Telling you what happened wasn't that bad per se, but the way it made me feel to think about it was.

Because it's just so embarrassing. So pathetic.

After all, there's no easy way to talk about your own faults. It just makes me sound like a loser, which I am, but if I don't talk about it—if I just brush it under the rug, as they say—then at least I don't have to confront that self-reflection of myself. That ugly reflection.

Okay, at this point, it's starting to sound a whole lot like I'm stalling, so here goes.

I did something so incredibly stupid that the mere thought of it makes me cringe with embarrassment.

What might that be, you ask?

Well.

I attempted to take my life.

And it was over Zoey.

I know. I know.

Not exactly the most original reason, but what can I say?

Brad was away when I climbed onto the windowsill of our fifth floor apartment. There, I contemplated my mortality as I stared at the concrete below. I remembered being surprisingly calm as I looked death in the face. I thought I'd be freaking out, unable to even scoot myself onto the edge, but I was wrong. It must have been the ease that came with acceptance.

I'd broken up with Zoey just two months prior and I was at the literal climax of my depression. It was such a dumb thing for me to do. I wanted to be with her, and judging by the way she broke down after I told her, she wanted to be with me too. I just couldn't shake my feelings of inadequacy. I didn't believe I was good enough. When you know your worth, and it feels like people are trying to bolster you up higher than you're meant to be, you can't help but feel shitty about it all. Like they're holding you to an unattainable standard.

Zoey would try to make sure I was on top of all my schoolwork and that I had my eyes set somewhere on the horizon. She had high hopes and goals for herself too, and she didn't want to be confined to a life of normalcy and mundanity. I didn't mind that kind of life, though. I felt like a simple, carefree life without many worries was the key to true happiness. Still, making sure she was happy made me happy too. You really don't know how true that statement is unless you're in that kind of relationship yourself. It does end up being like that sometimes.

However, as the years passed, it became too stressful to live up to her expectations, and as a result, I had the brilliant idea that cutting it off would fix things. Take some of the weight off that I didn't want to carry anymore. But look how that turned out. I honestly should have just kept my mouth shut and none of this ever would have happened.

It was the same situation with my mother.

I never should have told her that I saw Dad with another woman either. Then maybe the arguments wouldn't have gotten worse. Maybe he wouldn't have left. And then maybe Mom wouldn't have been sad.

Yeah, in both cases, I honestly should have just kept my mouth shut.

In my twisted logic, I thought it would be better if I never opened my mouth again, and in even more twisted logic, I thought the best way to do that was by making sure that I *couldn't* open my mouth again. It was a faulty thought process to begin with, but please forgive my previous mental state. I wasn't in exactly the right frame of mind.

I picked a day. I remember it was Saturday night and I waited for Brad to leave before I made my move. Of course, I had my doubts and reservations about the whole thing, but even then, around eleven at night I found myself sitting on that windowsill. On numerous occasions, I'd stare through that window whether I was absentmindedly doing homework or reading, and think to myself, "Gee, that alley is secluded. If someone were to die back there, no one would notice for a while." That wasn't verbatim what I thought, but it gives you the general idea of where my mindset was at. There was even a gate that prevented people from just walking into it.

I guess you can assume what happened next. I already told you that I *attempted* to take my life and seeing as I'm still here, explaining the situation, it only logically follows that the attempt failed. But it still wouldn't be completely honest to say that I attempted to take anything. What I mean by that is—

I changed my mind.

Maybe I just didn't have the guts to go through with it, or maybe I just didn't want to die.

Your guess would be as good as mine.

Moments before I decided to let go, the faces of all the people in my life came to mind. It was a small turnout, because I didn't interact with that many people, but it was still a harrowing experience.

At the center of that small group, the one that took center stage, was my mother.

Right before you're about to die they say your life flashes before your eyes. Within those flashes, I noticed something.

Why did Mom look so sad all the time?

Even when she was laughing.

Even when nothing seemed wrong.

Even when she should have been happy.

That small voice at the back of my mind, standing behind the crowd and struggling to be heard, shouted something out. Something I was able to hear.

Don't give her another reason to be sad.

After coming to this realization, I just had the overwhelming impression that this wasn't the right choice. I thought keeping my physical mouth shut was the answer, but I was wrong. It was that doubt in my head that needed to be silenced.

Luckily, I had that realization before I'd come face-to-face with the pavement because, at that point, I'm pretty sure my mind would have been on a lot of different things.

Hah... That was a morbid joke. It made me chuckle a little.

Anyway, at that point, the magnitude of what I was about to do finally dawned on me, and all that calm turned into fear and anxiety. The distance to the ground seemed to telescope away, getting further and further by the second. I became painfully conscious of my rising heart rate and my vision phased in and out of blurriness like the refocusing lenses of a camera.

The spot where I perched was cramped. I had to hunch my head forward so that I could sit uncomfortably on the ledge. I didn't realize beforehand that the space would be this narrow. Cliché as it sounds, my first choice was the roof, but you needed a key to access it, so that plan was a bust.

So, there I was, teetering on the edge of the window and my life, unable to turn around or move. I was panicking. My hands were clammy and the moisture under my armpits wasn't doing me any favors either. Perspiration ran down my arms and body, and that sudden sensory input grabbed my attention for a split second. I likened the feeling to having a pebble lodged in my shoe. It wasn't a major inconvenience, but it was distracting, and I didn't need to be distracted at a moment like that. For obvious reasons.

Despite thinking that, I unconsciously shifted my arm. It was something I shouldn't have done because the next moment, before I even knew what was happening, I slipped.

I was falling.

Whether it was the sudden change in weight distribution, or the removal of one of the vital pillars that supported me, I slipped and fell forward. Immediately, I was overcome with that feeling of having my stomach and all its juices wrenched upwards by inertia.

It all happened so quickly. There wasn't even time for me to scream.

I was falling.

I was going to die.

And I knew for certain that no one was going to be around to catch me this time, even if I wanted her to.

And I did.

I really did.

Reflexively, I did what I think anyone would have done in that situation, I frantically reached out for whatever I could grab onto. Something, anything, to slow my fall.

And my savior?

It was one of those air conditioning units that hung from the outside of your window. My fingertips latched onto it like my life depended on it. But I only managed to grab onto it with one hand, my left hand, the weaker of the two. I couldn't hold on for longer than a few seconds. The force of my fall and my sweaty fingers caused me to lose my grip again, but it had slowed me down just enough and diverted my previous course just enough.

I was falling.

When would I hit the ground?

It couldn't have been much further, but it felt like I was falling for hours, as if the moment was suspended in slow motion.

There was a loud *clunk* followed by a piercing pain that shot up the lower part of my back like electricity coursing through me all the way to the tips of my fingers and toes.

Then I settled on a sea of giant marshmallows, if those marshmallows were hard and lumpy and smelled like rotten garbage.

As I fell from the window, something else had slipped my mind. The only thing of any significance in the otherwise empty alleyway—a green dumpster that hugged the wall some feet to the left of my window. *The* green dumpster. The infamous green dumpster. Resting there open like the gaping maw of some emerald beast. In all the time I'd spent there I'd never seen anyone empty those bags of garbage.

Yeah, I'd fallen into the monster. Its open lid had swallowed me up.

And I just laid there.

My breathing was ragged, and my hands traveled up my body to make sure I was all in one piece, and from what I could tell, I was, except when I tried to get up.

I couldn't really move.

It wasn't like the windowsill situation, where I couldn't move because it was cramped or too tight. It was very spacious in that green dumpster. There was more room there than even the twin bed I had in my room.

No, I couldn't move because that pain in my back wasn't letting me. I was unable to twist my body without wanting to scream in agony.

I was helpless.

Stranded there, forced to bathe in a sea of trash and who knows what else, and with nothing else I could do, I stared up at the night sky. Now, I don't want you to get the wrong idea and think that the night sky was filled to the brim with stars or anything. I was living in the city, after all. With all the light pollution, you would only be able to see the brightest ones, and even then, they were faint enough to miss unless you were looking for them.

However, they were still there, if you were willing to look.

Seeing those few stars. Those few lights. It kind of reminded me of the faces of the people in my life, the ones that had flashed across my mind not even a minute prior. There weren't many, but they were still significant.

Hah.

I started to laugh.

It came from deep down inside. The situation wasn't funny and each heave hurt my body, but even then I laughed.

If there was one specific moment in which I realized things needed to change, that was the one. A lot of my choices have ended up hurting people. My mother. Zoey. And this choice. One that I almost made in the heat of the moment. This would have been the biggest, most painful one.

I didn't know what I needed to do.

There were so many things I needed to do.

Just this hadn't been one of them.

So, I continued to lie there. I'm not sure how long it took, but I waited until I was eventually able to move enough to pull myself out of the dumpster. By no means was it easy. Every movement I made caused me to relive the pain of the initial impact. Somehow I pushed through it and shuffled to the entrance of the alley, taking as long as I needed and using the wall as support. Thankfully, the gate wasn't locked at the time.

The light of morning had just started to peak over the horizon when I finally made it back up to my room. Traveling up that staircase might have been the most taxing thing I'd done in my entire life.

Having exhausted the last of my strength, I collapsed onto my bed and closed my eyes.

To this day, I don't know how serious the back injury was. When I checked the mirror in the morning, my lower back area was bruised and swollen. There was a nasty-looking gash and I thought I might have been able to see bone, though that might have just been a mixture of my paranoia and hallucinations.

I didn't tell anyone about it. Not until I had to explain to Mia, and I only did that so I wouldn't have my enrollment dropped. I didn't want to go to the hospital or anything. It was too embarrassing and pathetic of me. I knew if I did, it'd probably just be a shitstorm of trouble for me and everyone else.

If I kept it to myself, I could pretend like it never happened. It might as well have never happened. No one would have to worry about it. I made Mia promise not to say anything either. My impassioned speech probably touched the romanticist in her. She agreed on the condition that I allowed her to help me, and when I was ready, I would get it checked out.

So, for the time being, I stopped going to class. I couldn't move around, after all.

The cover story was simple enough.

I just explained to my professors, my mom, Brad, and anyone else who came around asking questions, that I'd caught some nasty stomach bug, or flu. That my immune system was compromised and that I needed as much bed rest as possible. They didn't ask that many questions, seeing as I looked and acted the part.

Besides all the work I had to catch myself up on, I didn't have many more problems after that.

Fast forward about four months and here we were now.

The pain in my back still flared up occasionally, enough that sometimes I occasionally had to excuse myself for a couple of minutes until it died back down. But I was used to that now. Might even say I'd grown a little attached to it. It's kind of like that cool scar you get in an accident that you show off to whoever was unlucky enough to bring up the subject. The only difference was that it wasn't cool, I didn't show it off, and I didn't go out of my way to tell that story to anyone. So, yeah, I guess the two situations were similar in the sense that they were both accidents.

Mine wasn't a source of pride either.

It was more of a reminder. A reminder of my shame. Even years down the road when the scar faded enough that it was nearly invisible, I'd still know it was there.

After saying everything that I wanted to say and everything that I needed to say, I turned to Yasmin. She'd been surprisingly quiet the whole time that I was weaving my tale of heartbreak and depression that

I was a little scared to see how she'd react. I'd never seen her this quiet before. It was like the calm before the storm.

What could you say after someone confides in you that they almost killed themselves? An apology? Asking for them to elaborate more on their reasoning for doing it? The whole thing just creates an awkward situation for everybody.

Yasmin sat motionless, staring at a spot on the ground, her hands placed in her lap. The docile and ladylike position was almost too serene for someone of her temperament.

"Uh, Yasmin?" I asked. "Earth to Yasmin, do you copy? Over."

As if finally registering my words, her head swiveled to face me while every other part of her body kept its fixed position. Her expression was calm.

"Chris?" she said simply.

"Uh, yeah?"

"Can I tell you something?"

I didn't know where this was going, but I was curious.

"Sure?"

"You're a fucking idiot."

Ah.

As far as reactions went, I couldn't expect anything less from her.

CHAPTER 16

So, after coming clean about my dark and troubled past to Yasmin, I think it was safe to say that we had taken the next step in our burgeoning relationship. The question now was whether the step we had taken was forward—or backward.

In a lot of ways, talking about death is the "end all and be all," as far as conversation topics go, especially regarding something as morbid and controversial as suicide. Just about all other topics pale in comparison. The questions I had about my relationship with Yasmin didn't seem like much of a big deal anymore.

Everything was in the open now, so addressing any outstanding issues was more a matter of course. Apparently, she must have felt the same way because she threw out a bunch of questions she'd probably been dying to ask. After all, there really wasn't much else that I could say that would surprise her.

Yasmin yelled in her rage that she'd sooner kill me herself if I ever so much as brought up wanting to die again. To make sure I understood that, she used her small fists to beat this point into my shoulder. This wasn't all. Yasmin was particularly mad for a couple of not-so-obvious reasons, but to her, they were probably the only reasons that had mattered.

Apparently, for one, I had no right to die until after her debt was cleared, or so she said. After having helped her as much as I had, she wanted to make sure that she was able to pay me back.

It was only fair, she'd said, as she hated owing people things.

Despite Humpty-Dumpty's great fall happening months ago, Yasmin seemed to have the idea that I was still harboring negative thoughts. I couldn't outright deny it was true; most such thoughts crept into my mind on nights I couldn't sleep, but I was convinced I wouldn't ever attempt to do something that stupid again. At least I hoped.

Secondly, she said I had made her feel bad.

I had made her feel bad, so now she was going to physically assault me as a result. What kind of crazy backwards logic was that?

Yasmin felt bad because of the things she said to me while I was acting as a model for her during our sessions.

"Twist your back more and look at me."

"Would it kill you to stand up a little straighter?"

"Stop complaining! You're going to do an upward-facing dog position and I'm going to have you hold it for an hour. If you give me any lip about it, I'll add another two hours to that!"

These were some of the more reasonable demands that had been called into scrutiny. Exhibits one, two, and three, respectively.

Yasmin could be quite the merciless dictator when she wanted to be.

"So, what does all of it mean then?" she asked after having reprimanded me violently for my idiocy.

"What does what mean?" I replied.

Her finger bounced between the two of us.

"This thing."

Ah. She was talking about our "relationship." I had just been asking that same question, I just didn't think it would get brought up so soon.

"Uh, I don't know," I said. "Can you be more specific?"

She rolled her eyes.

"Tell me again. State it clearly. Why did you try and—" Yasmin dragged her right thumb horizontally across her neck.

"First off, don't get the wrong idea about me. I didn't actually go through with it. I changed my mind. It was more of an accident. But to answer your question, I guess... I made a stupid choice and hurt someone I cared deeply about. At that moment, before my change of heart, I didn't want to live with that guilt or weight anymore. I'd been with her my whole life practically—so I was attached."

"That's dumb. Why didn't you just go back to her and apologize or whatever? That makes a whole lot more sense than getting angsty and trying to off yourself."

"I felt like I didn't deserve to. I don't know. Like I wasn't worthy. I owed a lot to her, so I couldn't face her on even terms." I thought about my next words. "You said it yourself just a couple of minutes ago. It's like I have an incredible debt to pay back, but my problem is the way I am now, I don't think I'd be able to do it. Everything would eventually turn out the same if I did. The only thing I can do is try to start over and build myself up. That's the only path I think there is. But, like I said, I don't know... Anyways, I feel like I'm rambling. Does any of this make sense?"

"I think I'm getting the big picture," Yasmin grumbled. "But this leads to the question I've been wondering this whole time."

"Which is?"

"Are you still not over her?"

That sounded like a loaded question. The kind of question that a guy had to tread around carefully, like when a girl asked you if a certain pair of jeans made her look fat. There was no right answer. The best choice was just to avoid it.

"I... don't know."

"How boring."

Yasmin sighed before getting to her feet. She walked to the far side of her room and for a moment, she stood there silently staring out of her window. It was afternoon and the sun had just begun its descent towards the horizon. Harsh rays of direct sunlight illuminated everything in the large apartment building.

"Fuck," she cursed. "They warned me about this."

"Who's 'they'? And what did they warn you about?"

"All those damn dating podcasts, articles, and books I've been listening to and reading."

She just said something completely unexpected.

"Wait, hold up. You're into that kind of stuff?"

"Just a bit," she said nonchalantly, brushing off the scrutiny with a hand motion. "I've only subscribed to fifteen different podcasts, nine different magazines, and read like seven different books on the subject."

"That sounds way more than a bit. It sounds like you're a certified expert!"

"That's nothing. I also watch a bit of porn too."

"What does 'a bit' mean to you exactly?"

"Forty hours a week."

"That's a full-time job!"

"It's fine. I only watch the raunchy stuff anyway. I kind of find vanilla boring."

"What depraved thoughts are crawling around in that mind of yours?"

This conversation had taken a sharp left turn into uncharted territory, and I didn't know where to navigate at all.

"Huh? Look who's talking."

"What do you mean? I'm the poster child for purity. I'm a total gentleman. Even my mom thinks so."

"Please," she spat. "I've seen the way you gawk at every woman who comes into your line of sight whenever we go out. It's disgusting."

"What are you even talking about? That doesn't happen at all! I don't gawk. When I'm inner monologuing I kind of just space out sometimes."

"Uh-huh, sure. What depraved thoughts are crawling around in that mind of yours?"

"You can't use my own words against me." I said. "And wait a second! When did this suddenly become about me? I was asking you why you were into that kind of stuff."

"What do you mean? I told you already. Vanilla porn is just too boring."

"Whatever! You can watch whatever porn you want. I was talking about the dating podcasts and the articles."

"Oh, that? I already mentioned that. Remember? It was back on the beach," Yasmin said. "Before we went out that day, I'd never been on a real date before, so I've been preparing for a while. Still am."

Huh... I do remember her saying something like that, mostly because of how surprising it was. Yasmin was a cute girl, so it was inconceivable to think that she wasn't getting any attention from the opposite sex. But, even if that was the case, it would only logically follow that she'd want to gather and learn more about the subject and, except for the part about the porn, reading about dating tips and boys seemed like a very girlish thing to do. Besides consulting these resources, a girl would also probably talk about these things with their girlfriends or better yet—their sister.

Ah.

All the pieces made sense now, and I felt stupid again for not realizing it any sooner.

Since after our first meeting, not one time had she made any allusions to having any friends or speaking to her sister. It's not like Yasmin was a shut-in or anything. She did go out to her classes and there were all the activities she participated in, but she always made it sound like she did them alone, unless I was there to accompany her.

Hm.

Just because one of her problems was solved didn't mean that they all were.

The root cause was still there.

Not dwelling on it any further, I decided now would be a good time to bring our conversation back on track. "I understand. What did they warn you about?"

"Guys who aren't over their exes are a red flag."

True… It was a sticky situation all around the board. I didn't know for certain if I could say that I wasn't over Zoey yet, but she did pop into my mind more often than I'd like to admit. So, that must have meant that I wasn't over her. Right?

Yasmin moved to the row of chairs that were lined up next to her kitchen counter. They were the high kind, like the stools you might find at a bar. For a few seconds, she struggled to climb up onto the chair before turning to face me.

"So, let me get this straight. You think you need to change yourself," Yasmin said. "And how are you going to do that? What's your plan?"

"I'm not sure. I've been thinking about that for months, and I had absolutely no idea how until…"

"Until what?"

"Until I met you."

Yasmin raised an eyebrow and gave me a look halfway between confusion and surprise.

"Me?"

"Yeah, you."

"Why me?"

"For most of my life, I had someone that I could rely on completely. Zoey did everything for me. When things got tough at home, she was always there to pick me up and make me feel better. It also made me feel useless, but I relied on her because it was easier, and I couldn't do anything myself. But you. You didn't have that problem, did you?" I said. "Yeah, your family was there, but you basically handled things on your own. You only relied on them for the bare necessities. That's why I know you're strong. Well, stronger than me, even though that's not really saying much."

"What are you trying to say, Chris? Did this girl tie your shoes for you and wipe your ass? Get to the point."

I sighed.

It was getting more and more difficult to find the right words. They never sounded right. So, throwing all caution to the wind, I just came right out and said what I was trying to get at all along.

"Yasmin, I need your help. Show me how I can be more like you. You say what you want, and you do what you want. I think if I can do that, then I won't have to feel so terrible about myself anymore, like I can't do anything or help anyone."

Though I tried my hardest to keep my voice from cracking, hearing those words come from my mouth, it almost sounded like I was pleading to her.

Pleading.

Another word for begging.

Both of which made me feel pathetic.

"Why are you making it sound like you're some helpless loser?" Yasmin said. "You're a loser, but you aren't helpless."

"Thanks. I feel better now."

"You know what I mean. You've been helping me for the past three weeks. You helped push me down the path of painting. Sure, I'm confident I would have done it on my own eventually, but you made me decide a lot sooner."

"It's not that..."

I thought back to the morning after our argument, when Yasmin had stormed into her room. I had stood there contemplating whether I should knock on her door and say something, but when I heard her crying, I'd left her.

Left.

Another word for abandon.

I'd done the same to my mother.

I'd done the same to Zoey.

Sure, I came back in Yasmin's case, but a strong, capable, and dependable person wouldn't have left them crying in the first place. They would have stayed. Zoey would have stayed.

"Please, Yasmin. Can you help me? I think you're the only one who could do it. I know you can."

Yasmin stayed silent.

She seemed to be contemplating my words while carefully going through the process of choosing her own.

"Before I give you an answer, I need you to answer something for me first," she said.

"Sure, go ahead. Ask away."

"You said you don't know if you're over Zoey. But how do you feel about me?"

Sheesh.

I didn't expect that one.

Today was quite a day, wasn't it? We were just going to air all the dirty laundry, as they say.

"I... like you."

But something wasn't there. Not yet, at least.

Those were the words that I didn't dare say out loud.

It was true. I did like Yasmin. I knew that much for sure. I wanted to see her. I wanted to talk to her. Strangely enough, even when I thought about potentially not hearing her insults anymore it made me sad. It was just that something was missing.

A spark?

Passion?

If I voiced that concern, she'd probably use some jargon that I'd never heard before to describe it, with her vast array of dating knowledge and whatnot, but for me this was the best way I could put it.

With Zoey, my feelings were more intense. She was always on my mind. By that I meant her influence. I still found myself asking, "What would Zoey say?" or "How would she handle this problem?" This was the effect that unwavering dependability had on me. She was the ideal I strived to be like.

Was that something I should tell Yasmin? I did want to be honest with her, but every way the situation played out in my mind ended with me at the bottom of the ocean sleeping with the fishes.

Then again, maybe she wouldn't care? Yasmin had spent a lot of time trying different things, but not many things held her interest. Who was to say that I would? If we did decide to go our separate ways, she'd be able to land a few dates in no time at all—if she made an effort to tone down her more violent tendencies.

She must have been able to read the expression on my face because she suddenly spoke up again, her eyes brimming with the intensity that I'd found myself growing more and more fond of. At the same time, that intensity was like a red flag. A flag that told me that Yasmin was about to do or say something unexpected.

And she did.

"Chris, I'm interested in you. You can even go so far as to say that I kind of maybe like you."

My heart fluttered at her words.

That was nice to hear. A lot of the time people are more guarded with their feelings to the point where most of it's left up to your own interpretations or, better yet, misinterpretations. This kind of confession didn't leave anything to the imagination.

Yasmin continued, "Over the past couple years, I've spent a lot of time trying different things, but it's not like nothing held my interest. I guess you've shown me that it's important to fight for those few things I do like, instead of being so quick to look for something else." Yasmin psyched herself up by slapping her cheeks a couple of times with both of her hands. "That's why I'm going to help you now."

"You will?"

Without immediately answering, Yasmin slid down from her stool. She then stomped towards me, and before I even knew what was happening, I was staring down the length of her index finger, which was pointed directly at me.

Finally in position, Yasmin spoke. "Yeah, after I'm through with you, you'll be cured of your overall spineless attitude. I won't quit until you can stand up straight with your head held high."

Her words were so firm as to be tangible, and I felt every ounce of weight in them.

They made me feel confident.

It seemed like my goal might actually be within my grasp now. If I followed her, I might be able to change.

Despite the obvious fact that my overreliance was my problem to begin with, it felt different this time around. I didn't know how or even why, but it was different. Maybe it had to do with the fact that this was a conscious decision on my part. I wasn't standing idly by anymore.

"But that's not all," Yasmin said, "I don't plan on giving you up so easily either."

"What do you mean?"

"From the way you talk about her, I can tell you're not over your ex. But I don't care. I don't give a single fuck about that because at that end of this, it's not going to even matter."

"I... still don't understand. What are you talking about?"

Yasmin rolled her eyes as if to say that she couldn't make it any clearer than that.

But.

Somehow.

In her usual Yasmin fashion.

She still found a way.

"You're going to choose me. I'll fucking make sure of that."

CHAPTER 17

Dependability is an interesting concept. And that's exactly all it is—a concept.

It's not tangible.

You can't hold it in your hands.

It can't be measured by any sort of device or machinery.

So.

The question was how would I know when I achieved that goal?

Dependability is something that can only be judged subjectively.

And, therefore, different people will have different ideas on what it means.

For instance, my definition of dependability—being someone that can always be called upon, and will never leave you or let you down—was very different from Yasmin's definition. She had her own idea of what it meant, which I was made painfully aware of when she presented me with her fool-proof (or Chris-proof, as she put it) guaranteed surefire plan for success.

To put it bluntly, it was basically a glorified workout plan, filled to the brim with overly complicated, seemingly pointless, and increasingly bizarre tasks that I needed to complete in order to be "dependable".

If you've ever seen *The Karate Kid* then you'll know exactly what I mean.

Except, though Yasmin had one fierce kick, she was no Mr. Miyagi. Not even close.

"Remind me again how doing your homework for you is going to help me?" I asked, my pencil scratching across a pad of paper.

"Who said it was meant to help you?"

"You did!"

"Oh, no, I just wanted my homework to be done. It was way too boring. But if it'll make you feel better, I can say that I *need* you to finish it for me."

Hah.

She was a smartass, but I guess when she put it that way, her reasoning could fit my definition—albeit loosely.

"So, what else do we have planned for today?" I asked. "I think I've been making some progress."

"Wait, did you already complete task number fifty-one? What was it again?"

"Fifty-one was to give a homeless person a bath. And, yeah, I did do it. Sadly."

I heard Yasmin stifle a laugh.

"You actually did it?" she said, barely holding herself together.

"Yeah, I did. And it wasn't pretty either. It was hard enough trying to sneak him into my apartment. The shower is completely filthy now, and he used all my shampoo."

"Ah, poor thing. You can have some of mine if you want. I have a bunch that I don't even use."

"No, it's fine," I grumbled. "I'm just not excited about all the things you're making me do next. I mean, right here you said you wanted me to slay a fire-breathing dragon to save a princess. This isn't Middle-Earth. Where are we going to get a dragon?"

"You're worrying about that insignificant detail? Don't you know? They say money can buy you anything."

"No, they don't. They say the exact opposite."

"No money can buy you nothing? Well, that's just obvious, don't you think?"

I didn't even know what to say to that, so I ignored it completely.

"Anyway," she said, "that's one of the last things on the list. You still have other things you need to do first, like cleaning my apartment."

"That's even more impossible than slaying the dragon."

"Shut up. It's not that bad. It's better than it used to be, so it won't take that long. I ran the numbers. If you start now, I figure you'll be finished by the time you graduate next year."

"What kind of math is that?!"

Or maybe the right question was how much junk was there for me to dispose of?

"You're at least going to help me, right?" I asked, glancing around the room.

Yasmin answered me with a long bout of silence.

Not that I was surprised by that. She hated cleaning.

Most of the tasks (labors, as she put it), were like that. It really did feel like a bunch of chores. At least Miyagi eventually told Daniel the point of it all. I didn't think that Yasmin would be that kind.

Another task included helping ten old ladies cross the road. In theory, that sounded simple enough. You see that all the time in movies. Unfortunately, I was forced to find out with my body that a lot of old ladies don't exactly want to be helped to cross the road. They're very much capable of doing that on their own. They, and the cops, assured me of that.

Also, did you know that the average purse can fit two full size bricks? Me neither. Those old ladies were the ones who were kind enough to show me.

Some other labors, not listed in any particular order, included: helping cats out of trees, offering to walk the neighborhoods dogs, cleaning gutters, giving out directions to people who looked like tourists, cleaning gum off the underside of the tables in our lecture halls, counting the clouds in the sky, and standing in front of the archway leading onto campus and offering compliments to everyone that passed by.

Everything I'd done so far had amounted to about a month of work, completed before and after class, on weekdays as well as weekends. Just about every free moment was spent doing them. I wasn't allowed to skip any or back out of them. They had to be completed in order, no matter how painful, embarrassing, or reluctant I was. If I was ever caught lying or cheating, I'd get my ass kicked.

But.

Anyway.

It was Saturday afternoon.

Once again, I'd found myself in Yasmin's apartment. We were in her studio room, and she was sitting behind her canvas and easel, sketching away with a charcoal pencil. I was sitting in front of her about ten feet away.

I didn't know what she was drawing, but I assumed it had something to do with me and the background cityscape of Oceanside.

Yasmin never let me see any of her work that was still in progress, especially if I was going to be part of the subject. In fact, now that I think about it, she didn't let me see any of her work at all. My knowledge of her skills was based entirely on the paintings she'd shown me when we first met. Could it be that she was embarrassed to show me her new piece? This thought made me even more curious. I wanted to see what she was working on. It was like Pandora's box. What was she hiding behind there that she wasn't allowing me to look at?

"So," I started, "Can I see whatever it is you're working on this time?"

"Sure," Yasmin said, her eyes still focused on her task. "Once I'm done."

I'd noticed a while back that whenever she was working on her art, her answers were shorter and not as abusive or aggressive. She told me that talking ruined her concentration and took her out her "flow," but it also had another unintended effect, one I wasn't even sure that she was aware of.

With her mind split between two different tasks, she wasn't as tight-lipped. It was easier to ask prying questions and get answers.

"And how will you know when you're done?" I continued. "You've done some other ones, right? I haven't seen any of those."

"The other ones?"

"All of the sketches and paintings you've done since we started doing this. There were a bunch. You used to have them over there, laying against the wall."

"Oh, I threw those away."

"You threw them away?!"

"Actually, my bad, I misspoke there. I didn't throw them away."

"Okay, that's good."

"I burned them all."

"No, that's worse! Infinitely worse!"

And how could she possibly mix those two things up? They sound nothing alike!

Yasmin shifted on top of her stool. I saw her hand stop moving and fall to her lap.

"They weren't perfect, so they didn't deserve to exist," she said.

"That's a terrifying way to put it."

"It's true. I just want to finish something that would be worth showing to you. You've been giving me a lot of your time. Nothing less than perfect will do. Those weren't good enough. All of them sucked. I'm sure if you gave a monkey a crayon, it'd do so much better."

"That would have to be one talented monkey."

"Well, we'll never know now. I sprinkled the ashes into the ocean last night."

"Sounds like a proper send-off. Hopefully, this current one fares better. When do you think you'll be done with it?"

"Hmm," Yasmin contemplated for a moment before answering, "a thousand years give or take."

"If it's going to take that long, I don't think anyone will be able to see it."

"That was just a highball estimate. I can't tell how long it'll take when I start a new piece. I take my time. You can't rush perfection. And who knows, maybe this one will be so good that they'll house it in some fancy museum for all to see. I'll fill galleries."

"That means you'll have to show people."

"Obviously. Do you think I'm stupid or something? I know what a gallery is."

"No, no," I said. "I meant that if any of your work gets put in a gallery, won't that mean I'll get to see it too?"

She didn't respond immediately, instead choosing to sit there in silence.

I couldn't tell what she was thinking, but I assumed it had something to do with how she was feeling just minutes before.

For some reason, Yasmin was shy when it came to her paintings.

She went out of her way to make sure I didn't see any of it, going so far as throwing a blanket over her work whenever I happened to try and walk behind her.

She was secretive. Not that she needed to be. Judging from what little I knew, she was easily the best artist I've ever met in person.

And yet.

It didn't quite seem that she believed it.

"Hmph, I guess it does," she said. "Hopefully I'll have something worth showing by the time that happens. Since you've been modeling for me, I can already tell that there is a spontaneity in my work that wasn't there before."

"Is that so?"

"Yeah. But for now, you're just going to have to take my word on it."

"Hah. That's fine. Take as long as you need. I can't wait to see what you create. I just wanted to say that I think you're amazing. The best. I'm sure anything you create will be great. I honestly believe that."

Yasmin quickly glanced at me and looked back.

"Thanks..." she said before resuming her work. "Now hold still, will you? You're moving too much. I swear if I mess this one up, then I'll be sprinkling your ashes into the ocean with it!"

"Yes, ma'am."

* * *

Our days passed like that for a while. It wasn't bad at all. I can say I enjoyed this time without any doubt. I'd even brought her over to my place a few times. At first, I was reluctant due to the difference in our living arrangements, but Yasmin didn't seem to mind at all. She was more surprised how I could put up with Brad, who she described as a "douche-bag frat bro." It's funny. I thought their personalities would have made them a perfect match, but Yasmin didn't like Brad, or she just found him incredibly stupid. They were both thrill seekers, but the way they went about it was different. While Yasmin wanted to have new experiences for the novelty of the opportunity, Brad seemed to do things because he thought his terrible ideas were good ideas.

Yeah, it was great. Bringing her into my life like this.

But if there was anything that was bothering me, it would have been one tiny detail. Much to my chagrin, there were no romantic developments to speak of. Zero at all.

This was in direct contrast to her bold declaration that I would choose her. That she was going to make sure of it.

After all this time in close proximity, something should have happened, right? Like seriously. I knew our connection was growing, but it wasn't progressing in any physical sense. There would be times when we'd be sitting on her couch watching movies on her huge flatscreen, and I'd get the inkling to wrap my arm around her. Brad had told me that was an all-time classic move and set-up. I was just never able to capitalize on it. Yasmin was always so stiff and rigid in those moments. As if she might have been expecting someone to barge through her doors at any second. Didn't help that she looked like she might assault me if I tried anything.

During those uncomfortable situations my arm would feel like lead, and before I knew it, the movie would be over, and I'd be walking home disappointed.

Thinking back on it, there wasn't any progression with Zoey either, and we'd been together for years. Sad, I know.

Don't get me wrong, it's not like I didn't want to do stuff like that. I did. I'm a guy. It's natural, but I just couldn't see myself doing any of that with her.

Zoey was too pure and sweet; to do that would corrupt her in a way. Well, at least, that's the justification that I'd use to explain away my cowardice.

The furthest Zoey and I ever got was kissing. And I had never initiated it. She probably felt that desire manifested in how sweaty and nervous I was back then and used that opportunity to go for it. To this day, they were fond, albeit awkward memories for me.

Yasmin didn't have much experience either.

If her first date was with me, if all her knowledge was based on what she'd read about and heard in articles and podcasts, then we were in the same boat. Two awkward adults trying to navigate through the human mating ritual. That could have explained our progress, or lack thereof.

Hm.

Zoey and Yasmin.

I could see the similarities in them.

Of course, Zoey was more pleasant to be around, and I never left her place with bruises, but their characteristic similarities were uncanny.

I guess that was what attracted me to them in the first place.

In both, I saw strong individuals that I could aspire to imitate.

If I were to look up dependability in my personal dictionary, I wouldn't have been surprised to see a picture of either of them. They were both there to help me. They didn't have to be, but they were.

In a relatively short time, I'd grown comfortable with Yasmin. It seemed like we had already cut through the bullshit, and we could be comfortable with one another, which was something I wasn't able to feel very often with other people. I mean, I can crack my jokes and be sarcastic with just about anyone, but it's just more natural with some versus others, you know? And I did tell her about my accident. I haven't even told Brad or my mother.

Any initial issues or reservations I'd had with her were becoming less evident. Subconsciously, maybe it was my own mind that was trying to find something wrong with Yasmin, when there wasn't anything wrong to find.

She was a keeper, and I didn't want to see her go. I was certain about that. I didn't feel alone when we were together and that was a feeling I was desperate to hold on to.

Since I'd met her, no other girl had surprised me as much as she had.

Which was true, until I returned to my room one day near the beginning of spring to find—laying on my bed, as if laying on someone else's bed was the most natural thing to do—Mona Lotta.

However, the fact that she was laying on my bed in such a natural way that it might have suggested that it was actually her bed she was laying on, wasn't the first thing I noticed about Mona. It was the set of two thick and bushy eyebrows that sat on her face like a pair of fuzzy caterpillars—eyebrows so prominent that they seemed to detract from the absurdity of the rest of the situation.

CHAPTER 18

"Uh, who are you?" I asked. "And what are you doing in my bed?" It was the afternoon, and I had just returned home from class hoping I'd get the chance to relax for a few minutes.

The girl, who hadn't reacted to the door opening, turned at the sound of my voice. She was under the covers. Mostly. From what I could see, it didn't look like she was wearing any clothes. She had the sheets pulled up, covering her breasts, yet revealing ample cleavage. Her skin was bronze, and she had curly, dark-brown hair, slightly disheveled. She looked at me through the lazy, seductive eyes that seemed almost sloth-like in nature.

It would have been easy to assume her sleepy expression was a result of her having just awakened, I mean, there are some people who just have that kind of face to begin with, the kind of face that always looks tired. But in regards to this mystery woman, it could be said that there was a pretty good reason for her to look that way.

It was because of her thick eyebrows, which weighed down her eyelids and gave her that sultry gaze. Most of her mental capacity was probably being used to keep her eyes from closing. Something about them seemed to lure me in, so much so that they were distracting enough to pull me away from the Grand Canyon of cleavage below.

The girl sat up and tilted her head, using her right hand to hold the sheets to her chest.

"Oh, it's you," she said.

"Don't say that, like I'm the one who's not supposed to be here."

"Oh. It's just you."

"That's even worse! Now it sounds like you're disappointed to see me!"

"Oh? It's only you?"

"Now it sounds like you were expecting more people to be here!"

"Hah, I'm just kidding," she said. Her voice had a peppy quality that contrasted with her sleepy look. "I'm very excited to see you. In fact, I've been waiting all day to see you, Chris. Come sit down next to me."

With her free hand she pointed to me and beckoned me toward her with a few flicks of her finger before patting a spot on the bed beside her. As if attached to her finger by a string, I followed her movements like I was her puppet.

Approaching the bed cautiously and sitting down next to her, I asked my obvious question again. "Okay, I'm here. Now answer me. Who are you?"

"My name is Mona. Mona Lotta. And if you ask around"—she ran a finger down my chest—"you'll probably hear that I tend to moan a lot-ah. Or, I guess you'll find out for yourself soon enough."

My jaw fell open, but after a brief moment, she tacked on, "Just kidding!" and threw in a wink for extra measure.

I didn't know what exactly she was kidding about, and a part of me was curious to find out, but I suppressed my urge to ask.

"Okay, Mona, if that is your actual name. What are you doing in *my* room? On *my* bed?"

"Your bestie, Brad, said that he had an uptight friend who was looking for some companionship. I agreed to do it, so he brought me here and told me to strip and wait in your bed for you to arrive. He said you had a kink for that kind of thing."

That jackass! He knew this wasn't what I meant when I said I was open to seeing other girls! I was going to strangle him the next time I saw him!

"Well, I'm sorry to break it to you. He was lying about that being my fetish. You didn't have to strip at all. Sorry."

"I know. I was just kidding." She smirked. "I stripped all on my own."

I nearly fell off the bed.

This girl was kinkier than me! Did she get off laying naked in someone else's bed? I didn't know if my heart could take much more of this temptation.

I sighed, and my eyes traveled over the contours of her body, lingering on some areas longer than others. Even through my sheets, I was able to see her curvaceous figure. "Okay, I see. I see. But, uh, I have another question now."

"Go ahead, sweetie."

"He didn't, uh, pay you, did he?"

Mona raised her thick eyebrows—the simple feat seemed like it took some effort due to how weighty they looked.

"Excuse me? I don't know who you think I am, but I'm not that kind of girl."

"Uh, I'm sorry. I was just making sure. I didn't want there to be some misunderstanding after the fact. I think it's important to clearly state these things at the beginning. Again, I'm sorry if I offended you."

"It's alright. It was an honest mistake." Mona nodded as if to emphasize her point. "But I'm a professional. I'll take the payment after we're finished."

"What?! That wasn't the issue I was addressing! And you will?!"

"Just kidding."

"…"

This was getting out of hand. She was making more jokes than even I could keep up with. At this point, she'd probably cracked more jokes than she said true statements. I couldn't believe a thing that came out of her mouth.

"Now, Chris, let's get down to business. Shall we?" She scooted over to me and placed a hand on top of my own. Hers was warm and soft. "Brad said something about you being lonely. Is that true? I can't believe that a handsome man like you doesn't have a girlfriend or two."

"Hah, yeah, I know. I guess you could say that I'm in a dry spell. I wouldn't say I'm lonely, but you know how it goes."

Mona leaned in even closer, and the scent of hazelnut filled my nostrils and assaulted my senses.

"Well, has any girl caught your attention?" She lowered the sheet an extra few inches.

Jeez. How much farther could that thing go? I thought I might be able to see something.

"Chris? Are you listening?"

"Yeah, of course I'm listening," I said, shaking some indecent thoughts out of my head. "Now what was the question again?"

"Is there any girl that you're interested in?"

"Like interested in as a person? There is this new female comedian that I've been listening to—"

"Don't play dumb, Chris. You know what I'm talking about."

Feigning ignorance had failed me yet again.

I didn't know why I even bothered at this point.

But, yeah. There was someone who interested me.

Highlighted by a dazzling array of flashing signs and billboards that even put the Las Vegas strip to shame, Yasmin's face popped into my mind. My mental image of her was lifelike, even managing to capture her expression of simultaneous boredom and frustration.

However, I wasn't entirely comfortable outright admitting that to someone I'd just met.

"There is... someone, I guess."

"Oh? Tell me more."

"I'd rather not."

"Why not?"

I lowered my voice and put on the sternest expression I could muster considering the situation. "It's none of your damn business. That's why."

Mona raised her eyebrows yet again. With how often she was doing that she was going to get a good workout today.

"That was so manly and cool!" she squealed. "I love a man that takes charge!"

"I know. That's why I said that."

She squealed once more. "You did it again!"

"Thanks. I could do this all day if I wanted to."

"I'm sure you can. You're just so witty and smart. I think I might already be falling for you."

Mona was dangerously close to me, but now she leaned forward, her head coming to rest on my shoulder. In a smooth, almost rehearsed motion, she looked up into my eyes. I could have counted the individual strands of her bountiful brows if I wanted to.

"Hi, there. May I help you?" I asked.

"You may."

"With what?"

"I think there's something on my lips. Can you please take a closer look at them?"

Before I could respond, Mona closed her eyes, tilted her head back slightly, and pursed her lips up at me.

Huh?

This situation.

Something felt completely off about this entire situation.

If I didn't know better, it all seemed like the contrived plot of some terribly acted porno.

Did that jackass Brad set up some hidden cameras or something?

Was this all a prank?

I wasn't going to fall for his stupid jokes yet again.

Fool me once, shame on you; fool me twice, shame on me, as they say.

"Your lips look fine to me. I don't see anything. Maybe they're a little chapped but all-around really solid. I'd give them an aggregate score of 8.6 out of 10."

Mona opened her left eye a crack and peeked through her long eyelashes.

"Are you sure?" she mumbled through her still pursed lips.

"Yup."

She scooted even closer and tilted her head back further. Her puckered, pink lips were right underneath my chin at this point. They would have tickled my beard hairs if I had any.

"Can you check again? I still feel something."

"Nope, there's nothing there. Wait, actually"—I used my fingers to brush off her lips—"I got it now. Just a little dust. You're all good now."

Mona pulled back and frowned at me, bringing her own hand up to her mouth.

"Thanks. They feel better now," she mumbled.

"Anytime."

After effectively shutting down the punchline of what I concluded had to have been a joke, we were now forced to sit there in awkward silence for the next minute. Despite doing what was necessary, I had to admit that I was still a bit disappointed. I was excited for a second there.

But now that I was beginning to calm down, I was able to think more clearly.

Why was she here? Did Brad really put her up to this?

In my twenty-one years on this rock, I'd never met a girl this forward. It was no exaggeration to say that she was throwing herself at me. It was obviously a trap. It had to be. But I wasn't sure how much longer I could hold back the levees of temptation and lust before they burst open. With Zoey, I made sure to keep those emotions more in check, but almost dying tends to change the way that you see things. It was important to get some more experience and perspective on matters of this nature.

"It's hot in here," Mona said out of the blue.

"It is getting stuffy, isn't it? Want me to turn on the fan—Ack!"

I turned to face Mona again and nearly had a heart attack.

The sheets she had been holding to her chest just moments before had sunk down even further. No, scratch that. She wasn't holding them anymore. They crumbled around her in a small pile around her waistline, revealing the bare flesh from her navel upwards.

She was naked.

She was just sitting there and letting it all hang free.

As if it was as natural as coming into someone else's room and laying in their bed.

"What are you doing?! Cover up!"

"What? Why?"

"I don't need to see all of that!"

"Wow, that hurts my feelings a little. You really don't want to see?"

I didn't need to see it. But whether or not I *wanted* to see it was a whole other issue.

Luckily for me, she didn't need to know that, even if she may have wanted to.

"That's beside the point! I'm telling you to cover up now!"

Mona blinked at my commands and made as if to touch her two elbows together in front of her.

"Are you sure? Seems to me that you're still interested."

"Yes!"

My hands shot forward to grab the sheets around her waist. However, in my desperation to bring them up to cover her, my hands connected with something soft and round. Two somethings to be exact.

"Oh! Mmm," Mona moaned.

"Sorry! I didn't mean to punch your boobs. It was an accident."

"No, I like it. Do it harder."

"Stop saying stuff like that!"

Eventually, I succeeded in covering her up again, but in the ensuing struggle she'd continued to make those strange noises. Also, even though I was trying to avoid it, it was obvious to me that Mona was attempting to rub up against me with everything she had.

"You're no fun."

"You know, you're actually not the first person to tell me that," I retorted.

Mona pouted. "Why don't you like me? Am I not attractive enough for you?"

"No, that's not it. I do like you! I like you a lot. You're very attractive. A ten out of ten!"

Mona looked up at me. She wasn't buying any of my excuses.

"You're lying! Why wouldn't you want a piece of all of this then? You're just like every other guy! It's because of *them*, isn't it?"

"Because of what, Mona?"

"Stop playing dumb! You know exactly what I'm talking about. You've been staring at them since the moment you walked into this room."

"Your... boobs?"

"No, *these*!"

She pointed to the two bushy patches of hair above her eyes. The way they were quivering now really did make them look like caterpillars.

"Your eyebrows?"

"Yes, my eyebrows! Do you have any idea how often people make fun of me? I have a figure that men would kill for, but when they see my face, they can't stop staring and laughing at me. They say I look like Groucho Marx!"

I couldn't help but stifle a laugh at that. I *thought* she reminded me of someone. The resemblance was uncanny. Now she just needed the mustache and glasses then her look would be complete

"It's not a big deal," I said "You pull them off well. And, hey, just think of it this way. If you don't like them, you can always just shave them both off completely."

Seeing the corners of the smirk that I was attempting to hide, Mona's lashed out.

"You think I'm ugly!" she shouted. "That I'm a butterface! That I have fuzzy caterpillars for eyebrows!"

"No! I told you already. I think you're sexy and beautiful. You're not a butterface at all and I love caterpillars! They're so cute. I love watching them eat leaves and move and do caterpillar things!"

With that, Mona's yells became louder, my consolations were doing nothing to calm her down. I didn't know what I should be doing or saying. It was obvious that she had a big complex about her eyebrows, but I honestly didn't think they looked bad—I really didn't. I just needed to find a way to make her feel that way too.

Drawing blanks and with no other options, I did the only plausible thing I could think of to placate the nearly naked girl beside me.

I grabbed her and pulled her in tight.

"Uwuh?"

Her face nuzzled into the side of my neck, and I could feel her warm breath through my black t-shirt. With how quickly I'd wrapped around her, she had no time to move her arms before they were both folded up against her body. She was completely secure within my embrace as were her two breasts that were now pressed into my chest.

The smell that I had only caught brief whiffs of before was now enveloping me. Hazelnut, with an added twinge of other tropical scents. She smelled lovely. It was almost intoxicating. My head was light, and my thoughts muddled by desire.

Trying to keep myself composed, I placed my lips next to her ear.

"Mona, don't cry," I whispered. "I mean it when I say that I love your eyebrows. They're the first thing I noticed when I saw you. They're stunning and you shouldn't let anyone tell you otherwise."

"Really?"

"Yeah, of course. I've never seen anyone with as lush eyebrows as you. They pull you in and I swear I could get lost if I stared into them any longer."

I'll be the first to admit that my words were corny. When you heard such things as dialogue on TV, they sounded smooth. But they were like nails on a chalkboard coming out of my mouth.

Despite my embarrassment, it didn't seem to matter.

"I want to believe you, but you're just saying that."

"No, I'm not. I mean it. They really are. You shouldn't be ashamed to have such a great feature. I wish I had something cool like that. Instead, I look like *this.*"

She chuckled, nuzzling herself deeper into my body.

"That might have been the sweetest thing that I've ever heard, Chris." She tilted her head back to look up at me. "Thank you."

"Feeling better now?"

She nodded.

"Good."

I loosened my arms and attempted to pull away, but she held onto the front of my shirt and stopped my retreat.

"Wait a moment. Please."

She closed her two eyes and pursed her lips up at me like she'd done before. However, this time around, it wasn't as forced. As Mona did this, a tear trailed down her face, finding refuge at the slope of her lips which now glistened from the moisture.

The temptation to do it was taunting me.

I mean… why not?

If it made Mona feel better and she wanted it, why shouldn't I do it? Technically speaking, Yasmin and I weren't together, so it shouldn't be a problem.

But I couldn't help feeling a little guilty.

We hadn't even kissed yet, so to do that with some other person first was a little—

"Hmm?"

Mona hummed a question at me and nodded her chin. She was waiting for me to make a move. If I didn't, who knows what she would do this time around, and I didn't want her to start yelling again.

Ah, what the hell.

There wasn't any harm in doing it.

I wanted to anyway. It'd been a while, and her lips looked so soft from this angle.

Closing my eyes, I leaned forward slowly, and feeling this movement, she did the same. My heart drummed against my chest, and I wondered if she could hear its erratic beat. On a side note, I also wondered if my breath smelled bad.

Did I even remember how to kiss?

No point worrying about that now.

With the short distance between our lips gradually closing, I braced for imminent impact.

Three, two, one—

And for a brief moment—the briefest of moments—our lips touched.

Thud. Thud. Thud.

The three loud knocks that came from the door shook the entire room, causing me to bump heads with Mona as I reflexively jumped backwards.

"Chris, it's me! Open the door!"

Thud. Thud. Thud.

"There's something I really want to talk to you about!" Yasmin's voice echoed through the wood, each word enunciated by the slamming of her fist.

Shit.

What perfect timing. I had to be the unluckiest man alive. Of course, Yasmin would come over unannounced.

My eyes bounced between Mona and the door more times than I could count. Now it seemed like my heart was racing for an entirely different reason.

But what did I have to worry about, right?

There shouldn't be any problem at all.

Right?

CHAPTER 19

"Hold on!" I shouted through the door at Yasmin. "I'm, uh, naked!"

I didn't see my feeble excuse as a lie. It was more of a half-truth if I had to call it anything. I needed Yasmin to hold on for a second, and someone was naked. It just wasn't me.

However, it was going to take more than some clever wordplay to get me out of this one.

Standing in the middle of the dingy, single and only room of my apartment, I frantically danced in place looking for some secret escape route or hiding place to stuff Mona into. A box, a closet, or trapdoor. But I knew there was none—that is if you didn't count the window. I wouldn't subject Mona to that though. Not even as an absolute last resort would I risk it. I couldn't.

"Ha, naked? Naughty boy. I hope I wasn't interrupting your private time." Yasmin laughed.

"Oh, dang!" I said. "You got me! I was really hoping I'd get the chance to, uh, relieve some stress before you got here. Do you mind giving me some time so that I can finish?"

"Yeah, I do mind. Whatever you're doing can wait! I got some exciting news so open the door now! Just put your pants on first."

So pushy. She couldn't take a hint at all.

I turned back to Mona. She hadn't moved a single inch from her spot on the bed.

"What are you doing?!" I said.

Mona sat there, oblivious to her surroundings, with a satisfied smirk on her face like she'd just accomplished a goal or won a bet. It didn't look like there was anybody home inside of her head right now.

There was no time for this!

I waved my hands in front of her face and pinched my shirt and pants to signal to her to get dressed, but she made no effort to do any of that. Instead, she directed her unfocused, sleepy gaze to me and spoke.

"Why do you look so stressed? Just come back to bed and relax."

Either I'd broken this girl, or she was completely nuts.

"No! Just get your clothes on! Hurry up!"

I picked up some articles of clothing that lay in a pile at the foot of my bed, clothes that looked too small and girly to be either Brad's or mine, and threw them at Mona. But when the massive ball of wadded up cotton and polyester hit her, her attitude and general demeanor didn't change at all. With a single arm swipe, she knocked her clothes back onto the floor.

"Chris?" Yasmin asked. "Open the damn door."

"Yes, I will, uh, just give me a second. The place is a mess and I'm trying to clean it up for you!"

As I raced around the room searching for what I knew wasn't there, Mona gave me a blank look before turning her attention to the door.

My mind was running at a million miles per hour.

Why was I this nervous?

I didn't have anything to hide.

We weren't official or going steady or whatever you called it.

We were just talking and getting to know each other at this stage.

So why?

My scattered thoughts eventually brought me to my window. Right now the distance to the ground didn't look quite that far. It may have just been a few feet. No, it was more like a few inches to the ground from our location on the fifth floor. Plus, if we aimed for the dumpster, we'd most likely not die.

Of course I was joking but still.

"Mona, I think I have an ide—"

My thought was interrupted by the sound of movement coming from behind me.

The sound of a chain lock.

More specifically, the sound of the chain lock on my front door being unlatched.

I spun around.

"Mona! What are you doing!"

She had finally moved from her spot on the bed and was now standing at the door, fiddling with the chain. Once she managed to unhook it, she released the tiny knob, letting it swing back and forth like a pendulum.

I had no time to react to what came next. I could only look on in horror as Mona's hand traveled down to the deadbolt lock, the last line of defense before the door could be opened, and turned it counterclockwise ninety degrees.

Under different circumstances, I might have enjoyed the view. Mona hadn't bothered to cover herself up and was instead standing there giving me a clear view of her assets—all of them. The way her hips cascaded outwards and opened up mesmerized me. As did her narrow waistline. She had that hourglass figure, but even without staring for too long, I could tell that I didn't have much time to ogle. My mind was already focused on the bomb that I expected to go off in three—

Two.

One.

"About time! You kept me waiting long enough!"

The door swung open, and Yasmin came face-to-face with Mona.

However, face-to-face wouldn't be entirely the best way to put it. Yasmin was a petite girl, it was one of her charms, and that meant she was short. Even standing on the tips of her toes she probably only came up to Mona's ample breasts—breasts Yasmin practically ran into like two airbags.

"Eh?"

Yasmin's eyes opened as wide as they could go. It was a look of pure surprise and disbelief. I mean, who expected to open a door and walk into a pair of large breasts when you were expecting to visit the guy you've been dating for a while now? Nobody. You'd have to be a fortune teller to see that one coming.

The eyes of the shorter girl first traveled upwards to Mona's eyes, then they moved down to the large breasts she had just collided with, before finally, they ended their journey on my cowering figure.

"Eh?" Yasmin repeated.

Like Mona, she might have been broken too—unable to process the events that were going on around her. She looked like a lost child.

"Hi, there, can we help you with something?" Mona asked.

Yasmin ignored the question, instead opting to continue staring at me.

"Chris, do you mind explaining to me what the *hell* is going on here?"

I shrugged my shoulders and flashed an awkward smile.

"I told you before you barged in here. I was trying to relieve some stress."

Hah.

I thought that was a good one.

But the death glare Yasmin was directing towards me said that she wasn't very amused.

If looks could kill, I'd be dead right now, as they say. I'd be dead a thousand times over.

Yasmin took two steps in my direction. Her face turned beet red while a vein was pulsating on her forehead. If I was close enough, I'm sure that I would have been able to see pockets of steam blasting from her ears and nostrils like a cartoon character.

Why was she reacting so strongly?

Was she even going to give me a chance to explain?

I'm innocent! The devil tempted me! Just let me plead my case!

Oh, right.

She already had given me that chance, and I squandered it by making a joke.

"Chris," Yasmin growled through clenched teeth. She was stomping towards me.

Time slowed down to a crawl.

Each individual cycle of Yasmin's steps was contained in their own eternity. I could already imagine the roundhouse kick that she would soon be sending towards my temple, going for the kill as she usually did, with nothing held back.

"Hold on a minute," Mona said, placing a hand on Yasmin's shoulder.

"Stay out of this, bushy-brows!" Yasmin shot back. "I'll deal with you in a minute And would it kill you to put a shirt on? No one wants to see your sagging cow-udders. It's gross."

The color drained from Mona's honey bronze face like someone had flipped off a switch.

"I'd rather have cow-udders than those pathetic things you have on your chest. My breasts haven't been that size since middle-school," Mona shot back.

Yasmin stopped in her tracks.

Just before her head grated back around to face her verbal assailant, I caught the glimpse of the hellish smile creeping onto her face. In a strange turn of events, I was just thankful that that smile wasn't directed at me.

"What did you just say?" Yasmin asked.

"My breasts haven't been that size since middle school—actually, elementary."

"Shut up! They're still growing!"

"I'm sorry, sweetie. If they were going to get any bigger, they would have by now. It's okay though. Some boys like that immature look, which is kind of weird if you think about it."

"Oh, yeah? And it'd also be weird for any guy to want to stare at such masculine eyebrows! I should buy you a weed whacker or something. Those things are getting out of control."

"They're full eyebrows! And some guys do like them! Chris was kind enough to give me the nicest compliment. Didn't you, Chris?"

Don't drag me into this! I was just about to escape out the front door while no one noticed me!

"Uh, I mean, yeah, they're, uh, nice."

"Well, Chris also said one time that he thought my boobs were bigger than he expected! Didn't you, Chris?"

"Uh, I mean, yeah, they're, uh, nice."

Now it was my turn to be broken.

For the next five minutes this sort of back-and-forth bickering continued without any real point, direction, or resolution—all the while I acted as the de facto mediator. I attempted to maintain impartiality in the proceedings, but whenever each of the girls made a good point, I couldn't help but buckle under their pleas for support.

I was a very weak-willed man indeed.

After they both had petered themselves out, Yasmin and Mona sat on my bed exhausted and unwilling to look at each other. Mona had finally decided to put her clothes back on. She wore a form fitting white tube top and a black skirt that fell about halfway down her large thighs. The sight of a skirt was a refreshing one. I had long ago thought they went extinct in the age of jeans, yoga pants, and leggings. It was nice to see that a long-lasting fantasy of men still existed in everyday life, especially on a college campus. In contrast, Yasmin was wearing a red hoodie, white shirt, and gray sweatpants. I knew she had nicer clothes, designer brands of every kind, but this was the kind of easygoing, comfortable attire I saw her in most of the time.

"Okay, are you two finished now?" I said.

They both nodded in unison, eyes addressing opposite walls.

"So, who's going to apologize first?"

"She started it," Yasmin was quick to fire off.

"Yasmin, come on!" I said.

"No, no," Mona stated firmly. "It's alright, Chris. I don't mind being the bigger person in this situation. The *adult.*" She turned her head to look at Yasmin without moving her body. "I'm sorry—sorry you're angry that your breasts will never be as big as mine."

"Mona, please!"

"Just kidding!" Mona smiled. "I'm sorry, Yasmin, I think we got off on the wrong foot. Besties?" She stuck her hand out towards Yasmin who took it begrudgingly.

"Fine," Yasmin muttered. "Whatever. I'm sorry too. But what were you two doing in here anyway?"

"Making sweet, sweet love."

Yasmin growled.

"Just kidding! We were about to before you rudely interrupted—"

"Okay, I think that's enough of that," I interjected. "I'm going to step in now before things get messy—again. Yasmin, nothing was going on. I came back here after class, and she was already laying there in my bed. Apparently, Brad put her up to it."

"Why would he do that?"

"I may have, sort of, kind of, said I wouldn't mind if he set me up with some girls he knows. The guy was worried about me. Don't blame him for it."

"No, it's fine. I believe you. Seems like a dumbass thing he'd do."

"You got that right. He's my bro, but he can't read situations that well."

Yasmin nodded. "But why didn't she have any clothes on though?"

"She just likes being naked, I guess. I don't know why. It's her kink."

"Are you bullshitting me right now?"

"It's true," Mona explained. "I stripped before Chris came in. I thought it would be funny."

Yasmin sighed. It seemed to be ninety-nine percent out of relief and one percent out of frustration. "How boring. I knew you didn't do anything. You should have just said so, then none of this misunderstanding business would have happened."

"Hah, I'll keep that in mind."

Well, there was a tiny something.

I didn't know if there was a three-second rule to kissing, but I know my lips came into contact with Mona's. I gave her a side-eye to see if she was thinking the same thing, but Mona was once again off in her own world.

I'd just tell Yasmin when we're in private. Not that I *had* too or anything, but it was just another thing that I didn't want to weigh on my mind longer than it already had.

I cleared my throat. "Oh yeah, you said you had something important to talk to me about?"

Yasmin nodded.

"Uh-huh. Really good news. I was so excited to tell you."

"What is it?"

"Well." Yasmin glanced at Mona. "I'll tell you later. Once we're alone."

"Don't mind little ol' me," Mona said. "Just pretend I'm not here."

"Nah, I'll wait. You were probably going to head out soon, *right?*"

Dang, absolutely merciless.

"How rude! I actually wasn't planning on leaving."

"What do you mean?" I asked. "You had to leave at some point."

Mona hesitated a second before speaking.

"I just—I don't have anywhere else to go."

"What do you mean by that? Don't you have your own place?"

"No, I don't."

That was a bombshell of a statement.

Even Yasmin held in any snarky remark she might have had loaded up.

Mona continued, "I usually just sleep at the place of whatever guy I'm seeing at the time. I haven't had my own apartment in a while now."

"How can you live like that?" I asked.

"Housing is expensive," she said simply. "Plus, it's not as hard as it sounds bouncing from place to place. Guys can be pretty gullible sometimes. As long as you give them what they want."

Something twisted in my stomach.

That statement could be interpreted in several different ways.

I just hope it didn't mean what I thought it meant.

"Okay, if it's so easy, then why are you here then?" Yasmin asked.

"I'm just in between places now is all," Mona said, matter-of-a-factly. "That's why I jumped at the chance when Brad said you were lonely and looking for companionship, Chris. It's also why I asked if you had anyone you were interested in or a special someone."

"..."

So.

She was just trying to be conscientious. At least in her own way.

Her actions made more sense now. It was less that she was throwing herself at me, and more that she was taking advantage of a potential opportunity.

I avoided giving her a straight answer about having a girl in my life, and she took that as her chance to jump in.

I couldn't blame her if she was desperate and had no place to go.

Mona had lain in my bed as comfortably as if it was her own.

How many different beds had she lain in for her to be able to do it so naturally? I couldn't even tolerate hotel beds. In fact, it took me months before I could even lie in this bed without tossing and turning the whole night.

But wait.

Was that the wrong question to be asking?

Maybe the real question was: when was the last time she had the chance to lay in a bed at all?

"But, hey, it's fine," Mona said. "I've just dumped a lot of personal information on you, and it looks like you're busy right now. So, I can just leave. Intruding wasn't ever my intention."

"Where are you going to go?"

"You don't have to worry about it. There are a lot of benches on campus, or I might head over to the park and find a spot there."

Mona walked past both Yasmin and I towards the door. She didn't stop to grab any of her belongings. She didn't have any. No bag of any kind, not even a purse.

All she had were the clothes on her back as they say. A white tube top that left her arms and upper chest exposed. A black skirt that only went midway down her thighs. And a pair of heels.

It was still cold outside, and the night air would be freezing.

"Wait a second."

With her hand firmly grasping the doorknob, Mona looked back at me from over her shoulder. She raised one of her thick eyebrows.

"Hm?"

Off to my right, I noticed Yasmin giving me a look of her own followed by a very subtle shake of her head. It was so slight that it was nearly imperceptible—as if she didn't want me to see it.

"If you have nowhere else to go... you can stay here."

"What?"

I walked over to Mona and put my two hands on her bare shoulders. She was already shivering. Gently, I pulled her away from the door.

"You just told me that you didn't have a place to stay. Did you really think that I'd let you leave?"

Mona raised her other eyebrow now.

"Yes?"

"Is your opinion of me that low?! What kind of man would leave a woman out in the cold? I won't abandon you. You can stay here until you get back on your feet. I'm almost certain that Brad wouldn't mind. In fact, he'd probably love the idea of a girl staying over."

"Do you mean that? Can I really stay?"

"Of course. As long as you don't mind that this place is small, a little rundown, the elevator doesn't work, and that I may have seen a few roaches in the bathroom, then you can stay. I'll sleep on the floor, and you can take my bed. Seemed like you were enjoying it anyway. So? What do you say?"

"I'm just surprised you'd do that for me... I mean if you don't mind. I'd appreciate that so much."

"Now hold on just a second," Yasmin said. "You're just going to let her sleep here? You hardly know her."

"What do you think I should do then? It's not going to be long-term. Just until she can find a more permanent place. And plus." I grinned. "I've already snuck a homeless person inside to give him a bath, so letting another one stay here isn't going to be much of a leap."

"Wait, are you saying I smell?" Mona asked.

Hah.

Yeah, this wasn't much of a leap at all. It was more like the next logical step. Again, I wasn't sure if this was the correct path, but something told me it was the right thing to do.

"It's just..." Yasmin looked between the two of us. "I... I have a better idea."

"What?" I asked.

"Ugh, I can't believe I'm saying this. But—she can stay at my place instead."

"Whoa, seriously? Why the change of heart so suddenly? You're not going to do anything to her are you?"

"Shut up! It just makes the most sense. Look at this place. It's a dump. You know that my place is bigger, and I have a spare bedroom that she can use. But I guess it's up to her. I don't care."

Yasmin turned away and folded her arms across her chest as if to highlight her nonchalance, but something about the motion was way too transparent—like she was trying too hard to play it off.

She obviously cared enough to voice her concern, so it was clear that she would have preferred for Mona to stay at her place rather than mine.

What could her real reason have been?

"I don't know what to say," Mona whispered. "I really don't know what to say."

"For starters, how about a 'thank you?'" Yasmin replied.

"Yeah, sure. Thank you. To the both of you. I mean it from the bottom of my heart." Mona wiped a tear that had fallen down her cheek. "I just feel like all your goodwill is wasted on me."

"Why would it be wasted on you?" I said. "Everyone needs help sometimes."

Mona sighed. "It's because I was just kidding the whole time."

"About what?"

"About being homeless."

"..."

For a second, the whole world went still as I tried to process the information I just heard.

But just for a second.

"What!" Yasmin and I both shouted in unison.

There was no way.

Mona had just played us both for fools.

Made us believe that she needed help. Took advantage of our kindness.

This woman was the devil incarnate!

"Look, I'm sorry! I just wanted to get back at Yasmin for how rude she was to me," Mona said, addressing the carpet. "I was just going with it, but I didn't expect it to get so serious and stuff. I didn't think you'd be so kind to offer me a place either! I just wanted both of you to feel bad for me. I'm sorry for allowing the joke to go on a little too far."

"You're a bitch," Yasmin growled. Strands of black hair were falling down her face making her look demonic.

"I said I was sorry!" Mona replied. "It was just a prank, bro! I really did appreciate how much you two cared!"

"Don't worry. I'm going to show you just how much I care." Yasmin cocked back her leg. The pent-up energy was causing it to tremble from all the tension. It would be released at any second.

"Yasmin, stop," I said. "Stop. Don't do it."

"Why not? You saw what she just did. I'm pissed. That was no joke."

She wasn't wrong.

I was partly angry too, and I felt that watching Yasmin send Mona to the upper atmosphere with her kick would have alleviated it.

But like I said. This anger only made up one part of what I was feeling right now—a very small part at that.

It might have sounded weird to say, but what I really felt was relief.

Relief that her situation wasn't as bleak as she made it out to be and that she wouldn't have to spend nights out in the cold. From my experience walking around after sunset, I knew there were many spots where the homeless congregated and slept both on campus and around the city. Despite their circumstances, each of them appeared to be more equipped for the environment than Mona.

I'm just happy none of it was true.

"Let's just drop it. She got us."

Yasmin frowned. "No, I want a piece of her. Once I'm done, then we'll be even."

"It's over. Stop."

Hearing the seriousness in my tone, Yasmin dropped her fighting stance and rolled her eyes.

"Fine. How boring..."

"Now, was that so hard to do?" I asked.

"Yeah, it was. It was complete bullshit." Yasmin turned to Mona. "You're lucky Chris was here to save you because I would have beat your—"

Yasmin's ringtone cut her threats of assault short.

With one last glare at Mona, Yasmin pulled her phone from her pocket and checked who it was.

"I have to take this. I'll be right back."

"Who is it?" I asked.

"I'll tell you later."

Yasmin sped to the entrance, bumping arms with Mona on the way out. Once the door slammed behind her, we could hear footsteps trailing off down the hallway.

Saved by the bell, as they say.

I might have ended up being a witness to murder if not for that call. It must have been important for her to so willingly drop everything.

"Sheesh, that was a close one." Mona, who looked a little more than relieved that she was spared, smiled peevishly.

"It was. She was going to hurt you. Yasmin's not a bad person though. That's just how she is. You get used to it."

"Seems like you're talking from experience."

"Yup. You can even say I have a 'Lotta' experience."

Mona giggled.

"A 'Lotta' experience, huh? Is she the one you were talking about? The person you were interested in."

I nodded this time, confirming her question.

I wasn't going to make the same mistake I made before.

"Yeah, she is."

"I see," Mona said. "You've piqued my interest, Chris. You really have."

"Well, I have been called 'The Second Most Interesting Man in the World.'"

"Okay, settle down now, cowboy."

"Seriously? Just going to shoot me down like that?"

"Just kidding."

At that we both shared a laugh.

Mona was a cool person. I wouldn't have minded the opportunity to get to know her some more. Speaking to her, I knew I would have to keep my guard up or else I'd fall victim to a never-ending loop of jokes. It was an interesting dynamic that led to our fun conversations.

"Well, I think I'd better get going then. It'll be easier for me to sneak away while Yasmin's distracted," she said.

"Good idea."

Mona wrapped her arms around me and gave me a tight squeeze. Through the thin fabric of her tube top I could feel her breasts squished up against my chest, something I wasn't complaining about.

She smelled nice.

I was already missing the warmth of her body seconds after she pulled away and moved over to the door.

"Chris. One more thing."

"What's up?"

"Hypothetically speaking. That offer Yasmin made me. That I could stay at her place if I needed to. Do you think she was serious?"

Mona's back was towards me, so I couldn't see her expression.

"Yeah, she may have anger issues, but she means what she says," I responded. "But even if she didn't, I already said that you could stay here too."

"And I wouldn't owe you any *favors*?"

"No, I'd prefer you didn't."

"You sure? I wouldn't mind. Whenever and however you wanted, I'd be cool with it."

"Get out."

Mona giggled.

But.

Was she trying to imply something by asking these questions?

Could it be that—

"Wait a second. Here, Mona. Before you go, take this."

I sprung across the room and snatched the napkin that had been sitting in the drawer of my desk. I placed it into Mona's palm.

"Chris, how sweet. But I'm not crying. I don't need—"

"Look at it."

Mona glanced down at the napkin in her hand. The neatly written digits of Yasmin's phone number were still as clear as ever.

"It's Yasmin's number. If you ever need to, just give her a call and explain your situation. And if she gives you any lip about it, just tell her I gave you her number."

"This..." Mona mumbled.

"Sometimes it's difficult to ask for help. Don't worry about it."

There's a lot more than meets the eye with people. You can't ever know for sure what they're thinking or why they do what they do. All you can do is stick out your hand and offer your help. In the end, whether they need it or not, it'll be up to them to decide if they want to take it.

"Thanks again."

"No thanks necessary, ma'am. I'm the hero after all."

Mona stifled a chuckle before opening the door. "Okay, just kidding. *Now* I have one more thing to say."

"Hah. Sure. What's up?"

"I was completely wrong about you," she said. "I kind of see what she was talking about now."

"Who?"

"Zoey."

And before I was able to question Mona any further, she gave me a wink and stepped out of the door.

CHAPTER 20

"Hey, where'd that bitch go? I wasn't finished with her yet."

"What?"

"The bitch. The Titty Monster. Eyebrows. Ms. Cow Udders. Liar-Liar Pants on Fire." Yasmin rapidly fired off the list of names she wasn't going to get the chance to use anymore en masse. "I'm talking about Mona. Just in case you didn't get that from my descriptions."

"Oh. I don't know."

Yasmin frowned.

"What's gotten into you? Did she say something? I can probably still catch her if you want me to kick her ass."

"No, it's fine. I'm fine. I don't know. Just had to sit down for a second. My back was hurting."

It wasn't a complete lie. My back was hurting. Mona did just drop something huge on me after all.

I always seemed to get back pains whenever Zoey crossed my mind—which was more often than I'd like to admit. However, I will say, the frequency has been going down in recent weeks at least. I guess that's why I had to sit down this time around, because this was an especially bad one.

I wasn't a spine doctor or whatever they're called, and I only looked up rudimentary information after the initial incident, so I couldn't tell you exactly where this pain originated. All I knew was that it was centralized around the lower area of my back where my spine connected to my pelvis. Basically, the spot where I had fallen on the dumpster. That damn green dumpster. My savior and torturer.

Ironically though, the turmoil in my mind was greater than the pain in my back.

Mona mentioned Zoey.

She knew her? From where? How? Why?

There were a lot of questions and zero answers.

And the most pressing question? Mona's last words.

I was completely wrong about you.

Wrong about what exactly?

With such limited information there was no way for me to know, and dwelling on the infinite number of possibilities, as I'm prone to do, wasn't going to be a productive use of my time.

"Oh, that's not good. Does it hurt bad?" Yasmin asked.

"Not too bad. Just feels like ten white-hot, metal rods have been inserted into my spine."

"You idiot! You should be in the hospital!"

"I also feel like I'm being burned alive."

"No, you should be dead!"

"It's fine. I've already survived one near death experience. What's one more going to do?"

"Bring you even nearer if not outright kill you!"

"I just need to focus on surviving then. They say whatever doesn't kill you makes you stronger."

"Not in these situations they don't!"

Our roundabout conversation was already making me feel better by taking my mind off the main issue. Yasmin's overreactions were funny, and they gave her the opportunity to show off her cute side, not that I minded or despised her typical attitude. She had her reasons. Being loud and vocal was the only way she was able to survive back in her home life, after all.

Still.

It would have been nice for us to share some of those "relationship" moments, I guess. The cutesy ones. Like those public displays of affection that you sometimes witness on your way to work or when you're out eating. You know what I'm talking about. The stuff that might make you vomit because of how sweet they were. Handholding. Light kisses. A picnic in the park. Was that too much to ask for?

We haven't even kissed yet.

Why was it that I felt like I've done more with Mona than Yasmin? And that's saying something.

Ugh.

Why am I complaining now? It's my fault that there hasn't been any forward progress. If I wanted something to happen, I needed to make it happen. I'd been complacent with Zoey as well and not much happened with her either. Oh well. I'd just have to be satisfied with our little verbal sparring matches. If I closed my eyes, I could even pretend that we were an old bickering married couple. The ones that argue about the most benign things, like whether to buy creamy or chunky peanut butter. Or two-ply toilet paper versus three-ply. You might think that their marriage would be on the rocks on account of all the arguing, but it couldn't be going any steadier than that. Straight relationship goals.

"If it hurts that bad, you should go to the hospital," Yasmin said again.

"No can do. I'm still kicking, so it's probably not that serious anyway. It's just a minor inconvenience. Also, if I did that, I'd have to answer too many questions. All those factors combine into a scenario I'm not too keen on letting come to pass."

"Fair enough. I wouldn't want to be put in that situation either, but if you aren't going to go, at least let me help you."

"Yeah, okay, I'd like that. How are you going to help me? Are you going to get me a brand new spine? You know—to replace the one you said I didn't have?"

"How boring," Yasmin said. "You always have to be such a wise ass. No, it's not a new spine. You'll have to grow that one yourself. And even if it was, how would we put it inside you? We would need to go to a hospital to do that, genius."

"Ah. Touché."

Yasmin's eyes narrowed. "If you want, I'll give you a massage."

A massage?

She was going to give *me* a massage?

"Okay, who are you and what have you done with the real Yasmin? I swear if you laid a finger on her."

"Shut up! If you don't want it, just say so. You don't have to be a jerk about it."

"No, no. I do. I do want it. I'm just surprised. What do you know about massages?"

"I had a book or two lying around at my place that I read over the past couple weeks."

"Are you telling me you want to be a masseuse now?"

"No, it's nothing like that. I just thought it would be... nice." Yasmin turned her face away from me. "Some of the dating advice I read also told me that gestures like this are important too. But don't get the wrong idea. It's not like I want to do this or anything. I just know your back hurts sometimes and I thought this would be a good idea to make you feel better."

As if my prayers had finally been answered, a cutesy event had been bestowed upon me.

She was trying to be nice.

Not only that, but she even dropped the line. That one line. It was a tsundere staple.

I could almost cry.

"Well, asshole? Say something or I'm going to change my mind."

"Sorry. I was just left speechless. It was as if you just offered me something truly magnificent. Of course, I'm not going to pass on this once in a lifetime opportunity!"

"Yeah, once in a lifetime is correct," Yasmin stated. "I'm never going to do this for you again. Also, don't expect too much either. I'm no professional or anything. Now, turn over and lay on your stomach."

With a large smile, I followed her demands and flipped over. My face sunk into the blankets that still carried Mona's lingering aroma. I'd made a fuss about having just cleaned my bed sheets, but they smelled better than before. Opening my arms and limbs, I stretched out my body in search of the most comfortable position.

Yasmin climbed onto the bed and scooted over to me. Compared to her usual demeanor, her movements were much gentler—softer even. She was handling me delicately. The same amount of care that she'd handle her canvas and supplies. She swung her leg over my body and mounted me like a saddle. Yasmin sat lower than one might expect, perching on my thighs in order to avoid my injury. She was light. Really really light. If not for the sensation of my body sinking deeper into my mattress, I might not have noticed her at all.

"Ready?" she asked meekly.

"Mmhmm."

She leaned her slender body forward and her small hands traveled up my back until they stopped on my shoulders. Her fingers curled over the humps of my traps and took their positions in two neat rows.

Despite the pain coming from my lower spinal area, Yasmin decided to start high and work her way down. There was an order to things, as they say. However, I didn't want her to put all this effort into me, so I opened my mouth to tell her that she didn't need to do all that. I didn't feel like I deserved this much of her kindness, especially after what I did——kissing Mona. Even if I didn't *really* have anything to be guilty about.

But.

When her palms began kneading my shoulders——I immediately shut up.

I groaned in pleasure, and Yasmin took that as her signal to proceed.

The sensations fanning out from my shoulders were heavenly. Pure bliss. A lifetime of worry, stress, and pain was melting away under the pressure of her fingertips.

I shivered in ecstasy.

I felt happy.

I didn't want it to end.

As I drifted in and out of consciousness from the gentle rocking, a thought dislodged from the back of my mind. I wanted to kick myself for not bringing it up earlier. It was the whole reason she had decided to come to my room in the first place.

"Hey, what was that thing you wanted to tell me about? Sorry, with all the commotion, it slipped my mind."

"Oh, don't worry about it. It wasn't too big of a deal anyway."

"I still want to hear it."

Yasmin's hands moved lower down my back.

"Well, I, uh," she stuttered. "I didn't think anything was going to happen. I did it for the hell of it. I would have been completely okay if they rejected me. I didn't think they'd be able to recognize my sheer genius."

"Okay?"

"But, yeah, I picked a couple of my favorite art pieces. The ones you've been helping me with—"

"You mean the ones that I've helped you with that you never end up showing me? The ones that you immediately lock away under armed guard once you're finished with them? Or burn? Those ones?"

Yasmin dug her fingers into my upper arms, causing me to yelp.

"Hey, easy back there!"

"You know I'm still not entirely comfortable showing off my work just yet. Especially to you."

"That statement implies that I should have seen at least a few by now or that you show off any of your work. Drop that 'entirely' bit and your statement makes a lot more sense."

She drove her nails into my arms again.

"Ow!"

I was just now beginning to realize how unfavorable a position I was in. I mean, I could have thrown her off in an instant if I wanted to, but not without the risk of hurting her. Right now, it was more like she was holding me hostage rather than giving me a soothing back rub. There always had to be a catch to everything.

"If you'd let me finish, then you'd know what I did," Yasmin said.

"What'd you do?"

"I sent a few pictures of my work to a gallery not too long ago."

"You did? What did they say?"

"That's what that phone call I got was about. It was to confirm my participation. The school's hosting a student and local artist event. They liked one of my pieces, and they wanted to put it into their upcoming show at the end of next month."

"Yasmin, that's great! See? I knew you could do it!"

I made a movement to spin around, but the sudden twisting of my back caused me to wince in pain and settle back down. In response, Yasmin immediately went to work on the area around my scar. She lifted my shirt up and used her fingers to gently massage me. My body was numb, but I still felt the warm touch of her fingers.

"Idiot! Don't move too quickly. Just relax. It's just a small show—nothing too fancy. I'm amazing, remember? It was only a matter of time until something like this happened. And this is just the first step. It's nothing to get too excited about."

"No, this is the exact kind of thing you should be excited about," I said. "I'm proud of you."

And I was. Yasmin was already making progress towards her dreams. She said this was just the first step, but she was being modest. Distilling and downplaying all the accomplishments she'd made in such a short time. This was more like her fifth or sixth large stride.

The initial step was obviously her decision to give the whole thing a shot in the first place.

After all her hard work, she deserved it.

Before, it seemed like we'd started off in similar positions, but now she was moving on up ahead of me.

Would I ever be able to change as much as her?

I was trying, but my situation still felt the same. I had no destination.

"Thanks. It wasn't that hard..." she murmured.

"For you? Of course not, ha-ha."

At that, Yasmin stayed silent, continuing her service on my back. The burning pain had died down. It was nothing more than a low simmer now. She was good at this.

As if on cue, another one of those awkward silences fell upon the room. Though I would be the first person to tell you that I didn't mind silence, the particular silence between the two of us right now was somewhat peculiar. Not that there haven't been long bouts of silence between the two of us. There were. Mostly during our art sessions. But, at least during those times, the lack of conversation was replaced by the sound of bristles on canvas or the scratching of a pencil.

Now, however, the background of silence was accompanied by a completely different set of sounds: the creaking of my bed springs as she straddled me, my occasional moans of pleasure, and her increasingly labored breaths as she pressed down on me.

Harder.

And harder.

Somewhere along the way, the whole atmosphere of the room had turned erotic—sensual even.

Was she getting that vibe? Or was it just me? I'm not overthinking anything am I?

Not waiting any longer to find out, I continued the conversation with another topic that had been on my mind.

"This is random, but Mona may end up calling you."

"Cow Tits?"

"Stop giving her those weird nicknames!"

"Is 'Sandbags' better? No, no. I got it. How about 'Cavewoman?'"

"No, they're not better!"

"The first name is because her big tits sag like sandbags. The second one is because her eyebrows make her look like a cavewoman."

"Yes, I gathered that! You didn't need to explain it to me."

"So, you agree with me then? That they're suitable nicknames."

"Eh? I'm not agreeing with anything. Stop twisting my words around. Her name is Mona. Just call her Mona."

"That's boring though."

"I don't care! How would you feel if you were given a nickname like that?"

I couldn't see from my position underneath her, but I could visualize Yasmin stroking her chin at this moment.

"Aren't nicknames terms of endearment?" she stated.

"Not when they're flat-out insults!"

"When I give them to you, I think of them as endearing."

"And what nicknames are you talking about?"

"Oh, where do I begin," Yasmin said, taking a moment to think. "Idiot, imbecile, moron, dumbass, and asshole—just to name a few."

"Every single one of those was an insult!"

"They're endearing insults."

"..."

I couldn't even begin to comprehend what was going on in this girl's head, so I just decided to let her live in her own fantasy world. It seemed like she had a fundamental misunderstanding on the difference between "nicknaming" and "name calling." It was a topic we would have to address another time.

"Well, anyway, *Mona* may call you. I gave her your number."

"Why would you do that?" Yasmin's tone shifted into annoyance. On my back, I could feel her fingers pressing down into my skin with more pressure.

"Despite what she said, she may actually need a place to stay."

"Is that what she told you when I was gone?"

"Yeah, that was part of it. And, I just had a feeling."

There must have been some purpose in asking if Yasmin and I were serious about offering her a place to stay.

"Okay and what do you want me to do about it? Sounds like her problem."

"I mean, did you mean it when you said she could stay at your place?"

Yasmin groaned.

"Is this what this is all about? No, I wasn't serious. I was talking out my ass. It was in the heat of the moment. I tend to do that sometimes."

"I see." I shook my head. "I guess next time I see her I'll tell her she can just stay with me then."

On my back, I could feel Yasmin's hands ball into fists. She started pounding on my back like a child. "Now wait just a second! You don't have to do that! Fine! She can stay at my place!"

"See? Why'd you flip-flop like that?"

Her fists stopped.

"It's not that simple."

"What do you mean?"

"Chris, I mean this in the kindest way possible," Yasmin said. "You're too goddamn naive sometimes."

Yasmin's hands opened again, and she continued her massage. Using her thumbs, she pressed down in smooth circles over my back.

"I didn't know you before your accident, so I can't describe how you were back then, but that doesn't mean that you have to stick your neck out for everyone. You have no clue who this Mona girl is, or what she wants from you. Absolutely no clue. For all we know, every word out of her mouth could be bullshit." Yasmin's fingers swirled down lower and deeper.

I could feel Yasmin shake her head. It reminded me of the subtle shake she had performed when I had offered to help Mona the first time—the shake that she subconsciously didn't want me to see.

"Ugh, this is hard to put into words," she continued. "I must not be making any sense right now. What I'm trying to say is that you don't need to go around helping every stranger who gives you a sob story. You don't owe it to them. It's okay to step aside and not get involved. There's nothing wrong with living your life that way."

"…"

Maybe not.

Possibly not.

Probably not.

I didn't know.

There was still an endless chasm of opportunities and choices spread out before me. Things I should do. Things I shouldn't do. Ways I should live my life and ways I shouldn't. Who's to say what was right or wrong? I was just taking the path that made the most logical sense to me.

Yasmin was right about a few things. She didn't know me before the accident, so she can't speak about that part of my personality, except through bits and pieces that I have revealed to her. But it shouldn't matter. I haven't changed.

Yeah, I didn't have any idea who Mona was or what her true reason was for showing up in my room like that. Apparently, she knew Zoey. Whatever that meant. I didn't know. If thinking about it was going to get me answers, I would have already figured it out by now.

My whole life I've been content with just going with the flow, carried along by some external force. Family. Friends. Girlfriend. Letting them choose for me was easier. It took the responsibility away from me.

This didn't mean that I never wanted to make a choice.

It's just that, the two times that I had made a choice—important choices made only to benefit myself—I had hurt two people I cared about very much.

My father was a cheater.

Seeing him with another woman tore me up inside. I remember just how sick it made me feel. Disgusted. Those hands of his that hugged me. Hugged my mother. Wrapped around some random woman. The smiles he gave weren't meant for us alone.

It was a half day at school and I had come home early to see Dad and that woman going at it on the couch. Nothing explicit, but the things I saw were damning enough to make me backtrack out of the house all the way back to school.

I couldn't live with the burden of carrying that knowledge while my mother was ignorant to it. It was tearing me apart and in order to make myself feel better, I told my mother. I told her everything that I had seen, hoping that the burden would be taken off me. And though my wish was granted, I didn't realize that it wouldn't have the effect that I wanted.

Screaming.

Arguments.

Fights.

That was what my choice had brought about, culminating in my father leaving and never coming back, which brought upon a host of its own problems. The burden I couldn't hold had been placed entirely on my mother who was left to take care of and support me by herself.

Maybe if I hadn't said anything, then everything would have been better?

Maybe if I had thought about how my choice would negatively affect my entire family, then I would have had the strength to carry that weight.

How would my life have changed if I hadn't made that choice?

I didn't know. It was something I thought about a lot though. It haunted my dreams and kept me up at night as I stared at that ceiling that hung overhead like the top of a wooden casket.

A different but equally stifling feeling returned when I started dating Zoey. A burden of expectation. I couldn't possibly live up to it, so I thought it was better if I just abandoned the idea entirely.

And we saw how that ended up.

"Chris? Say something."

"Sorry, I spaced out. What were we talking about again?"

"Were you really not listening?"

"No, I was. I'm just not entirely sure what you want me to say, Yasmin. I don't know why I do what I do. All my introspection hasn't gotten me any closer to any answers. It's all just speculation. And what I've deduced from that speculation is that I don't want to disappoint people anymore. The weight is too heavy. Unbearable for someone as weak as me. At the very least I know that if I put other people's interests before my own, offer help when they need it, then their lives can improve. I feel like I owe it to all the people who've put up with me so far."

"Are you happy living like that?"

"I sure as hell don't know, but I'd rather be inconvenienced or unhappy if that means someone else can be happy. I decided to act this way to atone for my mistakes. I still have a long way to go until I'm fully satisfied, but I'm doing my best. I do think starting to act like this may have been the most correct choice I've ever made."

"Why's that?"

"I met you, so how could it possibly be wrong?"

Yasmin sucked in a breath, her hands stopping on my hips.

"That—that was corny," she said. "I just want you to know that."

"Just because it's corny doesn't mean it isn't true."

I slowly moved to sit up and Yasmin slid off my back. As I turned to look at her, she looked away, out of my apartment's single window.

It was obvious she was trying to avoid any sort of eye contact with me. There was no grand view of the city outside that window like the one at her place. Instead, Yasmin stared intently at a brick wall, as if it were the most interesting thing she'd ever seen.

It was during these situations when we were having a 'moment' that Yasmin's headstrong, brash attitude was nowhere to be found. She was flustered. One of her fingers repeatedly tapped the top of her knee as if she was trying to communicate in Morse code, while two others on the opposite hand played with the hem of her sweatshirt.

Seeing this side of her.

This rare side of her.

What a treat to behold.

Yasmin was cute.

Moments like this highlighted that fact, and I wished I could have taken a commemorative photo. I'd keep it in my pocket and whip it out whenever I wanted to embarrass her.

But witnessing her cuteness factor was having another effect on my mental state.

Like I had with Mona, suddenly I felt a sort of temptation rising from somewhere deep inside. However, unlike with Mona, I wouldn't have described this feeling as being rooted in lust. It was something else, and I let that feeling carry my body forward.

If there was ever a time to make a move, it was now.

I placed my hand on top of hers.

"Eep!"

She made a surprisingly cute sound.

"Yasmin?"

"Yeah? What do you want?"

"Look at me."

With an awkward, unnatural smile on her face, she turned to face me. It looked like the forced smile of someone who was staring down the sights of a camera lens. Tense and strained. Ultimately, a very painful looking expression.

What was up with her? She looked constipated.

Right before I was about to ask if she was okay, Yasmin herself spoke up.

"Chris? You were telling the truth, right? Nothing happened between you and Mona, right?"

"That's still bothering you? I'm telling you nothing happened."

"Nothing at all?"

"Yeah, nothing. Actually—no, that isn't right."

There was that little something. Something I probably didn't have to mention. But something I probably *should* mention.

It was just for a second, less than a second even, but our lips did come into contact. Whatever you wanted to call it. A peck or a kiss.

Now would be the perfect time to mention that.

"Okay, don't get mad. Please don't get mad. We may have sort of kissed. It was just for a split second though. I didn't French her or anything. Even if I tried, I wouldn't have been successful with it. I probably would have ended up licking all around her face like a dog. Yeah, it was just lip on lip contact. Besides that, nothing else. I promise."

Yasmin's eyebrow twitched.

"Did you enjoy it?" she followed up, her question loaded with ominous and foreboding pressure.

Something was telling me that I better answer this question carefully or else! My life was on the line here!

"No! I didn't enjoy it. Not at all. And like I said, it was for less than a second. It didn't mean anything. I couldn't even feel it!"

"Good answer."

"So, you're not mad?"

"Not in the slightest. I'm totally secure. I mean, look at me. I'm the complete package! I'm absolutely perfect. People would die to date me. I could have you replaced in a second."

Said the girl with no prior experience.

Her confidence was completely unfounded.

It seemed to me that Yasmin was putting on an air of nonchalance now that she knew Mona wasn't a threat.

"That's a relief. I thought you were going to be more jealous," I said.

"Jealous? Are you kidding me? I'm not jealous at all. It'd be a total downgrade if you went with Cow Tits. With her massive chest, huge ass, flawless skin, tiny waist, and perfect hair."

"Uh, right."

Turned out some of that insecurity was still managing to seep through.

"I can forgive you for kissing another person behind my back," Yasmin continued. "I kind of asked for that to happen by saying it wouldn't matter because you'd choose me. But we aren't official or anything. And despite me being better than her in every way imaginable, I could see how a weak guy like you might have been tempted by her charms. I just didn't know what I was going to do if you said that you liked it. I might have had to do something drastic."

"Drastic? In what way?"

"Let's just say you'd both be so horribly disfigured that no one would be able to identify you. Not even your mother."

And just like that, Yasmin was back to her usual self.

Where did the cute Yasmin go? I missed her already.

"Then it's a good thing I didn't enjoy it!" I said.

"Yeah. You're right about that. That's also another reason why I would have wanted her to stay at my place rather than here. I didn't want to give her any more opportunities to seduce you. And I should know how easy that would have been. I had you wrapped around my finger the first day that we met."

"Wow, someone's grown awfully confident. Just a second ago, you got all embarrassed from a hand touch."

"Shut up! I wasn't embarrassed at all. You just surprised me! I had already given up on you taking any initiative at all!"

"Given up? How am I supposed to try anything when you're so angry and stuck-up all the time? You wouldn't pet a growling dog, would you? I would do something if I had a chance!"

"Oh, yeah? Prove it then! Do something now. You got the perfect opportunity! Doesn't get any more perfect than this!" Yasmin gestured up and down her body. "Lay one on me, big boy!"

"Alright then! You asked for it!"

Yasmin and I glared into each other's eyes. She had a smug smirk on her face; all her previous meekness having been washed away.

But this false bravado was betrayed by the single bead of sweat rolling down her temple.

Hmph. If she wanted it, then I'd give her what she wanted.

I just needed to snake my arm around her waist—like this.

Pull her in.

I calculated the advanced formulas needed to estimate the trajectory and distance to impact.

And—

And—

I closed my eyes and went for it.

My lips gently connected with something soft, and I sort of just let them stay there. It was the first kiss between us—a long awaited one at that—so I didn't really plan on what kind of kiss I wanted. I'd say this one would suffice. I wouldn't win any awards for "Best Kiss" or anything like that, but I was satisfied. This was a small win. I did it. The small kiss that I previously shared with Mona hadn't been a fluke. Going for it again had just proved that to me.

"There! Told you!" I gloated.

Yasmin didn't reply to that. Her eyes were wide, and her lips hung in the air at their previous position. The same position where my own mouth had just been.

She brought her hand up to her lips and traced all around them.

"My first kiss..." she whispered.

"Wait? That was your first kiss?"

It was a shock to hear that, but it made sense. She hadn't had a boyfriend and she had to resort to a plethora of outside resources to get any information on matters of the heart, so to have never kissed anyone before didn't seem like a stretch by any means.

So, I was her first, huh?

I hoped she enjoyed it.

"My first kiss..." she repeated. "My first kiss... My first kiss... My first kiss..."

"Uh, how was it?"

Her eyes flicked onto me, breaking through the glazed look that had previously been on her face.

"It sucked!"

"Wha—?"

"You ruined it! I want a do-over!"

And with that Yasmin lunged forward and closed the distance between us in less than a second.

She kissed me.

If you could even call that a kiss.

At the very least I had tried to be gentle with mine. I thought girls liked gentleness?

If that was the case, then Yasmin must not have been a girl.

She didn't care about tenderness at all.

Her lips were rough and callous as she slammed her mouth onto mine with the tact and softness of a battering ram. The repeated collisions of our two front pairs of teeth sounded like their own tap-dancing concert.

But it was a concert I wasn't listening to.

I was too engrossed in the way that her lips and body made me feel.

After a long and arduous past few weeks, today was finally the day that we had our first kiss.

It was also the day that we had our second, third, and fourth.

CHAPTER 21

"So, Christian, how have things been going as of late? You seem to be having a ball."

"Things have been going well, Mia. I can't complain."

"Do tell, do tell. And please address me as Mrs. Lee."

"I think I've narrowed down some of my options and may finally be ready to make a decision."

"On a career path? That sounds splendid! What were you thinking?"

"Uh, not that. I'm still mulling stuff over in that regard. Sorry." I scratched my temple. "I'm talking about the whole dating schtick I mentioned last time."

"Oh." Mia somehow managed to sound both excited and disappointed. "That's still wonderful news to hear. What have you decided?"

"I'm leaning a lot closer to picking Yasmin. You know, like, fully committing to it."

"Was any other woman in the running?" Mia asked.

"Yeah, I mean, it's me we're talking about. I don't have to try *that* hard to get girls. I just put an ad in the paper and the girls line up at my door."

"Hm, that sounds illegal."

"You know what I'm talking about!"

Monday afternoon.

Mia's office.

Today was another one of the usual scheduled meetings to give her updates on my rehabilitation efforts. However, unlike the *usual* usual scheduled meetings that I had with Mia, this time I had more good news to share with her. Whenever I had good news that I wanted to share, this whole therapy business felt less like a mandatory hassle and more like a mandatory convenience. Something that was still required, but was nice to do occasionally.

In my excitement to share my unusual bit of good news, I had arrived at her office around ten minutes before our scheduled meeting.

Mia, who was sitting at her desk, had her nose buried in a book, and I could only see her tightly bound bun sitting on the top of her head like a dumpling. She lifted a finger as if to silence me before I even spoke a word.

It must have been a good book she was reading because though I had come ten minutes early, I stood there for a good fifteen minutes waiting for her to put her finger down.

"My deepest apologies," she had said, wiping a tear from under the rim of her wide-circular frames. "It was just getting good."

The book was one of her favorites. It was one of those old ones. The kind that bored millions of kids out of their minds back in high school literature classes. Not necessarily because the stories were boring, even though they usually were, but because of how they were written. It was older English and every time I ever attempted to read anything like that my eyes would glaze over, and I'd end up having to reread the same paragraph many times before I was able to comprehend anything at all. It was torture. Now I don't want you to think that I hated books. That couldn't be further from the truth. I loved them. I just preferred if they were written sometime this century.

"So, you believe Yasmin's a keeper," Mia said, taking a sip of black coffee.

"Starting to feel that way, yeah."

"Hmm, do you have any reservations? If you like her then go for it. From what you've told me, it sounds like she's also quite fond of you. You two would make a cute couple."

"A cute couple. A beautiful couple. I've been told. But you know what I've been through. I can't be going around and making choices like this willy-nilly. In fact, you're the one who asked me if I was even ready to start dating again."

"Yes, I did. I remember that. However, seeing the way you speak about her has slowly warmed me up to that idea. Yasmin has been a good influence on you and vice versa."

"Yeah, I guess so."

I had helped her a little and she had helped me. No arguments there. It was safe to say that because of each other, we've been able to get out of our comfort zones, even if it was only due to the competitiveness of our more-than-just-friends friendship. She'd shown me the benefits of going out and trying different things. Meanwhile, I'd helped her make some beneficial choices as well, some that had already begun to bear fruit.

"Speaking of which," I continued, "Yasmin actually got a piece accepted into the student gallery show."

"Bless my soul! Quite the budding artist! I'm so proud!"

"I was proud of her too. She kept saying it wasn't a big deal, but you should have seen the look in her eyes. She was happy about it."

"As she should be." Mia nodded approvingly. "I confided in you before that I wished to be a writer at one point, so I know that the arts can be a trying and perilous road, but Yasmin has already begun to make progress down that path, something I wasn't ever able to do."

"What made you stop?"

Mia placed a hand on top of the large book that she had been reading.

"It just seemed to be a distant romantic dream for me."

"I mean, you can still try. It's not too late. And you're not too old."

She smiled.

"Yes, I guess not. But I have a job right now: to make sure that all my young wards know what they should be doing first. Maybe in the future—yes, in some future. That's when I'll try my hand at writing again."

Behind the lenses of her glasses, I could see Mia drifting away to far-off worlds and places that she'd only ever visited in her imagination. It was a look I saw quite often on the face of Yasmin.

Their personalities couldn't be any more different even if they tried, but Mia and Yasmin shared that commonality at least.

If I hadn't helped her, would Yasmin have ended up like this?

There was nothing *wrong* with Mia, but from the way I heard her talk about books and writing, it seemed like there was a deep well of regret residing under her docile, caring, and professional exterior. A measure of lingering sadness as well.

On the surface, and by most accounts from the student body and those who had Mia as an advisor, she was a cheerful woman—happy, an envoy of sunshine and rainbows. She lit up whatever room she walked into with her smile. Not only would she never hurt a fly, but she'd also actively go out of her way to nurse one back to health. She was the kind of woman that men would proudly go to war for, or better yet, start wars over. That's how much of a national treasure Mia was.

That's why I was surprised whenever I heard those tidbits of sadness in her tone.

Dang.

It just blows your mind.

Sometimes you think you know someone, but you end up only knowing exactly what they've shown you.

"By the way, when's the show?" Mia asked.

"At the end of the month. To be honest, Yasmin didn't want me to tell anybody about it. She's still shy, so she didn't want to draw all that attention to herself, but it would be great if you could stop by and invite anyone else who may be interested. I wanted to surprise her with a large group. You know, so we could embarrass her and stuff."

"Does the young miss not have any other friends to speak of?"

"No, I don't think she does."

Just a couple days ago, I'd confirmed what I had long speculated. Yasmin's friend situation.

After a morning class, I wanted to grab some food at one of the campus cafes. I had half an hour before I'd head over to my next lecture so I went to find a small spot where I could sit and savor my food, a yogurt parfait. It was a full house that day, but I was lucky to grab a seat off to the side. The last one open.

As I was about to sit, I saw Yasmin.

Due to her height, she stood out among the crowd. But even if she wasn't a shrimp, I'm almost positive I would have picked her out.

She went into the cafe and then a minute later she walked out carrying one of those premade sandwiches that they sell. I never had one, but they were popular. Yasmin then looked side-to-side as if she was about to cross the street.

Obviously, there were no seats left. I'd just grabbed the last one.

Now, the reasonable thing for me would have been to flag her down, but I wanted to observe her in her natural habitat, unbeknownst to prying eyes.

The girl walked around aimlessly with a scowl for a good five minutes before a spot opened up to her. And there she sat down and ate. She simply ate.

She didn't glance at her phone once.

She didn't talk to anyone around her.

She just sat there and stared at the other people who were laughing, talking, and having a good time.

She looked... lonely. Or at least that was the impression I got.

I say this because, though the situation may not have looked bad or unusual, that's how I felt sometimes. I had Brad, but we never texted. Yasmin was the only one who texted me. Contacting me at all times of the day to hang out or keep her busy, which she happened to do a minute after she finished eating. I received a message saying how bored she was, and that she wanted to meet up later that evening.

Maybe it wasn't rock-solid evidence, but I got the vibe that she had no one else that she could talk to.

"You didn't even need to ask, Christian. I'll invite everyone I can! To see at least *one* of my advisees succeed is such a monumental accomplishment."

"Right."

That kind of sounded like she was taking a jab at me.

I was trying. In my own way.

"So, you'd like to surprise her, huh? That sounds so romantic! Young love! How it makes my heart flutter so!" Mia swooned and brought her right wrist to her forehead.

"If showing your support for a friend is all that's needed to be considered romantic these days, then the bar really is low. I can only imagine what you'd call it if I told you we had our first kiss."

Mia covered her eyes. "Out of wedlock? How salacious! How lewd!"

"Not even close!"

Since when was kissing seen as overtly sexual?

Wait. Why am I even asking that question? Mia was the one who was behind the times. After all, in those books she loved so much it was considered vulgar to show too much ankle. I couldn't even imagine being sexually aroused by someone's ankle. That's weird.

"Christian," Mia said, still hiding behind the veil of her hands, "at the very least please tell me that you covered up."

"Yeah, our ankles were completely concealed. I wore my thickest socks. Double layered them even just to be sure."

"Though that makes me happy to hear, that wasn't what I was talking about."

Now only covering her eyes with one hand, she reached under her desk and grabbed a small basket loaded to the brim with an assortment of shiny, wrapped plastic squares.

"Are those what I think they are?!"

"Yes, Christian, you need to be safe and cover up. Please take a condom. Or ten. Or rather how many ever you need."

"What did you think I was doing with her?"

"Unspeakable things, Christian. Unspeakable things."

"..."

I thought it would be best to leave it at that.

Yasmin and I didn't get any further than kissing, but I wasn't sure if Mia would believe it or not. Seemed like she had her own idea of what kind of person I am. An inaccurate one.

"Anyway, I think we've gotten off-topic," I said.

"That we have, but I'm still curious and had wanted to ask if there was anyone else that you were planning to invite."

"Yeah, actually... there was one."

And here was the most recent predicament that I found myself in.

Yasmin didn't have a whole lot of friends, so there weren't that many people I could think of to invite to see the show. However, even among that small select group, there was only one that I felt that I needed to make sure attended—

"Who might they be? Maybe I know them?" Mia inquired.

"Bernadette. Yasmin's sister."

It was still a touchy subject to bring up around Yasmin. A subject that usually resulted in strings of unbroken profanity and shouts. Despite everything, Yasmin still had not made-up with her sister yet. They barely talked. Actually, that wouldn't be entirely accurate. From what I've seen, Adi frequently did reach out to her hot-headed younger sister. Occasionally, when Yasmin was away from her phone, I'd see that she received a message. The recipient? The name changed frequently. There was the "Back-Stabbing Bitch." Another was "Sell-out Bitch." Also, "Daddy's Little Bitch." The last time I checked, the name that popped up was, "Brown-Nosing Bitch."

I think I was starting to see a trend in her nicknames.

The only reason that I knew the messages were from the same person, let alone Adi, were due to the contents of the messages. Either Yasmin didn't care or didn't bother to hide the messages, so they showed up clear as day on her screen. It made sense I guess, because if not for that, she never would have opened the messages to read them anyway.

The messages usually started out with some variation of the same greeting:

Hey, sis. Hope everything has been well...

The messages were never long, but they usually wrapped up with Adi telling Yasmin that she'd be there for her whenever she needed it, and for her to be well. One time she even mentioned my name too. I was surprised she remembered me.

But, yeah. It was kind of obvious that things were still more than a little rocky between the two sisters.

If I was a psychiatrist, I might have even said that Yasmin's desire to experience so many different things was her way of filling the void of something missing in her life. An Adi-shaped void.

But what did I know? I just had an inkling of a feeling. A small one, but it was there, that this whole thing wouldn't be a lost cause.

That's why I hoped getting Adi to show up to the art show would be the nudge in the right direction to get them all sorted out.

It sounded simple enough. This worked in the movies, after all.

However, whether this was really possible wasn't the real issue. There was another feeling that I couldn't shake. That it was going to be a monumental pain in the ass for me to even get them in the same room together.

And as it would turn out, that assumption wasn't too far off.

CHAPTER 22

I didn't know where to begin.

I seriously had no idea.

Ever since that fateful day at the bar, the day that I had wooed and charmed Adi with my awesome suaveness that would have put James Bond to shame, I hadn't spoken to or seen her. She gave me Yasmin's number, not her own, so I wasn't quite sure how I was to get into contact with her.

I guess I could've asked Yasmin to give it to me, but that didn't seem very smart no matter which way you looked at it. I could already imagine the barrage of questions she'd ask about why I needed it.

"What the fuck were you going to do with that?" or "Were you going to try and hit on my sister now, you sick fuck?" were just some of the more *nicely* worded questions she'd probably ask, believe it or not.

Didn't Adi have a boyfriend anyway?

Yasmin had no reason to feel threatened.

But I decided to just let Brad ask Yasmin anyway. It'd be an in-character thing for him to do and Yasmin already saw him as the "Horndog." A very apt nickname indeed. I had to give it to her because she nailed that one on the head.

"So does the plan make sense or not, Brad?" I asked. "I really need you to do this." The gallery show was in a week, and we didn't have much time.

"Bro, you're fussing about nothing. I totally got this. When have I ever steered you wrong, huh? You know I always pull out when I need to."

"Something about that statement doesn't sound quite right."

He probably meant pull *through*.

Yet, strangely, what he said still worked. And both statements could be considered true.

I wasn't going to admit that to him, though. Not right now.

"Brad, don't even get me started. Especially not with that Mona business. Who even was that? How did you know her?"

"Aye, that wasn't my fault. I just asked around for you, trying to hook you up with some girls, and she was one of the few that approached me about it. How was I supposed to know she knew Zoey? That was my bad. A one in million coincidence."

That day when Brad had returned to the apartment, I recapped him on the entirety of the events he had missed. It was true that he'd let her in the room, but he had no idea about the other stuff. He was just trying to set me up with her because he thought she was hot, and that I needed some extra variety in the "chest department" as he described it.

"Just be more careful next time," I'd said.

"Say no more, say no more, my guy! I'll be running complete background checks next time around. Also, an STD check and drug test and alcohol test. The next one will be squeaky clean, I promise."

"Whatever."

Nighttime.

At the bar where I'd first talked to Adi.

After another round of exams, I decided to tag along with Brad, partially to celebrate and partially to elaborate my plans for Yasmin's surprise party.

Though Brad came here frequently, I hadn't returned since that initial night. I didn't think I had a reason to.

"So, all I have to do is ask Yasmin for her sister's number and give it to you?"

"Yeah, easy peasy, no complicated plan necessary."

"And you couldn't do it because?" Brad asked for the fifth time.

"Because the party is supposed to be a *surprise*. If I asked for her sister's number around this time, wouldn't it seem, uh, I don't know, kind of obvious?"

"Bro, I think you're overthinking things again."

"Just get the damn number."

Brad shrugged his shoulders and took a swig of his beer.

"One more thing," he said.

"What?"

"If I get the number, can I use it for my personal benefit?" Brad grinned at me.

"She has a boyfriend."

"So?"

"What do you mean? She's taken."

"Bro, you still have so much to learn. We'll see what she does after she's met *me*."

"Probably call the cops."

"That's fucked up. That only happened one time."

"You deserve it. Now, let's get this over with. Here's Yasmin's number. Just call her and ask. Don't say anything unnecessary, all right?"

"Got it. But, hey, where are you going?"

"I'll let you handle this right now. I'm going to head to the toilet. All this water I've been drinking is running straight through me."

"What! What if I don't know what to say? I need you here by my side to lend me emotional support! Yasmin is scary!"

"Big tough guy like you? You should be fine. I seem to remember you leaving me to fend for myself in the past. Just get the number at all costs. I don't care how. Now, I'll be right back."

Before he could protest any further, I made a beeline through the crowd and down the hall to the restrooms.

If I told you that I didn't have any reservations about this plan, then I'd be lying. It seemed like another instance where I was sticking my nose somewhere it didn't belong. Was this okay? It was a family issue, and I didn't know all of the dynamics behind their relationship. Just one side of the coin—Yasmin's side.

The way she described it was that they used to be close when they were younger, before the money. When their home life started to change, so did their relationship.

In Yasmin's words, Adi had basically sold her out for money. Abandoned her and sided with her parents. Yasmin was the only one who didn't reject their previous life. That poor life. That life that Yasmin herself didn't mind.

The two of them were twins, the fraternal kind, and to have literally the closest person to you reject you like that? I couldn't blame her for being sore about the subject. I would have felt the same way in her shoes.

I could only hope to get Adi's side of the story one day. Hopefully, it'd fill in the blanks, as they say.

After I relieved my bladder and washed my hands, I made my way back to the bar. As I approached, I could see that Brad's face was planted in his hands and his shoulders were slumped forward. The feeble position was a stark contrast to his usual large and boisterous stature.

"What happened to you? You look like a dog after they've been brought in to be neutered. Where's that familiar Brad gusto?"

Brad just shook his head, not bothering to look up at me.

"That girl, Yasmin, she's a demon."

"Yeah, she's a little rough around the edges. But she doesn't mean anything by it. That's just how she is."

"She called me a pea-brained, moronic, walking pile of cat vomit."

"Okay, so she's rough around the edges."

"She also said that if I died in a ditch out in the desert no one would care."

"All right, that's just excessive. She obviously didn't mean that. That's just way too cruel."

"She also said that she obviously *did* mean it when she said it."

"Oh, okay then, but for what it's worth, I'd care if you died in a ditch out in the desert."

"She also said that she'd make the ditch large enough for the both of us."

"Wait a second! How did I get dragged into this?!"

Brad shook his head and simply held up the palm of his hand.

"Don't worry. I got Bernadette's number though..." His tone was flat and devoid of life.

"That's good. I guess. I'm surprised you managed to get it after all of that."

"You said at whatever cost."

I took down Bernadette's number and entered it into my cell phone. Ironically, her number was just a few digits off from Yasmin's.

Brad remained in his huddled position, balled up on the top of his bar chair, looking utterly defeated and emasculated. In the years that I'd known him, I'd never seen him have this reaction to anything. Sure, I remembered days when we'd be out and he'd be hitting on girls at the club, in class, at a cafe, at a library, at a sexual harassment seminar, basically anywhere there were members of the opposite sex, and he'd get completely shot down. It was bad. I'm talking looks of utter revulsion, girls laughing, drinks splashed in his face, and campus security getting called on him. However, despite a string of failures, Brad always seemed to bounce back from any and all adversity, even finding quite a bit of success.

But, now he looked as if he wanted to give up on life.

Yasmin took this much of a toll on him.

It was messed up to say, especially in my friend's time of need, but I couldn't help but wonder if I had looked this pathetic back a couple of months ago.

That was a depressing thought.

"Zoey was never this mean to me," Brad said.

"Yeah, Zoey was an absolute angel, but she isn't around anymore, is she?"

"Maybe instead of the whole Yasmin plan, this should have been a plan to get you back together with her. She never called me a pea-brained, moronic, walking pile of cat vomit."

"I... I don't know. I still haven't seen or spoken to her since."

Since the break-up.

The thought caused a pain to shoot up my spine like electricity.

"Just food for thought, bro. Being with someone like this who is so outwardly abusive and toxic can't be all that good for your mental state."

"She's not that bad, but I'll keep that in mind," I said. "Anyway, I'm going to call Adi now."

I entered her number and the line started to ring.

All right, how was I going to play this?

Like usual, I had no idea what I wanted to say.

Should I just come out and tell her the whole reason I was calling? You know, cut straight to the chase, leaving no room for any bullshit whatsoever? I just didn't know the dynamic between their whole relationship. Maybe if I mentioned Yasmin's name too soon then Adi would just decline straight out. If that happened, then there wouldn't be any hope for this reconciliation plan.

As the phone finished its fourth ring, I settled on an adequate game plan that would at the very least get my foot in the door. The fifth ring was cut off midway, signaling that someone had picked up the line.

Now, whenever I call someone, especially someone that I've never called before, there's this thought that always crosses my mind. It's a simple thought, one I'm sure that everyone has had at one point or another.

The thought?

What was the first thing that the person on the other line was going to say?

If you didn't think about it very hard, it seemed like a logical question to have, especially for someone who has a certain amount of anxiety when talking to people on the phone. However, there weren't that many responses one could get, were there? A simple "Hello?" was the most likely thing that someone would say when they answered the phone. It was the best multifunctional response, serving the purpose of a greeting as well as a polite way of asking, "What the hell do you want?" In contrast, if it was a restaurant or business or service of some type, they'd probably say something along the lines of, "This is such-and-such, how may I help you?"

It may sound like I'm getting off-topic, but it's relevant. The thing was that most of the time you didn't need to question what the person on the other line said first, you just needed to have what you wanted to say prepared so that the conversation could transition smoothly into the matter of why the call was made in the first place.

Unfortunately, this wasn't one of those times.

Not that it even mattered anyway because I couldn't ever have anticipated what I was about to hear.

"Please... I beg of you. Stop calling me. Just leave me alone. Go away. I... I don't want to talk anymore."

What the hell?

And just like that I had forgotten everything I had planned on saying and even my initial reason for calling in the first place.

Was that Adi? It'd been so long that I wasn't sure.

The voice was shaky, virtually a whisper, and I strained my ears to hear it.

"Adi? Are you alright? I don't know if you remember me, but this is Chris. We met at the bar a few months ago. You gave me Yasmin's number."

On the other side, I heard someone clear their throat followed by some rustling in the background. "Oh, Chris. Yes, of course. I remember. How are you doing?"

"I'm fine, but forget about that, what about you? What was that all about?"

"Hah, I'm okay, and it was nothing."

"It didn't sound like nothing."

"You're mistaken."

"Uh, are you sure?"

"Very sure."

I scratched my head and turned to Brad who was looking back at me with a confused expression.

Obviously, something was up. Didn't take a genius or the world's greatest detective to figure that one out. But it was more a matter of whether Adi wanted to tell me what it was or if I should press her.

I took a moment to think about it before proceeding.

"Well, if you say so," I replied, deciding to let it go. "I just had something I wanted to ask y—"

My question was interrupted by a series of thunderous knocking sounds in the background of the call followed by what sounded like muffled shouts.

Adi gasped. Her breaths came out in short heaves as if she was running. Sprinting for dear life. There was more rustling before I heard a door slamming in the background.

No, I couldn't let this go.

Something was definitely wrong.

"Adi? What was that just now?" I asked.

"Chris, I'm scared." Her voice had taken on a certain echoing quality.

Did she just lock herself in the bathroom?

"Adi, what's wrong? Tell me!"

"I'm scared. He won't leave me alone."

"Who? Who won't leave you alone? Where are you right now?"

Adi broke down into tears, and despite her fragmented speech spoken between sobs, I was still able to make out her next words.

"Please, Chris... Can you help me?"

CHAPTER 23

Less than fifteen minutes later, I found myself outside of the address that Adi had given to me over the phone—her apartment complex.

I was huffing, my own heart threatening to burst out of my chest like some alien life form. Both my hands were planted firmly on my knees as I took a minute to catch my breath.

It wouldn't be an exaggeration to say that this might have been the fastest that I'd ever run in my life. Seriously. I wasn't much of a runner or an exerciser for that matter, but this was the fastest option. After all, waiting around for an Uber was out of the question, especially when someone's life was potentially in danger.

By my estimation, I probably saved about five minutes of time by not waiting. May not seem like much, but every second counts.

The apartment complex wasn't too far from my neck of the woods anyway, so I knew exactly where to go. I'd left Brad back at the bar. During my conversation with Adi, he'd gotten distracted by a pair of girls that looked like supermodels, and wandered off. I couldn't have dragged him away from them with heavy machinery. So much for always pulling through...

Adi's room was on the second floor, and I jogged up the steps and down the hall to room 206 before knocking on the door.

"Hey, it's me!"

Adi had originally wanted me to stay on the line with her as I raced over, but my phone was already on the verge of dying, and it suddenly shut off about ten minutes into my journey over to her place.

"Who is it?" a weak, timid voice replied.

"It's Chris. I'm here now. Sorry, my phone ran out of batteries."

There was a long moment of silence before I heard the deadbolt turning in the lock. The door creaked open, and a head framed by long raven hair peaked out from the other side. She gave me the once over, her eyes lingering on my facial features for no longer than a second before shifting left down the hallway, then right, then left again, and finally right again.

"Did you see anyone outside?" she whispered.

"No, I don't think so."

The coast had been clear when I walked up. Nothing out of the ordinary from what I could tell. It was around 10:30 p.m., or at least it was the last time I checked and there weren't any more people than usual out on the streets at this time. A perfectly normal night by all accounts, other than the predicament at hand.

"Then please hurry and get inside before he comes back!"

Adi grabbed me by the collar of my shirt and pulled me into her room.

I stumbled inside as she closed the door behind me and made sure to lock it securely. She even turned the knob and pulled the handle to double check.

She was very thorough.

Or just really scared.

Possibly a mixture of the two.

"I'm very sorry about all this," she said. "So very sorry. Please forgive me."

"It's fine. Don't worry about me. I'm as tough as a mule. I'm more worried about you. How are you holding up?"

"A mule? You're a mule?"

"Eh? No, it's an expression. It means I'm strong." I flexed my nearly nonexistent biceps. "See?"

Adi, whose gaze had been focused on her fingertips, turned up to face me. Despite being twins, she wasn't as short as her sister, so her eye level was just a few inches below mine.

Her eyes were red. If not for the situation, I might have thought she was stoned with how bloodshot they were. Even the surrounding areas were swollen, making the two bags that hung underneath her eyes look like fleshy, red pockets.

She wore an ensemble of black clothing from head to toe. Her shirt had faded to a grayish-color that made it look vintage. It was a little small too, and I could just ever so slightly see her navel peeking out from the bottom. Her jeans were distressed around the knees and upper thighs.

Adi gestured at a small table that sat near the right side of the room, next to her bed. Upon it was a stack of crumpled tissues that rose toward the ceiling like a great white mountain of paper, snot, and tears, threatening to collapse at the slightest touch. Off to the side, there was a small wire waste basket that overflowed with another mound of tissues. Adi took her place at one end of the table and I joined her.

"Sorry," she whispered, attempting to force the white balls of tissue into the overstuffed waste basket. She picked out a few of the less soiled ones to keep her company. Was she that concerned with conserving tissue?

We both sat in silence.

Adi's gaze had fallen back down to her hands, which were now fidgeting nervously with one another like she didn't know what to do with them.

The sight of it made me feel nervous, so I let my gaze wander the room.

I had to admit. I was surprised at what I saw.

"Nice place you got here. Very cozy," I let slip out.

"Uh, thank you."

I mentioned before that I didn't have many frames of references for what a girl's room should look like. Most of my limited knowledge came from TV shows, movies, and other sources. For some reason, they were always filled to the brim with stuffed bears, a shitload of pink things, and posters upon posters of effeminate looking guys who used way too much hair gel. However, now I was starting to think that the whole image that I've grown up mystified by was nothing more than Hollywood bullshit.

Yasmin's room was an outlier. Back when I first walked in, I was amazed at just how much stuff she had. She had everything. That wasn't an exaggeration either. She literally had everything.

Oh, the things money could buy you.

It couldn't buy happiness, as they say, but it could get you just about anything else.

Seeing as the two of them were sisters, though estranged, barely talking, and at complete odds with one another, I pictured Adi's room to be somewhat like Yasmin's. I'm talking multiple rooms, expensive, modern, and filled to the brim with cool, rich people stuff. Basically, luxury the likes of which mere mortals of the lower middle class couldn't even hope to comprehend.

The area she lived in should have tipped me off that this wasn't the case.

I couldn't have been any further from the truth.

I mentioned she lived in my neck of the woods, and that was true, but those extra few blocks made all the difference. In other words, it was a rough area. I hadn't spotted many people lurking outside, but I wouldn't have felt comfortable going for walks at night. I could only imagine how a girl like Adi must feel about the area.

Things just weren't very well lit at all. Especially right now. You couldn't be sure whether a shape or shadow was a person looking for any opportunity to shank you and steal your wallet or something like that. At least where Brad and I lived was considered a common off-campus apartment complex, which meant there was no shortage of students and traffic bustling around the area. And that kept the ne'er-do-wells at bay.

As for the room itself?

The best way I could describe it was... small. Very small. Or rather 'cozy' like I said.

Unlike Yasmin's, it was a single room studio, so there wasn't much to see. But I didn't think there would have been much to see even if it was any bigger.

The room had all the basic amenities that one would need, and not much else. A small connecting kitchen with a stove and a microwave, and a bathroom with a metal tub equipped with a shower nozzle.

Yeah, and that was pretty much it.

A very spartan living arrangement.

No decorations or anything that personalized the room in any way.

Adi patted her eyes with the crumpled tissue as if she was applying make-up.

"I'm sorry," she said again.

Was that the fourth time she'd apologized? Or the fifth? I'd already lost count.

"It's okay. You don't need to keep saying that. I don't mind."

"I'm sorry..."

"Hah," I chuckled, scratching the back of my head. "Anyway, can you tell me what's going on now? The suspense is killing me."

"It's killing you? You're dying right now?"

"What? No, the suspense. I'm just worried about why you were crying. You said you needed help, right?"

"Oh, sorry."

The conversation wasn't going anywhere.

I needed to change my tactics.

"Adi, just tell me what's wrong."

"Yes, of course." She repositioned herself and pushed back a few strands of hair that had fallen in front of her face. "Well, it's about my boyfriend. Ex-boyfriend."

"He's the one that I heard shouting over the phone?"

She nodded.

"I decided to call it quits with him a few days ago. For a while now, I'd been trying to hold this relationship together. I did like him. I really did. He has a temper, but I've grown to love his soft and tender side. It's just that he's been getting worse lately. Ever since I originally brought up my reservations about his behavior. That night he begged me to stay. Told me that he would do everything he could to change for the better. Promised me he would. He even said that he couldn't live without me. That he didn't know what he would do if we broke up. I didn't know what to do. I was scared.

"So, I gave him another chance. I trusted him and gave him the benefit of the doubt. But things didn't change for the better like I hoped. They got much worse. He became overly possessive and obsessed. He tries to monitor my location, prevents me from talking to my friends, and"—Adi paused to massage a spot on her arm that was covered by her long-sleeved shirt—"other things. Sorry, I really don't want to talk about it."

"It's fine. Tell me what you want, and leave out everything else. I think I'm getting the big picture. What did you do next?"

"A couple days ago, I realized I couldn't take it anymore. I called him and tried to end things, but he just flat out refused. He said I was just being stupid and ever since then he's been harassing me. Calling and texting me non-stop, leaving multiple voicemails and messages. He's even been coming over unannounced and hanging around my building, banging on my door."

"How many messages did he send? That's a good way to judge things. Give me a ballpark estimate."

"Maybe like fifteen to twenty."

"Oh, that's not too bad."

"Thousand."

Okay, that actually was pretty bad.

Why didn't she just block his number?

At that moment, as if the person in question had been listening through the door, Adi's phone began to vibrate. She jumped a little and her knees collided with the small coffee table we were sitting around, causing her fearful expression to mix with a wince of pain. When she recovered, she didn't reach for the phone; in fact, she seemed to shrink away from it, inching closer to the far wall. We both waited awkwardly for the phone to buzz halfway across the table before falling silent.

It was a precarious situation she was in. I had heard about things like this happening. Abusive, toxic relationships. Her ex was being completely manipulative. Saying things like he couldn't live without her. That he didn't know what he'd do if they broke up.

Hearing stuff like that really pissed me off.

Maybe because I had found myself on that side not too long ago. Not that I had threatened Zoey, but that I felt like I couldn't live with the weight of the choice I had made.

Threats like that weren't something anyone should ever throw out so casually. It was disgusting.

What was a person to do when someone threatened you like that?

I completely understood why she felt afraid and trapped.

"Why didn't you just call the police or campus security?" I asked. "They take things like this very seriously. I'm sure they could have handled the situation."

"I know. That's the first thing I thought of too. But it's just that—I didn't want to get the police involved. Too many questions and paperwork. And my parents would be notified too. I don't want to burden anyone unnecessarily."

Shit.

She had a point.

For me to criticize her would make me a hypocrite.

That was the exact reason that I didn't want to go to the hospital or notify the authorities about my accident either. Way too messy and a lot of people would have gotten dragged into it as well.

Similar to me, she was willing to suffer in silence the whole time. Carrying that weight upon herself.

"I understand. Trust me, I understand your sentiment completely. But have you told anyone else about it?"

It was a general question, but I was thinking of a particular face when I asked it, even though I almost certainly knew the answer before she even replied. If Yasmin had known about this, I couldn't see her sitting quietly by, while her sister was in danger, despite their circumstances.

Adi shook her head.

"Just you."

"Just me?"

"Sorry. Of course I didn't plan on dragging you into this. It's just that when you called, it felt like it might have been a sign from God—that you were sent to help me once again. Despite not even knowing me, I still remember that you offered to help me back when we first met at the bar. You know, by giving me relationship advice in regard to my boyfriend. Or rather, ex-boyfriend now. I really did appreciate it."

"Wait, hold up. The guy you were talking about back then is the same one that's harassing you now?"

"Yes."

"Forgive me if I'm wrong. Didn't my advice convince you to stay with him?"

"Yes?" Adi replied with a confused expression. It didn't seem like the magnitude of the situation had fallen on her just yet. Or maybe it did, and she was just being nice.

"Woah, woah, woah. Let me get this straight. So that guy is the same guy that is harassing you right now, stalking you, and blowing up your phone?"

"Blowing up my phone? Like a bomb? No, it's right here."

"It's just an expression! As in bombarding your phone with endless calls and text messages. Obviously, he didn't blow up your phone! That'd be attempted murder and he'd be in jail by now!"

Adi's eyebrows scrunched together. "Oh, sorry."

"It's fine. You don't have to keep apologizing. Seriously."

"I'm sorry."

Once again, we'd fallen into the usual exchange.

I don't know why, but for some reason my interactions with Yasmin came into my mind at that moment.

Were these two really sisters? Let alone twins.

It really was something how different they were.

She probably already apologized more times than Yasmin had in my whole time dating her. It just wasn't a very "Yasmin" thing to do. Yasmin always had to be right and get her way. She'd rather die than admit defeat of any kind and was willing to plow forward, headstrong over any obstacle.

In contrast, her sister, Adi, seemed like the kind of person who changed directions with the slightest breeze.

"Oh, no. I did it again. Didn't I? I'm sorry. I just wasn't thinking."

"You're good. It's fine. Don't worry about it at all."

"No, it's not Chris. With the whole situation. I just have a lot to think about right now. I'm afraid to go outside. Because of that, I've already missed a couple of classes and even a few homework assignments. I just don't know what I'm going to do."

"Hm..."

She didn't have many options, especially if she didn't want to involve the police.

It was a conundrum. One that was directly interfering with her personal and social life. And to make matters worse, she didn't have anyone to turn to for help—except me, that is. But even that was just a coincidence.

But even if it was a coincidence, it didn't mean that I couldn't do anything, right?

The way she sat across from me, her head and shoulders hanging, reminded me of a defenseless puppy. And what kind of person would just stand around while cute, little puppies get kicked? For sure not me.

"I'll take care of it for you."

Adi whose eyes had once again fallen to her fingertips looked back up at me.

"Huh? What do you mean?"

"I'll tell that guy to leave you alone and get off your back."

"My back? But he's not on my back."

"Are you making fun of me?!"

Maybe in the past I would have let something like this go. I mean, I most likely would have gone out of my way to make sure I didn't get involved. And maybe that's what I should have done before. In a roundabout way, this was my fault. Adi should have just broken it off beforehand, but in all my brilliance I had done something stupid and had convinced her not too. This whole situation was a consequence of me butting in where I didn't belong. I thought that I could do the right thing.

That same thought process resulted in my father leaving.

In me breaking up with Zoey.

In me nearly killing myself because of that weight.

And now this.

Maybe I haven't learned a damn thing after everything?

People were still getting hurt because of my choices.

So much for being dependable. I was the opposite of that. It was like I was a liability to everyone around me.

But.

But.

Now I had a rare opportunity to right that wrong and solve the problem that I started. So, sure as hell I was going to take it.

"How are you going to do it?" Adi asked. "He's scary and I've already tried. He won't listen."

"Well, look at me. I'm a tough guy. Probably in the top 5000 for toughest guys in this school. I'll set him straight. You don't have to worry about it."

"Okay, I just don't know how you're going to do it."

Bzzt.

The phone vibrating on the table caused Adi to jump once again, and it once again caused her knees to bump the table and wince in pain.

"Is it him?" I asked.

She nodded slowly, her eyes fixated on the cellphone that was now rumbling across the table in her direction—only to be stopped by my hand.

In one swift movement, I picked up the phone and answered the call.

"What the hell do you want? Do you have any idea what time it is?"

I went straight for the jugular.

Based on Adi's character, I couldn't even imagine her coming off as forcibly as I had, and I hoped that my unexpected attack would throw the caller off balance.

I mean, he was probably expecting a feeble-willed hello, right?

"What? Who is this? Where's Bernadette?" The voice that replied sounded surprised as well as deep and intimidating. I could feel myself shrinking ever so slightly behind the cellphone, but I held steady.

"Don't worry about that. I'm just here to tell you to leave her alone."

At that the voice laughed.

"Look, buddy. I don't know who you are or where you got those big balls of yours, but you better put her on the line right now."

"No, she doesn't want to talk to you anymore so lay off."

"Put her on now, asshole. Or else."

"Yeah, or else I'm going to kick your ass!" I shouted. "You better not show your face around here anymore. Adi's with me now so get lost!"

Spurred on by a sudden rush of adrenaline, I quickly cut the call before the voice could respond and slammed the phone on the table to emphasize the point.

"And that's that! Problem solved!"

Adi stared at me with wide eyes from across the table. It was as if she never would have expected me to do what I had very clearly just done.

Ah.

I couldn't help but notice that her eyes were the same exact shade as Yasmin's.

CHAPTER 24

After all the excitement, Adi's general demeanor became much more positive. She thanked me profusely and lavished me with all the praise and recognition that I didn't know that I needed or wanted. I felt like I'd done something right. And I was finally being rewarded for it. Not that I needed any physical or mental reward. Adi's warm smile was reward enough. It was a relief to see. I didn't know if my heart could have taken any more of that pained expression. It tugged on my heartstrings.

Having the weight lifted off her shoulders, she apologized for how she'd been such a terrible host for not offering me any sort of refreshments or food. Then she got to work putting tea on the stove. As was proper etiquette, I politely refused, but in a very Yasmin manner she brushed off my concern and told me to make myself comfortable while she had everything prepared.

I spent a few minutes twiddling my thumbs before she presented me with an old, chipped mug filled with the translucent brown liquid and urged me to drink it.

The mug was an interesting one.

It was shaped like an elephant, and its long trunk curved upwards acting as the handle. It even had two floppy ears embedded onto its surface. The cup was gray or at least I thought it used to be, but now it was severely discolored. Stains dotted the cylindrical surface along with hairline cracks that traveled through the ceramic like a series of tributaries. I was afraid one wrong tap might have caused the cup to explode, splashing me with a near boiling hot liquid, and ruining one of my only good pairs of jeans. But as fortune, or misfortune rather, would have it, I'd set my sights on the wrong danger and approached the situation the incorrect way.

And as a result, I paid the price for it.

Not watching where I placed my lips, I cut myself on the rim where there was a fracture the size of a quarter.

"Ouch!"

A small stream of blood started to run down my lip, intermingling with a tiny dribble of tea. I already didn't like how the tea tasted, but now that it mixed with my blood? It wasn't for me.

I'd been served tea at Yasmin's, and it tasted nothing like this. The quality was night and day. Black and white. Apples and oranges.

"I'm so sorry!" Adi chirped as she grabbed the tissue box from off the shelf and snatched the last remaining tissues. "Here, take these."

I was a bit embarrassed that she was fussing so much over such a minor cut, and even more embarrassed at how she watched me with the level of concern a neurosurgeon might give one of their patients.

"I'm sorry. I'm sorry. I'm sorry! After all the help you gave me, I'm still causing you trouble."

"I'm alright. Trust me. I've dealt with much worse," I said. "But how bad is it? Do I still look handsome, or should I give up on my modeling career?"

"I didn't know you modeled. If your entire career was ruined because of me, I don't know what I would do!"

She didn't get it. For some reason, Adi didn't seem to quite grasp the concept of sarcasm, which was basically my native tongue. Having to explain to her whenever I was joking or not was already getting tedious. I was either going to need to expend the effort to be more literal or—

Make my sarcasm so outlandish that there was no possible way she could mistake it for reality.

As far as options went, I'd have to go with the latter.

"Yes, I'm a model. My face is plastered on billboards all over the country, no, the world! I was voted 'People Magazine's Sexiest Man on Earth.' Most of my days are spent reading the trucks full of fan mail that I'm sent every day."

"That's amazing! I can totally see it. You're very handsome."

What?

She believed me? And even called me handsome at that.

I guess I needed to take it even further.

"Yes, thank you. I'm so handsome that there's even talk of the government cloning my DNA. In the not-so-distant future everyone's going to be able to have a clone of me!"

"You can bet that I'll be the first one in line to grab one. You're so helpful after all."

Still?

I'll take it even further!

"In the far-off future, everyone's going to end up looking like me! Men, women, children, everyone!"

"If everyone was as beautiful a person as you then I'm sure that all the world's problems would be solved. There would be no famine and no war."

I give up.

There was no winning against her.

What good was a comedian without an audience to entertain?

Looks like I'd have to be completely literal with her from here on out—if that was even possible for me.

I grabbed the mug and took a sip, careful to avoid the sharp edge of the rim this time around. All the while Adi continued to watch my movements. The awkwardness of the situation caused me to notice something.

"You're not going to drink any?"

"Oh, I will. Once you're finished."

"What? Why?"

She pointed to the mug that I was still holding underneath my nose.

"That's the only mug that I have."

"Urk!"

I restrained the sudden urge to spit my mouthful of tea all over her.

"What do you mean this is your only cup?!"

"I'm usually the only one who drinks the tea, so I didn't think I needed more than one cup."

"I mean, that makes sense, I guess, but don't you think it's a good idea to have some spares just in case it breaks, or you have guests?"

"I don't have many people who come over and it's a sturdy cup. I've had it for years."

"Still..."

To only have one single mug?

It didn't matter her reasoning, that wasn't very smart. And it begged the question—

"What about your other dinnerware and things? There's no way you only have one of.. everything..."

"No, that's correct. I only have one plate, one bowl, one fork, one spoon, and one knife."

"Ah, I see."

I didn't really see at all.

Her and Yasmin were both rich, right? If she wanted, Adi could have had a lot more than she did. She could have even lived in a better area too, closer to her sister. Yet judging by the way she was living now, you wouldn't have been able to tell.

"Anyways," Adi said, changing the subject, "I can't even begin to express how thankful I am for your help, Chris. I do mean that."

"Again, it was no problem. I heard you crying over the phone, so of course I was going to help. I needed to save the damsel in distress."

"Yes... I was in a great deal of distress." She looked down. "But it makes me wonder why you called in the first place."

"Oh, yeah. Right."

I had nearly forgotten. I'd come here for another purpose besides saving her.

"Actually, it's about your sister, Yasmin."

"Yasmin? Is everything okay?"

"Yeah, yeah, everything's great. I just wanted to invite you to a surprise party I'm throwing for her. One of her art pieces got accepted into this gallery show, so I was asking some people to come and see it on opening day."

"Really? That's amazing!" Adi's body perked up at the news and it even looked like she rose a few inches off the ground. However, her reaction was short-lived, as she sank back down almost immediately, settling into a much smaller position than she was previously in. "I'm proud of her."

"I am too. That's why I'm doing this in the first place. I think it'd be great if you could show up."

"Sorry, but I don't think that'd be a very good idea. I... think she hates me."

"What makes you think that?" It was the million-dollar question.

I had my suspicions, obviously. I had heard Yasmin's side of the story, but now it seemed like I was finally going to get some details from Adi. What secrets would she end up spilling about her and her sister's lives? I couldn't wait to find out.

There were two sides to every story as they say.

You needed to have the complete picture before you could draw an accurate conclusion. Of course, in the end, people tended to see whatever they wanted to see. The facts could be staring someone dead in the eyes and they could just choose to turn away or play dumb.

"I hurt her badly. She doesn't answer my texts or calls, and I can't even blame her for that."

"She still talks about you occasionally."

"She does?" Adi's shoulders rose again. "What does she say?"

"Uh, you sure you want to know?"

Adi nodded vigorously as if she was a human proportioned bobblehead.

"Well, she refers to you as the 'Brown-nosing Bitch,' and sometimes the 'Sellout Bitch.'"

"Oh." It looked like Adi was about to burst into tears. Drops of moisture pooled at the corners of her eyes, only held at bay by the few lashes that lined her lower eyelid. "She always did like her nicknames."

"Someone needs to teach her the difference between name calling and nicknaming."

"Yeah, that's true."

Adi grabbed another one of her crumbled tissues and dabbed at her eyes.

Why did I go out and say that? Even for me that was a dick move. But I was sure the root of the issue would be found in the origin of those nicknames or whatever the hell we were going to refer to them as. Usually, Yasmin's insults held some semblance of truth, that's why she used them. They made her feel clever. She'd even outright told me that once. But from what I could tell, Adi was a gentle girl, and those names didn't fit her in the slightest.

"Adi? You good? I'm sorry for bringing that up."

"No, I should be sorry. I deserve those names."

"I can't see how that's possible. I thought Yasmin was just being difficult like she usually is."

"Hah. That's the thing. She wasn't always so brash. And that's the reason she hates me. You see. We used to be very close. I'm sure she must have mentioned that we didn't have a great deal of money when we were younger. That meant that we had to get creative. So, we did everything together and shared everything. It wasn't much of a problem though because we were twins, after all. Me being the older one by a whole minute." Adi smiled, but it wasn't at me. It was directed to someone who wasn't there. "That means it was my responsibility to look after her and make sure she was okay.

"Due to our financial situation, our parents would always argue about money, and I saw how much of a toll the constant shouting and yelling had on Yasmin. I tried to interject whenever I could to stop them. However, that kind of thing isn't very easy for me to do—as you can tell. I wasn't very successful at dealing with our parents and I felt like I was failing at my role as a big sister. I eventually started to resent our financial situation as well; it made me feel like a failure that I was unable to hold our family together. It was my one responsibility. But then everything changed—"

"When the Fire Nation attacked?"

"What?"

"Uh, nothing, never mind. When your father won the lottery."

"Yes, and after that it seemed like our entire life changed just like that. Our parents no longer argued and instead of having to share everything—a room, a cup, clothes—we were both given our own things. I'll admit. It was nice not having to share for once and having all that new stuff to myself. I think I did enjoy the freedom and individuality I was given. It felt like I didn't have to watch Yasmin too closely any longer. However, even I could see that she didn't feel entirely the same way as our mother and father did. She'd come into my room whenever she had the chance, to sleep together, play, and just to talk. She'd much rather play with me and share a toy or a book with me than to be alone."

Yes.

Yasmin had said something of the sort.

Despite the arguing and the fights. Their family was much closer before. They enjoyed and were thankful for the simple things that kept them together. Even though money had pulled them out of their abject poverty, who was to say if their condition *actually* improved? It was more like the fundamental problems and hardships had just moved across town. Into a more affluent area. They exchanged one problem for another.

"For some reason though, even though I'm not sure why, my parents didn't like seeing that. They thought she was being ungrateful of our newfound fortune. That she was wasting what we had been given. Maybe now that they had seen what being rich was like, they didn't want to be reminded about how they used to live? I don't know. The main reason I'm telling you this is because, in a way, I felt the same way as them. Maybe not entirely. Maybe not as much as them, but I know... I know that a part of me, no matter how small or large, felt that. And it just so happened that our parents saw that too. I promise you that it wasn't supposed to be forever or even long term, but in order to convince Yasmin to change her mindset, our parents praised and gave me expensive gifts every chance they got, while only giving her what she needed."

"That's..."

Sad?

Terrible?

Messed up?

I'm not sure if there was even a turn of phrase that could describe that level of cruelty. I'd have to check the statute, but it might have even fallen under a cruel and unusual punishment, if not low-grade child abuse.

"Please don't misunderstand. My parents aren't bad people. They loved us. They loved her. That's why they wanted her to appreciate our blessings."

"Is that what they told you?"

"No... it's an assumption," Adi said. "But, anyway, I went along with it, their plan. In my mind it seemed like the easiest and fastest option to bring us all back together. Do you see what I'm trying to say? It was either changing Yasmin's mind or changing both of our parents' minds. That's how I rationalized things and it made it easier going forward. And adults *are* supposed to know better, right? At least more than us kids. I just didn't realize how much it was going to hurt Yasmin to do that."

"You saw that it was hurting her, and you still continued to do it?"

"I didn't see it, per se. She's good at hiding her innermost feelings—always has been. But I noticed her outward demeanor change. She started lashing out more. Screaming. Voicing her frustration. Cursing and calling people names. The names didn't used to be so nasty. Some were sweet and thoughtful. That's actually where 'Adi' came from. It's what she used to call me when we played when we were younger. She couldn't pronounce my name Bernadette for the longest time, and it just stuck."

What a turn of events.

Yasmin thought her family was rejecting her and flaunting their wealth to punish her. In reality, they thought she was missing out, and wanted to lure her to their side by forcing her to see the difference between poverty and wealthiness.

Of course, there wasn't any defense or excuse for Adi's actions. But her motives made sense. Somewhat. Enough for me to draw my own conclusions.

And what conclusions might they be?

Adi wasn't a bad person.

Adi regretted what she did. I heard it in the way that she spoke to me and described the events. She didn't mean to hurt her sister like she did. I think that sentiment was enough to warrant her deserving another chance.

"I made the wrong choice. There's no number of apologies I can give that can make her forgive me. But still... I just want things to go back to how they used to be."

How they used to be.

Back when they didn't have much money.

Back when they lived in a cramped apartment that looked like it was even too small for one.

Back when they had to share everything—clothes, bed, even their dinnerware.

Back when both sisters acted like sisters.

Things couldn't ever go back to exactly how they used to be, but at least their relationship could be rekindled.

"Come to Yasmin's surprise party then. Tell her what you just told me. She'll forgive you." I said it, of course, not knowing if it was true. I didn't know how Yasmin would take it. I didn't even know if I should be putting these two in the same room. Yasmin could very well end up burning the entire place down to the ground. However, what I did know was that sometimes you needed to say things with conviction. That's the only way people would put their faith in you. To be seen as a dependable person. I'd make things come true if I had to.

"Do you really think so?"

"Yeah, definitely."

Adi smiled.

"Yasmin is really lucky to have someone like you. I kind of feel a little jealous that I didn't keep you to myself."

"Well, like I said, they'll be cloning me sometime in the future."

"I can't wait."

Dang.

It was true what they said about women strolling into your life one after the other and flirting with you right after you started dating someone somewhat seriously.

It was just my luck. And it was way too convenient.

We chatted for about another fifteen minutes. I gave her the details and my plan for the surprise party. Adi seemed excited and hopeful now. Seeing her happy made me happy.

"Whelp, it's getting late, so I'm thinking that I might bounce on out of here," I said, standing up.

"Bounce? Like a ball?"

"Not this again!"

She giggled behind her hand.

"Sorry. I'll walk you out."

Adi stood up and led me to the door. She unlocked the deadbolt and we both walked outside—where the cold night air that I still wasn't fully used to nipped at my exposed skin.

And where—across the hallway—a large figure stood waiting.

"That's—!" Adi's voice wavered behind me.

A very large figure.

Male. From what I could tell of his angular features and short hair.

Not only did he stretch to the ceiling in his dark hoodie and jeans, but he also stretched outwards toward the walls of the hallway, large enough to block the path to the staircase like a sleeping Snorlax.

Of course, that wouldn't have been the best way to describe his appearance because he wasn't fat or sleeping. He didn't have a gut of any kind and I could tell that his body was shaped like an upside-down Dorito chip. A small waist that opened into wide, broad shoulders.

It was muscle. He obviously worked out.

Before I could admire his stunning physique any longer, his deep and menacing voice echoed towards me.

It sounded just like it had over the cellphone. Just clearer. And more threatening, especially now that I could see the face behind it. It wasn't just some disembodied voice. A person was saying these words to me.

Did I mention that he was very large?

"So here I am," he said. "Now, what was that about you kicking my ass?"

CHAPTER 25

You may not believe it if I told you, but I wasn't scared, even if I had plenty to be scared about.

For one, I had very limited fighting experience—next to zilch if I'm being honest. Most of my experience comes from watching professional wrestling and superhero movies as a kid and trying to mimic those moves on pillows and imaginary enemies and whatnot—hence, very limited. Most of those moves probably weren't even practical in real fights. Of course, as a kid, I didn't know what I was watching was fake. I thought it was as real as anything else, like Santa Claus and the Easter Bunny.

I even remember losing some of those imaginary fights too. I'd pretend that I'd be battered, close to death, laying on the battlefield. I'd be on my last legs, and someone would come and save me. And the role of my savior and hero usually ended up falling onto my exasperated, annoyed mother who just wanted me to clean up the huge mess that I'd made of the living room; the one she was tired of having to clean every day. She'd punch the empty air a few times, but to me, that nothingness could have been a vast array of robots, ninjas, or anal probing aliens.

Another reason I should have been scared was because this fellow was very large. Tall, dark, and gruesome as they say. It seemed like he could snap a twig like me with a look. Maybe if I knew how to fight, I could make up for the physical difference in our strength, but I didn't, so I was basically screwed.

Yet, despite the culmination of these factors, I was calm.

The reason I felt calm when my body's fight-or-flight responses should have triggered, was because I didn't think a fight was going to even happen—that there wasn't *actually* a real problem or threat towering over me. Street brawls over women were totally just a Hollywood construct added for the sole purpose of drama and entertainment. No rational human being would risk getting arrested for assault and battery. It was dumb.

Using this rationale as a sort of protective bubble, I walked in his direction. The second floor of Adi's apartment complex was an open balcony and off to the left, over the low wall, you could see the lights of passing cars and buildings oblivious to the confrontation that was playing out overhead.

"Don't do it, Chris, I don't think you can win," Adi whispered. She was trying to hide behind my back.

"I don't either, but I'm not going to fight him. I'm just going to talk. I'm sure that we can work something out if we communicate like a pair of reasonable adults."

"Amelia is many things, but I wouldn't describe him as reasonable."

"Wait. His name is Amelia? That huge, scary looking man?"

"Yeah, don't bring it up though. He kind of has a complex about that. Apparently, his parent's always wanted a girl. He usually goes by Mel."

"Ah, I see."

I had more questions about that, but I didn't have time to dwell on the issue as I'd closed the distance between the two of us.

Except for his initial statement, Amelia hadn't said another word. He just stood there smiling down on us like we were his prey. Therefore, in order to start the peaceful negotiations, I took it upon myself to begin the dialogue.

"Okay, look Amelia. I think we got off on the wrong foot. I don't want to have to get the authorities involved. Let's try and talk about th—"

"Shut up! Don't call me that!"

A right hook traveled in a long arc towards my cheek—which was the only possible explanation for why I was able to dodge it reflexively. I wouldn't have been fast enough otherwise.

My quick step backwards caused me to lose balance, but I recovered as his arm drew back in preparation for the next attack.

Something told me that he didn't throw that telegraphed punch out of the kindness of his heart, like someone might fire off a warning shot. No. From the way he grunted and twisted his torso, putting his whole body and weight behind the strike, I knew he was going all out. He had sacrificed speed for a more devastating blow.

What would have happened if that would have connected with my face?

Hopefully, I wouldn't have to find out.

"Chris, look out!"

The next strike came from the left. This one was faster, the aim truer, and I wasn't able to dodge it completely this time. Tracing the shortest path to its target, the blow nicked my shoulder. A sharp pain shot down my arm, but was quickly replaced by a fuzzy numbness.

"What're you doing?" I shouted. "Stop!"

Amelia took a step forward and I responded by jumping back, towing Adi along with me as I grabbed her wrist.

"Eek!"

I tugged harder than I probably should have, but I needed to create some more distance between Amelia and us.

I'm sorry. I usually don't handle women so roughly!

Within my grip, I could feel something shaking. Adi's wrist was trembling. Or maybe it wasn't her at all? It very well might have been me that was shaking. I couldn't tell. It wouldn't have been a stretch to assume as much. My heart rate was elevated now, and adrenaline was shooting through my veins. Both characteristics of the fight-or-flight response that had been absent just moments before were a little late—or maybe just right on time.

Was I being a fool for thinking things wouldn't end up this way? Devolving into senseless violence.

I mean, it wasn't very Hollywood at all!

This antagonist never gave his speech, no monologue, no real build up. Just an anticlimactic, unprovoked assault, unless you counted the earlier conversation over the phone as the lead up to our fight.

No.

That was wrong.

This wasn't a fight.

It shouldn't legally be called a fight.

If someone pitted a giant silverback gorilla against a puppy, you wouldn't call it a fight.

It was a massacre.

The result was nothing but inevitable.

And yet—

"Adi, get back!"

I shoved her behind me, but even then, she moved no more than a few steps away. Her body was stiff, but from my peripherals, I could see her slowly raise her hand out to me.

"Chris... you can't win."

She was right.

I couldn't.

And yet—

"Sometimes you still have to try!"

Amelia kicked off the ground and threw a wild haymaker at me.

In order to change things up, I raised my arm to block his strike, but it only made the difference in our strength more apparent. His punch crushed through my guard, sending shockwaves throughout my body and nearly knocking me off my feet and onto my ass.

What monstrous strength!

Blocking would be useless against Amelia. It hardly prevented any damage at all, and he'd eventually whittle me down if I resorted to it too heavily. It was doing nothing but delaying the inevitable and solidifying my defeat. If I hoped for the outcome to be any different, I had to do something else. I had to attack!

I threw a desperate punch with all my strength. There was no technique or strategy behind it, just the force of my body.

My fist connected with a wall of pure muscle where I had thought I'd be hitting soft flesh. I could feel my fingers crack under the pressure of my own blow, which had done more to me than to him. His body was not only built for offense, but defense as well.

Amelia snorted.

"Seriously?"

He sent another punch towards me before I could think of any response. I knew I had to dodge it, but I was too slow to react, and his blow landed in the pit of my stomach. My body immediately went limp in his hand as I felt the contents of my stomach sent up to my throat. It would have probably been an effective attack if I threw up all over him, better than my lousy attempt at a punch, but I held the acidic liquid down.

Amelia continued his relentless assault, not giving me any time to recover, as if I was no more than a punching bag to him. His fists were like steel. Strike after strike hit various parts of my body, each one momentarily causing me to black out. Through my daze, I did the only thing I could do and raised my arms to protect my head and face.

A sharp pain in my thigh buckled my knees.

While I had focused my defenses on my upper body, he'd taken the opportunity to strike my defenseless legs.

In my opinion, it was pointless; he didn't have to do that. Against me, every strike was an opportunity, an opening. He didn't have to resort to attacking my weak points to beat me. It was complete overkill.

Where was this rage and brutality coming from?

Through the building fog in my mind, I heard someone calling out behind me.

"Stop it! Don't hurt him!" Adi shouted.

The combination of punches stopped.

Amelia, who was grabbing the collar of my shirt, paused his attacks, giving me a brief second of reprieve. I was finally able to breathe, albeit barely. At this point, I was lapsing in and out of consciousness and their voices sounded as if they were coming from miles away. I could barely hear them over the sound of the persistent buzzing in my ears.

"You're leaving me for *this*?" Amelia shook me. "This pussy?"

"Please… stop. Leave him alone. I'll do whatever you want."

"You're damn right you will."

No.

I wanted to shout that out, but his grip was cutting off my airway.

She shouldn't go back to him. That was the wrong choice. I had to do whatever I could to stop it. Even if my previous punch had been useless, I still had to try. What I had wasn't a plan. It was much simpler than that. I'd just have to punch harder than I did before. Even if the result might be the same, I just had to punch harder.

It might have been a dick move, but while he was distracted with Adi, I delivered another strike; this time aimed squarely for his face.

"Unh?"

Amelia's head snapped back a few inches as I left my hand planted on his face. He looked back down at me over the top of my arm and frowned. He then released his own drawn fist, and though I couldn't see it myself, I was sure that my head snapped back further than just a few inches.

Amelia tossed me to the side, and I slid across the ground. But he wasn't done. He walked over and stomped on my chest.

One.

Two.

Three.

Four times.

Probably many times more, but I lost count after that. I was fading out of reality. I saw the light at the end of the tunnel.

To top it all off, as if to say he was finished, he directed a kick at my spine, knocking the wind out of me as I spasmed in pain. I hadn't felt such agony since my accident.

"And stay down," he spat. Satisfied with his work, he stepped over me and turned his attention to Adi.

Ugh.

He didn't have to tell me that.

I couldn't get up.

My body and the voice in my head was forcing me down. Didn't help that my legs were numb now. I could barely feel them.

It was over. The inevitable outcome that everyone predicted came to be. What was the point in the end? Did I even accomplish anything by fighting back? These were some of the thoughts crossing my mind as I lay there watching Amelia advance on Adi, who had backed herself into the corner.

In the end, I was just as useless as ever. Had I done the right thing? I didn't know. It seemed I didn't know a lot of things. I just felt like this was what I had to do. Was that a good enough reason? Adi needed me. She was miserable, trapped in a situation she couldn't get out of. I... just thought I could help. I didn't have to do anything, but I still chose to.

That's right, I didn't *have* to do anything. But neither did the people in my life who had hoisted me up, like I was their burden. Just dead weight. It wasn't too much to ask that I didn't want to be a burden all the time, right? It would have been nice to be seen as the dependable one occasionally.

However, the only way that could come to pass was if I stood up and did things. Take the lead. Be a perfect example. Not waiting to be led by the hand like a scared little boy and be told what I was doing was right or wrong. It had to be of my own volition. I needed to evaluate the situation and do what I could.

And right now, Adi needed me.

She was ready to rekindle her relationship with her sister.

I wanted to make sure that I saw that through.

I just needed to overcome a seemingly insurmountable obstacle. I was going to have to endure a lot more pain before this was over. I didn't know if my back was going to be able to handle it.

And yet, I still had to try.

Something told me that the source of the answer, and the path to my victory, was in Amelia's *why*. Despite being on the ground, I could stop him if I understood his *why*.

No rational human being would risk going to jail for assault and battery. But Amelia wasn't rational, was he? He swung, spoke, and acted like he had something to prove. He wasn't fighting me.

Something clicked.

Adi said he had a complex about his name.

Maybe growing up in a household that wanted a girl instead of a boy had caused him to act this way. That very household that wanted a girl so much that they even gave their newborn boy a female name.

What other things could his parents have done to emasculate him? To undermine his masculinity to the degree that he had to overcompensate in other ways to make up for it. Overly muscular body. Picking fights that he didn't need to pick. Controlling aspects of another person's life. It all culminated in a vicious circle.

He wasn't a girl, but he was named as such and probably treated as such. Seeing a name brings up a series of stereotypes and preconceived notions about the person or thing behind the name. This meant that people would already draw a conclusion about you before they'd even met you.

I didn't know for sure, but I could assume that he was made fun of for that name. Kids could be so cruel. At least most adults had the ability to filter their thoughts so as to not hurt others, but kids usually didn't have that restriction, and if they did, they didn't care. They said what they wanted. I knew that as well as anyone else did. The kids, mostly girls if I'm being honest, back in the ol' schoolyard made fun of me all the time when I showed any interest in them. They pointed and laughed in my face.

I could only imagine what they would have said about Amelia.

He was a boy, now a man, he wasn't a girl, and it seemed he wanted to make sure people understood that. And if they didn't, he was willing to force them to, whether it be through his body or actions.

"Ugh." I propped myself back up even though my spine was screaming at me to stay down.

I could sympathize with his motives, but I still couldn't forgive his actions. We all coped with pain and grief in different ways, like changing the way you choose to live your life, buying needless things to distract you, giving up something of yourself to survive, and even shutting out the people who care about you. Obviously, they're not all beneficial; some could even be seen as avoiding the issue entirely but taking your pain out on others should never be the choice that you choose.

That's why—

"Hey, Amelia! That is your name, right? It's very cutesy. I think it suits you perfectly."

I said those words as I rose from my position on the ground.

I was surprised I could even speak through the pain I was experiencing.

Amelia stopped in his tracks. He glared back at me over the top of his shoulder.

"What did you say?"

I'd taken everything a step further and shouted something I knew would rile him up. A string of words that would hit him where it hurt, that would pierce through his psyche. And, luckily, it had the effect that I wanted.

Only steps away from Adi's crumpled figure, Amelia turned completely around and stomped his way back towards me.

I was wobbling, but at least I was back on my feet now. That meant I wasn't completely defenseless, but I still wasn't able to move from my position. My legs wouldn't budge. It would only take one or two blows to put me down for good. Maybe even just a strong gust of wind.

Good thing winning the fight wasn't exactly the point.

At this moment, I'd succeeded in getting him away from Adi. Even if it was just for one second.

That was a win in my books.

From the beginning, this was all my fault anyway. She was in this situation because of me. I felt responsible for this, and I had told myself—promised myself—that I didn't want to be responsible for anyone's pain anymore because of my stupid choices.

My mom.

Zoey.

Adi.

In a very small way, I had righted one of my wrongs. Even if it was just for a second.

Amelia was now looming over me, and he pulled his fist back behind his head as if to charge up his final attack.

Hah.

It was kind of funny though.

I didn't know why, but for some reason, he didn't seem that large to me anymore. Not that it mattered. My arms were dead weight at this point. I couldn't lift them to defend myself.

"What did you say again?" he repeated. "I couldn't hear you."

I racked my brain trying to think of something even wittier to say, but my head was swimming with a lot of different thoughts, so I settled on just repeating myself. You couldn't beat simplicity after all.

"You hit like a girl."

Hah.

I had my last laugh.

I closed my eyes and waited for the blow to come—

"I fucking hate when people say that."

A voice said from behind me.

One that I recognized all too well. Even in this moment, it still managed to sound both bored and irritated at the same time.

I turned my head over my shoulder just in time to see a roundhouse kick flying over my head.

Yasmin?!

The lightning fast kick that connected with Amelia's chin was followed by a loud crack like thunder. Despite the difference in size, Yasmin still managed to stretch her leg to its utmost limit in order to reach that impossible height.

He staggered back holding his jaw.

Judging by his expression, Amelia was just as hurt by the blow as he was surprised.

"What?" he bellowed.

Yasmin held her fighting stance but glared down at me.

"You look like shit."

"Yeah, kind of," I choked out.

I honestly couldn't believe Yasmin was here. There were so many things I wanted to ask her. Why? How?

She must have read my expression because she answered my questions.

"That pea brained loser Brad said something was happening to my sister. He also said that you'd gone off to help her, so I called you to ask what was going on," Yasmin explained. "But you wouldn't pick up your damn phone. No one ignores me."

"Uh..."

Come on! Even in this situation she felt the need to berate me. I'm bleeding here. In pain. Barely able to stand. Would it kill you to give me a break?

Yasmin's frown softened ever so slightly.

"I'm sorry it took me so long though. This place was all the way across town, so I ordered an rideshare service, and you know how long it takes for them to come sometimes. Probably would have been faster if I just ran over here. I'm thinking I could have gotten here about five minutes earlier at least. Then maybe you wouldn't have been slapped around so much. By the way, One-Eyed Joe says hello."

Amelia, who had recovered from Yasmin's blow, took a step forward in our direction.

"Who are you?!" Amelia asked.

"Yasmin!" Adi yelled from down the hall. At the sight of her sister, she had snapped out of her daze. One of her hands was clutched firmly over her chest.

"Adi!" Yasmin's eyes flicked to Adi before focusing back on Amelia who was still advancing. "What did you do to her? I swear, if you hurt her!"

Amelia bared his teeth in a chilling smile. They were red and stained with blood.

"Trust me, bitch. It's going to be nothing compared to what I'm about to do to you."

Yasmin's second kick smashed right into Amelia's cheek bone.

It almost looked like his head swiveled all the way around.

Her kick was so fast it was impossible to see coming. And, therefore, it must have been impossible to block. Compared to the kicks I'd see her practice on her punching bag or even throw at me, these were on another level. Had she been holding back in our fights? What a terrifying thought. It reminded me of fighting games I've played. Being hit by one of her stray light kicks was already painful enough. I couldn't even imagine the force behind one of her heavy kicks.

In a roar of pain, Amelia began flailing his arms wildly with no target in mind. He was simply trying to destroy whatever was in his path. One of these strikes grazed my ear and I winced in pain.

"That's enough!" Yasmin yelled. She launched a set of rapid-fire kicks at Amelia, each one with enough power to stagger him and push him back. Face, stomach, arm, shoulder. No target was spared from her barrage. She even sent some blows under the belt, going against all conventional codes of ethics and honor that people would usually expect out of a fight. She must have been angry. The small fires that I usually saw lit behind her eyes were now a set of raging infernos.

The ground shook as Amelia fell to his knees under Yasmin's rain of blows. He was the one that was wobbling now, and I half expected a deep voice to come out of nowhere and tell us to, "Finish Him!" but cool as that may have been, it was only Yasmin who had some final words.

"Hey, listen to me." She slapped his face to snap him out of his stunned state before continuing. "You think this is bad? Well, think again. I wasn't even trying. This was not even a fraction of my true power. And if you have any intelligence at all, that should scare you. Do you understand what I'm saying?"

Amelia blinked.

"Now I better not catch you around here anymore," she finished.

"Or... else... what? I'll be back. You can count on that. I'm not through with any of you."

Yasmin frowned. "How boring."

Yasmin turned back around to face me. She had on her denim short shorts and a white crop top underneath a red plaid flannel shirt. Not necessarily weather-appropriate clothing, but she must not have thought to change before coming. Her eyes traveled up my body and lingered an extra second or two on my face. She gave me a smile.

In a fraction of a second, Yasmin's body twisted around, and she performed a spinning kick on Amelia that sent him flying. It was magnificent. A real sight to behold. The way his back arched as he traveled into the air was beautiful enough to bring a tear to my eye. He got some serious hang time. If not for the wall that he crashed into which caused him to crumble in a heap at Adi's feet, it wouldn't have surprised me if he had been able to soar across the entire country. I wasn't exaggerating. He had blasted off.

Yasmin nodded, looking at me over her shoulder this time.

"Well, Chris? What was that about hitting like a girl?"

CHAPTER 26

After the conclusion of our battle with Amelia, we did end up calling the authorities. They hauled him away to wherever they take people like that. It could have been the campus police station. I wouldn't have even been surprised if it was the hospital after what Yasmin had done to him. But it was all speculation. I didn't know nor care. After we answered some questions and declined all medical services, we headed back into Adi's apartment like a party of adventurers who had survived some great ordeal.

Though Yasmin talked a big game, saying things like she wasn't even trying or that she only used a fraction of her power, somehow, I knew that the situation had shook her up just as much as the rest of us. You don't see two people you care about, who were hurt physically and mentally, and come out completely unscathed.

But anyway, yes, I said that Yasmin had witnessed *two* people she cared about in distress. And she *did* care about her sister. No matter how nonchalant and aloof she played it, she did.

It just took them a while to speak to each other.

The tension was as palpable as can be, so much so that even I could feel its overwhelming pressure. Together they supported me and awkwardly laid me down on Adi's bed, but like magnets of the same polarity, their eyes seemed unable to meet, clearly bouncing around each other or staying glued upon me who watched on in awe.

What were they doing?

It was so obvious. And because it was so obvious it was painful to watch.

One of you should say something!

Adi where was that confidence from before? You were eager to rekindle things, right?

And Yasmin—where was that smart mouth that said whatever it wanted?

So desperate to avoid the subject, they even spoke to me in turns, so they didn't have to talk to each other. It was like we weren't all in the room at the same time. Whenever one of them spoke to me, it was just the two of us. The sister who remained silent would become an ephemeral presence or maybe some inanimate object you didn't pay much mind to. Like a lamp.

"How are you feeling now, Chris?" Adi said. She was kneeling by the bedside, her body angled as far away from Yasmin as possible.

"I'm good. I feel like a million bucks."

"A million bucks? That's an awfully large amount of deer to be feeling."

"Never mind. I suddenly feel worse."

And then Yasmin's turn.

"Hey," she said.

"Yeah?"

"What were you thinking? Why did you try and fight that guy?"

"It wasn't my first option. I had originally assumed we could just flip a coin. Leave it all to chance, you know? Heads—he leaves. Tails—I leave."

"Oh, yeah? What happened to that? Would have spared you the bruises."

"None of us had a coin."

Such pointless exchanges went on for almost half an hour. Don't get me wrong—I liked them, at first. It showed they cared about me enough to ask and make sure I was okay and whatnot. But, in the end, I was getting annoyed. How many bushes could they beat around? They were literally scraping the bottom of the barrel to find topics to talk about.

"Is that a new haircut?" Yasmin asked.

"No. Same hair I've had all year."

"Hm." She stared at my scalp for a couple of seconds. "Are you sure?"

"Yes, I'm sure! It's my hair! Why wouldn't I know when it was last cut?"

And now Adi.

"Chris, if you don't mind, can I ask you a question? It's kind of important."

"Sure, sure. Ask away."

"What's your opinion on the financial outlook of the United States in the next decade?"

"That *is* an important question! Very important! But even if I said it was okay, is now the time to be asking something like that?!"

"Oh, sorry. It was on my homework assignment. I'll just skip it for now and come back to it later."

I had no idea where to even begin answering. She should ask her professor or consult some online journals if she wanted to know that badly.

But enough of this!

Clearly, if anything was to progress, I was going to have to mediate between these two numbskulls before I got any more frustrated. These conversations were getting me heated and I suddenly noticed how dry my mouth was. All this talking had made me thirsty.

I cleared my throat.

"Adi, could you grab me some water, please?"

"Yes, of course."

For the first time since we had entered, Adi stood up and walked a couple feet into the kitchen. I noticed Yasmin side-eyeing Adi's movement, still deciding not to look directly at her.

There was the sound of clanking and running water, and a second later, Adi returned holding that elephant-shaped mug that I had cut my lip on. She wasn't kidding when she said that was her only cup. She must have had to wash it first before filling it with water.

While Adi was walking towards us, she held a hand underneath the mug in order to catch any stray droplets as the water sloshed against the sides.

"Here you go," Adi said, making a movement to hand me the cup.

"Thanks."

I reached out to grab it.

"Is—Is that?"

From Adi's left, near the foot of the bed where she had been the whole time, Yasmin spoke. Her eyes fixated on the outstretched mug that her sister was still holding as if it were on display.

"Is that our old mug?" Yasmin finished.

"Yes, yes, it is."

"Can I see it?"

Adi nodded and held out the cup to Yasmin, who carefully grabbed it from her hands.

Yasmin studied the mug. She traced her fingers over the design, following the elephant trunk-shaped handle up to the rim and around, stopping at the chipped edge. A smile came across her face.

"Isn't this from when I accidentally dropped it? It was that one day during winter when mom and dad had stepped out to try and buy more blankets because it was cold."

"Yes, it was."

Yasmin's gaze stayed fixated on the mug for another couple of seconds before she looked up at her sister and both of their eyes finally met. They were twins, but Yasmin was still noticeably shorter than her sister. While Adi was more mature and developed for lack of a better word, Yasmin was smaller and looked much younger than she was. That stark contrast didn't accurately reflect the single minute difference in time between their births.

Both were finally acknowledging each other.

It had taken a while—years even, but it was finally happening.

"Dad told us before he went out not to touch anything and to just lay in bed," Adi said. "They still didn't completely trust us to be home alone, but both of us were feeling under the weather."

"Yeah, I remember," Yasmin said. "Hah. But I still wanted some of that tea, so I decided to do it myself. When I was carrying it, some of the boiling liquid splashed on me and I got startled."

Adi laughed. A tear was forming at the corner of her eye, which she wiped away with her sleeve. "You dropped the cup and the water spilled over everything. Mom and Dad were so angry. I thought he'd never stop yelling."

"But you covered for me."

There was a moment of silence.

"Mm-hmm. Of course. You are my little sister after all. But it looks like you're the one protecting me now."

"Yeah." Yasmin looked down into the mug and swirled the water around.

Adi took a deep breath. She looked at me, and I nodded my head slightly.

"Yasmin, I—" She stumbled over her words but quickly recovered. Tears instantly replaced the ones she continued to wipe away. "I'm sorry."

She did it.

Adi did what she had wanted to do all along.

She apologized.

It was years in the making.

Whether or not this would be the last one between sisters was another issue entirely.

And Yasmin's long-awaited response?

"You're a bitch."

What the hell? How cruel! How brutal and cold-hearted!

"But... let's go back to how things used to be," Yasmin finished with a smile.

Adi chuckled through her tears.

"Yes, I couldn't want anything more."

The two sisters met in an embrace. It was awkward and clumsy. They hadn't done it in a while and they didn't know where to put their arms or where to grab onto, but it was heartwarming, nonetheless.

"By the way," Yasmin muttered from her position nuzzled into Adi's chest, "you don't happen to have any of that old tea Mom and Dad used to buy would you? I forgot the name of it."

"I do. I'll put some on now."

At that moment, they both walked over to the stove, carrying with them the elephant-shaped mug and a conversation between sisters.

Even though I was still thirsty, I decided not to speak up.

I didn't want to risk interrupting their tender moment.

* * *

"Owie!"

"Hold still, you idiot!"

"Don't wanna!"

"What are you? Five? Do I have to knock you out too? To get you to stop moving? Trust me I will."

"I'm four and three quarters, actually," I said, dodging Yasmin's hand like it was the head of a looming cobra. And please. You couldn't even if you tried. I'd beat your ass, in a non-domestic-violence kind of way."

"It looked like you were getting your ass beat plenty before I showed up."

About an hour later.

We were sitting on Yasmin's couch back at her apartment. Littered around amongst the random assortment of objects were some gauze strips, bandages, and other first-aid paraphernalia stuff that I couldn't pronounce or didn't know the name too. If it wasn't obvious, she was trying to treat my wounds, but whether it was because she was inexperienced or she was doing something wrong, it wasn't going well. I don't want to sound like a baby, but it hurt. Every time she dabbed my forehead with one of her little cotton swabs, that burning sensation made me want to curse up a storm.

It was around two in the morning now, and the fatigue, soreness, and plethora of bruises that splotched my body was taking full effect. I would have done anything to be laying in my warm bed right now counting sheep, but Yasmin was having none of that. She practically forced me to come back here in order to make sure I was okay. And I was. For the most part. My lower back still hurt from that kick, and my face was swollen like I had a severe allergic reaction to a bee sting, but besides that, I was a-okay.

"Ouch! Go easy, will you!"

"I haven't even touched you yet."

"You're clearly touching me! I'm looking right at you!"

"Oh, no. He must have gotten hit on the head hard. Possibly even a concussion. He's hallucinating."

"I'm not hallucinating at all! Stop trying to make me sound like I'm crazy when I'm not! And who are you talking to?"

"Chris, it's just you and me in this room. There's no one else. Are you sure you're okay? You're acting crazy."

"You tricked me!"

And you're the one who acts crazy most of the time!

"The sooner you hold still the sooner I'll be finished!" she yelled.

"That's what you've been saying for the past fifteen minutes!"

"Okay, then just one more bruise. Let me dab just one more."

"That's what you've been saying for the past fifteen bruises!"

"Is that my fault? You've yet to stay still at all!"

"Yeah, it is your fault. It shouldn't be burning this much. Do you even know what you're doing with that thing?"

"That's what she said," Yasmin shot back.

"Can we please not resort to jokes from the early 2000s? And plus, I have no idea how to interpret that in this context!"

Was a woman even supposed to use that joke?

It was rare to see Yasmin so gung ho about trying to patch me up. *Caring* would never have been the first word I'd pick to describe her. She did care about things, I couldn't deny that. But what she cared about was more sinister in nature. Namely, Yasmin cared to revel in my pain and misfortune. Whenever I stubbed my toe on the corner of a coffee table or bonked my head on a branch, she'd laugh in the face of my pain and tell me something along the lines of "Suck it up, buttercup!" like some grade school girl who stumbled upon the magic of rhyme schemes.

In a surprise attack, Yasmin's hand juked the arm I had propped up in defense and shot straight towards my face. However,It managed to swipe the cotton ball out of her hand before it made contact with its target. It flew through the air and floated down slowly, landing on a pile of soiled clothes.

"Denied," I said.

Yasmin's swatted hand hung in the air above her head for a full five seconds. She looked at me and frowned.

"Fine. Last time I ever do anything nice for you."

"That was basically the first time you've ever done anything nice for me."

"Fuck you." She thought for a moment. "I gave you a massage that one time."

Ah. She did. After the Mona thing. My back was hurting, much like it is now, and she offered to massage it. That was nice.

"Alright, one thing. You did one nice thing for me."

"I let you kiss me."

"You make it sound like you did me a favor! And you asked me to do it! Twice even!"

"You should be grateful that someone like you was even able to kiss such a fair, lovely maiden like myself."

Setting aside that she referred to me as "someone like you," which is almost always used in a negative context, the girl in front of me had referred to herself as a fair, lovely maiden. The maiden bit was arguable at best, but fair and lovely? Not even close.

She was cute though.

And those short shorts did show off her tight calves.

Not that I was staring.

"I'm not even going into why that's fundamentally wrong." I sighed. "I know you're stubborn, but I'm just curious why you're more adamant than usual right now. I'm good. Perfect." I raised my arm up but my involuntary wince of pain betrayed me. "See? Perfect."

Yasmin grabbed another cotton ball from her first-aid kit and squished it between her index finger and thumb.

"It's obvious," she said. "I shouldn't have to tell you."

Ugh. Not this.

Could someone explain to me why women always play this game? The whole, "I shouldn't have to tell you" thing. Or the "I'm mad because you don't know why I'm mad," shtick. Sometimes a guy literally has no idea what's wrong. I'm not a mind reader. I'm dumb. You have to tell me things directly or else I won't get it.

"Yasmin, why the long face? If you really want to pretend to be a nurse or whatever—then I won't stop you. I was just being difficult. I'm sorry. I didn't want you fussing over me too much. Being a burden makes me feel uncomfortable."

"That's it. You just said it," Yasmin said. "I told you. I told you that you'd end up getting hurt if you kept butting into other people's business."

I sat there in silence.

"I'm not saying that I'm not thankful for you helping my sister. I am. I truly am. In a way, this was my fault too. All your bruises and the pain you experienced. If I had talked to my sister sooner and answered her texts, I probably would have been able to save her myself a long time ago. But I was too stubborn. I was still carrying all that resentment. I should have just let it go and moved on. I don't know why I didn't. I just... don't know. I hate it. But just trying to do right by you makes me feel better. So please, let me do this."

As if asking my permission.

As if pleading.

Ah.

So that's why.

She was blaming herself, much like how I was blaming myself too. Though I felt like I was *more* at fault, seeing as I basically told Adi to stay in that relationship without knowing all the details. I knew it wasn't a dick-measuring contest, but still.

"Fine, fine," I said. "Go ahead. I won't stop you. Just go slow. And be gentle too."

In a very uncharacteristic way, Yasmin cheered and got back to work, and I begrudgingly resisted the urge to wince in pain every time she pressed down on the button-like welts on my face. You couldn't blame me though. It was a completely human reflex. It would be more worrisome if I didn't flinch or wince at all.

"Good, I'm going to make sure you're in tip-top shape," she said as if she might have been preparing me for a dog show.

She leaned closer to me until our faces were mere inches apart. We hadn't kissed since the other day and it was my very desire to do it again that welcomed it.

"Uh, why's that?"

"To see the art gallery exhibit. It's next week."

"Oh, I completely forgot about that," I lied.

"You're going to be there, right?" Her question came out soft.

"I'll have to check my schedule. I'm a busy guy, you know."

"Oh, okay..."

Urk.

Something just kicked me in the groin of my heart.

Was that disappointment I heard? And was she pouting too?! She was! Her bottom lip was sticking out so far I thought it was scraping the floor, collecting dirt like a dustpan.

Resist it, Chris. It'll result in a bigger payoff later when you surprise her with everyone else. Do not succumb.

I failed.

"I'll be there."

It just hurt me too much to see Yasmin so disappointed. As long as I was around, I never wanted to see her that way. Whether it be through my hilarious jokes or my sporadic idiocy, I wanted to see her smile and laugh, hopefully not entirely at my expense, but I'd take what I could get.

"Really?" She perked up again. "I mean you don't have to, if you don't want to."

Which is it, woman? What's with all the mixed signals? Your words are saying one thing and your body is saying another.

"I'll be there. I want to."

"That... makes me happy to hear."

Yasmin wrapped her arms around me and rested her head on my chest. I wondered if she could feel how fast my heart was beating at that moment? It couldn't have been comfortable for her.

"You promise?" Yasmin said.

"Pinkie promise. I cross my heart and hope to die. I swear on my mother and my unborn children. I wouldn't miss it for the entire world." I grabbed her pinkie with my own and gave it a shake.

"Seriously? Even if the world was ending?"

"Yup. The ending of the world would have to wait until after the gallery show. I'd tell the big man upstairs to postpone his business because there was something more important that I needed to do."

"That's so stupid. You're dumb," she said, her voice muffled. "But thanks."

"No problem."

I tightened my embrace, and she sighed.

"After getting my hopes up this much, you better be there. I'll never forgive you if you don't show up."

"Yeah, yeah, yeah. Whatever you say."

"I'm serious. You can forget about dying because I'll make sure you experience a fate worse than death."

Yasmin had a real scary way of turning heartfelt and romantic moments into threats of violence. But—I liked that part about her. What did that say about me?

Seeing the perfect opportunity right before my eyes and spurred on by a tugging in my heart, I took her chin in my fingers and tilted her head upwards. I then leaned forward and kissed her. Yasmin melted into my arms—my body, and it felt as if we became one.

It was a bold move on my part, but my body moved on its own.

After a long moment that ended up feeling like only a second—I was the first to pull back. Not because I wanted to. I didn't. I wouldn't have complained if we stayed like that for another hour, but I needed to breathe.

"How's that for an answer?" I said with a grin.

"Better..."

I won't bore you with the rest of the details, but I ended up staying the night. It was actually something of a blessing if I was being completely honest. Her bed felt much better than mine. It probably had something to do with the thread count.

CHAPTER 27

"So, uh, I think I really like this girl, Mia."

I said those words from my position in the leather chair directly across from her. It took me a lot of courage to come out and say it like that. Actually, it'd be more appropriate to say that I blurted it out in a stream of word vomit, mostly due to my anxiety. I'd been thinking about the wording all morning and the type of response that I might get once I finally told Mia. Was she going to be surprised? Worried? Angry? I didn't know. And the feeling of not knowing went hand-in-hand with the feeling of unease from not knowing.

The thing that kept me going was that there was a mutual trust and bond between two individuals that share the difficult things. And I'd already shared a lot of the difficult things with her, so this shouldn't have been hard to do.

But why did it feel like I was a teenage boy after he told his mom that he'd just gotten his girlfriend pregnant?

Mia didn't respond immediately. She just sat there looking at me through the rims of her large frame glasses that were about twenty years out of style if I had to guesstimate. Along with the row of neatly trimmed bangs that fell over her forehead, the frames did a good job of hiding her eyebrows and masking her expression. I couldn't tell what she was thinking.

"Yasmin? And please address me as Mrs. Lee."

"Yeah, Yasmin."

"I see."

At this point, I'd been visiting Mia for around half a year. Obviously, the first couple months were rocky, and it took me everything not to convince her to report my accident to the relevant authorities. Mia wasn't even a psychiatrist or therapist or anything. She just cared about me. She didn't want to see me fall into the same situation twice. Back then I was required to visit her more frequently. I had to check in with her at least three times a week to let her know how I was feeling. It was mandatory as were the terms of our agreement. However, now that I'd been doing better, she'd eased up on me. But I always tried to make time to meet her whenever I could. She was my Mom away from home.

"How do you feel about it?" she asked.

"It feels strange. Different even. I know I've been in a relationship before, but this time around, I don't know, I just feel... different."

"So, to put it in a not so nice way, the feelings that you experience with Yasmin are different than Zoey, I presume."

"Yeah, I guess you could put it that way."

"Golly," Mia said, rearranging and straightening a pile of papers on her desk. "How often do you still think about Zoey or reminisce about your time with her?"

A direct attack.

Had she wanted to ask this from the beginning?

"On occasion. Not as much as before—but somehow, I still do. Usually in a comparison to Yasmin. How they move, talk, and... other things."

I decided to leave it at that. Hopefully, Mia would get the idea. I didn't want to elaborate any further.

"That doesn't seem very healthy at all—comparing the two that is. In my opinion, it sounds as if you aren't completely over Zoey yet and are trying to see bits of her in Yasmin."

"Possibly."

Possibly.

More like probably.

Zoey still found ways to creep into my mind, forcing her way out of the basement of my deep subconscious. Seeing her smile in someone else. The flick of blonde hair in the crowd. The glint of her eyes in a window reflection. Her hurt voice that haunted my dreams.

"Not to reduce and trivialize your experiences down to words on a page, but this situation comes up quite often in my novels that I adore so much." Mia gestured to the shelf of old hardcover tomes, each one the size of a brick.

"And what ends up happening?"

"Hmm. Mostly they end up staying with the new man or woman in their life—the main love interest. Through their experiences together, the protagonist learns to let go of his past. Or something along those lines." She repositioned her glasses on the bridge of her nose.

"Sounds a little cliche," I said. "Why read if you know what's going to happen next?"

"I know they're a bit cliche, but much of the fun is the reasoning and events that led up to that decision. The epiphany that leads the protagonist to make the right choice in those circumstances."

The right choice, huh?

As I've been saying, I don't know anything about that.

I'm just going with the flow, as they say.

And my main goal right now was just focusing on not screwing things up.

"I'm over Zoey. I'm ready to let go and put my failures behind me. Yasmin is the one I want to be with right now."

I think.

I kept those last two words to myself.

Mia nodded. "I very much hope so. As long as you know what you want, that's all that really matters. And, by the way, what time are we meeting again? And at what location?"

"It's the coffee shop a block away from the gallery. You know, the one close to the main gates of the campus. The gallery opens at 11:00 a.m., so I'm thinking we'll meet around 10:30."

I'd already planned everything to a tee and notified all the relevant parties. It wasn't a big group or anything, just a couple familiar faces. I even got the opportunity to ask One-eyed Joe to stop by. He was excited to hear that the "beautiful couple" was still going strong.

"Splendid. I'm excited." Mia bounced in her seat.

"Me too."

"Good," she reiterated. "But now that we've taken care of all the fun stuff. Let's get to the nitty gritty, shall we? There's still the issue of your future, young man. With all the shenanigans you've been up to, you haven't been giving it much thought at all, have you?"

"Actually, I have."

"Seriously? I'm surprised. Okay then, Christian. Where do you see yourself five years from now? In other words, what would you like to be after you graduate college?"

I thought for a moment.

"A dependable person."

CHAPTER 28

"And that should do it."

I just finished going over my checklist one last time before I went to sleep.

My clothes were laid out. So were my wallet and my keys. Everything was ready to go. There would be no problems at all. I was prepared for any circumstance.

Tomorrow was Yasmin's big day.

Hah.

It was funny that I was the nervous one. Though I didn't have a reason to be, the jitters were keeping me awake. I wasn't sleepy at all, like a kid the night before his field trip. But I knew it would be a good idea for me to try and get to sleep. I didn't want to wake up cranky.

I climbed into bed and grabbed my phone. The alarms were correctly set, I'd made sure of it. There would be no stupid mistakes tonight.

I reached over to my table and flipped the light switch off before shutting my eyes.

...

......

Ugh.

I couldn't sleep.

I tossed and turned, trying to reposition myself in the most comfortable way, but it was a futile endeavor. After a minute, I eventually landed back in my starting position—straight on my back.

I couldn't place my finger on it.

It was a nagging feeling in my gut. It was telling me to do something.

If Brad was here, I would have gone over the plan with him again. Just to make sure. But he happened to be out on another one of his nightly rendezvous, so I was left to wallow by myself as usual.

I pulled out my phone again. In the darkness of the room, the blinding light from the screen illuminated my face in a white glow. I had to wait a couple of seconds for my eyes to adjust, but once they did, I started aimlessly surfing the web, hoping in part that I'd eventually get tired enough to fall asleep. But a whole fifteen minutes passed, and nothing changed.

The internet was too mentally stimulating; if I wanted to fall asleep, I had to do something boring. At that, I started checking my school email and looking at all the assignments I had coming up for my classes. When that didn't work, I went through my text messages to see if I had forgotten to respond to someone. Everything looked good though. Everyone in the "Yasmin Surprise Crew" group chat had confirmed that they were attending and that we'd meet at 10:30 sharp, so it wasn't that.

What was it then?

I wasn't forgetting anything, or at least, I didn't remember if I had.

Not knowing what to do, I mindlessly scrolled through my phone until I stopped on a familiar name. A name that I still had saved in my contacts.

Zoey.

It'd been a while... Since we talked. Since everything happened.

We were childhood friends. People had said we were inseparable. Back then I never would have believed it if someone told me this was how things would have ended up between us.

Since we'd met this was without a doubt the longest period of time we'd gone without talking to each other–or seeing each other.

Hmm.

But perhaps it was time to end that. Maybe it was time for me to reach out again.

A part of me was saying that I shouldn't, but the other side was saying that it was something I had to do. This was a long time coming, after all. I'd wanted to do this forever. I just wasn't ready before.

Not wasting another second, I typed out and erased about ten different messages before settling on one that I liked.

I wasn't the same person I was a few months ago. Maybe I still couldn't live up to her image, but I was much closer now. Thanks to Yasmin and everyone else supporting me, I believed I could at least see Zoey's back in the distance.

I hit send.

And staring at my phone, I patiently waited for her response.

CHAPTER 29

A buzzing at my bedside woke me up.

I rubbed the grogginess out of my eyes with one hand and reached for my phone with the other. I was having more trouble getting up than I was used to. My entire body felt like lead.

Hm?

The light peeking in from my window was unusually bright.

What time was it?

It couldn't have been that late, otherwise my ten alarms would have notified me as well as the entire building.

I glanced at the screen of my phone where, surprisingly, a handful of messages were waiting for me.

But that wasn't what I was focusing on.

No.

My eyes were glued to the time at the top of my screen that read 10:40.

CHAPTER 30

"Shit! No. No. No!"

Despite my best efforts and the hours of preparation, I was running late. Both figuratively and literally. On the day that the gallery was to open no less. The most important of days.

It felt like the entire world was standing in my way, trying to prevent me from getting to my destination on time. But I knew that wasn't entirely true, even if I didn't want to admit it.

This was my fault.

I'd slept through the alarms I'd so painstakingly set—all ten of them.

An ironically human error, but an error nonetheless.

I bet roosters never had this problem.

It was 10:40 a.m. when I rolled out of bed. My first thought was that my eyes were playing tricks on me. I couldn't believe it. But no matter how hard I rubbed them, the numbers didn't change.

Until they did.

It was now 10:41 a.m.

In a weird way, I was just thankful that I woke up at all. I don't remember what time it was when I finally fell asleep. All I remember was that I was staring at my phone, waiting for Zoey's response. The response that never came. It was already late when I sent it too. Why did I think that she'd get back to me so soon?

It was stupid of me.

I was so stupid!

I ran around my room, hastily trying to get ready. You're supposed to expect the unexpected as they say, but this was way too unexpected. If it wasn't thanks to that text notification, I'd still be asleep.

The message was from Yasmin.

I'm actually a little nervous so hurry up and get here so you can keep me company.

It was such a vulnerable-sounding message I almost thought it wasn't from her.

Yasmin even threw in the crying face emoji for good measure. Something even more out of character. Something I could never picture her doing without vomiting.

I'll be there, I replied before setting my phone back down.

I cannot be late. After all my big talk, a punishment worse than death would have been warranted.

I lifted my arm and braved a whiff of my odor. It was passable—I didn't have the time to take a shower anyway. I rubbed my stick of deodorant over my armpit a couple extra times for good measure before throwing on the clothes I'd prepared the night before—jeans, white tee shirt, and a blue flannel—and bolting out the door. I jumped down the steps three at a time and found myself in the lobby in under ten seconds. A new record.

If I kept this pace up, I'd make it just in time. It'll be like I didn't just wake up ten minutes ago. Just so long as Timmy hadn't fallen down the old well, I'd be able to make it.

Down in the lobby, I had to beeline through a random assortment of furniture strewn about as if it was a yard sale. On the street sat a large white moving van. Cardboard boxes were stacked up beside it.

Was someone moving in?

It didn't matter.

I had to hurry!

Lumbering towards me dangerously was a guy that looked around my age, struggling to move a two-seater couch all on his own. It was obviously way too heavy for him, and he was teetering from side-to-side, nearly colliding with pedestrians who cursed at him, but were too busy to help.

"Hey… can someone… give me… a hand here?"

The guy suddenly swerved in my direction, but I was able to dodge him and grab the opposite side of the couch, balancing it out in the process. Good thing that I did too. The couch was just about to squash a small child into paste all over the wall.

"Thanks," the guy said.

"No problem," I responded hastily.

"If… you aren't… too busy, could you… actually help me… move it up… to the sixth floor?" he said through wheezes.

"I'm actually kind of running a little late."

More than just a little now.

"This… is the only thing… I can't handle… on my own. It won't take long. We'll use the elevator."

Balancing the couch with my knee, I used one hand to pull out my phone and glance at the time.

There was still time.

This person needed my help and I couldn't leave him. It sounded like he was about to pass out from physical exertion.

"Yeah, let's hurry though."

I pressed the up arrow, and was surprised when I heard the cables and gears creaking inside of the shaft. I always used the stairs. It was good exercise and most of the time there was an old out-of-service sign hanging outside the elevator anyway. However, despite the lift technically working, it really wasn't of service to me at all. It was a hindrance if anything. Waiting for the elevator to reach the lobby was almost unbearable.

Hurry up! Hurry up! Come on! It probably couldn't go any slower if it tried.

Ding.

The doors sputtered open, and we hoisted the couch up. After some maneuvering and coordinating miscommunications, we got it inside the narrow metal cage and sat it against the far wall. I was on the right side, closer to the door, so I had the honor of pressing the button for the sixth floor. His room was above mine as it turned out.

"My name's Kris by the way," the man said.

"Oh, me too. My name is Christian, but I go by Chris."

"Ha-ha, what a coincidence. I'm Kristopher though. With a K." He gave me a warm smile, sweat dripping down his face. "But anyway, thanks again, Chris. Sorry for taking up your time. My girlfriend was actually supposed to be here to help me, but she bailed."

"I think it's time you get another girlfriend then."

"Ha-ha, nah, she's great."

Boy, if I thought the elevator took a long time to go down, then I was way off. Going up was an entirely different beast. The gears and cables screamed as we climbed up each floor. Combined, we shouldn't have been anywhere near the weight limit, yet it still climbed so slow. So painfully slow.

Come on.

Come on.

I glanced down at my phone again.

The time read 10:50.

I had ten minutes.

Also, it looked like the group chat had been messaging me asking where I was over the past twenty minutes. I'd better let them know I was on my way now.

Change of plans, I'll meet you guys outside the gallery and we'll walk in together before the reception starts. I'm almost there.

Send.

The elevator had just passed the third floor… fourth floor… fifth floor.

Ding.

I had already stooped down in preparation to lift the couch, my fingers curled underneath the bottom, eagerly waiting to hoist. I felt like a racing horse, once the doors opened, I'd force this couch through with all my strength and be on my way.

Once the doors opened.

If the doors opened.

"Huh?" Kris said.

I let go of the couch and pressed the button that had two outward-facing arrows.

Nothing happened.

I pressed the button again. Over and over. Still nothing.

No. Not like this. I jinxed it. I fucking jinxed it.

"What's wrong?" Kris asked.

"Can't you tell? We're stuck," I retorted, agitation seeping into my words. And to make matters worse, the previous group text message I sent hadn't gone through. There was no reception within the confines of our metal prison. Such a convenient development. That meant no way to ask for help and, more importantly, no way to let anyone know where I was.

Yeah—roosters really never had these kinds of problems at all.

CHAPTER 31

By the time my phone read 12:36 p.m., I had already resigned myself to my fate. I was late. Not fashionably late. Just plain late. The stars had aligned to stop me. No other way to put it.

Or what was that other thing? Murdock's rule? No, it was Murphy's Law. That's what it was called.

Murphy's Law was an old adage that dictated that whatever could go wrong would go wrong. I wasn't sure where the term came from, but I know that one of my old teachers from high school mentioned it once. Coincidentally, it just so happened that that teacher, Mr. Garretson, ran late on the day he taught that class. He rushed into class twenty minutes after the bell saying his car was acting up. Then he realized he'd forgotten his briefcase with all the quizzes we were supposed to take. Also, the projector wasn't working. Neither was the Wi-Fi. It was at that point that he sank down into his chair, face in his hands, and started bawling. Honest to God bawling. As if his pet had just died, which I learned a few days later that it had. Mr. Garretson blamed Murphy for everything.

The only reason I could even remember something so insignificant was because of how worried I was that day. Not for Mr. Garretson, though. It was for that quiz. I hadn't studied at all.

I glanced down at my phone again.

Who was I kidding? There was no way in hell would Yasmin be buying any of this Murphy's Law nonsense. I was just searching for something to blame. No doubt she was pissed at me right now. More than pissed. I was sure once I got out of there, I'd be experiencing her wrath. Whenever that was.

Despite not having any service in the elevator, I started typing out a message. It wasn't like a last will or anything nor was it long and complicated. I thought of it as a sort of therapy—to alleviate some of my guilt and stress. I made sure to read it over before I pointlessly hit the send button.

I'm sorry.

I closed my eyes and leaned my head back.

All things considered, there was one good thing about the situation.

This was a really comfortable couch.

If I had to lean my back against the hard wall, I couldn't have endured long.

Over the first half hour of entrapment, we exhausted just about every avenue of escape that Kris and I could think of. First off, the red call button didn't work because, of course, it didn't. Wasn't the point of all those regulations and certifications to make sure everything was up to standard? I glanced up and saw the little certificate hanging above the buttons and skimmed the faded text.

Yeah, the elevator had passed all the safety regulations—twenty years ago.

Kris laughed when he saw that.

"Ain't that something," he said. "Now I know why this place was so cheap."

Next, we attempted to pry open the doors. Since I had forgotten my crowbar back in my room, we ended up having to use our fingers. It was a lot harder than I thought it'd be. How come in the movies they made it look so easy? Despite our combined efforts, it didn't budge at all; not even an inch. Out of sheer desperation, I even held my hand out and said, "Open Sesame!" a couple of times. The doors didn't open, but Kris got another good laugh at that one.

Lastly, the next logical thing was to open the ceiling hatch. The thing was, we couldn't even figure out how to get it open. It must not have been opened in years. The latch was covered by a metal grating that we were unable to remove. So, we ended up giving up on that as well.

Both red in the face, we fell back onto the couch exasperated, Kris once again out of breath. The action caused the entire elevator shaft to shake. From above we could hear the cables screeching.

Much like with the seasons, it seemed like each of these failed attempts coincided with the transition of my moods. At first, I was eager and frantic to get out. Pacing around trying to find any structural weakness in this impenetrable metal prison of ours. But as each minute after 11:00 a.m. ticked by, I grew more and more dejected. My strength and vigor drained away, swirling down into the pit of despair. Finally I had no choice but to accept the situation, and so I sat on that very comfortable couch, absentmindedly staring at my reflection.

The elevator was basically a giant mirror, each of the four walls casting an infinite reflection that went as far as the eye could see. I couldn't see my face clearly due to the years of wear and tear, but if I could, I'm sure I would have seen a defeated face staring back at me endlessly.

"How are you doing over there, Chris?" Kris asked with a smile, his series of reflections peering over at mine from across the couch. "You don't look so good."

Not bothering to turn and face him, I addressed the mirror.

"You think?"

Now that things had de-escalated and I had nothing better to do than wait for help to arrive, I had a chance to get to know Kris a little better. Not that I had a choice; he was the one initiating conversation.

He was a few inches taller than me, which meant he stood over six feet when wearing shoes. His hair was almost gravity-defying, as it hung in the air, unmoving, like some kind of abstract black sculpture sitting on his head. It created the kind of look you might see models sporting in magazine advertisements. The stubble on his chin and upper lip highlighted an angular jaw and pronounced lips. I couldn't deny that the guy was the spitting image of conventional attractiveness. I would not want to stand next to him if we were taking pictures.

Apparently, Kris was from the area. The lease on his former place had finished and he decided to move a little closer to cut down on transit costs. He was a third-year student like me, but unlike myself, he knew exactly what he wanted to do with his life. He was going the pre-med route and was already looking at graduate schools to apply to.

His life was pretty much set.

"I'm telling you now, I'm going to be rich in the future," he boldly claimed.

It seemed like he was bragging, but I was perfectly okay with that, because Kris had a way of talking that made you unable to hate him. Despite being here because of him—I couldn't dislike him.

I'm not sure what it was. It was a special quality that he had when he spoke. He was just so excited, full of life, and animated, as if he was trying to pull you into his world. He laughed at everything and even bantered off of my quips. He was doing whatever he could to keep morale up, and I respected that. Compared to the push-and-pull conversations I've had with others, ours felt relatively normal, as if we were on an equal playing field. Eventually, as I watched his laughing reflection from the mirror, I noticed that I was smiling back at him.

"So, you don't think that we're going to run out of oxygen, do you?" Kris asked. "Because I can't hold my breath for very long."

"No, we won't. From the look of it the elevator isn't hermetically sealed. That being said, you don't have permission to fart in here."

"Damn. Good thing you told me that, because I was just about to let one loose."

"Please don't. Probably the last thing I need right now."

"If I were to interpret that statement a different way, you basically said you needed me to fart. Just not now."

Ugh. He'd gotten me, but I wasn't ready to admit defeat. I absentmindedly glanced down at my phone again before taking the conversation in another direction.

"Hey, Kris. Can I ask you a question?"

"You just did."

"Please no dad jokes."

"What about mom jokes? Are those off-limits too?"

"They're even more off-limits than dad jokes."

"I'm just going to assume brother and sister jokes are a no-no too."

"You assumed correctly," I said. "Besides, something about jokes of that nature sound inherently wrong. But, anyway, let's get back on track."

"Sure, go ahead and ask me whatever you want."

I paused for a moment and stood up to reposition myself on the couch and to stretch my back. The small movement caused the elevator car to shake slightly, and the wires squealed again.

"You seem to be taking this whole situation really well," I said. "How do you manage to stay so positive?"

Kris smirked at me. "Does it look that way?"

"Yeah."

Kris chuckled. It was subdued. As if he'd laughed at a funny thought. "I'm happy to hear you say that, but I don't feel that way."

"You don't?"

It was a surprise to hear that coming from him. Nothing he'd done up to this point had tipped me off. Whereas earlier on I'd taken out some of my frustration on him, he'd just taken it all with a smile.

"This whole thing sucks, but I know from experience that being angry and frustrated about the situation doesn't help things."

"Uh-huh."

"You see, I used to be a sickly kid when I was younger. My body didn't work all that well."

"Like what? You were physically weak? Bedridden?"

Kris nodded. "A little of both. Can I show you something?"

"Sure, why not."

Kris stood up and lifted his shirt up to expose his chest.

His torso was pale and slim, without much fat, and he even had a little muscle—more than me at least. So not bad. He probably didn't feel very self-conscious taking his shirt off at the beach or at a pool. However, despite my observation, the point of his display wasn't to show off his physique.

On the right side of his chest Kris had multiple scars; some darker and more noticeable while others had already begun to fade. If I had to describe what they looked like, the first thing that came to mind was bullet wounds. As if some cylindrical objects had been inserted into his chest. And by that account I wasn't that far off.

"I collapsed my lung multiple times growing up. These scars here"—he pointed to his side—"are where they inserted the tube to pull out the extra air that was caving it in."

"That looks painful. How did it happen? Did you fall or something?"

"Nope. It was random. Doctors said they were spontaneous. One day I'd be fine and the next, I'd be having trouble breathing."

Random.

Without any apparent reason.

But wait—

"Didn't you say it happened multiple times?"

"Yeah. Six different times. And every time it happened, I had to spend a few weeks in the hospital until they said I was good to go."

Six times.

How could that be called random?

Maybe if it was only twice, it could be a coincidence. A happenstance. But six? Obviously, at that point anyone would think that something must have been causing it. But from the sound of it. That wasn't the case.

Everything that could go wrong, would go wrong.

Something suddenly occurred to me.

His asking for help to lift the couch. The wheezing. His comment from earlier about running out of oxygen. In retrospect, his concerns made complete sense. Those were exactly the things that someone with his condition would have to worry about. Even though there had been no way for me to know, my lack of tact in the matter made me feel like an asshole. I even went so far as to say he looked "positive" in this situation. Enclosed spaces inherently had a way of making it difficult for people to breathe, so I had to wonder how he truly felt.

And despite all these factors, he was the first one to ask me if I was alright.

"Hey, Kris. How are you holding up then? Are you good? And you can put your shirt down now."

"I'm fine. Sorry. I didn't mean to bring down the mood. The whole point that I was trying to make was that complaining or feeling down about the situation didn't make it better for me. Of course, you can't control emotions, but you can change how you react to them."

"I see."

It was a fine way to live, I couldn't deny that. In fact, that advice would have come in handy before. Not that I would have been in any sort of mental state to follow it. Both of us seemed to have our own set of scars—his chest and my back—but it was how we dealt with them that was different. He was so quick to show me his, but I couldn't bring myself to do the same. I didn't want people to know about that part of me if I could help it.

"You can't stop your emotions, but you can change how you react to it, huh?" I said. "That's deep. Where'd you hear that?"

"A fortune cookie."

And there we had it. We were now learning about life from a few simple words on a strip of paper. Not that I was complaining, I just expected a more—credible source.

"Back home, my family and I lived upstairs from a little Chinese restaurant. Not going to lie to you, the food wasn't very good. I even got food poisoning I think, ha-ha. But it was the most meaningful $7.68 that I'd ever spent."

"That's a good way to look at things."

"Yup, and that's exactly the point," Kris said. "And as a whole, things have been turning out all right for me lately. Considering the circumstances."

Considering the circumstances. My life would have turned out differently too if I was able to maintain such an optimistic outlook despite my negative feelings.

I wanted to say something in response to that, but I was having trouble finding the words. In most conversations, there was a give and take. You offer something up, whether it be a bit about your past or a personal insecurity, and though it's not expected, the other party usually tells you something about themselves in return. Anything was better than nothing. It didn't have to be something of equal weight, but the gesture of opening up was important if you wanted to create bonds.

But I still couldn't bring myself to do it, and I felt the scales tipping in his direction.

While we sat in silence letting our previous conversation sink in, a sudden lurch nearly threw us out of our seats and onto the floor.

"What was that?" Kris asked.

"I don't know." I glanced down at my phone. It was now 1:05. "Maybe someone's finally noticed, and they sent some help."

The elevator lurched again—more violently this time. Both of us held the walls to steady ourselves.

"I sure hope so," Kris said, "Also, I noticed you keep looking at your phone. Any messages get through?"

"No. Nothing. These walls must be lined with lead or something. Even Superman wouldn't be able to see us."

"Ha-ha, yeah. Same here. Zero bars. Sorry again, by the way."

"No, don't worry about it. It's okay."

"You have somewhere you need to go, right?"

"Yeah."

"Wouldn't be meeting a girl, would you?"

"Kind of..."

"A date?" Kris pressed forward with a grin.

As sure as day turns to night. As sure as Newton's Laws of Motion. It was a guarantee that if two guys talked long enough that the conversation would devolve into women. Whether it was because it was always an interesting topic to talk about in order to get bro-points or because it was some biological process in our male brains—it would be brought up without fail. This wouldn't have been a problem if I knew how to navigate the conversation around my so-called relationship with Yasmin. But I didn't. So, it was a problem.

"Not exactly. She has an art thing," I said.

"A fart thing? Well, good thing she isn't locked in here with us then."

"An *art* thing! A-R-T."

"Oh, my bad, ha-ha. I thought you said fart. But, if she did have a fart thing, it would explain why you wouldn't want to go on a date with her. I don't like fart things. Not that I'm prejudiced against them or anything. You like what you like, but if my girlfriend had a fart thing, I don't think we'd have made it this *far*—t."

"That wasn't even remotely funny!"

"Just imagine how awkward all our sex would have been if she just couldn't stop farting. Especially if I didn't like it."

"Okay, no more saying *fart*. I've had enough!"

Kris keeled over, clutching his stomach and laughing. Probably the loudest it'd been since we'd been stuck. He was practically dying over something as childish as a fart joke.

As he wiped a tear from his eye, he recomposed himself enough to speak.

"Ha-ha, I couldn't resist."

"Just get it all out of your system."

"I'm good now, I'm good," Kris said, wheezing and holding his hand over his chest. "I tell you what. In order to make up for all of this, how about I take you out to dinner later tonight? You can invite your lady friend and I'll invite my girl. Like a double date. It's the least I can do since I caused you to be late. And don't worry—" Kris started snickering behind his hand again.

"Don't say it!"

"She doesn't have a fart thing."

The elevator jerked again, falling a few inches this time, which stopped me from throttling Kris with my own two hands. He'd killed the joke a long time ago—buried it even.

"Okay. Okay. I'm done for real this time." Kris's tone changed into a more serious one. "But I'm being honest about my offer. Join us. I think my girl would get a kick out of you."

"Oh, yeah? How long have you two been dating?"

"About two years, give or take a few months."

"Must be serious if it's been going on for that long."

Especially with how handsome the guy was. He shouldn't have had that much trouble playing the field if he wanted to. I always had this belief that good-looking people had it easier in the dating field even if it wasn't the case. I wasn't bitter about it, I was just saying. Brad was a fine example of that.

"Yeah. She's amazing. I really like her. I honestly didn't think it'd work out with us."

"Why's that?"

Kris chuckled and scratched the back of his head.

"It's a funny story. When we met, she was seeing this other guy. Apparently, they were childhood friends, high school sweethearts even, from this small town downstate that I've never heard of. They had decided to go to college together. The whole shebang, you know? I didn't even think I had a chance, but I still wanted to get to know her and stuff. She was smart, caring, and even laughed at my jokes, so she was basically all I could want. As I talked to her more, I learned that she wasn't satisfied in her current relationship. She loved the guy and was even there when he was going through some rough times with his mother, but something wasn't right. She had this nagging feeling that she was completely out of his league or something. That he didn't deserve her."

A feeling that I couldn't explain washed over me. I was sinking. All my internal organs and blood drained down into my feet.

It couldn't be.

"This guy..."

"Was a total idiot, right? She didn't tell me any specifics at all. She wanted to keep things separate. So most of this is speculation on my part. But even with what little I knew, the guy sounded like he was just being selfish. What an asshole." Kris sounded agitated. "The thing was she couldn't leave him. No matter how much I urged her too. She said that she still cared about him. Also, she made this silly childhood promise. When they were kids, she told him that she would never abandon him or something like that. I'm not hating, but it was a little naive for that guy to force that on her."

It wasn't possible.

This kind of coincidence.

"Even though she wasn't willing to leave him. She still wanted to see me. We spent whatever time we could together and even started to hook up. It was killing me back then, because I thought that this was all we'd ever be. Went on for over two years, man. Can you believe that? Honestly, if I wanted something more, I should have just left, but I couldn't. I was invested in her."

I was having trouble breathing.

I wanted to throw up.

But somehow, I was still able to speak in a voice that wasn't my own.

"What happened next?"

I had to know. Even if I didn't want to. Even if I wouldn't be able to bear what I was hearing. I still had to know.

"About six months ago, everything changed. She called me late one night sounding distressed. Apparently, the guy had dumped her that day. Out-of-the-blue, he just went and left her with no explanation. He never said why. What a complete asshole. It pisses me off thinking about people who're that selfish. She still cared about him, and he just cast her off like that." Kris shook his head. "But I guess it doesn't really matter. Even though the whole thing came as a shock to her. I was relieved that I could spend more time with her now. So, in the end, everyone got what they wanted."

He left her with no explanation.

No, why.

An unimaginable pain was coursing through my back, and I was having trouble holding myself up. I felt so heavy. I desperately wanted to lie down now, even if I had to lie on the floor to do it. I just needed to lie down. My head was spinning at a hundred miles-per-hour. I couldn't think.

Chris, why?

The question she asked me. The one I never answered.

"So, yeah, that's pretty much our little love story," Kris said. "But, hey. Want to see her? It's sappy, but I have a picture of us as my phone wallpaper. Honestly, I never thought I'd do something like that, but you never know what's going to happen in the future."

Without waiting for my response, Kris excitedly dug into the pocket of his jeans and retrieved his phone.

I wanted to see it.

And I didn't want to see it.

This would be the final confirmation. I'd know without a doubt. But did I want to? Sometimes the fear of not knowing could stifle you, preventing you from acting. But sometimes it could save you too.

Could it really be...?

"Isn't she perfect? Her name is—"

Suddenly the elevator jolted again, dropping about a foot and throwing both of us onto the ground. Kris's phone flew and landed on the floor, sliding to a stop underneath me——screen upwards.

I didn't know if it was because it had just fallen, but the entire surface of the screen was cracked. Dozens of tiny pieces were chipping off and crumbling, yet I was still able to make out the face looking up at me.

A face that I recognized all too well.

I can't remember what exactly happened next. There was a loud sound of grating metal and in the next moment we were falling. All three of us. Spiraling down.

Down.

And down.

My body was floating—weightless. The same exact sensation that I had when I'd fallen from my window.

And the last thought that I had before everything went dark was just how sorry I really was.

CHAPTER 32

White.

Blinding whiteness.

That's what I saw when I finally opened my eyes, and it was just as disorientating as you'd expect. Reflexively, I tried to bring both of my hands up to block the light and give my pupils a chance to readjust, but only one of my arms was able to move. The left to be exact. My right side was numb, and I couldn't feel any sensation from that part of my body besides a sort of warm pressure.

Was I dead?

What had happened?

I racked my brain trying to remember anything, trying to make sense of the scattered details.

The university art exhibit... I was running late... Kris... The elevator.

The elevator.

That's right.

The elevator had fallen.

I tried to run my hands up and down my body to make sure that I was all in one piece, but my right arm still wouldn't move. Was it because of the elevator? How serious were my injuries? Everything felt so heavy and stiff, like I was submerged in mud.

"Mmurgh."

A groan came from my right and though it took some effort, I looked down to see what it was. Much to my surprise, Yasmin was sleeping there by my side. She looked terribly comfortable too, using my right arm as a pillow for her head and hands like that. It was literally cutting off all of my circulation, preventing me from moving or feeling anything.

Hah, that was a relief. I was getting a little nervous there. I was right-handed, so obviously it was important to me.

The expression on Yasmin's face as she slept was a tranquil one, I'd even go so far to call it peaceful too. Not a care in the world. Her eyes and mouth had a soft edge about them. Seeing that look on her face put me at ease. If she was able to sleep this soundly, then things were probably okay.

It was the same expression she had when I lay down next to her, the night after she made up with Adi.

That night, Yasmin had been defenseless.

She'd opened her heart to me and let me inside her bedroom. And in terms of sanctity and sacredness, the feeling I'd experienced in that moment was second only to the sensation of stepping into an actual church. It'd been a big step forward for us. Our budding relationship had been a precarious one up and to this point. I liked her, that much was true, but I still had some mental roadblocks to navigate before I'd be sure of my feelings.

However, I will admit, I'd forgotten what it felt like sleeping beside someone. It was warm. Maybe a bit cramped, even on the king-sized bed that seemed to take up most of her room. All the extra folds and bedsheets didn't matter because we ended up nestled in the middle of the bed, in a space where only we existed. At that moment, I had nothing on my mind except her.

It was nice.

But I wasn't in her apartment anymore.

This was a hospital room, and it looked exactly like you might've expected a hospital room to look like. The walls were a sterile white, the curtains were a sterile white, the sheets were a sterile white, and the bed was a sterile white. Everything was suffocatingly clean to the point that it was off-putting—unnatural. There was more dust piled up on me than there was on anything else. Nothing was this clean. No matter how white, sparkly, and spotless it was. What were these people trying to cover up? They weren't going to fool me. That's why seeing Yasmin's mass of black hair, which made her stand out against the background, was comforting. I was in a strange place, so it was reassuring to have that point of familiarity.

I hadn't noticed it before, but there was a tight pressure around my waist that made moving difficult. It was a brace of some sort. Not only that, a whole crayon box worth of colored wires—the sixty-four count ones, you know with the sharpener in the back—ran up my arms and connected to multiple monitors and contraptions above my head. I felt like I was a cyborg. More machine than man.

"Ugh." Yasmin groaned again, this time opening her eyes slightly.

"Hey," I croaked. It hurt to speak.

"Chris?" Yasmin sat up and rubbed her eyes. The gesture reminded me of a small child who'd just been woken up. "Are you okay?"

"I mean, I'm still alive, right? Or is this just a figment of my imagination?"

"Of course you're alive. Don't be dumb."

"Sorry, just checking," I said. "I wasn't so sure. I feel dead."

A small smile crossed her face, but I could tell something was off about it. It wasn't one of your patented Yasmin smiles, ones that were rooted in assholery and mischief. There seemed to be more meaning hidden behind it then she was letting on.

Yasmin glanced down at my legs before quickly turning back to me. "That's good to hear."

"How long have I been out?"

"Three days."

"Three days?!"

"Yeah, you probably don't remember, but you did lapse in and out of consciousness a couple of times."

"No, I don't remember any of that."

Three days, huh. That was such a long time to be asleep.

"Kris. What happened to Kris?" I asked.

"What? Why are you speaking in the third person now?" Yasmin asked. "Are you sure you're okay?"

"No, no. The other guy that was with me."

"Oh, he's over there. Behind the curtain. They brought you two in here together." Yasmin directed her thumb over her shoulder. "He's doing much better than you. He's asleep now, but he woke up around two days ago. Also, he was talking about you a lot. Are you friends?"

"Nah, I just met him."

Yasmin frowned.

"The doctor said you two are lucky. You shouldn't be alive right now," she said.

"Then we'll do great in Vegas."

"How... boring. Still cracking jokes in inappropriate situations, I see."

"You know me. I just can't read the room."

Damn.

It felt good hearing her catchphrase again. You usually don't think about it, but it was the little things about people that could bring you so much joy. The small characteristics that you wouldn't initially notice, but eventually grew to be synonymous with the person themselves.

I attempted to shift my position in order to get a better look at her, but my legs were stiff and heavy. They wouldn't budge, and I couldn't feel much sensation even down into my extremities.

"So, uh, looks like you've been here a while," I said. "Did you want to be the first person to see me wake up?"

Yasmin's cheeks turned red. Grabbing her chair, she scooted a foot away from me.

"Please. Don't get full of yourself. I just got here," she claimed, tufts of hair sticking out in every direction.

"Right. And what's that over there?"

In the corner of the room there was a bulging backpack, sleeves and pant legs sticking out of the various pockets.

"I, uh, just a spare change of clothes and my homework. I always do that."

"Sure, whatever you say," I said, not buying any of it. "To be honest, I'm just happy that you're not yelling at me or trying to kill me."

"Why would I do that?"

"Because I missed the art exhibit opening. And for what it's worth, I *was* trying to make it there."

"It... doesn't matter."

"Hah, you don't know how relieved I am to hear that. I wasn't in the mood to get my ass kicked."

At that, Yasmin's expression changed. Her eyes went wide, and she looked down. She seemed hurt.

Was it what I just said?

It wasn't usually like her. I was expecting some snarky response. The thought of apologizing even crossed my mind before she suddenly spoke up again.

"Chris, what happened in there? In the elevator."

"Nothing really. Kris, the other guy, asked me to help him move that couch, but when we put it in the elevator shaft and tried to bring it up to the sixth floor, the elevator stalled."

That was basically the gist of the entire thing.

Or at least, the kind of answer that Yasmin was probably looking for when she asked me that question.

I didn't see how the conversations I shared with Kris were relevant—even the last one. Yasmin didn't need to know about that. I planned to keep that bit of information to myself and mull it over when I was alone. It hurt too much to even think about. It made me sick, and I could already feel my hands trembling. I couldn't explain what emotion I was feeling at that moment.

"Is that all?"

"Uh, yeah. We were just sitting there."

Yasmin sighed and rubbed the bridge of her nose.

"What?" I asked.

"It's nothing. It's probably nothing."

"Just come out and say it then."

My tone sounded harsher than I intended, but I couldn't help it. My frustration was now seeping into my words. It was clear that she knew something that I didn't. Some bit of information. And now she was trying to trip me up and make me admit something. I had nothing I wanted to admit though. Nothing she needed to know or was relevant to the elevator getting stuck. Yet she was still pressing me and acting exasperated. There was nothing more for me to say. Nothing.

"It's about Zoey."

My heart leapt up into my throat.

Why would she be mentioning her name now?

"What about her?"

Yasmin paused for a moment. Our eyes met and we held that contact for I don't know how long. Temptation urged me to pull away first, but before I could, she beat me to it.

"You were screaming her name," Yasmin stated blankly. "Remember how I just told you that you lapsed in-and-out of consciousness a couple times? You'd wake up in this daze, yelling her name, and thrashing your arms around. They had to restrain and sedate you in order to calm you down."

"Seriously?"

"Yeah, but ironically, that wasn't the thing that bothered me."

"What do you mean by that?" I asked.

"After the first time, Brad mentioned something to me. I'd never seen him look so serious. It was kind of off-putting if I was being perfectly honest. But, anyway, he mentioned that this wasn't anything new. You'd done this before. There would be times at night when he'd hear you calling Zoey's name in your sleep. Sometimes it'd be no more than a whisper and other times you'd be yelling at the top of your lungs. Screaming bloody murder as he put it. Does any of that sound familiar?"

"I... don't know. I can't remember."

"You can't remember?"

"I mean sometimes I'd have some nightmares, but I didn't think anything of it, so this is all news to me. What else did Brad say?"

"Well," Yasmin said, pausing for a second, "he said that these episodes of yours had been happening less and less. Four months ago, they were happening a couple times a week—maybe even more. It spooked him so much that he tried to avoid coming back to the apartment to sleep. He hated to leave you alone, but he couldn't handle it. But lately, he told me the frequency had gone down. He said that you hadn't had an outburst in over a month. Until a couple days ago, that is."

I squirmed in place, trying to find a better position to situate myself. The bed had suddenly become very uncomfortable.

"That wasn't all," Yasmin continued. "As weird as it might sound, I could have just brushed off your nightmares. Considering what happened to you and what you almost did, it's only natural that your experiences had scarred you and left you traumatized. So, I wasn't wholly surprised when Brad told me about it. But when *he* woke up, I knew that there had to be some other reason that must have triggered you."

"He?"

"The other guy that was brought in with you. Kris, I guess."

"I don't understand. What happened?"

"It was what he did when he woke up. I was here when it happened—doing my, uh, homework. Right after he had gotten situated with his surroundings, and the doctor had talked to him, he asked to borrow someone's phone. There's nothing weird about that. Anyone would want to call their family to let them know what happened and that they're okay, but his mom and his dad—they weren't the first people he wanted to call. The first person he wanted to talk to, who he practically begged to talk to, was his girlfriend."

"..."

Yasmin looked at me silently. Her face was sullen, none of that usual fire that I'd grown to appreciate and that marked her distinct character.

"It's her, isn't it? There's no way that could have been a coincidence," she asked.

"Yeah."

Yasmin sighed before repeating her previous question—the one that had started this whole conversation in the first place. And the one that I dreaded because I knew it was coming.

"What happened in there, Chris?"

Should I tell her?

Was there even a point in trying to avoid it now?

No, one way or another she was going to get the answer out of me, so it was better for me to tell her of my own accord.

"They've been dating for over two years," I said in a roundabout way, hoping that Yasmin would be able to understand the nuance. I didn't want to say the c-word. The one that started with "ch" and ended with "eat". Verbalizing words had a wonderful tendency of giving them power, as they say, and if I said it, then the concept would become real, as if I'd breathed my own life into it.

"Holy shit. Does that mean?"

"Yeah."

"Didn't you say you guys had been dating since you were kids?"

"Yeah."

"And didn't you break up with her like six months ago?"

"Yeah."

"What a cheating bitch."

I winced at her insult.

Maybe it was warranted. Maybe she'd called it like it was. But even then, that's not what I wanted to hear her call Zoey. Someone who still had an influence on who I was as a person.

"Please don't call her that," I said.

"What? Why? That's exactly what she is. That's fucked up. If she actually cared, she wouldn't have done anything like that."

"It's just… not that simple."

"Seriously, after all this time you're still hung up on her? Even now?"

Even now.

It was Yasmin's turn to add a bit of nuance to her question.

A nuance that wasn't really nuance at all. It wasn't subtle and I didn't think it was meant to be either. It was as if it was spoken loud and clear from an intercom straight into my heart.

Even now.

After everything Yasmin and I had experienced together and the night we had shared. After—all we'd been through.

"I'm just trying to understand my feelings right now," I said. "A part of me still can't believe that she'd… do something like that. The whole time I had no idea. Just—all the emotion I feel right now. It hurts. There's just this overwhelming sense of dread I can't shake."

Was… this what my mother had felt?

"Dread?" Yasmin asked.

"Yeah, it's exactly what I thought would happen. I knew it. It's because of how pathetic I am."

"It's in the past though. Why does it matter?"

"It matters."

"She made her choice. That has nothing to do with you. Why does it matter?"

"It just does."

"But why, Chris? Why?!" Yasmin's voice came out agitated, almost pleading. "Why does it matter? Why does any of it matter? Maybe I'm the last one to be saying this considering everything you've helped me with and all the obstacles I've overcome in just the past few months with you, but at this point, why does it matter that she cheated? That was in the past, even if you just found out now. You haven't spoken to her or seen her for months! You can't keep obsessing over that image you have of her. You have to let it go. I really feel like a fucking hypocrite saying all of this, but you saw how getting hung up on the past affected me and my relationship with my family—with Adi. I know how hard it could be, but I always hoped that things would return to how they used to be with her. I just needed to forget the past and my anger and hatred and move on. That's what I learned from spending all this time with you. But why can't you take your own advice?! Living like this, putting yourself on the line to help people. You don't have to do this to make up for it."

Yasmin was shaking her head. Her hand squeezed mine while her eyes glistened under the fluorescent lights that sterilized and washed out everything underneath them. She was frustrated—at my indecisiveness and at my inability to make the logical choice, the one that any rational person could make to move on. To look at the past with a sort of amused recognition instead of brooding over it and holding every future decision under its lenses. But how could I?

It always came down to this.

It always seemed to be a matter of why.

That was the question wrapped around every choice.

What good was any choice without its reason?

"It matters because I fell from my window and nearly died," I said. "And the reason I even put myself in that situation was because I thought I did the wrong thing. Zoey used to tell me that she'd never leave me. Ever since we were little and even before we started dating. She had faith in me. When I left her, I thought I betrayed her commitment and love. My motivation to never hurt anyone else like that was what set me on this path in the first place, but I didn't feel good enough. The reason you and I even met was because of my desire to change. The reason I went out of my way to try and help people, help you, was because of this. I wanted to change and be like her."

Yasmin remained silent, trying to make sense of my words. But I had yet to make the main point, so I continued.

"But it turns out I was right. I *had* done the right thing. And it's not even because she was cheating. Though finding out she did that—it still hurts. I still can't wrap my head around how I should be feeling about that. There's a heavy pressure in my chest I can't explain, but that wasn't why I was right to break up with her. The reason was because she felt trapped in our relationship. That I was holding her back. That I wasn't giving her what she needed. She felt all of this, and yet, she was still going to stay with me. That was her *why*. Her reason. Zoey must have thought I was so hopeless without her. She couldn't leave me because... she thought I needed her. So, breaking up with her was the right thing to do. I did her a favor. All my fears and insecurities that I wasn't good enough were true. I guess I always knew that, but I hoped it wasn't completely true. I believed she must have seen something in me. Like I had something deep down that she adored or respected. But it turns out I didn't. If I had this realization in the past, instead of being left alone in my mind unanswered, allowed to ruminate and fester, so much of my emotional trauma could have been avoided. It makes everything feel pointless."

"She would have stayed with you? If you didn't break up with her?"

"Yeah, that's what the other Kris implied."

Yasmin sighed. She let go of my hand and pulled away.

"You sound as if that's something you would have wanted," she said. "Sounds an awful lot like you hoped she'd take you back."

"..."

"So, everything else feels pointless to you now. Like none of *this* matters." She pointed between the two of us.

"That's not what I mean..."

But wasn't it?

It sounded exactly like it meant.

If I didn't go through that emotional ordeal, I would never have decided to live in the way that I thought she had. To start reaching out to others, to look to others in need.

It was safe to assume Yasmin and I would have never met.

I wouldn't have offered friendly advice to Adi who looked like she needed someone to listen to her.

"Alright, it's fine. I was having some doubts of my own too," she said, brushing everything off with the flick of her hand. "Like I said in the past, those dating articles warned me something like this could happen, so this is partially my fault too."

Yasmin stood up and walked to the corner to grab her bag.

"Where are you going?" I asked. The conversation seemed unfinished, like we had stopped in the middle of a paragraph. It didn't feel right to let her walk out when things were like this.

"I'm going to go let the doctor know that you're awake now. He's going to want to talk to you."

Before I could respond, she walked over to my bedside and pulled something out of her pocket.

"Oh, yeah. I forgot. Here's your phone. They gave it to me when they changed your clothes." Yasmin haphazardly tossed it onto my lap. "You're probably going to have a lot of notifications. Do me a favor and just delete all the ones from me."

"Wait, you're coming back, right?"

Yasmin replied by slamming the door on her way out.

* * *

When the doctor walked in five minutes later, my eyes were unfocused, lazily fixed on my phone that was still in my lap. I hadn't grabbed or looked through it yet. I hadn't moved from my spot for that matter either. Not that I could have if I wanted to. And I did want to. I kept telling myself that at least. If I could move, I would have chased Yasmin out of the door, and stopped her from leaving.

No.

That wasn't entirely correct.

Right now, it only sounded like I was trying to convince myself that I would, so I could ease the shame I was feeling.

"Mr. Christianson?"

The friendly voice caused me to look up, and for a split second, I thought I saw Yasmin's figure poking out from behind the man in the white lab coat, but my eyes were just playing tricks on me. Making me see what I wanted to see.

"Your girlfriend just told me you woke up. How are you feeling?"

"I've been better," I said, ignoring his first comment. It wasn't worth the effort to explain.

"I bet."

As he walked over, the doctor examined something on Kris' side of the curtain before moving over to me. He stood near the foot of the bed, flipping through pages attached to the gray clipboard he had in his hands.

"I'm Doctor Henry Stevens. I'm the one who's been monitoring your condition and taking care of you. There are some things I want to go over with you. Are you prepared?"

"Would you still tell me if I said I wasn't?"

The doctor chuckled drily.

"You got me there. But I just wanted to make sure you were ready."

"Go for it, Doc. I don't think there's anything you can say that can make me feel any more terrible than I already do. Do your absolute worst."

Of course, I didn't know it at the moment, but I'd later regret that I had said that. Like I was calling upon my own misfortune.

That was because Doctor Stevens *did* do his worst.

He really did.

CHAPTER 33

The next few days slogged by so unbelievably slowly that I was almost certain time wasn't moving at all. The hands on the clock would move, but they didn't go anywhere, like they were perpetually stuck.

Most of the time consisted of lying flat on my back, staring up at the white ceiling panels, and passively trying to count the little pin holes in them. 3,459 was where I was at now. It was a mundane and difficult task, but that was the point. It took my mind off everything and focused it on nothing. A hopelessly pointless task. Nothing would happen if I did end up counting those dots. There was no reward or cookie waiting for me, but I did it anyway because that was all I could do.

Occasionally, I'd lose my place, but I wasn't too bothered by it. I just ended up starting over—at number one. That first hole was in the panel directly over my face, in the bottom far-left corner. I could have sworn that it looked slightly bigger than the rest and it had a distinct shape too.

When I wasn't busy with that, Doctor Stevens would come in occasionally, or one of the many nurses whose names I didn't care to learn. They'd run some tests, ask how I was doing and if I needed anything, and empty out the little urinal I had to use whenever I needed to pee. It always hung within arm's reach of me, but even then, it felt like a massive ordeal to lean over, grab it, and use it. Not that I was lazy. The doctor just didn't want me to move around all that much. They did offer me a diaper, but I declined.

One by one, Brad, Adi, and Mia came to visit. I honestly felt a little bad about it. I knew Brad probably had his swimming practices and Mia must have had other counseling appointments to take care of, but they still found the time to come.

It felt nice to know that they cared, but that was canceled out by the feeling that I was once again being a burden on people. With that net gain and net loss, I was ultimately ambivalent to the entire thing.

Brad carried on about all the fun stuff we'd do when I got out of there. "We're getting drunk, bro," was what he said, conveniently forgetting that I didn't drink. Adi was more silent, and we watched a few TV shows together while she offered to spoon feed me my hospital food slop. I think she took it literally when the Doctor said I shouldn't move at all, and I half-expected her to chew my food for me first. Mia left a stack of her favorite novels at my bedside, and even took the time to read a chapter or two to me. I couldn't remember a thing about what she read. Her voice was a lullaby stronger than any sleeping pill. Even though the three visits were very different, I knew my friends were all trying to cheer me up in their own ways. I appreciated it.

When I ended up telling them the news—what Doctor Stevens had told me the other day, they all basically had the same reaction. Muted surprise followed by sad, knowing nods.

I figured that they must have already heard, but I didn't press them for details. It would have explained all their efforts to try and cheer me up.

If they knew, that must have meant Yasmin knew as well. And though I may not have wanted to admit it, I was disappointed every time that door opened and I didn't see her scowling face.

Was she still upset about what I said? That everything felt pointless.

Everything including the complicated thing between us and all the things we experienced—the things we shared.

Every one of them.

Pointless.

Everything felt that way.

But that didn't mean they *were* that way, right?

These were the questions playing through my head on an endless loop.

I could message her. My phone hadn't moved from the nightstand next to my bed. I saw all the notifications, and it seemed like too much of a chore to handle.

But maybe in the end, this was for the best. She may not want me anymore in the first place after all.

That's because the doc had said that I was broken.

A broken husk of a man.

Forever to be looked on with empathy, sympathy, and a couple other words that ended with "-thy".

Okay, he didn't *actually* say that. I figured if he was the kind of doctor that did say things like that, he wouldn't have ended up being a doctor for very long. People don't like to be told bad news. It might have been expected, but they didn't like it.

What the doctor did say could be distilled down to about five words.

You may never walk again.

Once he'd hit me with that one, probably the worst he could have done, my mind had gone blank. I couldn't remember much of what came after—just fragments of the rest of our conversation.

Looking at some x-rays and the clearly defined scar, Doctor Stevens noted that the structural integrity of my back had already been compromised before the elevator fiasco, making me far more susceptible to serious and lasting damage. The back pains I frequently experienced were a symptom of that.

"How'd you hurt your spine before? I don't see any records of it."

"I don't know."

He frowned, probably realizing asking any further wouldn't be worth it.

At that point, Stevens went on a long-winded explanation, but the gist of the matter was that he seemed to imply that it hadn't healed properly before. If I had gone to the hospital when this mysterious accident happened, they would have made me wear a back brace to hold my spine in alignment until things were mended, and I wouldn't have had any problems with it. Things weren't for certain, due to all the swelling, but they'd be running some tests and monitoring my condition closely in the next few weeks.

Knowing that he probably just dropped a lot for me to process, Doctor Stevens left me with a small consolation prize made for the sole purpose of helping me see the big picture. To see the forest for the trees, as they say. It came in the form of an offhand comment.

"Despite the injuries you sustained, you two are lucky to be alive," the Doc said. "You were saved by a miracle."

Well, if we're getting specific, it was that couch that saved both of us. There were some other safety measures in place that slowed the elevator down, but the cushioning from the couch was what ultimately did it. It acted like a giant airbag and drastically reduced the impact that both of us experienced. We might have been killed otherwise.

Hearing him call me lucky reminded me of my previous joke about Vegas, and I almost reused it too, but it reminded me of Yasmin and suddenly I had no desire to be funny anymore. It would be for the best if I attempted to keep this conversation serious. I had nothing to laugh about. But despite my rather sour and melancholic mood, a mood that I might have selfishly claimed as my own, unable to be felt by anyone beside me—I wasn't the only person who seemed to be feeling some sort of way.

I longed to see Yasmin every time that door opened, and Kris was waiting for someone too. I'd even go so far as to say that he was hurt every time it wasn't her. It was an emotional pain, but by the way his face twinged, it very well might have been a physical one as well.

We'd drawn back the curtains separating our beds and he'd talk to me excitedly in the same manner as he'd done in the elevator with that unhateable and captivating quality he had.

"Chris, I'm telling you. You're going to like her. She said she'd come to visit me. I'm kind of excited. Do I look okay? I mean my hair—it's not too crazy, right?"

But as the hours passed, Zoey still didn't show up.

Zoey.

The girl who he was desperately waiting for.

My childhood friend and former girlfriend.

She didn't show up.

"I told her all about you since we're hospital mates and all," Kris droned on. "Said you were a funny dude to talk to and that you saved me."

"Saved you?"

"Yeah, you don't remember? When the elevator started falling, I was literally frozen in place. I couldn't move. But you forced me onto the couch. You're my hero."

I didn't remember that at all.

Did I really do that?

"What—what did she say?" I asked, trying not to let on how much I wanted to know.

"Uh, she had no comment."

"Ah."

Of course not.

Kris' injuries were far less serious than mine. A minor concussion and some fractured ribs. If not for his medical history they would have sent him home sooner, but they wanted to make sure there were no complications. Still, he patiently waited with a smile on his face for Zoey to walk through that door, oblivious to the fact that the reason she hadn't already was because of his 'hospital mate' lying just a couple feet away from him.

I noticed his smile waver every time one of my friends walked in. Brad, Adi, and Mia. He'd give me the side-eye the entire time they were there, just focusing his attention on the door.

"You're a popular guy, Chris," he said, after Mia left.

"Uh, do you think so?"

"Yeah, I didn't know you had a thing for older women."

"She's married!"

"Older and married? Even better."

"Don't twist my words around like that with a smile on your face. It's creepy."

"So, it'd be okay if I did it with a frown?"

"Considering the context? No, it'd be even worse! It'd be like you were planning to do something terrible. Just don't do it in any kind of way."

"Sure thing." Kris nodded. "What I meant to say was that you have a lot of friends."

"Not really. You just saw all of them."

"That's not true."

"It's close enough that it might as well be."

Kris chuckled. It sounded devoid of some of the life I expected.

"Did your lady friend come by? The one with the *art* thing."

"She did, but that was the day before yesterday. I would have introduced you to her, but you were sleeping."

"Ah, okay."

He turned his head and glanced over at the door. I'm sure that if I was keeping track of how many times he'd done that, it would've surpassed the number of those pinholes on the ceiling.

"My girl keeps saying she'll come, but..." He stopped and shook his head.

Though I hadn't known him for long, less than a week even counting the days I was unconscious, I'd say I had a pretty decent bead on the kind of person Kris was. He was an eternal optimist—able to laugh off every situation he'd found himself in. This happy-go-lucky attitude had been built up from his own life experiences. Having found himself in the hospital more times than the average person, he'd learned that frustration and anger got him nowhere. He'd said that he couldn't change his emotions, but he could change how he reacted to them. And his default reaction was laughter. I earnestly believed he could find the bright side—the silver lining, as they say—of any situation. Nothing could stop this man. Yet now, that cheerful ambience was nowhere to be found.

"I'm having a hard time trying to laugh this one off," he said.

It was getting hard to look at him.

I felt guilty.

I wanted to disappear.

I was a broken husk of a man.

And in those moments of weakness, with my broken husk lying there next to Kris, I wanted to tell him about my history with Zoey. To spill my guts to him. I figured it would put him at ease and explain why she wasn't coming, but I couldn't bring myself to do it.

There were plenty of chances to do it too, so I couldn't use that as an excuse, not that I wanted to. Just about every hour consisted of sixty opportunities to tell him, which was characterized by those empty passing minutes of silence.

It wasn't even that I didn't know the words to use. I had already gone over the conversation in my head hundreds if not thousands of times. I was confident that I knew just about every response and branching path that the conversation could have taken. Multiple times the words were sitting on the tip of my tongue, hammering at the back of my teeth, begging to be let out. But to keep my mouth shut would be to silence these words and thoughts. To kill them before they were voiced. And that desire to keep my mouth shut always ended up winning out in the end, until the whole mental battle began again the next minute.

My will was getting weaker though.

Every time the door opened, I had to hold my breath. After all, it was all speculation. Zoey could have just been busy. She could be walking down the hall this very second. I didn't know. I had no idea what Zoey was thinking, but it only made sense to me that it would be an awkward experience if she walked in here with both of us—a Chris and a Kris—lying there. It's not exactly a thing that I would have wanted to do myself. It's not about being a coward, but you'd need much more than bravery to weather that level of tension.

I looked back up to the ceiling, where the pinholes were waiting for me, and decided to put off any more of these oppressive thoughts. I'd have an easier time contemplating the meaning of the universe than to understand the inner workings of the female mind. We really were two different species or from two different planets.

Ah.

I lost count.

I guess I had to start back from zero.

Where was that first hole again?

Before I could locate it, there was a sound from the door. Both Kris and I zeroed in on it like missile guidance systems. It creaked open and a figure floated through.

A woman.

It wasn't any of the nurses.

It wasn't Adi, Mia, or Yasmin for that matter either.

I almost didn't recognize her.

In fact, I probably wouldn't have recognized the woman—if it weren't for those massive eyebrows of hers.

CHAPTER 34

"Mona?" Both Kris and I said in unison as we pointed our respective index fingers at the curly-haired woman. We then reflexively turned back to look at one another.

"Wait, you know her?" I asked.

"Yeah."

"Really?"

"Yeah, would I have called out her name if I didn't know who she was?"

"True, and I could be saying the same exact thing."

"Fair enough," Kris replied.

This quickfire exchange may have read like it came one after the other, but it all happened almost instantaneously. So fast that I was surprised that the only bystander in the room, Mona Lotta, was able to keep up.

"Oh, whoops, I think I have the wrong room," Mona said, a finger on her chin as she looked between the both of us.

"Seriously?!" we both said.

"Just kidding."

She giggled and skipped over to our bedsides as if she was playing hopscotch. All the while, the mounds of fatty flesh that you'd call her breasts bounced with the supposed rhythm of her steps.

After a few hops, Mona landed with both feet together and threw her arms up like she was a gymnast who had just completed her floor exercise. She turned to me first and arched a single eyebrow.

"You like what you see?" she asked.

"I wasn't watching."

"I saw you staring."

"I did nothing of the sort."

I hated lying, but that didn't mean I was going to come out and admit that I'd been captivated by her breasts the entire time she'd been hopping towards me. There wasn't any way to put it in a positive light. However, considering who I was talking to, that probably wasn't entirely accurate. She would have enjoyed the praise. Relished it even. But I wasn't going to give her that little victory over me. I needed to maintain control otherwise I'd be swept up in her flow.

It'd been a little over a month since I'd last seen Mona, in my bed—naked no less. She never did end up calling Yasmin about needing a place. For all intents and purposes, that brief experience with her was a fleeting dream. I had no idea what the point of it was.

"Mona, is Zoey with you too?" Kris asked, looking back at the door.

"Sorry, sweetie... She couldn't make it."

"What? Why not?"

"She has some *womanly* matters to attend to." Mona gave me a look. She stared straight into my eyes before turning back to Kris. "I was just with her. She sent me to come and talk to you and to apologize."

"But... it's not her time of the month."

I stifled a gag.

Did he really know that?

I didn't even know that.

I didn't want to know that, and I dated her for over twelve years.

"Hm, it worries me that you know something like that Kris," Mona said, looking visibly disturbed.

"She brings it up often enough. I just happened to notice the pattern."

"Sure, honey, we'll go with that."

The two of them talked on for the next couple of minutes while I watched and listened. I didn't know the connection between the two, but it was obvious that there was a level of rapport built up between them. They bickered like two siblings arguing over who got to ride shotgun—Mona being the older one. She seemed to have the acute ability to instantaneously get underneath Kris's skin. Pressing all the right or wrong buttons to cause the irritation in his voice to rise.

"You two seem buddy-buddy," I said when there was a lull in their conversation.

"Does it look that way?" Kris replied. "I think she's annoying."

"How mean! It's the eyebrows, isn't it? You think I'm annoying because of my eyebrows! I knew it!"

Kris turned to me and rolled his eyes.

"Mona never fails to find an opportunity to inject her eyebrows into every conversation. I don't think she realizes she's only drawing attention to them."

"Hellooo. Excuse me. I'm standing right here."

"They are massive though, aren't they?" Kris continued. "I was thinking about shaving them off in her sleep and studying them for science."

"I can still hear you."

"But, besides her constant neediness, she's an okay person."

"That's the exact vibe I got from her too," I said. "How'd you meet her?"

"Second-year, we took an advanced biology class together. It was a prerequisite for the major."

"Seriously? She wants to go into the medical field too? That's... surprising. I've heard rumors about biology classes."

Mostly that they were GPA suicide.

"No, that wasn't it," Kris said. "Mona, why don't you tell him why you took that class?"

Mona smiled.

"I needed that super-duper easy A."

"That's the exact opposite of easy!" I retorted.

Describing myself as a chronic window-shopper of classes, I had heard the horror stories revolving around the biology classes at Oceanside University. A crucible. Hell on Earth in many aspects. No set of classes had resulted in more failures and droppers in the history of the school. They say less than 5% can make it through alive and even then, many are left emotionally traumatized and scared for the rest of their lives.

Did that mean Mona was a certified genius?!

"It is when you copy the smart kids."

"..."

Wow.

She wasn't wrong, but still. To openly admit to breaking every academic integrity agreement so casually. People cheated, that wasn't anything unusual. However, it was still a taboo subject in most regards. One that gave people a reason to look down on you.

"I just needed the grade, and that was the only class available in that time slot. I don't care about sciency stuff or math. What would someone in the performing arts do with anything like that anyway?"

"That's true, I guess," I said. "And I didn't know that you wanted to be a performer."

Mona shrugged.

"You never asked," she stated plainly. "But it's been ever since I was little, when my dad would sit me down in front of the TV screen. He was a big fan of the old-timey stuff that he grew up with, so naturally that's what he wanted to show me. To have the chance to play different characters with different backstories seemed like an exhilarating experience. Glamorous too. It's either that or modeling." She finished by striking a pose that I'd seen in more centerfolds than I could remember.

Well, all things considered, it made sense. Mona had that vibe about her.

She knew what she wanted to do, huh.

I just couldn't shake the notion that here I was, sitting or awkwardly lying to be more accurate, and I'd stumbled upon another person who knew what they wanted to do in their life. People like me, who didn't know specifically, really were on the endangered species list.

"Yeah, and after we were made lab partners," Kris said, "guess who was the one that had to do all that work. That work that she copied off. *Me.* So many sleepless nights. So many."

"You're still complaining about that?" Mona said. "I made it up to you, didn't I?"

"How?"

"I mean, I did do that one thing with my mouth that you like."

"Don't insert sexual innuendos into our conversation where they don't belong. What will Chris here think?"

"Oh, don't worry about that. He already knows exactly what I mean." She winked at me.

"Leave me out of this. I have absolutely no idea what you're talking about."

"Hmph. Men. Always so quick to jump the gun and make assumptions. I didn't mean anything sexual by it. I meant that I'm a smooth talker. You know, you use your mouth to talk too."

That was a stretch by every definition of the word. If this was a trial, I'm sure that this would have been classified as misdirection.

She was grasping at straws, as they say.

"In other words," Mona continued, "Kris, wasn't I the one who set you up with Zoey in the first place?"

Wait.

What the hell?

Did I just hear what I thought I just heard?

Did she just say what I thought I just heard her say?

"God, you always fall back on that one too! Yes, you did. And I'm thankful. You can't just rely on that one forever. Let's just call it here and now, with the other Chris here as our witness, that we're even."

"Stevens," she said.

Wait a second.

You have to go back.

I didn't quite catch that.

They just glossed over an important plot point.

"Anyway, enough about me. Chris, how do you know Mona?"

"Ah."

It took me a second for my mind to get back on track. I attempted to reposition myself on the bed, but of course, I couldn't move all that well, so it must have looked like I was having a seizure.

"He's one of my many male conquests," Mona spoke first.

"No, I'm not," I croaked out.

"We're two star-crossed lovers from rival families caught in a doomed romance."

"If I was Romeo, you certainly wouldn't be my Juliet."

"We're simply lovers then."

"You have a lax definition of what it means to be lovers."

"Lovers of good food and entertainment."

"Just about everyone would fall under that definition!"

Kris laughed.

He was enjoying himself too much. I figured he was just having a good time not being on the receiving end of Mona's antics for once.

Mona had that effect on people.

Through and through, she was an irritating and difficult person to talk to.

"In all honesty," she said, "you can say that he's a friend of a friend. *Ex*-friend."

I glared at Mona and at that, she stuck her tongue out at me.

What was she planning?

In this situation, I was completely defenseless both physically and mentally. Mona seemed to be the one holding all the cards. There was nothing for me to do but play along and hope she didn't expose me right here and now.

But ultimately, would it even be a big deal if I was exposed? I couldn't explain why I was so anxious right now. We were adults and adults dated different people. That wasn't a big deal. Yet my body was reacting in such a way that suggested that it was, in fact, a big deal.

"Oh, do I know this ex-friend?" Kris asked.

"You do actually."

"Who is it?"

"It's on a need-to-know basis," Mona said, "and you don't need to know. I was just sent here on behalf of Zoey to relay her message and to see how you're doing. That's all. She said you sounded down lately. I can assure you that she wanted to be here. She just couldn't."

"I understand. Thanks for coming. At the very least, getting a visitor, even if it was you, was nice..."

"I'm going to ignore that extra remark and take that as a compliment. So, you're welcome, bestie."

As if on cue, the door opened again and one of the nameless nurses scurried into the room. She looked at the three of us, apologized, and then moved over to Kris's bedside to check his vitals.

"Alright, Kris," the nurse chirped, "ready for your last round of tests and X-rays? The doctor said if everything looks good, then you'll be free to go."

"Really? Dang, okay. That's great news. I can't wait to get out of here." Kris' doom-and-gloom attitude seemed to have all but dissipated as he climbed out of the hospital bed. He stopped at the door and turned back to me. "Sorry, no offense. I've just spent too much time in hospital rooms."

"None taken. I understand."

With that, he was gone.

And then there were two.

It was strange. In the blink of an eye, our lively atmosphere had transitioned into whatever it was now. Virtually dead silence. Awkward, oppressive silence. The calm before the storm in many respects. Mona continued to stare at the door as if she might have been expecting it to open again—for Kris to storm back in saying he'd forgotten something or for another nurse to come and whisk me away too.

"He's a sweet guy," Mona said. "A little too optimistic at times, but that has its appeal too."

"Yeah."

"A good pick for Zoey, wouldn't you say?"

"I mean, sure, I guess."

I didn't have an opinion. That simple statement already took me a great deal of effort to say. There wasn't anything wrong with him in my eyes. He was an upstanding individual. The kind of guy that, if you brought him home to meet your family, your dad might not outright threaten. Also, he seemed to have his life together. So all-around, he was a good catch. I'd give him an 8.5 out of 10.

And—most importantly—he was better than me.

That's all he needed to be.

"Don't be too hard on yourself. You're not that bad."

"Whoa, how'd you know what I was thinking?"

"I didn't, but I could assume. I was able to deduce that much from what I've heard and know about you, the context of our previous conversations, and because of the expression clearly written all over your face."

"Wow, it's that obvious?"

"It's elementary," she said smugly. "But anyway, I think now that we're alone, it'd be a good time for us to have a little chit-chat."

I nodded.

Though it might not have initially seemed that way, maybe Mona was a genius after all.

CHAPTER 35

Mona plopped down on Kris's bed, filling the vacancy that he'd just left behind. As she did so, her breasts jiggled like water balloons. I had to tear my eyes away lest I went on along-winded tangent about her assets and how they could do no wrong. How they made the impossible possible. How they—see! That's what I'm talking about. I almost fell into that trap! Control yourself, Chris! Stay on topic.

"Do you think he'd notice if we did it on his bed?" Mona asked as she dragged her long nail across the sheets.

"Did what?"

"You know. *That.*"

"I do know, but I really hope I'm wrong. That's why I'm asking for clarification before I make an ass of myself."

"It's rude to make a girl say *it.*"

"So I was right?!"

"I'll just put it this way," Mona said. "We can have a little wrestling match. One-on-one. Mano a mano. Or maybe it'd be more accurate to say—*mouth to mouth.*"

"Can you stop italicizing those words?! It's making me think they mean something they don't!"

Mona and her double entendres were going to be the death of me and I wasn't talking about the ones on her chest.

She giggled.

"I meant if we could talk. If we could have our conversation on his bed. I didn't mean anything sexual. I promise."

"Yes, you did," I said. "But I can't move anyway, so it doesn't matter." I shook a bit to emphasize the point.

"Is it that bad?"

"They have me strapped up really good. They don't want me moving at all."

Also, I can't feel my legs, I amended.

"All that from the elevator? I heard it was a miracle for you two to be alive, but that's seriously crazy."

"It... wasn't all from the elevator."

"Huh?"

I didn't reply to her immediately. There was a mental checklist I had to go over in my mind before I was okay with revealing any part of my troubled past. I'd run over that same checklist with Mia and then Yasmin. Considering the context of those two situations, I had no choice but to do it in either. But could the same be said right now? I couldn't say with any certainty that I even knew who Mona was or if she could be trusted. However, it did seem to me that she had a good heart. Her actions and words always had another meaning or motivation layered underneath, but for some reason, possibly my own stupidity, I never got the vibe that those reasons were malicious. They were deceptive and manipulative, but not malicious. Mona did seem to have a deep connection to Zoey too, so in a way, I figured she was involved in this somehow, even if indirectly.

I took a deep breath before I exhaled the rest of my reservations.

"I... kind of had an accident around six months ago," I started slowly. It still wasn't easy saying it whether it be due to embarrassment or shame. I had to ease myself into it. I was the type of person who slowly peeled off a bandage. To me, that was always less painful because the pain was spread out. A little pain over a long period of time was more bearable than all at once. "I was sitting on my windowsill. You probably remember from when you came over. It's small and tight. So, yeah, I was sitting there, and I tried to climb back through, and I slipped. I fell all the way down. There were a couple of air conditioning units that slowed my descent, but I basically fell the whole way. I landed on the edge of this green dumpster in the alley. I screwed my back up bad, but I was too embarrassed to go to the doctor or anything. I didn't want to have to explain what I was doing."

"Why were you up there?"

"No reason. I was just thinking."

"About a certain girl I presume."

"Yeah."

"Hm, the timing adds up," Mona said, nodding her head as if she was counting. "It would have been after you broke up with Zoey, right?"

"How'd you know that? And don't say you read it from my facial expressions. Where did the two of you even meet? She never brought you up at all, and she told me everything... Or at least I thought she did."

Mona leaned back using her arms as pillars for support. Without saying a word, she stared at the ceiling and absentmindedly kicked her feet over the edge of the bed.

I didn't reiterate my question. I was sure she heard me. She was probably thinking of a response.

"It was all the way back in our first year. You know how they throw a mixer for the new freshman students? That's where we bumped into each other. It was besties at first sight."

"..."

I did remember something like that happening. Zoey had asked me if I wanted to go to it, to try and be social and make some connections, but I obviously declined. Too many people. I don't do good with too many people. I get exhausted having to put up a front.

"When I wasn't talking to her about my escapades, you were a topic that came up a lot in fact," Mona said. "She was always talking about you. So, I should know a thing or two."

"Hopefully, not too much."

This was news to me.

Growing up, Zoey and I had the same friend group. That meant that I had no fear of people learning too much about me because they already knew who I was. My friends could already see how I acted.

"She told me a great deal," Mona continued. "But that doesn't mean I still don't have some unanswered questions."

"Like what?"

"Like why you did it. Why'd you break-up with her?"

I knew this question was coming. I could have seen it from a mile away.

It was the question I asked myself every night before I went to sleep. And every night the answer that came to me before I dozed off was slightly different. They were mostly interchangeable, but each one had their own subtleties.

"Where do I even begin?" I said. "It's because I wasn't good enough for someone like her. I couldn't live up to what I thought she deserved. I just kept letting her down. All these things. Ever since we were little, she'd been doing all the work and leading me around by the hand. I wanted to be like her. But I couldn't. So, I just thought I'd be doing her a favor by breaking up with her. I instantly regretted it, though. She looked so hurt. I wanted to take it back. But judging from what Kris said, I made the right choice. I was a loser. A spineless coward who couldn't deal with his own insecurities."

Mona brought a finger up to her chin.

"A coward, huh? I see. I'm starting to see everything. So, that's what you think?"

"I mean, at this point, it's all true, isn't it? Kris basically confirmed it."

"It isn't quite like that."

"..."

What was the point of this conversation?

I hoped Mona wasn't trying to cheer me up because she was failing—terribly.

"Zoey and you... Both of you are really similar, you know."

"Oh? What similarities could I have had with her?"

Mona sat up straight and frowned, her eyebrows fusing together in a downward angle. She looked upset. I hadn't seen her this upset before.

"She told me about the night you two first met," Mona said.

"Ugh, that? You mean she told you how she practically saved my life at the park when I slipped off the jungle gym? Geez, that's so embarrassing."

"That's not how she saw it."

"What? What do you mean?"

I was confused.

What other way was there to see it? That's exactly what happened. I was sitting up there, and she caught me as I was falling. She saved me. A trend that would carry on for the next twelve years.

Mona sighed, her gaze falling to her own feet, she began to speak.

"'When I saw that boy from my window—that young boy who couldn't have been any older than seven or eight—playing alone at the park that night, I couldn't help but think... that he must be very... brave. And even though I was scared to go out alone. I wanted to go meet him.'"

Mona spoke in a tone that wasn't hers. Neither were the words she chose. Using her acting chops, she'd almost perfectly encapsulated Zoey's mannerisms of speech. Despite not hearing it for months, I could still recognize that much.

But brave?

Me?

That was laughable.

I doubted that Zoey would have called me that. Mona must have been kidding as she usually was.

That's what I wanted to think, until I remembered Zoey's own words.

Kids aren't allowed to be here at night. It's dangerous.

What had sounded like admonishment when I heard it for the first time, underneath this new light, could be interpreted differently. But I still didn't want to buy it.

"All I did was complain to her about my problems that night. How I'd left my mom crying, and how I couldn't do anything to help her. A brave person wouldn't do that."

"It takes a brave person to admit what they've done wrong and all their faults. From that conversation, Zoey must have come to realize that you were a person who cared about his mother, and that the choices you made weighed heavily on you."

"That's a stretch. A *big* stretch. No way she saw it that way. That manner of looking at it—"

It was like seeing a glass that was half empty as half full.

The exact way that Zoey saw things.

"Believe it or not, Chrissy boy, she isn't the perfect person you think she is," Mona said, "and this is me talking as her friend. She wasn't angry or upset at you because she thought you were pathetic. Trust me. I know. We talked. We still talk. Like all the time."

"She must have. I was useless without her. I let her do everything, and she never let me down. Kris even said that she thought I was out of her league. The only thing I did—that I could do—was stand there and just watch."

"Exactly."

"Exactly what?"

"With your eyes always on her, the only thing she could do was try her best. To be the person you expected her to be. She constantly strived to be the best version of herself."

"Huh?" I was having trouble understanding.

Mona's words weren't confusing or obscure, but I couldn't comprehend the meaning behind them. They conflicted so drastically with my own perspective. I'd viewed things from a certain way for so long, I couldn't just automatically switch like that.

"Okay, but what does that have to do with similarities? Zoey wasn't useless at all."

"Ah, you're dense. Sooo dense. This is what she meant, isn't it?" Mona groaned before standing up and closing the distance to my bed. "The thing that was bothering her. *Actually* bothering her—the expectations you put on her to be perfect."

"..."

The expectations that I put on her to be perfect...

I still didn't quite get it.

What expectations was she talking about?

I was the one who felt inadequate.

I needed more time to process what I was hearing and to pick through my past and memories with a fine-toothed comb. However, Mona interrupted my thoughts.

"She said she'd never leave you, right? When you were kids? I'll be the first to admit that that's cute. Sounds like something from an old school Disney fairy-tale romance. Nowadays they're shying away from that message and stuff, but I wished some guy would come along and tell me that. It's romantic. But that kind of thing—it's a lot to live up to, you know?"

So that's what it was.

I hadn't looked at it from that perspective before. All these months, I'd only framed my thoughts around me and not her.

After you make a bold declaration like that, to never leave someone's side, the only thing you can do is put your everything into it. If you don't—you'd fail. There was no middle ground. It was the type of goal that required your all.

Of course, it was a lot to live up to. Overly idealistic and self-destructive.

Zoey and I both had the same problem. Managing our own self-worth. It's not that either of us was inadequate. It was the unrealistic expectations that we were putting on ourselves that eventually tore us apart.

"Though she wouldn't hardly admit it, her life didn't revolve solely around you and making sure you were satisfied," Mona said. "She did have her own desires and dreams, but because of that promise, she was willing to let them go. Doing both wouldn't be possible."

"She didn't have to."

Hearing this was twisting my insides. If I could, I would have climbed out of bed and run out that door, but I was locked in place. There was no escape. I was required to listen even if it was too much to bear.

"You know she did. You should know that better than anyone else. You were the one watching her. She didn't want to disappoint you. To be honest, I just thought you were a dick who couldn't see what you were doing to her and were taking advantage of her kindness. So, like the amazing friend I was, I decided I'd help her out. Give her a little escape from whatever obligations she had. I set her up with a capable, sweet guy from my biology class."

"Kris."

"Yup. Complete coincidence that you two basically had the same name. In hindsight, that's kind of weird, but it wasn't all that important. He was nice, and I figured his demeanor would cheer her up too. It did. My plan worked. I have to say I was quite proud of myself. I got to play matchmaker. I thought it didn't matter to me if she was cheating, if the guy she was cheating with was an improvement."

Gee thanks. I appreciate it.

Considering the state I was in, it was like I was the captured hero and Mona was playing the part of the criminal mastermind—the one who had orchestrated everything from the shadows. It would have been great if she could fast-forward through the monologuing and the explanation of her nefarious plan and just killed me already. Killed me in some overly-complicated and impractical way.

"But I was wrong," Mona continued. "I didn't think she'd be so busted up when you cut things off with her. I think—I think she must have thought she failed you, like she wasn't good enough and that she couldn't be the person you needed her to be." Mona was standing over

me, her arms crossed. The stern expression had softened into a pensive melancholy as she looked down at my legs.

What?

Immediately those words brought me back to what Mona had said the last time I'd seen her. Her cryptic parting words as she had walked out my door.

I was completely wrong about you.

"In what way?" I said, trying to glean even the smallest hint from Mona's hazel eyes.

"You're not completely helpless," Mona said, tapping her finger to the beat of her words. "You're not totally pathetic. And you're only moderately useless."

"I can't tell if those are compliments or thinly veiled insults—especially that last one."

"You can take it whichever way you want to. I won't judge. A little experimentation makes everything fun."

"And now you're doing that sexual innuendo thing again."

"No, I'm not. That's just how I talk."

"Whatever," I said. "Let's not get derailed. Can you be more specific about what you meant when you said you were wrong?"

"You're a totally capable person, Chris. I found that out when we met. You weren't anything like I imagined."

"But what made you think that? I didn't do anything."

"You offered me a place to stay," Mona replied without missing a beat.

"Yeah, but that..."

That couldn't count for anything.

I thought she was homeless.

Any rational, normal person would have done the same thing in my situation. In fact, it was safe to assume that it would have been weirder if a person didn't offer to help. My character as a person had nothing to do with it. Nothing at all.

"But nothing," Mona said, her voice rising in excitement. "Hearing Zoey talk about you made me think that you were a spineless wimpy excuse of a man. That's why I wanted to see for myself. When I heard that your friend Brad was parading around trying to set you up with some girls, I saw the perfect opportunity. Zoey used to mention him too. Said he wasn't the best influence on you."

"Yeah, he probably isn't. He's my bro though."

"Let's just say I was pleasantly surprised with the man I met that day. I could tell you weren't a complete pushover. You even kissed me. Very bold of you."

"You were literally throwing yourself on to me."

"I know, that was kind of the point. I still didn't think you'd do it. It was a test. One that you passed with flying colors, if I do say so myself. I got the impression that you might have been gay. I mean, you barely made any moves on Zoey, and she's a complete babe. That bothered her and made her think that you weren't attracted to her. Even I thought about shooting my shot with her more times than I'd like to admit." Mona smiled. "That kiss showed me you had some balls. I knew there was more to you than meets the eye, or rather ear, especially by the way that bratty miss with the potty mouth looked at you and talked to you. I have a feeling she'd think the exact same thing."

Yasmin.

The thing that initially drew me to her was how much she reminded me of Zoey. In my eyes they were both strong individuals.

But then I'd said it was pointless.

It was a dumb thing to say, sure.

I don't want you to think this was an excuse, but back when Yasmin was talking to me a couple days ago, I was feeling particularly nihilistic. Maybe deep down, though I didn't want to admit it, I was hoping Zoey would take me back if I changed enough and became someone she deserved, but it was pointless to think about now. She'd moved on, and Kris adored her. I wasn't going to butt in between them.

Especially when there was someone else I'd fallen for.

"I'm not so sure about that anymore," I mumbled. "I think I screwed that up too."

"Then do something about it, Chris. This is how the whole thing began in the first place isn't it? You told me you liked her, so do something."

"What do you expect me to do? Crawl out of here and go find her? I can't move."

"You have a phone don't you? Just call her or text her or do something. She's probably waiting. I could tell as much from looking at her. Girls have a sixth sense for this sort of thing, after all. She likes you."

"Nah, I think I'm just going to let this one be. I'm done. Plus, considering how I am now"—I attempted to move my legs—"I can't see Yasmin wanting me now. I don't want to cause her any more trouble."

I believed that this was the correct path. By now, it should have been clear that I wasn't cut out for relationships. I'm always thinking about myself. I couldn't even see the person that was hurting right in front of me for twelve whole years. And though I'd vowed that things would be different, there hadn't been much growth at all. Maybe things would have been better if I just—"

"Shut up!"

Mona jumped on top of me.

More accurately, it was a belly flop—right on top of me.

"Oof! What are you doing? Get off!"

With the weight of her body pinning me down, I was at a severe disadvantage. I was pinned. As I struggled to break free, Mona held on that much tighter.

"Stop thinking! Stop thinking! Stop thinking!"

Unable to do anything else, I leaned down and chomped down on her shoulder. Even through the cotton fabric of her sweater, I could have sworn that I tasted cinnamon.

"Eek! That hurt!"

Mona flipped around and climbed up my body like a spider. She then sat up, making sure to use her legs to lock my arms against my sides.

"Let me go!"

"No!"

In the next instant, Mona smothered my face with the two fun bags on her chest, muffling my pleas. To paraphrase a famous movie tagline, in the space between a woman's breasts, no one can hear you scream.

I felt like in any other circumstance, this would have been a dream come true for me. What guy wouldn't want this? In fact, I'd even rank suffocating in the boobs of a woman in my top three best ways to die, right next to peacefully in my sleep and sugar overdose. The thing was, no matter how pleasant it felt or how lovely it smelled, suffocating still sucked. Didn't help that I had wasted a lot of my precious oxygen trying to yell for the doctor or any of the nurses. They were never here when you needed them.

"I won't let you go until you stop thinking!"

"That's the same thing as being dead!" I mumbled into her chest, but it came out as a garbled bunch of words that she probably didn't understand.

So, this was how I was going to go, huh?

I had to say that it was a fun ride, except for all the parts that were completely lame.

As my head started to feel light and my already blackened vision began to fade into unconsciousness, the familiar image of Yasmin strolled into my mind. Of course, she had a scowl. The folded arms. The hip cocked contrapposto. Interestingly, despite being posed in a way that was typical of her, she didn't look annoyed or irritated. If anything, she looked disappointed.

I didn't like it.

You're supposed to see happy stuff at the end of your life. Why was it that I always saw depressing things? I don't want to die that way. I don't want any more regrets. If I got one more chance, I think I'd apologize to Yasmin. Meeting her wasn't pointless at all. It was fun.

Suddenly, right as I was about to pass out for good, Mona lifted her body off me and stood up.

"Well, have you stopped thinking? If not, I'll get back on top of you and finish the tit job."

"The what?" I said as I clutched my chest, gasping for air.

"The tit job. You know, like an assassination."

"That's a hit job."

"Oh, same thing."

"You know it's not."

Mona giggled. "Either way, it looks like you enjoyed it."

She pointed to my lower body, prompting me to quickly cover my immodesty with one of the pillows supporting my back. Hey, it was a natural male reaction. Completely natural. I didn't know why she was acting so surprised. I was just happy to know it still worked.

"Well, it seems like your resolve has been hardened, so with that I'll take my leave," Mona said as she patted the wrinkles out of her sweater.

"Uh, thanks," I replied.

"No, you don't have to thank me. It looks like I inadvertently caused you a lot of... trouble. I sincerely apologize. If I didn't clear my conscience, I'd never be able to get my beauty sleep. And, just so you know, I'm going to leave it in your hands. If you fuck things up with Yasmin, it'll be all your fault this time."

"I won't."

With that, she gave me a wink and pranced out the door.

CHAPTER 36

I've always had difficulty apologizing. I knew that wasn't a wholly unique experience. It was something I could say about myself, but probably something that could be said about most people as well. I'd long since learned that I'm not as different from others as I think I am.

As to when exactly this difficulty started becoming a recurring trend, I could trace it as far back as my elementary school days. Back then was when you'd first begun interacting and apologizing to other children after all, quickly learning that you weren't the center of the universe.

Before I continue, I want to clarify that this was not to say that the act of apologizing itself was difficult. I'm sure that any person in the world can shoot off a casual, "sorry," or a "my bad," or something along those lines. I mean, those would be the exact things you say in passing after bumping into someone on the sidewalk or accidentally stepping on their foot. When such events happen, hasty apologies always come out as a gut reaction utterance—usually without any thought involved.

That's where the key difference resided.

The apologies you had to think about, the ones where a simple, "sorry, my bad," wouldn't cut it, those were the ones that I found so difficult to navigate around. The "I really fucked this up," apologies.

The key to making this kind of apology work was usually by adding a gesture. A grand gesture that showed that you learned from the mistake, and you were asking for forgiveness. It was almost a necessity.

Huh.

I guess that's where another distinction was.

Apologizing and asking for forgiveness.

Those were two different things.

Though often done in tandem, the former was meant to acknowledge fault and the latter was meant to return things to a previous state—the status quo.

Going back to my wonderful elementary school experience, a particular story comes to mind. To give you a rough timeline, it couldn't have been any further back than first or second grade, so I was very young. It was lunchtime and all the kids from my class were in the cafeteria, which also doubled as our auditorium, sitting on these long tables and benches that folded and extended out of the walls. The school tried to fit all the students from a single class onto each of their respective tables, so most of the time it was very cramped. Shoulder-to-shoulder even. Back then, I used to swing my feet back and forth, not consciously, but the way a child just does when they are unable to touch the floor.

The next day, I was called into the principal's office where, to my surprise, my mother was waiting for me. I didn't know it yet, but I was in serious trouble. Not too long ago, the mother of another student had called the office—furious. What was it about? She said that her daughter had come home the day prior crying with welts and bruises all up her legs. She said that I'd been kicking her underneath the table during lunchtime. The thing was—I just didn't remember it. Specifically, I didn't remember kicking her because I didn't notice I was doing it. She was a quiet girl who spoke softly, if at all, and she never made me aware that I was hurting her. But this is not to downplay what I did. I was sorry, but back then, when I was that young especially, it was difficult to wrap my mind around the concept that something was your fault, or you were in trouble when you were unaware that you did anything wrong.

At home, after being adequately disciplined, my mother told me that I needed to apologize. I didn't know how I was supposed to do it, so I settled on the idea of making that girl an apology card. On the front, I drew a simple picture of her, as crude and innocent as any drawing made by a kid that age, and I sprinkled the words "I'm sorry!" all over the front and back. I probably wrote it over a hundred times. I kept telling myself that I needed to add one more. It needed one more. Back at school, I handed the finished card off to the principal who said she'd give it to her.

I never got to see that girl's reaction or find out if she ever got the card. It turned out that the girl's mother decided to pull her out of our school before I was able to see her again.

I can't really find a moral in that story, not that one was needed. It's just that I tend to remember it at times like this, and as long as I live, I'm sure that it's not something I'll ever completely forget.

I'd made a grand gesture back when Yasmin and I were getting to know each other. I'd showed up at the door to her apartment in a bathrobe and the tightest speedo I've ever worn. The first speedo I'd ever worn. I'd asked for forgiveness by offering to support her in her pursuit of art, something I was able to tell that she loved greatly.

In fact, Adi did the same thing. She showed her younger sister that she had kept a precious item from their childhood after all the years. That was enough to show that she still cared about her sister despite their estranged relationship.

I think the thing that could be said with certainty was that, despite her cold outside demeanor, Yasmin was vulnerable too. Words and actions could have just as much effect on her as anyone else. Sure, she may have had more violent reactions to things, but she was still a human being, a prideful one, and she deserved to be treated well like anyone else.

A cold, prideful, violent, and vulnerable human being.

That's what Yasmin was.

It's for this reason, as I was holding my cell phone next to my ear, that I was convinced calling wouldn't work, but what other choice did I have? It was a step up from texting, but multiple steps down—flights even—from doing it face-to-face or anything I'd consider grand. This was the bare minimum I could do, but the bare minimum, ironically, wasn't enough.

To expand on the previous joke, my resolve had been adequately hardened by Mona, who convinced me that I needed to make things up with Yasmin, but in the face of this current situation that resolve was softening quickly. I was nervous and unsure of how to proceed, and no two things killed a man's confidence faster than that. That's why, when the call went to voicemail, I was both disappointed and relieved.

She didn't pick up.

Maybe she was just away from her phone at the moment or maybe she saw who it was and decided it wasn't worth answering?

Thinking this way made my resolve shrink further.

She didn't like me anymore.

She hated me.

She wanted nothing to do with me.

As you could see, I was having a lot of negative thoughts. They weren't unfounded. They were based on the facts of the situation. I'd once again hurt her feelings, and I believed that no one should have to put up with anyone that hurt them—physically or mentally.

But I still wanted to talk to her.

Except that didn't matter at all if she didn't want to talk to me—if she no longer cared about me.

If that was the case, there was nothing left for me to do but give up and let her go.

With a tap, I ended the call before it could start recording a voicemail. No one uses voicemail anymore, right? Ironically, it felt like such an archaic way of communication. No one had time to record a message or even to listen to them nowadays, especially if they were grainy and you couldn't hear. Though text messages weren't as formal, they were in fact many times simpler, faster, and easier. This sentiment of mine was reflected when I returned to my home screen where I could see all those notifications that I still hadn't cleared yet. From the looks of it, they were basically all from the day of the student art exhibit.

There were five missed calls.

And fifty missed text messages.

Fifty.

That was a lot. Well, a lot for an unpopular person who didn't get messages that often.

Now you know why I'd put off going through them. It didn't help that I'd been in a somewhat depressed mood either, and I figured reading them all would just make me feel even worse.

Scrolling through the calls first, three came from Mia and one each from Adi and Brad. No doubt they were wondering where I was that day. I hadn't arrived at the arranged meeting spot when I said I would, even after making such a big deal out of it and forcing them to swear that they wouldn't be late. I bet their first reaction was how hypocritical I was.

Yeah.

In our group text chat, Brad had asked where I was a few times, which was echoed by the other two. That was right around 11:00 a.m. Altogether that accounted for six of the text messages.

Another three were spam asking me to meet hot and horny singles in my area. MILFs even. Very tempting.

And one was to remind me to schedule a dentist appointment, which I'd been putting off lazily for the past two months.

Altogether this accounted for ten out of the fifty total.

The rest were from Yasmin.

My initial reaction was that she went a bit overboard. More than a bit. It was completely overboard. If I didn't answer after the first five messages, shouldn't it have been apparent that something was up? I could only imagine the insults she had thrown at me. This could easily account for about a year's supply worth! There was probably enough here to fill out the first volume of a giant insult encyclopedia.

Not knowing what to expect, I took a deep breath, clicked her name, and started from the top.

The first message was the one that I had woken up to that day, and my reply to it. She had asked me to get there a little early to keep her company. I remembered how shocked I was to see that because it didn't sound like her at all. She'd sooner die a thousand deaths than to express that level of weakness. From there, the rest of them must have been sent when I had no service.

Cool. I'm in the far right corner

Where are you now?

This guy is trying to talk to me,
its kinda creeping me out

He won't leave me alonnnne.

Fuck. He just won't stop talking.
I think he's hitting on me or something.
I'm just staring at my phone but he isn't getting the hint

He just asked for my number. Plz kill me.

Alright, I told him that I was waiting for my boyfriend to get here, so you better fucking pretend. I'll pay for food later to make up for it

How much longer? More people are starting to walk in

Hey, moron, where you at?

Hello?

Whatttt, Adi and the others just showed up. Were you setting up a surprise for me? I'm so fucking embarrassed. I told you to keep this private. I'm gonna kick your ass when you get here. And I'm not paying for food later.

They told me that you said you'd meet them, but you didn't show up? What's going on?

Okay, I'm just gonna spam you until you answer

Hellooooooo

Answer me

Dumbass

Idiot

sjdkjdsndsl

wwadafssdjs

ckskdsmdsl

Moron

Fucking answerrrrrr

You're gonna miss it, I'm supposed to go up and talk about my art piece in a few minutes

Hurry

I'm up next

Chris?

Seriously? What the fuck. You better have the world's greatest excuse. I swear to god you better be dying.
You said you'd fucking be here. You promised.

I can't believe you right now

Never talk to me again.

Geez.

I figured that she'd be pissed, but this was taking it up to eleven, as they say. Despite having an excuse, reading her words was still tearing at my heart.

On the surface and to any outsiders, this may have seemed like a small thing, but it was obvious the art event was something that she cared about, and she was hoping that I'd be there to experience it with her. To her, it was a big deal.

And to make it better, she wasn't finished yet.

The next set of messages, much to my surprise, started with one of my own. It was the one that I had tried to send when I was in the elevator when my cell phone had no reception. My simple and feeble, "I'm sorry." Once I regained service, the text must have automatically been sent.

That text was one of those thoughtless and banal apologies. One without substance, a gut reaction, that was unable to capture the nuance of the situation. It was an apology that wasn't worth the effort to read or even consider. If I was being honest, it was embarrassing to look at, especially when compared to the walls of text that sandwiched it on either side. I expected that Yasmin was once again going to rip into me and shred whatever was left.

Finallyyyyy. you better be sorry.
And, hey, I told you not to speak to me again

Never mind, that was harsh. Reading back my previous messages, I sound like a crazy bitch. I can see why you didn't respond. You're probably scared haha. Where are you by the way? Everyone's getting freaked out. They keep telling me that you were really trying to be here. Mrs. Lee said you were trying to plan this from the beginning and that's why you wanted to make sure that I made up with my sister beforehand, so that she could see too. Thanks, I appreciate that. You don't know how much that means to me and I feel like I don't express that enough. I don't want to make any more of a fuss about this, of course if you were busy or something came up you didn't have to come. We'll talk later. Just let me know where you are, so I can let everyone else know

I'm getting really worried. Just let me know you're okay.

Hey, I'm leaving early and I'm heading over to your place now. I'll be there in a couple of minutes. There's a shit ton of sirens

Street's blocked off

What the hell is going on? U ok?

Cops and ambulances surrounding your place. They're not letting anyone go in

People saying the elevator collapsed or something. Two people were inside

Let me know you're ok. I'll feel better even if you tell me one of your terrible jokes. I just want to know you're good

Chris, please.

Please say something

That was the final one.

I kept reading her messages over and over. I'm sure that I read them enough times that I would have been able to recite them all by heart. Despite only being words on a screen, I could hear Yasmin's voice reading them back to me as perfectly as if she was right there by my bedside. It carried all of her tone and inclinations down to her signs of frustration, snarky retorts—and even her concern.

Ah.

I was a fool.

A dumbass.

A moron.

An idiot.

She *did* care.

How I was able to think for even a minute, no, even a second, that she didn't was beyond me. This girl did care about me and that meant that everything was worth fighting for. I needed to see her again and talk to her face-to-face. If I didn't try and clear things up, I knew that it'd haunt me for the rest of my life.

But apologizing over text wasn't optimal. Messages had a miraculous way of capturing and expressing emotions, but I wanted to do this right. Yasmin wasn't picking up my phone calls, so I needed to send a message that would draw her attention. One that I'd know she'd see and would have to react to. A tiny reaction to open her back up to talking to me was all I needed. It wasn't a question of whether she would be angry or happy, only whether she'd respond. That was the first step.

I couldn't help but feel like this was a familiar situation. It reminded me of the very first time I texted Yasmin. Back then I had no idea what to do, so I just said whatever popped into my mind and luckily it worked. However, things are different now. Now, I knew exactly what I wanted to say.

That must have meant that I'd grown as a person, didn't it?

I hit send, admiring my work.

Something.

Yes—I'd grown.

It just wasn't that much.

CHAPTER 37

I was dragged out of my not-so-deep slumber by the sound of rustling, clattering, and movement. The noises were faint but persistent—just barely loud enough to wake me up. My first thought was that it was one of those nurses trying to discreetly go about their business without being too noisy. I figured they needed to clean up the other side of the room so that it'd be ready for any future patients. Kris had been discharged earlier that day after his X-ray results and tests came back looking good.

Kris had returned to the room a little while after Mona had left, looking hopeful. And when the doctor stopped by a little after that to confirm the results, Kris burst out in excitement. He practically started jumping on the bed, and I expected to see streams of confetti shooting out from behind him. I wouldn't have been surprised if the doctor called the nurses in to hold him down and sedate him; he was that excited. It really was a heartwarming display though. I couldn't help but feel excited for the guy.

As he was leaving, he came to my bedside, grabbed my hand, and told me that he'd never forget me. That he'd write about my greatness and spread my tale. He emphasized this by calling me his hero more than enough times and saying that his offer for the double date dinner was still on the table as soon as I got out of there. The literal second, I got out of there, he said. For better or worse, he was really trying to make sure the dinner happened. In response, I hit him with the typical non-committal "I'll think about it,"—everyone's favorite choice to avoid having to answer questions they didn't want to—and I watched as he skipped out the door. He told me that he'd be waiting for my response.

Well, to be completely frank, I didn't *need* to think about it.

I had my answer.

I had it a while back, relatively speaking, seeing as we'd only met roughly a week ago.

The thing was I just didn't have the heart to outright tell him no.

Even though people say that you should freely express your feelings, it would come off rude no matter how you say it. That's because an unwritten rule of life was that, a lot of the time, honesty and politeness didn't always go together. Anyone who's ever had to give a false compliment should know what I'm talking about.

So, I held my tongue, as they say.

I didn't want to ruin his mood, after all.

He was a good guy, and he didn't deserve it.

But now.

Back in the present, I decided to keep my eyes closed and pretend to be asleep for that very same reason. If I sat up now while the nurse was still here, then the conversation would naturally steer towards the "Oh, did I wake you? I'm sorry!" and the "No, you didn't. It's okay." That seemed like too much of a pain in the back to deal with. Yeah, I'd been woken up. Naturally, it would just be rude to come out and say that, though, so I thought it'd be easier for everyone if I just kept my eyes and mouth shut. That was my initial plan at least, but the nurse was making my polite effort difficult to follow through.

The ruckus around the room was growing in volume.

It sounded like things were being banged against each other with no care whatsoever. It was followed by the sound of zippers being zipped and the high-pitched screeching of metal being dragged across the vinyl floor. If you thought nails on a chalkboard sounded bad, this was much worse. It took most of my self-restraint not to smother myself with my own pillow.

What was going on?

Unless I cautioned a peek through one eye, I wouldn't be sure what it was or if any of this noise was necessary to begin with.

Maybe after seeing that I hadn't been disturbed in the slightest by their initial ruckus, my intruder decided to forgo stealth and tact entirely. They were probably of the mindset that it was best to just get everything over with quickly, and I could respect that. But did they have to be so loud?

There was a choir of screeching. Followed by a brief intermission before the sound was replaced with a rapid drumming, not unlike the sound of a rapidly beating heart. Not unlike the incessant tapping of someone who was quickly losing their patience.

Did I dare open an eye to see what was going on?

Surely, any normal person would have just woken me up directly if they needed me. No normal person, especially not a nurse, would resort to such roundabout measures of waking someone up. Right?

"Ahem."

A voice cleared its throat.

It was female.

Slightly gruff.

Definitely irritated.

I was able to tell all that from that one noise.

Still, I decided I wouldn't react to it.

"Ahem... ahem."

A double this time.

I shut my eyes slightly tighter.

"Ahem... Ahem... Ahem!"

Was something wrong with her throat?

If I could've turned on my side, away from the noise, I would have, but it turns out curiosity got the better of me. I opened my eyes to see what was causing all the commotion. There at the foot of my bed, sitting on a stool behind her easel and canvas, was Yasmin. Her head was sticking out around the side, staring directly at me. However, when she saw my eyes open, she quickly retreated behind the enormous canvas.

"Uh, Yasmin?" I asked.

She didn't answer immediately. Instead, she kept her face hidden away and grabbed one of the charcoal pencils she liked to use from out of her bag.

"Oh, did I wake you?" she said. "I didn't mean to. I'm sorry."

"No, you didn't. It's ok—Wait a second! You were obviously trying to wake me up!"

"Prove it."

"Uh, I mean, I can't, but you obviously did it."

"If you don't leave behind any evidence then it basically didn't happen," she said. "Trust me. I know that better than anyone else. I'm speaking from experience."

"What experience could that be?"

I hope she wasn't talking about anything illegal.

"If I tell you, then I'd have to kill you."

"Okay, just forget I asked."

So definitely illegal.

It made sense. The act of telling someone would fall under the category of leaving behind evidence, and I didn't want to end up just another loose end to be tied up. Or end up sleeping with the fishes, as they say.

Over the next handful of minutes, the two of us remained silent. The only sign of any activity would have been Yasmin's frequent peeking from behind the easel to look at me before going back to work. All I could do was just sit there. I was waiting for an opportunity to say something, but she looked engrossed in her task, and I wanted her attention to be completely on me before I started. Just not in the way it currently was.

I was surprised. I didn't expect to see her so soon—if at all.

She didn't reply to my genius message, but I'm pretty sure she saw it. Yasmin always checked her notifications. It made her paranoid if she didn't. She wanted to make sure that she didn't miss anything cool or exciting. I swear that I even saw her perusing the spam section of her email once to look for anything interesting.

Yasmin hadn't given any indication that she was coming to see me. I was beginning to think that my message was a bit out of place and only pissed her off more. But it had been a risk I was willing to take.

To see her now was a surprise, and I was caught off guard, especially since everything felt... normal. Besides the overwhelming pressure between us that is.

After another ten minutes, my anxiety finally hit its breaking point.

I should say something.

I couldn't wait any longer. I needed to get what I wanted to say off my back. It didn't matter if she accepted me or not at the end of it.

"Uh, Yasmin."

"What?" Her voice was ice cold.

"So, did you get my text message?"

"What?" she repeated, more aggressively this time.

I gulped.

"The text message I sent you yesterday afternoon. You saw it and, uh, decided to come visit me, right?"

"That moronic thing? Yeah, I saw it. It was so stupid that I was literally about to delete your number and block you. I got secondhand embarrassment from just even looking at it. I wanted to gouge my own eyes out. If anything, that message made me not want to show up."

It wasn't that bad. A little stupid, but it was still funny.

These were the thoughts I didn't dare voice out loud.

"Lucky for you," she continued, "I'd already made up my mind."

"You did?"

"Yeah... Mona gave me a call yesterday. She was crying, and she convinced me that I should come and see you. She said that the doctors said you were dying and that you didn't have much longer to live, and if I wanted to get anything off my chest before you passed, then now would be the time. But from what I can tell, she must have been kidding again. That lying bitch. I should have known."

Mona.

This was her way of helping me out one last time, huh?

She knew I had no way to get to Yasmin, so she ensured that she'd come here.

Hah.

And, just so you know, I'm going to leave it in your hands. If you fuck things up with Yasmin, it was all your fault this time.

Mona...

Thank you.

I took a deep breath and clenched my fingers around my bed sheets. The skin around my knuckles turned white.

"Um, can we talk for a second, Yasmin? I have some things I need to say."

"Great. So do I."

Eh.

That didn't sound good.

"Okay, then do you want to go first? Or I can go first. I'm cool with whatever."

"You go. I'm almost done."

"Alright. Just give me a minute to gather my thoughts."

I'd already had close to half an hour to think about what I wanted to say, but being put on the spot managed to flush away all that progress. I knew that I just needed to come out and say it—to apologize. There was no way I was going to be able to make it sound smart. I just needed to be raw and unfiltered. Hopefully that'd be enough for my emotion to resonate. I'd have to convey what I'm feeling with sheer tenacity!

I took a deep breath.

My throat was dry, and I needed water.

Was it getting hot in here or was it just me?

No!

Enough excuses. Just speak! Nothing would happen unless I made it happen!

"I'm sorry!" I shouted at the top of my lungs. The words came out louder than I expected, and I could see Yasmin, who was still behind the canvas, jump in her seat.

"I'm sorry! I'm sorry! I'm sorry! I'm sorry!"

I repeated it many times over. It wasn't eloquent or thoughtful, but I couldn't come up with anything else. The simple words were just that—simply what I felt. Everything unnecessary was discarded. No excuses or explanations for why I said what I did.

It should have been obvious my time with Yasmin wasn't pointless at all. It was fun. Even if it was only for a few months, I wouldn't have exchanged that time for the world. These were the things that I wanted to voice, but the stream of repeated apologies wouldn't stop coming. Soon it began to blend into one long, single sound.

"I'msorryI'msorryI'msorryI'msorryI'msorryI'msorryI'msorryI'msorry I'msorryI'msorryI'msorryI'msorryI'msorryI'msorryI'msorryI'msorryI'ms orryI'msorryI'msorryI'msorryI'msorryI'msorryI'msorryI'msorryI'msorry I'msorryI'msorryI'msorryI'msorryI'msorryI'msorryI'msorryI'msorryI'ms orryI'msorryI'msorryI'msorryI'msorryI'msorryI'msorryI'msorryI'msorry I'msorryI'msorryI'msorryI'msorryI'msorryI'msorryI'msorryI'msorryI'ms orryI'msorryI'msorryI'msorryI'msorryI'msorryI'msorryI'msorryI'msorry I'msorryI'msorryI'msorryI'msorryI'msorryI'msorryI'msorryI'msorryI'ms orryI'msorryI'msorry."

My dry throat was cracking now and at any moment I was sure a nurse or doctor would come rushing in. I was screaming bloody murder, but that didn't matter. The thought that I might never have got to express my regret to her was enough for me to power through every other reservation I had. I'd hurt her. Even if I didn't mean to do it. And I was sorry.

Just one more.

"I'm sorry!"

The last one I enunciated with everything I had left while clasping my hands together and bowing my head.

I hoped that was enough. I hoped that was all I needed to do. Did my message get across to her? Did I need to be any clearer?

Since she was still hidden behind the canvas, I couldn't see Yasmin's face. That obviously meant I couldn't read her expressions either, so I had no idea what she was thinking. Not even a hint. It didn't help that she'd remained silent the entire time. The subtle sounds of her charcoal pencil scratching against the grittiness of the canvas had stopped, and she was sitting motionless on her stool.

What was she going to say?

I didn't care anymore. Just please say anything at all.

"Uhhh..." she started, maintaining that note for half a beat too long before proceeding. "For what?"

"..."

For what?

Did she just ask me—for what?

I laughed nervously. "What do you mean for what? You don't know? You really don't know?"

"No, I don't know what you're apologizing for..."

So, the worst possible thing just happened. I'd failed. The message didn't get through to her at all.

"Well, it was that whole big deal when you were here. I said that bit about feeling like everything was pointless. And the whole thing with Zoey cheating. Remember I was saying how if I had known all of that I probably wouldn't have made such an effort to change. Then we never would have met."

"Oh, that. I'm not upset about that at all. Honestly, I completely forgot you even said it until you just brought it up. Obviously, I knew you didn't mean that. You think I'm an idiot? I'm not that dumb to completely take your words out of context again. Remember that first night you came over to my place when I got angry? I learned back then. I know just how terrible you can be at explaining things."

"Ah, I see."

Wow.

Just wow.

I was speechless.

What an anticlimax.

My apology, or apologies, was what was feeling completely pointless now. Unnecessary and blown out of proportion. I'd overthought everything once again. This was embarrassing. Maybe if I hid away behind my hands and underneath my covers, she'd forget I'd exist.

"That's a relief," I said. "So that means we're good."

"No, we're not."

"I don't understand."

All these sharp turns in the conversation were giving me whiplash at this point. Could it be that I missed some big issue entirely?

"Sorry, I phrased that wrong. I didn't mean it that way. It's just hard for me to put into words. You're good, Chris. Great." Yasmin was still addressing the canvas in front of her, and it gave her voice an echoing, far-off quality, like she wasn't there with me—as if there was a wall between us.

"Then what's the problem?"

She sighed.

"It's me."

A cliche answer, but one I still didn't see coming. There was nothing wrong with her in my eyes.

She rustled in her seat, seemingly retreating further away, which was something I didn't like. With the barrier between us, I wasn't sure if it'd even be possible for us to connect. I wanted her to look at me when she spoke, and I'd do the same.

"Yasmin, come over here and we can talk—"

"No, I can't," she interrupted, her voice soft. "I don't think I'll be able to say what I want to say if I could see your face—if I could see you. I'm going to need you to just sit there and listen to me, not that you have a choice. It's hard enough as it is, and I don't want to repeat myself. Am I being clear?"

"Yes, ma'am."

"Okay, good.

Coming from Yasmin's direction I heard a series of loud breaths, and as she braced herself for what was to come, so did I. Clearly, she was having trouble. More trouble than what I'd expect from her.

But my heart was racing too.

Somewhere along the way, the heavy pounding had crept up on me, and I couldn't even hear my own thoughts. But my thoughts weren't what was important. It was the words that I was eagerly waiting for Yasmin to speak that had me at the edge of my seat.

After one more deep exhale, Yasmin spoke.

"I've been having some shitty negative thoughts lately. About you," she started, before pausing once again to find her words. "About a promise I made to you."

"The promise?"

"Yeah, the promise. You helped me. You're still helping me. And I wanted to do all that I could to help you overcome your own issues too. Whatever they were. All of them. That's what I promised to do."

"..."

Yeah, after I'm through with you, you'll be cured of your overall spineless attitude. I won't quit until you can stand up straight with your head held high.

I vaguely recalled her saying something like that, back after I told her about my past and insecurities. Not only did she remember it too, she clearly felt very strongly about it.

"But I don't think I can do it," she said. "I'm not the kind of person who can do that. I'm just too selfish."

"Yasmin, I don't think that at all."

"Hah, sure," she scoffed. "Just let me finish."

She cleared her throat, but this time it held more significance than it did before. It wasn't just for show. Her words were brittle—as if her voice would crack at any second.

"Back when they brought you here into the hospital, I was here with you. I felt terrible about all those texts I sent to you, so I thought it was the least I could do. I was just relieved that you were alive. However, before you woke up the doctor told me how serious your condition was and about the spinal injuries that you already had. He said that there was a possibility that you may never walk again. And do you know what was going through my mind? What I was thinking when he said that?"

Though she couldn't see me—I shook my head.

"The first thing that I felt—literally, the first thought—was contempt," she said. "Not concern. Not about how you may feel. It was contempt and doubt. Doubt about my ties to you. I immediately started to think about how not being able to move your legs would affect every other part of your life—the things it would prevent you from being able to do. Things that I still wanted to do. There are still so many things I want to try and if what the doctor said was true, you'd never be able to do them. And... I thought, maybe I shouldn't see you anymore. Why should I have to sacrifice aspects of my life for this person that I didn't even know a couple months ago? It wasn't just a passing thought either. It stayed on my mind the whole time. Despite saying how I'd help you—I only thought about myself and how that news would affect me and the sacrifices I'd have to make to uphold my promise... Fuck... I'm such a shitty person, aren't I?"

"You're not."

I'd be lying if I said her words had no impact on me. They hit me hard. My chest was heavy, and my breaths were coming out shallow. I could see why even Yasmin was having trouble saying those words to me. She was carrying these feelings inside her the whole time. That must not have been easy for her.

"Hah, even now, you're still just trying to make me feel better, but it's only making me feel worse," she muttered. "I was able to push those feelings away myself. I knew how terrible it was for me to think that way. I just thought it was a moment of weakness for me. I didn't plan on saying anything. I was just going to pretend it never happened. That was before you brought up Zoey again. How she always told you that she'd never leave you. Even when she might have not felt the same way about you—she said she'd never leave you. That's when all those emotions and the doubt resurfaced. I can't be like that. I can't compete with an ideal like that. I'm not perfect. I just don't know what I'm supposed to do. I don't know how I'm supposed to help you at all. I know I act confident and seem independent, but I couldn't have made all these changes without your help. Pursuing painting. Rekindling things with my sister. Those are the two things I never thought were possible. It's all because of you."

Near the end, her words were becoming harder to understand. They were caught between her breaths, and she stumbled over them.

She said she couldn't compete.

It was never a competition, but somehow, I made her feel that it was.

Yasmin was conflicted knowing that she'd have to sacrifice so much to uphold her promise, and she didn't think she could do that. Or maybe some part of her didn't want to have to do that. Her words hurt me—but I couldn't blame her or how she was feeling. It was a lot to ask of anyone. It's not something you should ever ask of anyone either.

The expectations and obligations a person carries are sometimes too much to handle. I knew that better than anyone else. Yasmin cared about me, but there was still so much we didn't know about each other. These past couple months only represented a small fragment of our entire lives and histories. In other words, I knew that it wasn't my place to occupy such a large portion of her future. She shouldn't have to make such a big decision over someone she basically just met. It wasn't my place. She had no real obligation to me, even excluding such a childish and naive promise.

"Tell me what I should do, Chris," Yasmin whispered, her words were so soft they were almost inaudible.

Hearing her request, I didn't have to think about my next words.

The answer was obvious.

"You don't have to do anything."

My voice was firm.

The words I spoke were as clear as my conviction.

I continued, "I don't expect you to do anything, Yasmin. I just want you to live your life the way you want to live it. You don't have to make sacrifices for me. You don't have to force yourself."

Behind her canvas, I was able to see the corner of her arm move up towards her face.

"But... my promise."

"You think I'd want you to put your life off to the side for my sake? No way. I only want you to do what you want to do. Don't worry about me."

"I don't know what to say. It still doesn't feel right to me. You've helped me so much. I got to make it up somehow. I have to do something."

I sighed. "You're as stubborn as always, huh? You can't just let me sacrifice myself. But, I figured you'd say something like that. That's so you."

And it was.

No matter what she always had her own way of thinking. She was stubborn. She contradicted me. She called me out for what I was. Some unworldly force inside of her caused her to oppose everything I said and interject her own thoughts whether she was right or wrong. She didn't seem to care. She just wanted things her way. No matter how inconvenient or unreasonable.

That's why—

I sat up as straight as I could. My lower body wasn't cooperating, if anything, it was trying to stop me, but I persisted.

I peeked over the side of the bed.

Jeez.

It looked like a long way down from up here.

I curled my fingers over the railing and dragged myself over to the edge as close as I could, the wires doing nothing to hold me back except tighten in protest.

Everything was trying to hold me back.

"What are you doing?" Yasmin asked, quickly standing up from her seat and knocking her easel to the side. It fell to the ground with a loud clatter.

"I'm a selfish person, too. Don't think any of this was easy for me either."

I looked down at the floor one last time.

Hopefully, this works or else this is going to hurt a lot.

Without waiting another second, I pulled myself over the edge of my bed and fell.

"Chris!"

It wasn't a long way down, obviously. It couldn't have been more than four feet. However, in that short amount of time, Yasmin was able to use the force of her legs to kick off the floor and catch me right before my face connected with the ground. The machinery that had been monitoring my vitals crashed down with me—entangling the both of us.

She held me. Her arms and hands, so small, gripped me tightly. So tight. It was hard to breathe. Was she trying to caress me or strangle the life out of me?

"What the fuck are you doing?! Are you suicidal? Is something wrong with your fucking head? You're an idiot!"

With nothing between us anymore, I was finally able to see what I couldn't see before.

Her face was wet with tears, showing none of its usual strength and determination. It was a face that she never made a habit of showing. Still, that didn't mean it wasn't a representation of who she was. It was still an embodiment of her true underlying feelings. Seeing that face, I couldn't help but want to tease her.

"Sorry, for a second there I thought I could fly."

"Bullshit!"

I laughed.

I couldn't help it. This wasn't the time for me to be making jokes, but it was still in my nature. It made everything easier for me, and in a way, it was a method for me to express my inward feelings too.

"In all honesty, I wanted to show you that my legs worked just fine," I said.

"Clearly, they didn't! You should have been able to tell without doing that!"

"That wouldn't have worked. I had to show you."

"Why?"

"If I could show you, then you wouldn't have to worry about anything. The main problem would be solved. Then it would be like I wasn't holding you back anymore. Both of us would still be able to do all the things you wanted to do."

Yasmin's voice caught in her throat.

I might not have thought it was possible, but she squeezed even tighter, her fingers digging into me. She was sobbing into my shoulder now, her wails muffled by the fabric of my thin hospital gown. I gently placed a hand on the back of her head.

As we continued to hold each other, my eyes focused on the large object that had landed at our feet. Despite viewing it from an angle, I could still see what it was.

It was her canvas.

On its surface, in a sea of black splotches and smears, was Yasmin's charcoal drawing of me, the spots where her tears had fallen only served to make it more beautiful in my eyes.

CHAPTER 38

The next month went about as well as you'd expect.

I don't know why, but for some reason, a statement like that—wrought with copious amounts of sarcasm—seemed to imply that things weren't going all that well. That things were actually going poorly. In some cases that was true, even if I didn't want to admit it. I couldn't blame anyone for thinking that way, especially considering all the events of the past handful of months. I had a tough go of things. Life had taken its toll on me both physically and mentally.

But I didn't regret any of it.

For the most part, everything I did was my own choice.

If I could go back in time and restart everything, like a New Game Plus mode in a video game keeping all my memories and experiences, I believe I'd still choose to do things the same way. At least 99.99% of the time. But what about that other unaccounted for .01%? Well, that's easy to explain off. Obviously, you can't be certain about everything—right? There's always a matter of risk. I just hoped that, most of the time, I was able to be the person I wanted to be. That's all anyone could ever really ask for after all.

However, what I do know is that, without the experiences I gained along the way, and the people who helped me, things wouldn't have turned out as well as they *did.*

"Hey, moron, you think you're ready for this? If you don't give it your all, I'll kick your ass."

"Be nice, sis. You should apologize. Of course, Chris will do his best."

"Yes, Christian is quite capable when he applies himself."

"My bro's got this. I know he does."

"Thanks, everyone, I feel so loved," I said, smiling at the group that stood around me. "I should be fine."

Any minute, the nurse would stroll through the door to take me away. Today was my first day of physical rehabilitation. I'd be lying if I said I wasn't a little nervous; I mean who wouldn't be? I still had a long, perilous road ahead of me, wrought with more dangers and struggles than I was prepared for. I probably wouldn't survive.

"How's your back feeling, by the way?" Yasmin leaned in close to me as the rest of the group chattered away amongst themselves. She was so close that I could feel her breath against my cheek. It tickled—but that wasn't the reason I smiled.

"Better than it's felt in a while."

"I'm happy to hear that," she whispered. "Just hurry up and get better alright? I'm not going to wait for you forever. We've got things to do."

"Hah, that's a lot of pressure you're putting on me. I don't do well with pressure."

"You'll do great."

Yasmin shot a look over her shoulder to make sure no one was watching before giving me a quick peck on the cheek.

Finally, some affection!

That was just what I needed.

Nothing could stop me now.

Yeah...

It looked like a lot of people were depending on me to get better, and I didn't want to let any of them down. Expectations could be a heavy burden sometimes, enough to cripple even the strongest individuals, but in the right amount, it's not that bad.

Well, that's what I say.

But what do I know?

Thank you for reading a MoonQuill original novel. To experience more exciting stories, visit us at moonquill.com

To know when we release new books, join our mailing list from our site and receive three books for free!

We will never spam you!

To talk with other members of the MoonQuill community, check out our community Discord.

Finally, we would really appreciate it if you could take a moment to review the book. Every review greatly helps the author and supports their ability to continue writing fantastic books for us to enjoy.

www.ingramcontent.com/pod-product-compliance
Lightning Source LLC
LaVergne TN
LVHW090546110826
845146LV00001B/35

* 9 7 9 8 8 8 9 9 3 0 1 3 6 *